Hamill, Pete,
Loving women : a novel of
the Fifties /

AUG 1 8			
AUG 3 1	NOV 2 7		
SEP 5	DEC 9		
SEP 8	DEC 2 9 1989		
SEP 1 3	MAY 3 1991		
SEP 2 5	JUL 1 5 1991		
OCT 3			
OCT 7			
OCT 1 1			
OCT 2 1			
NOV 1 1			

MAY 2 3 1989

LOVING
WOMEN

LOVING WOMEN

A Novel of the Fifties

PETE HAMILL

RANDOM HOUSE | NEW YORK

Library of Congress Cataloging-in-Publication Data

Hamill, Pete.
Loving women.

I. Title.
PS3558.A423L68   1989   813'.54   88-42995
ISBN 0-394-57528-8

Manufactured in the United States of America
98765432
First Edition
Book design by JoAnne Metsch

To the Memory of

SAL COSTELLA

NICK OCHLAN

AND

MILTON CANIFF

A gone shipmate, like any other man, is gone forever; and I never met one of them again. But at times the spring flood of memory sets with force up the dark River of the Nine Bends. Then on the waters of the forlorn stream drifts a ship—a shadowy ship manned by a crew of Shades. They pass and make a sign, in a shadowy hail. Haven't we, together and upon the immortal sea, wrung out a meaning from our sinful lives? Good-bye, brothers! You were a good crowd. . . .
—Joseph Conrad, *The Nigger of the* Narcissus

> Well, I'm driftin' and driftin' like a ship out on the sea
> Well, I'm driftin' and driftin' like a ship out on the sea
> Well, I ain't got nobody, in this world to care for me . . .
> —Charles Brown, "Driftin' Blues"

Ah for another go, ah for a better chance!
—Henry James

I was stationed at Ellyson Field in 1953–54. But this is a work of fiction. The characters and events are imaginary.

PART
ONE

Anchors aweigh, my boys, anchors aweigh.

1987

I AM ON THIS bed in a cheap motel listening to the growl of the Gulf. My cameras remain in their silvery Halliburton case. I have hung the shirts and jeans in the closet. On the wall there is a fading photograph of the Blue Angels flying in tight formation over Pensacola. There is no room service and I am hungry, but I don't care to move. It is a week now since my third wife left me, and I am 1,536 miles from home.

It was easy to pack my bags and drive down here, to the places I had not seen in more than thirty years. I was weary of many things: New York and the people I knew there. Photography. Myself. We were in a time of plague. All around me people were dying, as a fierce and murderous virus spread through their blood and destroyed all those immune systems that had made them so briefly human. Each day's newspaper carried the names of the previous day's body count. I knew some of them. Their names filled my head as I remembered them in life and tried to imagine their painful final days, but after a few hours they just became part of the blur.

In restaurants with my wife, Rose, in the final weeks, I heard other names staining the air around me: Bernie Goetz. Donna Rice. Ivan Boesky. Fawn Hall. Oliver North. A hundred others. They were chewed along with the food, their squalid tales consumed like everything else in the city that season. I would gaze around, and see the young in their West Side uniforms talking about junk bonds and arbitrage and leveraged buy-outs and treacherous partners, and I would feel suddenly old at fifty-one. I smoked too much, and most nights was growled at in restaurants by the lean young men with the health-club tans, while their women pawed self-righteously at the smoky air. The cigarettes marked me as part of another generation, my style and attitudes (though not my work) shaped by Bogart and Murrow, Camus and Malraux, those once-living icons who jammed cigarettes in their mouths as signals of their manhood, inhaled a billion of them, and died. Worse, I was twenty pounds overweight in a time when eating was paid for by hours at a Nautilus machine. I was not yet old and no longer young, and on the night of my birthday, Rose leaned over and asked me in her gray-eyed, direct way: "Michael, what *is* it that you want?"

I was quiet for a long while, looking out at the spring crowds parading on Columbus Avenue. I told her: "1953."

She didn't understand. In 1953, Rose Donofrio was not yet born. In the months when we were, as they used to say, courting, she would have smiled, and asked what I meant and tried to pry some answer from me. But that night she didn't really care. That night, Rose had other matters on her mind. That night, Rose blinked at me and shook her head; her gaze drifted away, and when she came back, she told me that she'd met another man and wanted to go and live with him. Her eyes were suddenly liquid, as if she expected some melancholy response from me or some explosion of protest. I couldn't give her either. That was the problem. That had been the problem for a long time. Rose gave me this fresh information, this trembling admission of betrayal, and it merely drifted like my cigarette smoke into the great blurry fog of other information, along with the contras and the calorie count of sushi. I waved at the waiter and asked for a check and Rose and I walked home in silence. By midnight, we'd agreed that she could keep the loft and I would get the country house. She packed three bags and said she would spend the night at a girlfriend's house, a fiction to spare my feelings. We'd call the lawyers in the morning.

"You never loved me, did you?" Rose said at the door.

"Yes, I did. More than you'll ever know."

She closed the door, all teary now, and I looked at my watch and thought: *I'd better go down soon, and buy the* Times. Rose had a gift, inherited from her Italian mother, for the melodramatic gesture and the venomous aria, the cutting word and the slammed door. In a way, that was what had attracted me to her when we met, four years earlier at a party on East 71st Street. But I didn't, or couldn't, respond any more. There was nothing left in me of such theatrics.

Maybe I was just too old. Maybe I had seen too many real bodies in too many real places for too many years. Passion had killed them all. Political passion, or religious passion, or personal passion. And I had known for years that the greatest occupational hazard I faced as a photographer was indifference. So I never plunged into her dark Sicilian storms. And I felt nothing about her abrupt and treacherous departure. It had been a long time since I'd felt anything at all.

But late on that first night alone, emptying my file cabinets and packing cartons in one of the sad ceremonies of departure, something shifted in me. I had little interest in the old tear sheets of my work, the yellowing pages of magazines (some of them dead), the folders full of birth and death certificates, licenses and diplomas. I was too old to be moved by the snapshots of people I'd once loved, and I couldn't bear to read again the letters from vanished friends, postmarked Saigon or Lagos or Beirut. And then I came up short. Lying flat on the bottom of a file drawer was a thick, dog-eared folder. It was marked in large tight lettering, done in India ink with a Speedball pen, *Personal Stuff.* There were some letters inside, a group of drawings held together with a rusting paper clip, a few slips of paper bearing phone numbers, and The Blue Notebook.

I was seventeen years old when I had first started writing in The Blue Notebook—a kid in the Navy. And here it was, intact. Improbably, that sweet and serious boy I used to be had survived in its pages into the years of manhood. I set the Notebook aside. I finished packing the files and stacked the cartons along the wall beside the door. I took some pictures off the walls: a drawing by José Luis Cuevas, a painting of city rooftops by Anne Freilicher, a watercolor of Coney Island by David Levine. Over the fireplace was a nude photograph of Rose Donofrio, her hair streaming forward, her features obscured. I left it there. I filled a steamer trunk with winter clothes. I packed three more cartons with records—all those people Rose could not bear to hear: Charlie Parker and Sinatra and Dinah Washington and Wynonie Harris. A hundred others. I sealed the cartons with masking tape, then went down and bought the *Times.*

But toward morning, lying alone on the futon, staring at light patterns on the ceiling, listening to the slow murmur of the early-morning traffic, my head began to fill with long-gone images. Faces. Sounds. I heard the clatter of palm trees in the Florida night and

Hank Williams singing on a jukebox. I smelled great tons of bacon frying in a mess hall. I saw the faces of men I used to know. And a woman I once loved more than life itself.

When I woke that afternoon, I thought I had better go South.

From The Blue Notebook

Journey. *n.* 1 Travel from one place to another, usually taking a rather long time. 2 A distance, course, or area traveled or suitable for traveling. 3 A period of travel. 4 A passage or progress from one stage to another.

I've said good-bye to everybody now. I am going away. They have said their good-byes too, but I don't think they even know who I am. Not my friends. Not my family. Not the girl I loved. They see me now as Michael Patrick Devlin, USN, a sailor. Just like they used to see me, only a year ago, as a high school student or a stickball player or the crazy kid who drew his own comics. I could tell them (or anyone else who asks) that I was born June 24, 1935, which makes me seventeen and a half. I could tell them that I went to Holy Name School in Brooklyn for eight years and Bishop Loughlin High School for three. I could tell them I have dark blond hair and blue eyes that are turning gray and that I'm five-foot-eleven and weigh 178 pounds. I'm a Dodger fan (of course). For fourteen months I boxed (not very well) at the Police Athletic League as a middleweight. I could tell them that my father was born in Ireland, in the city of Belfast, and that makes me Irish-American. I could tell them that my mother was born in The Bronx and is dead. Catholics. What else? I could tell them I have two younger brothers and a sister. That the greatest book I ever read was Rabble in Arms *by Kenneth Roberts. That I want to be a comic-strip artist. But even if I told them all those things, it wouldn't add up to me.*

They don't really know me, not one of them, and I'm not telling any of them.

I'm going away.

On a journey.

Every Navy man has two jobs: he is a fighting man and a specialist. His fighting duty at his battle station comes first; his daily work and his special jobs are important, too. Each man's job may seem small, but it is part of the fighting efficiency of his ship. Every man's job is small compared to the ship as a whole, but if one man falls down on his job, the ship may be lost.
—The Bluejackets' Manual.

Aunt Margaret asked me when I came home from boot camp what it was that I wanted. I couldn't tell her. It would have felt as if I were asking her for something, and I don't want to ever have to ask anyone for anything. But there were some things I wanted: a Parker 51 pen. A television set for my brothers and sister. A telephone too. Rooms with doors. I wanted Craftint paper so I could draw like Roy Crane. A set of Lionel trains. Every one of the Bomba the Jungle Boy *series. I wanted to wake up one morning and discover that I looked like a combination of William Holden and Chet Baker. I wanted a new girl. But when she asked me, I just shrugged and said, "Nothing, Aunt Margaret. I don't want anything at all." A complete lie.*

Love. *n.* 1 The profoundly tender or passionate affection for a person of the opposite sex. 2 A feeling of warm personal attachment or deep affection, as for a parent, child or friend. 3 Sexual passion or desire, or its gratification. 4 A person toward whom love is felt; beloved person; sweetheart. 5 A love affair; amour. 6 A personification of sexual affection, as Eros or Cupid. 7 Affectionate concern for the well-being of others. 8 Strong predilection or liking of anything (the ~ of books). 9 The object or thing so liked. 10 The benevolent affection of God for His creatures, or the reverent affection due from them to God.

Chapter

1

AND SO, EARLY one chilly spring morning, the sky still purple, I drove out through the Holland Tunnel. Slowly, then vividly, the images of an old journey began to emerge, like a photograph in a developing tray. I began to hear voices and music and the sounds of travel. And then I was on a Greyhound bus. It was New Year's Eve, 1952, the bus was heading South. I was desperate for the love a woman.

I stared at my reflection in the window and wondered again how women saw me. My white Navy hat was pulled rakishly (I thought) over one eye, the collar of my pea jacket was up high, and I kept trying to set my mouth in the weary, knowing way that Flip Corkin used in *Terry and the Pirates.* To be sure, my hair was still too boot-camp short, my nose too long, my teeth in need of work. I would never be mistaken for a movie star. But I looked at myself a lot then, and it was not just some adolescent exercise in narcissism. I simply wondered how I looked to others, especially to women.

The snow was falling steadily when the bus reached the iron of New Jersey. The boy I was then stared at the fat wet flakes and wondered how everything had gone so wrong that Christmas, with a girl named Maureen Crowley (the name living on for years in my head when so many others had joined the general blur), and why all the guys he knew had girls, even wives, and he had none. The boy wished his mother was alive, sure he could ask her questions about such matters. He couldn't ask his father anything. My father was big and gruff and strong, with eyebrows that met over his nose; he knew a lot about electrical wiring and radio circuits and the construction of lamps. He just didn't know how to explain anything to me about the mysteries of the human heart. Or so I thought on the last day of 1952. The old man was from Ireland and my mother was from The Bronx, a mick and a narrowback joined in holy matrimony, and if he never said anything sweet or tender to me, well, in my presence he never said anything human to her either.

I was sure then, as only young men can be sure, that he didn't even say much of anything when she was dying in the public ward at the hospital. The doctors wouldn't let me watch her die, because I was only fourteen and tuberculosis was contagious and there were other people dying there too and I could never be expected to understand any of it. Not yet. Sex and death in those days were only rumors and whispers. And besides, I was the oldest and had to mind my brothers and my sister every night while my father went to visit her. I stayed with them each night, listening to *Gangbusters* or *The Inner Sanctum* or Jimmy Durante on the radio, hearing the voices of cops and gangsters and comedians, when what I most truly wanted was to know what it was I was supposed to do to make a woman love me. My mother would know. But she was kept hidden as she died, and my father was silent and I was full of questions, right up to the evening he learned that he didn't have to visit her ever again. I do know that he cried in his bed that last night of my mother's life. I heard him. But he never said a goddamned thing to me.

So I sat in the dark on that empty bus, the uniform identifying me as a man prepared to die for his country, and told myself that 1952 had turned out to be rotten but maybe 1953 would be better. Neither could ever be as bad as the year my mother died. And in some way, I was happy to be on the road, going out of New York, away from Brooklyn. This had nothing to do with the new president; Dwight Eisenhower was a famous general with a baby face and a simple smile, and he told everybody he would go to Korea and end the war. But the truth was that, in our part of Brooklyn we never cared much for generals and didn't care at all for Republicans. Even when Douglas MacArthur came back after Harry Truman fired him, and they kept playing "Old Soldiers Never Die," and there was talk about impeaching Truman and making MacArthur president, we sided with Truman. So when the radios played MacArthur's song in the bars, most of the men answered it with "Anchors Aweigh." There were some soldiers from our neighborhood and a few Marines, but mostly we were Navy. When our people fought for their country, they went to sea. So it was no big deal that when I was old enough to go, I dropped out of high school and went to boot camp in Bainbridge. Like almost everybody else.

Deep into Virginia that long-ago New Year's Eve, the snow was still falling thickly. I remember staring through the steam-glazed windows at the white world, thinking that the storm would never end. For miles, I followed the traceries of telephone lines. And saw, off in the distance, snug houses behind screens of skeletal trees.

Those houses. In blue icy fields. Blinking with Christmas lights. Inside, men had women who held them tight, who talked to them about life and kids and music and the weather. They slept under thick blankets while the snow fell steadily, and when the moon played its light over the frozen world, they fucked. I wanted a woman who would hold me, too. Who would talk to me. Laugh at my jokes. Fuck me good as I fucked her. The boy I was then didn't really want the houses. Out in the country, far from the cities of the world: that wasn't my life. But I wanted the woman.

By noon, the heater had surrendered to the storm and it was very cold in the bus. And I remember saying to myself: *Pensacola.* Then again. *Pensacola, Pensacola, Pensacola,* like beads on a rosary. I had never even heard of the town until the Navy assigned me there in a thick packet of orders issued before Christmas leave. But when I got home, I looked up the town in Nelson's *Encyclopedia* (worn red bindings, double columns of tiny type, bought a book at a time by my mother, clipping coupons from the *New York Post*) and tried to imagine the place from the volume's few lines. Sitting in the living room, on the frayed couch beside the kerosene heater, I felt Pensacola come to me across 1,536 miles in bright pastel colors.

Pen-sa-co-la I whispered on the bus (and repeated it now, in the Datsun 280-ZX, following myself South). And saw rounded forms, brown and glowing from the sun, smooth, polished. *Pensacola.* Brown breasts and brown thighs and brown bellies, too. Women glistening with oil. Hot to the touch. For surely Pensacola was a woman's name. Pensacola Brown. Yeah. The name was full of lazy hills and the *Pensa* seemed buttered to the *cola,* not locked hard and bolted tight, like *Stuttgart* or *New York.* It was a name very much like *Florida.* Hi, I'm Florida Brown and I want to fuck you . . . Except that Florida was green with drooping palms and the sounds of spring training on the radio and blue with the sea. And it was too short and smooth and familiar to be a woman's name. Pensacola had hard little bumps in it, like tits.

I looked out at the blizzard and closed my eyes, and saw palm trees withering under the snow and a gigantic glacier shoving the beaches into the sea and heard the north wind howling, claiming victory over the sun. I opened my eyes in a moment of panic. There were a half dozen other passengers in the bus, most of them sleeping. I remember the driver's back. He inhaled deeply, then exhaled in a weary way. And I closed my eyes again, and invented a world of heat—to help the driver, to defend Pensacola, to warm myself. I was on the beach at Coney Island, on Bay 22, under a hammering sun. I was on the rooftop of our house in Brooklyn, gazing at the Manhattan skyline in a sweltering August stupor. It was too hot to sleep, and down on the street old people sat in folding chairs, fanning themselves with the *Daily News,* drinking hot tea because they all believed that it cooled you off and its leaves cured sunburn. I thought of *The Desert Song,* the movie that made me volunteer in boot camp for the naval air station at Port Lyautey in Morocco. I was Dennis Morgan. The Red Shadow himself. Riding across the sun-baked desert. Leading the Riff against the hated French, singing:

> *"You'd better go, go, go,*
> *Before you've bitten the sword . . ."*

In my tent, a masked woman in silky pajamas. Deep black eyes. Huge golden earrings. Jeweled rings on her toes. Her toenails painted. She opened her arms and touched my face. "Michael," she whispered in some exotic foreign accent. "You must do it to me now. . . ." Later, I fell asleep in her arms.

Ah, youth.

When I woke up, everything had changed. The snow was gone. Purple light spilled down valleys. I could not afford a watch, so I had no idea what time it was or how long I'd slept, but the land was black now, and there were few lights. The bus was fuller, too, although the seat beside me was empty. I heard a woman's phlegmy snoring in the dark. And then smelled the thick fatty air of the bus, a mixture of farts, cigarette smoke, and engine fumes. I felt vaguely sick. Then addressed myself: *You are Michael Devlin, USN 4640237. You are almost eighteen years old, not a child. You cannot get sick in a bus.* And I didn't.

But I could see Maureen again. I stared out at the dark forests, trying to get rid of her. But there she was, pale and beautiful, standing among the trees. She would not go away. I was far from Brooklyn, but I could see her (as I see her now) wearing a maroon coat and turning around, her back to me, snow melting in her hair. *Oh, Momma, let me talk to you.* I was calling her name as she walked quickly down the snow-packed path in Prospect Park. Her head lowered against the wind. Hands jammed in her pockets. Maureen, I called. But she chose not to hear me. *Maureen.* And once more: *Maureen.* My voice was muffled, but I knew she could hear me. And then at last she turned. I came closer, moving clumsily in the snow. And saw the fear in her eyes. *Fear,* for Christ's sakes. Her face trembled. And then she started to run. Out of the park. Out of my life.

The Greyhound was moving with fresh power now, and I thought: *That was only nine days ago and it seems like ancient history.* I didn't run after her. I couldn't do that. Couldn't beg. Not for her. Not for anybody. But I saw her again on crowded beaches, on the empty slopes of summer hills. She was on the subway with me, coming back from a movie in Manhattan, her head burrowed against my shoulder. "Maureen," I whispered on the bus, and thought about her skin. And then, hundreds of miles from her and going farther away by the minute, she gave me what she had given me so many times in that long ripe crazy summer before I joined the Navy. Off to the side along my thigh, forced there by the tight crotch of the Navy blues. Once, when I was still an altar boy at Holy Name Church, I imagined God in possession of a hard-on counting machine. That was the beginning of the loss of faith. He was up there in heaven, seeing all, knowing all, and He would spot my hard-ons, logging them in His gigantic counting machine along with billions of other impure hard-ons all over the world. In His rage, He looked to see if I touched myself. Or far worse, whether I played with myself. And certainly He would need another, much larger counting machine to keep track of all the jacking off, one that would have to handle billions of entries in Brooklyn alone. And thinking about this (on the altar of the 8:30 Saturday Mass) I laughed. That was the way faith must always end. After all, if there was a God, why would He care about my hard-ons anyway? Was he nuts, or what? A grown man, counting hard-ons? But I was also still a Catholic, and naturally, after I laughed, I felt guilty. For about a minute. And then felt certain that I'd never stop burning in Purgatory and was already too far behind to ever get even with God, so I might as well enjoy sin. I was fourteen. The year my mother died.

So within a few weeks I went forward to the worst sin of all. I was serving as altar boy at a Saturday afternoon wedding. The bride was a hot-eyed Italian, with creamy skin and gigantic tits and I could see when she looked at the groom (as Father Kavanaugh was rattling on about sickness and health until death do you part) that she wanted to fuck him right on the spot. And I realized that within a few hours he'd have his cock in her, and those huge tits in his face. And I got a hard-on right there on the altar. I was wearing a cassock and surplice, so nobody could see it, but it wouldn't go away. Even when I thought about Jerry Lewis. Or a Spanish Main movie. I kept seeing the bride's hot eyes. And after the wedding, when the priest went down the aisle to say good-bye to the happy couple and pick up his tip, I hurried into the empty sacristy, lifted the skirt of my cassock, trembling with the certainty that God would blast me with a lightning bolt, and jerked off down the flower chute.

There were no lightning bolts. Not that day. Nor on other days and nights. But I couldn't do that now. Not in a bus. Not in Navy blues, for Christ's sakes. So I laughed then, and the hard-on vanished and so did my image of Maureen. She was part of my most shameful secret. I was old enough to die for my country, but I was still that most rare and suspicious kind of sailor: a virgin. I could tell this to nobody. But it was true: I'd never slept with a woman. Any woman. I'd fallen in love with a few girls, most terribly and drastically with Maureen Crowley. But because I loved them, I couldn't sleep with them. And I couldn't sleep with anyone else, because that would be a betrayal. So I looked out again at the countryside, plunging into America, a sailor without a ship, assigned to shore duty when all my friends were going to sea, a warrior without a war, now that Eisenhower was in and the generals were meeting in Korea to end the fighting. And I felt like a child. But after a while, I felt better: Somewhere down this road, somewhere in the mysterious South, lay my salvation. Here, far from home, I would find my woman.

Chapter

2

I REMEMBER WAKING UP in the dark, with the bus stopped outside a Howard Johnson's restaurant. I used the john. I sipped a cup
of coffee. Nothing else. I had nineteen dollars left after Christmas
leave, and they would have to last me all the way to Pensacola and
for a couple of weeks after that, until I'd get paid. At the counter,
I tried to get a red-haired waitress to look at me by wearing a
wounded look on my face. Like Bogart. But she was too busy for
my secret wound, so I picked a newspaper off a stool and read the
comics.

I didn't see *Steve Canyon*, which I was sure was the greatest comic
strip in the world. But the paper did carry *Buz Sawyer*, the other
great one. I'd clipped *Canyon* and *Sawyer* from the *Mirror* and the
Journal-American since I was twelve, filing them neatly in #10 envelopes. I filled sketchbooks with copies of the characters, trying to
use a brush the way Milton Caniff did on Canyon (and on *Terry and
the Pirates*, which I'd collected in the comic-book editions), trying
to draw women the way Roy Crane did in *Buz Sawyer*. Crane used
a special paper called Craftint that I'd read about in a book about
cartooning. You used one chemical on the special paper and got a
gray tone made of lines going one way. You used the other chemical and the lines came out crosshatched and darker. So Crane's
panels were beautiful, with the two shades of gray, the dead whites,
the juicy blacks. But Caniff had better characters. His dialogue was
hipper. His women were smarter and sexier, real women who knew
the world. Not just the Dragon Lady from *Terry*, who everybody
knew about. Or Burma, singing the "St. Louis Blues." But Copper

Calhoon and Deen Wilderness and April Kane and Feeta Feeta and Fancy, too. Oh yeah, I loved the girl called Fancy. I wanted to go to a movie or a dance with Crane's women or give them a feel on a beach somewhere. But I wanted to fuck the women drawn by Milton Caniff.

I sipped my coffee at the counter and stared at *Buz Sawyer,* and tried to enter the story. There were no newspapers in boot camp, so I'd lost track of most of them. I'd asked my father to save the strips for me, but he couldn't understand why a man old enough to be in the United States Navy would care about such things, so he didn't bother. He couldn't even imagine why I wanted to be a cartoonist. That was something like aspiring to be the Pope or the president of Argentina. He didn't get it. I was Irish. I should be a cop. A fireman. An ironworker. Like the sons of every other donkey who ever landed in Brooklyn.

So I looked at *Buz Sawyer* as if I were engaged in a monumental act of defiance, hoping that somehow my father would walk into this diner in the middle of America and get furious at the sight. The comics were what we had instead of rock 'n' roll. I didn't know the story, but I did recognize the character in the first panel. His name was Harry Sparrow. He had a large bald head, like Doctor Huer in *Buck Rogers,* and a monocle hanging from his right eye and he was dressed in a cutaway tuxedo complete with striped pants. Harry Sparrow was an international crook. A hustler. A guy who dealt in guns. Somehow he was now involved in a plot to run guns to a Central American country called—I remember the name—Salvaduras. Crane was always putting Sawyer or Easy in some Central American country and owned the region the way Caniff owned China. And in 1952 Central America was still a comical place made up of banana republics, where the revolutions were lots of fun. Nobody called the bad guys the moral equals of the Founding Fathers. Nobody shot peasants or nurses or schoolteachers and called it liberation. Certainly not in *Buz Sawyer.* In the strip (which I tore out and slipped into The Blue Notebook, where it yellowed for thirty-five-years), Harry Sparrow was listening and smirking as a sexy woman named Fifi talked on the telephone to one of the Salvaduran leaders. Behind them was the gilt frame of a painting.

"More sugar, Fifi," Harry said to the girl. "More! More! Pour it on!"

"I am ZO unhappy, Adolfo, *chèri,"* she was saying to the guy on the other end of the telephone line. Fifi. *Chèri.* She must be French. "DINNER," she said. Her right hand was playing with her blond hair. The left hand caressed the telephone. She had a star on her left cheek. Her breasts rose fiercely off her round compact body. "Just the two of us. . . ."

Then I heard the horn honking outside and I finished my coffee and folded the newspaper and hurried back to the bus.

"Happy New Year," the driver said.

"Yeah," I said. "Happy New Year."

That year we still called black people Negroes, and there was a Negro soldier with pomaded hair sitting in the aisle seat beside mine. He stood to let me in and I nodded at him. He looked like an old welterweight named Tommy Bell, who once knocked down Sugar Ray Robinson. Five other Negro men were dozing on the wide back seat. Two leaned against each other. Another sat with his arms folded. The bus was now full.

I looked up and saw the driver standing beside the steering wheel, looking down the aisle. His lips moved as if he were counting passengers. He leaned forward and said something to the sleeping Negro in the first seat. There was no reaction. The driver squeezed the man's shoulder, and when the soldier didn't move, the driver shook him, and then the soldier was suddenly awake, backing away with his hands up, like a fighter. The driver shook his head sadly and whispered to the man. He stood up, blinking, and looked down the aisle. Now the driver was waking the large black woman in the third row. The soldier jerked a duffel bag off the overhead rack, slung it onto his shoulder and came stomping down the aisle.

"Now, where in *hell* my spose to sit?" he said loudly. "Huh?" He turned to the driver. "Answer me that! There ain't no seats back here!"

"Jest a minute," the driver said. The Negro woman was now in the aisle, like a giant plug. Her jaw was loose. She was mumbling. The driver lifted down two shopping bags from the rack.

"I ain't gonna stand all the way to no Atlanta!" the soldier shouted. "I jest ain't gonna do it!"

"Hold on," the driver said. "Jest hold yer hosses." He waited until the woman took the shopping bags, then he allowed her to lead the way down the aisle. The driver's eyes squinted; his face seemed more yellow as he scanned the faces in the rear.

"This is boolshit!" the soldier said. "Goddam one hunnid pissent *boolshit*!"

The driver turned harder. "Take it easy, soldier. This ain't my idea. It's the law."

"The law . . ."

The man next to me watched in silence. His hands clenched and unclenched. "We crossin' the Mason-Dixon lahn," he said to me. "Or like we calls it, the *Smith and Wesson* lahn." He smiled in a bitter way. "Some country, ain't it?"

The driver told a thin, redheaded white woman to get up and sent her to the third-row seat vacated by the large Negro woman. Then he helped the redhead take down a cheap plastic suitcase, tied together with a stocking. The redhead took it from him quickly, shielding it with her body as if ashamed of its condition. The driver turned to me.

"Okay, sailor," he said. "You're goin' to the first row and this soldier's takin' your place." I started to get up. The pomaded Negro shook his head. "Some shit," he said. I reached up for my sea bag. I said to the driver: "What's this all about, anyway?"

"The South," he said wearily.

There was a white man sleeping against the window in the first row. He was an older man, maybe forty, with thinning blond hair, a long nose, a bony face. He was wearing a checked sport jacket. A black raincoat was drawn tightly up to his chin like a blanket. He had his shoes off and there was a flight bag at his feet. I sat down and the bus finally pulled out. Soon we were back in the rhythm of the road. Dark forests. Distant houses. I thought about Harry Sparrow and Fifi. In bed together.

All I needed was another useless hard-on. So I shook Fifi out of my mind, and watched the road and the ease and skill of the driver as he moved the huge bus around slower-moving trucks. I didn't know how to drive. I was from Brooklyn, where nobody I knew had a car. Including my father. We used the subway to go places. In boot camp, guys laughed when I told them this. *You cain't drahv? Shit, man, what's yore p'oblem?* I tried to explain, but they couldn't believe it; most of them started driving when they were twelve, thirteen. I guess I admitted I couldn't drive to avoid talking about the more terrible failure: The dark secret of my virginity.

. . .

Somewhere near Greeneville, the driver picked up a small microphone clamped to the dashboard. He glanced at his watch, then
flicked a switch.

In a hoarse voice, he said, "Ladies and gennulmen, in exactly ten
seconds, it'll be January the first, nineteen hunnid an fipty three."

I heard some applause, but when I glanced around most of the
white people were asleep. It was hard to see the Negroes in the
dark. Back home, everybody was celebrating, drinking and shouting while Guy Lombardo's band played "Auld Lang Syne" on the
radio. The worst band in the history of the world. The people were
probably celebrating because they wouldn't have to hear Guy Lombardo for another whole year. My father was probably down the
block in Rattigan's, somber and silent while the other men were
singing loud and drinking hard; my brothers were banging pots on
the fire escape and throwing snowballs at drunks.

And somewhere tonight, I thought, *right this second, while this bus
takes me where I've never been, right now Maureen is with her accountant.
She's at a party with him. Sitting on a couch. Tony Bennett is singing
"Because of You" on the phonograph. She's wearing her blue dress. Or
maybe the white one. The accountant is holding her left hand. Or maybe
the right. He stands up and she follows. The room is dark, a small lamp
on in a corner, maybe thirty watts, maybe red. He starts dancing with her.
She moves close to him. In the dark, does she think her accountant is me?*

"Here, sailor," the driver said, and passed me a pint bottle of
whiskey without taking his eyes off the road. The dark-brown glass
of the bottle was cool in my hand. There was no label.

"Thanks," I said, unscrewing the cap and taking a belt. "Happy
New Year." I didn't much like whiskey, the way it burned when
it went down, the way it stayed in you so that you reeked of it for
days after you'd drunk it. In that, at least, I was like my father. We
both preferred beer. But I drank from the unmarked bottle anyway.
It was a New Year's gift. A long way from home. I felt it open like
a warm blossom in my belly.

"Yeah, happy New Year," the driver said. "An' gib some to the
gent nex' to you, swabbie."

The man next to me was now awake. He nodded in greeting as
I handed him the pint. His hands were very thin, with veins standing up like blue ropes.

"Thanks, buddy," the man said.

"Thank the driver. It's his whiskey."

"Maybe we oughtta git off this thing. All we need is a drunk bus driver."

"He doesn't look the type," I said.

"They never do."

The man took a second belt of the whiskey, then gave it back to me and I passed it on to the driver, thanking him.

"Hi," the man beside me said. "I'm Jack Turner." I told him my name and we shook hands in a cramped way.

"Where you headin', sailor?"

"Pensacola."

"Why, hell's bells, so'm I."

"You Navy?"

"Yeah, bo'," he said. "Seventeen years, man an' boy." He dug into the bag at his feet, found another pint bottle and cracked the seal. "Three more years and I'm done. The Big Two-Oh. Twenty years in this man's Navy. Then it's back to the world."

I waited; this was the first Old Salt I'd talked to man-to-man. In boot camp, the salts were all ball-breakers: yelling, shouting, marching us around the grinder till we dropped. Maybe it was because Turner wasn't wearing a uniform. I don't know. But he seemed okay.

"You must've seen a lot of the world," I said. "In seventeen years, I mean."

He handed me the bottle. Four Roses. I took a swig, but held it in my mouth for a while before letting it go down.

"Yeah," he said. "I been some places. Seen some shit. But places ain't the world. Not the real world."

The whiskey was spreading out of the core of my stomach now. "What is?"

Turner glanced out the window into the darkness. "A woman. Kids. A house. A car . . . All that boring shit. That's the world . . . Pass that bottle on to the driver. He's a good ole boy."

I tapped the driver's elbow and offered him the Four Roses. But he shook his head no and smiled. I handed the bottle back to Turner.

"You don't travel in uniform?" I said.

Turner laughed. "Hell, no. Not if I got money to pay my way. Maybe hitchhikin', the uniform's an advantage. But you got the money, peel that sucker off," he said, pinching the sleeve of my blue jumper. "I'll tell you why. People see a sailor, they always

laugh. They think sailors are crazy and crazy people strike most
people as funny. And you know sumpin? They're right. Sailors *are*
crazy. You're out on some leaky tub, with all that goddamned
ocean around you. For weeks, months, years, like we was in the
war. I mean *years.* Nothin to see all around you but ocean and
sailors. Crazy goddamn bad-ass sailors. All goin crazy. Some goin
queer. Until finely, they come home to port, crazy and horny, and
they go *ape* shit. Truly fucking crazy-ass apeshit. You ever see a
sailor walking along sober on a Saturday night? You ever see one
in church? Or in a lib'ry? Fuck no. You see sailors fallin down in
the street, you see them laughin and pukin and rollin in piss and
sawdust. You see them gettin locked up. And you know somethin?
Nobody ever gets mad. They see jarheads doin this shit, they get
pissed off. They see some army guy grab a girl by the ass, they want
t' lynch him, even if he aint a nigger. They see some flyboy gettin
fucked up in public, they write to the gahdamned newspaper." He
took a belt from the bottle. "But they see a sailor with blood all
over his whites, fallin on his ass in the gutter, with a hooker on his
shoulders and puke on his fuckin shoes, and they *laugh.*"

I laughed too. "I see what you mean."

But Turner wasn't laughing. "You see, I don't like people to
laugh. Because sailors aint funny. Sailors are the saddest, most
fucked-up, most lonely-ass people on God's pore lonesome fuckin
earth."

He look a longer swig this time, swallowing it slowly.

"So I travel in civvies," he said. "Wherever I end up stationed,
I get me a locker club first thing, and when I go ashore, I change
into civvies. I don't want anyone laughin at me."

Neither did I. I liked Turner for that and I wished he was going
all the way to Ellyson Field with me. I'd have someone to talk to,
to show me the ropes. He was an ordnance man, first class, going
to Mainside to show young pilots what guns looked like. He was
happy about the billet too. It could've been Shit City. Norfolk. Or
it could've been another aircraft carrier and he hated aircraft carriers. *There's four ways of doing things in this man's Navy,* Turner said:
The easy way, the hard way, the Navy way, and the Midway. The
Midway was his last aircraft carrier.

He was quiet for a while and then he asked me if I had a girl.
I said no, and he looked at my face and saw something there, I
guess, and said, "That bad, huh?" I told him that the truth was I

got a Dear John letter while I was in Bainbridge and he passed me
the bottle and I sipped and my stomach burned and I was very
hungry and he said, well, it was better to get a Dear John early than
late and I shouldn't feel so damned bad because everybody gets
one, sooner or later, every sailor gets one, and he took a sip and
so did I, and he told me he had gotten five Dear Johns in his life
and three of them were from wives. I said that was terrible and he
said Nah, wasn't so terrible, they were right, probably, I was no
bargain, no sailor is. But I loved them all. Right up to the minute
it was over. Tell me about them, I said. And he did.

Chapter

3

What Turner Told Me

JUDY, SHE WAS *the first, sixteen and red-haired and saucy and hot. Damn she was hot. Rub that gal's elbow and she'd come. Hot, brother. I married her in 1938 in San Diego, just before they shipped me to the Far East. She was from Shreveport, down Luziana way, staying in Dago with her sister, who was married to a bosuns mate. The bosuns mate was out at sea and I met Judy in a sailor joint with her sister and we went home together, the three of us, and we woke up together too. But Judy was mine from the gitgo and I had some leave for a week and we got married. I was on a cruiser passing Guam when I got a letter saying she was knocked up and I should start picking out baby names. I shoulda known better, I guess. Because she tole me she was too damn lonely there in San Diego and she wanted to go home to this little place near Shreveport where her folks sharecropped, go home there and have the baby there, and I wrote back, Sure, okay, that sounds fine. Well, that Pacific tour was eighteen months. This was before the war and we just went all over the damned place, and when I got home and took the bus from Dago to Shreveport, the little boy was crawlin and Judy was sleepin with the sheriff. Everybody knew it too. They knew it in the town. Her folks knew it. And when I went into that little shitass town, six miles from Shreveport, everybody looked at me, like theyuz wonderin what I was gonna do, and they had this look on the face, pity, hell, tell it true, contempt. And when I went to Judy with what I saw, with what I felt from everybody, when I said Hey, woman what is this shit? She looked at me and turned her back and said, I want the sheriff. I want him, she said, not no long-gone forty-dollar-a-month sailor boy. She wanted the damned sheriff and the damned sheriff wanted her, and if I didn't like it why didden I go down there to the courthouse and tell the sheriff what was on my mind? So I drove around all night in her Pa's car, with a shotgun in my lap and drinkin white lightnin. And I stopped in some honky-tonks and listened to the damned jukebox. And I watched the god-damned courthouse. All the time thinkin, I'll just drive over to that whore-house halfway to Shreveport and get me a piece of ass and then I'll go shoot the goddamned sheriff. And that's what I started in doing. But after I got laid I went out to the car and fell asleep with the shotgun in my lap and when I woke up I left the car there and the shotgun and I hitchhiked into Shreveport and got me a bus and went all the way back to San Diego. I only heard from her one last time. She sent me a letter, saying, Here's your copy of the dee-vorce, Sincerely, Judy. I always loved that word. Sin-cerely. Everytime I hear that goddamned word I think of Judy. She had the roundest sweetest ass in Shreveport, boy.*

My second wife's name was Ginger, and right off I shoulda known better. You fuck girls named Ginger. You don't marry 'em. She was a hostess in a dancehall in Honolulu when I met her. A long-legged high-hipped woman in a flowered dress like they all wear out there, and small titties and a big ass and skin that glowed like gold. I think maybe there was a little Jap in her, the way she had them high goddamned cheekbones and small little titties, but if that was so, well, her ass sure wasn't Jap. No sir. She tole me she was nineteen and I believed her and she sure looked great in that dim light in the hall with the smoke and everything and Glenn Miller playin and all of us sailors drinkin hard and the weather so damned hot that her dress with the flowers on it stuck to her ass like a tattoo. Oh I was in love, boy. Right there. Took me about nineteen minutes and I wanted that woman for the rest of my life. Later on, I learned she was really twenty-seven (I was twenty). Later on, I learned she'd been married once before and had two kids she never tole me about. Later on, I learned she had the goddamned clap, too—this while I was two months out at sea and married for three, and I knew this because she gave it to me. I had some dose, boy. I was dripping with it during the battle of Midway and after I talked to the medics in sick bay I went to the yeoman's office and told him I wanted to stop sendin checks to dear wife Ginger and I filled out all the forms and sent her a letter with one damned sentence it. Dear Ginger, I said. I got yore clap, bitch. Sincerely. I put that in. Sincerely, and signed my name. The next time I was in Pearl was 1943 and she was workin in a whorehouse and I had her blow me for three dollars before talkin about the de-vorce. A real sincere woman, Ginger.

There was a lot of other women too. Yeah. Young girls and old girls, and colored and Chink. But the third wife was the one. I thought she'd make the whole damn thing come together. Her name was Susan and I met her in San Francisco after the war. Small dark-haired girl who worked in a bank and lived alone and wore glasses cause she was nearsighted. Lived in this small house on Mission Street. She didn't want to have nothin to do with me, me bein a goddamned sailor. She just give me the brush. Right off. When I went into the bank to get change for a twenty-dollar bill. I aint no Errol Flynn but I had my share and so when she gave me the brush naturally I wanted her so bad I hurt. So I stayed on her, every day, sometimes twice a day, while the ship was in drydock, and I plain wore her down. I married her, I guess, just to prove to her I was serious, not some horny damned swabbie. Why not? Hell, she didn't have no sheriff, she didn't have the clap. So I tried one las' time to live the life of a married man.

Right off I seen she was a nut about neatness. She had a million rules for everything, all that shit about a place for everything and everything in its place. At first this didn't bother me. Hell, I was Navy. I'd lived a long time in little tight spaces and I obeyed the rules cause sometimes the rules saved your life. So at first I thought it was terrific. She was kinda military, you know? But then I found out she was a Christian too. A God-fearin Bible-readin black-hearted Christian. And that type of a Christian is all rules, boy. She wouldnt let me smoke cigarettes in the house cause it stunk up the wallpaper. She wouldn't drink whiskey with me. She got mad if I didden go to church with her and if I was late for dinner. If I got stuck at the ship or stuck in traffic or stopped for a few whiskeys with a couple of sailors, she'd go nuts. In the closets in the house in Mission Street, she put everything in little cellophane bags and gave them all labels, like panties or slips or bras. The inside of the refrigerator looked like something in a supermarket with everything in rows. And if I put a milk bottle on the vegetable shelf, she'd scream at me. She wouldn't have sex during her period, of course, and for four or five days before her period she was nutty and pissed off and I wasn't interested. Naturally, she thought a blow job was a sin. Naturally, using a rubber was a sin too. She would only fuck me in the bedroom, with the light out, between nine and eleven at night. She wouldn't fuck any later than that cause she needed her rest to get up on time for the bank. I said to her, You don't work at the bank on Saturday or Sunday, baby! But on Friday night she was too tired from

*the whole week of workin and on Saturday night she was restin to get up
for church on Sunday.*

*Well, after a while I started coming home late. And some nights I didn't
come home at all. Then I was there one Friday night and after dinner I
was sittin in this big chair beside the fireplace, just like I always saw men
do in pictures in magazines, and the fire was burnin cause it gets cold there
in San Francisco. And she started screaming at me for leavin the newspaper
on the floor. You always make a mess, she yelled. You can't do anything
without makin a mess. Yellin at me, the top of her lungs.*

*So after a bit, I stood up. I lit me a cigarette and blew the smoke on the
wallpaper and she yelled What are you doin and I put the butt out on the
rug, mashin it in real good. Then I lit another and walked past her smokin
and opened the refrigerator and messed everything up and then I pissed in
it. Right into the goddamned fridge. I remember the butter meltin in the
butter dish. Then I got a pint of whiskey from my coat and chug-a-lugged
it and got sick and puked on the doormat. Never said a word all the time.
Well, little Susan ran right outta there.*

*She didden come home that night, or the next one either. So I wandered
around the house with the radio blastin, smokin and drinkin and takin
shits with the bathroom door open. On Sunday morning she still wasn't
back. I got drunk twice that day without leavin the house and even to me
the place was beginnin to stink. On Monday morning, I took a long cold
shower and got all dressed real neat in civvies and went down to the bank.
She wasn't there. Called in sick, her boss said. Lookin at me funny. Sick
of me, I reckon. So I hit the bars, feelin lower than whaleshit and playin
the jukes and callin home every hour. She never answered the phone and
I realized that I didn't really know much about her, didn't know where
she came from, where she might of run. I didn't know her folks. I didn't
even know the name of the damned church. All I knew was she was gone.
And I was through. By sundown, I was loaded. I couldn't hardly walk,
but I got on a bus and went to Mission Street and went to the house to pack
my clothes. I kept writin a note to her in my head, all about how I was goin
back to the Navy where I belonged and I was sorry I was so rotten to her
and she should find a nice guy for herself and let him put the papers on
the floor once in a while. And of course I was gonna sign this letter
sincerely. I opened the door with my key. And heard a noise from upstairs.
From the bedroom. Not the kind of noise a burglar makes. I tiptoed up them
stairs and when I opened the door, she was naked on the bed, goin down
on a fat bearded guy I'd seen one day at the bank. The fat guy looked scared
shitless, but Susan didn't stop. She looked at me with her eyes all crazy and*

her mouth full of dick and kept goin at it with the fat guy. I went out in the hall and packed my clothes and never saw her again. A week later I got a good-bye letter from her, typed and neat. It was like the charges in a court martial. Or a bank statement. She never said nothin in it about the fat man.

Chapter

4

I HEAR HIS VOICE now. Hear the warnings. Hear the Old Salt telling that boy something about the price of love. Or sex. Or both. And the boy thought: *That's his story; those were Turner's mistakes, and I won't repeat either. I'll find my own woman. I'll know.* Such courage makes the young fight old men's wars. But the woman was not far away, waiting in the shadows of the South. I remember that we changed buses outside a large, badly lit bus station in downtown Atlanta. We had about an hour to wait. And then Turner said it would be better if we got on board the second bus and found window seats. That way, he said, if it ain't a full bus, we can stretch out and sleep the rest of the way. I thought he must be right. He had been on a lot more buses than I had. And a lot more women too. I found a seat in the seventh row, Turner in the second. There were more Negroes sitting in the rear, and a lot more empty seats. Pensacola. I was almost there.

She got on just before we left.

I first saw her standing beside the driver, her skin almost olive in the diffused light from the terminal. In all the years since, that simple image has remained in me. I've photographed models standing in empty buses, bathed in that oblique light. I've tried to capture the same mood on buses in the hills of Nicaragua, or the highlands of Kenya, or moving around Washington Heights. It's never worked. The pictures in your head are always more powerful than the ones on paper. But there she was, with curly black hair and an oval face and the sort of long, thin nose that I'd once seen described as aquiline. She was wearing a black turtleneck and blue jeans and she was lugging a small, beat-up suitcase. *Come to me,* I thought, trying to send messages to her through the dark air of the bus. *Sit here, woman. Sit beside me and learn to love me and I will meet you every night and you can wear a veil and look at me with dark eyes and I will love you more than all the earth. Here. In this empty seat. Beside me. Please.* She started down the aisle, looking left and right, and stopped at the empty seat beside me.

"This taken?" she said. There was something scared in her hoarse voice. If she was wearing makeup, I couldn't see it. Her lips were full, and she had a mole on her left cheekbone.

"No, it's open," I said, standing up. "Need a hand with that?"

I took the suitcase and heaved it up into the baggage rack. The bus was moving now.

"Thanks, sailor," she said. I sat back down and she seemed to collapse in the seat beside me. She put a large leather purse on her lap. Her legs were clamped together but I could see strong thighs under the jeans. *Go ahead,* I thought. *Talk to her. Say something. Say anything. Speak. She is here. You wanted her here. Speak.*

"Goin' to Pensacola?" I said. *Oh you dumb kid. You asshole. Asking a dumb-kid question.*

"I guess," she said.

"Me too," I said. "I hear it's beautiful."

"I wouldn't know. Never been there before."

Her accent was Southern, but the rhythm was odd. It wasn't like the corn-pone accents I'd heard in the movies or on the radio. Her voice was more slurred, like the voice of Billie Holiday. I looked at her face again. There were tiny lines around the corners of her eyes and a little pad of fat under her chin. The skin was pulled tight across her cheekbones. I couldn't tell how old she was. And that excited me even more. All I was sure of was that she wasn't a kid.

"I never been there before either," I said. "I'm looking forward, you know. See it . . . "

"Well, you'll be comfy there, I reckon. It's all sailors, so I hear."

"One of the biggest bases in the country."

"Imagine that."

She was curt, in a polite way, but she wasn't freezing me out. She just seemed to have something else on her mind. Then, without willing it, my eyes drifted to her chest and she must have felt my look and turned slightly to the left, pulling the leather bag close to her body. Even then, she didn't cut me off.

"You're a Yankee, right?" she said.

"Yeah. Well, I'm from New York. But we'd go nuts where I came from if you called us Yankees. I'm from Brooklyn and we hate the Yankees. The ball team, I mean."

"Well," she said, and smiled, "you're in the right part of the country f' hatin' Yankees."

Please, do that again. Smile like that again. And say "part" like it was pronounced "paht." And smile that wide smile, with those hard white teeth. Please.

She turned to me. "Mind if I smoke?" Saying it *mahnd.*

"No, no, go ahead." She took a pack of Luckies from the purse and lit one. The movement was pure Ida Lupino. But in the match's flare, I saw that she had ugly hands. The skin was raw and her veins jutted up and she had chewed her nails down close. Then she took a drag and exhaled and the smoke drifted up into the darkness and I forgot the hands and wanted her to teach me everything she knew.

"Sure don't feel like New Year's, does it?" she said.

"It sure doesn't," I said, wondering *What does my voice sound like?* "How'd you get stuck on this bus tonight, anyway?"

She turned and looked at me. Her eyes were dark brown and lustrous and she looked straight at me. Really *looked* at me. None of that flirting stuff that a thousand generations of women had been taught back home. "How did *you?*" she said, a little annoyed curl in her voice. I smiled and told her I was assigned to Pensacola. That they gave me a Christmas leave but insisted I report to Pensacola on New Year's Day. She smiled and glanced at my body and turned away and took another drag on the cigarette. I was right: she wasn't wearing lipstick.

"Who knows?" she said. "Who ever knows?"

She tamped out the cigarette and put her head back and closed her eyes, holding the purse tightly. When her face relaxed, the lines at the side of her eyes widened. Under the eyes, there were bluish smudges. Fatigue. Or age. I couldn't tell. The bus was moving into open country now and I could see her only in glimpses of light from passing cars. Suddenly, I wanted to draw her, defining her hair with a million pen lines, all curling, twisting, moving, making the shadows with a brush fat with ink. I wanted her to take off the turtleneck and stand before me and let me draw her. On paper, she would be mine. Her eyes opened.

"Why are you starin at me, child?"

" 'Cause you're beautiful. I guess." And wished I hadn't added that "I guess." I didn't need doubt. Or qualification.

She was quiet for a moment, and then said, "How old are you?"

And I said (taking it from a movie or a story or from somebody else), "Old enough."

She smiled again, showing those teeth.

"Old enough for *what*?"

She giggled when she said that, and I thought of Turner: *People laugh at sailors.*

"Old enough to tell you you're beautiful."

She fumbled for a fresh cigarette and sighed. "Well, I sure don't *feel* beautiful. But I guess I'll take the compliment. Thank you, child." She lighted another Lucky and offered me the pack and when I shook my head, she tucked them away. She held the cigarette in her left hand, which was bent almost at a right angle to her arm. "You got *any* vices, child?" I hated that "child." It sounded as if she was playing with me. Keeping me at a distance by treating me like a kid. And I thought: *Give her the worldly look, the Flip Corkin set of the mouth.* I assumed it, and shrugged off her question in a weary way. She said "You got somethin wrong with your mouth?"

Shit.

"No. Why?"

"Never mind." She took a deep drag and leaned back and blew a perfect smoke ring, then a second smaller one. Just like the Camels sign in Times Square. And I thought, *She's performing for me. Maybe she's trying to act as cool for me as I am for her.*

"Where'd you learn to do *that*?" I said.

"A sick damn cousin of mine. And I mean sick in the head. That girl knew everything bad there was to know. Started me smokin when I was eight."

"You're kidding. Eight?"

"Well, I tried it when I was eight. Just puffin and like that. I really started serious when I was nine."

I laughed and so did she.

"Where you from?" I said.

She paused. "Down here. From the South."

"Any special place?"

"No."

She was avoiding an answer, pushing me back. She stared at her cigarette. Then in the back of the bus someone started to sing:

"Should auld acquaintance be forgot . . . " She turned, as if to listen, then took a small nervous drag. *"And ne'er be brought to mind? . . . "* Others were joining in, and I was humming, and she started to sing too, very quietly, and tamped out the cigarette and closed her eyes. *"For auld lang syne, my dears, for auld lang syne . . ."* The bus was loud with the song now, with New Year's Eve, with the sadness of the old words in a sad bus heading south. *"We'll tak a cup o' kindness yet . . ."* She opened her eyes. They were brimming. When she closed them, tears slipped down the sides of her face. *"For auld lang syne . . . "*

She didn't open her eyes again. Her hands clenched and unclenched. Then they were still. The bus grew quiet. We passed through an endless region of blackness. Then, on a long wide turn, she fell gently against me. Deep in sleep. And didn't move. I could smell her hair. Clean and washed. She smelled a lot better than I did. There was a slight snore coming from her. Her right arm was flat and still on my thigh, lying there for a while, and then her hand took hold, hugging my leg in the dark. My heart moved quickly, pumping excitement through me. I was sure this was a signal, a moment of intimacy, a display of confidence and safety. I was desperate for the love of a woman. And here she was. We'd met in the dark on a New Year's Eve and she was telling me from sleep that there were joinings that did not depend on words. I could feel her breath against my arm, the rhythmic rise and fall of her body. Old enough, I thought.

Chapter

5

ALMOST AS SOON as she had appeared in my life, she was gone.
I woke up suddenly in a world full of morning green. The woman's
seat was empty. I turned and saw other empty seats on the bus, and
a black man with gray hair looking at me in a knowing way and
Turner four rows in front, sleeping with his head against a window.
But the woman wasn't on the bus. She'd talked to me and slept
against me and had gripped my flesh and now she was gone. Like
that. While I slept. I didn't even remember falling asleep and
cursed myself for weakness. And then thought: *Maybe it was a
dream. Maybe I made this up. Maybe my desperation for a woman had
invented her, brought her on board this bus on a lonesome New Year's Eve,
with her oval face and rough veined hands and wild hair.* But I checked
the ashtray. And like one of those scenes at the end of a fairy-tale
movie, there was physical proof of the angelic visitation: her
crushed Luckies.

So I gazed around, full of her leaving (even now, all these years
later, I fear a woman's departure during sleep). And angry with
myself. I was such a goddamned kid that I didn't find out where she
was from and where she was going. I hadn't even found out her
name. I stared at the passing country, my eyes drowned in a billion
shades of green. Dark, bright, rich, glossy. On all sides of the road
as the bus rushed along on its ribbon of tar. *She's out there somewhere,*
I thought, as the meshed greens rose like walls when we picked up
speed on a downslope, and then separated as the bus settled. I could
see foliage at the edge of the road and beyond that a swampy river,
and, away off, a haze hanging in the branches of the forests. *She's
here in the green southern world.*

This was before I knew the names of the natural world. But I was looking at broom grass and blackjack oak, elder and sassafrass, honeysuckle and sycamores and water oak and willows. And in a blur I felt her hand move in the drowsing dark, holding my cock, her voice small and fearful, my hand led under the black turtleneck to the fullness of her breasts. That was real. Or it was a dream. I'm uncertain even now. I looked for reassurance to the Luckies in the ashtray. And turned away to see the river moving sluggishly in its swampy channel, and saw (but did not recognize) banks of abandoned sugar cane, Spanish moss draping live oaks, sudden movements in the darker green, insects hovering like helicopters and then suddenly jabbing the surface of the opaque water. *Her veined hand, her breasts.* I saw abrupt saddles of dry land covered with shivering grass *as her voice shivered in the blur* and then we were again in the darkness of the swamp. Trees rose monstrously, blocking the sky. There were mangrove trees among them, their roots plunged into the water, gnarled and knuckled, like huge hands frozen while searching for some smooth and agile quarry. *I will find her.*

And then the swamp was gone and the bus moved into a zone of luminous blond light. The earth itself was lighter, sandier, the grass bleached, and I began to see houses off in the distance, made of silvery unpainted boards, with plumes of blue smoke drifting up from brick chimneys. In the lee of a small hill, three crumpled-looking cows lay under a giant shade tree and beyond them a white boy galloped bareback on a chestnut horse.

I had no sense that any of these things were real. The woman who had sat beside me in the night: Was she real? And were these real rivers and trees and swamps and insects, real shacks and cows and horses? I wished I could stop the bus and wander around in this strange new morning world. This South. Wander until I'd found her. *Please stop the bus, driver. Let me touch the South. Let me find my woman.* I wanted to see it with her, understand it, read books and maps, ask a million questions, find out the names of the trees and the towns and the people. I wanted to know what armies had fought across the landscape and who the heroes were. And the villains. And the explorers. And the wild men. *The South. I'm in the South.*

I swore that I would find her. Track her down. Discover where she got off and retrace the steps. Just like a detective. Like Canyon. Or Buz Sawyer. Like Holmes or Philip Marlowe. Ask people and describe her. And finally meet her at dusk somewhere, and she'll say, *How old are you?* And I'll say, *Old enough.* And she'll say, *Don't you have a woman back home?* And I'll say, *Not anymore.* And she'll say, *Well, you might as well spend the night.* Yes. Like that.

Then up ahead there was a gigantic brightening, the sky suddenly fuller and whiter. The bus heaved up a long sloping rise and the trees became sparse and then at the crest of the rise I could see the land falling away for miles, and the smudged air of many chimneys and the first gas station and a restaurant called Mom's and a sign saying BAIT and then groups of Negroes, men and women, walking along the sides of the road and cars falling in behind the bus and flatbed trucks moving toward us in the other lane. I opened the bus window and was slapped by a hot, damp wind. And then, beyond the buildings and the smoke and the scrubby mottled surface of the land, out past the trucks and the Negroes, I could see the wide blue waters of the Gulf.

"Well," Turner said, standing in the aisle beside me, stretching the muscles of his face, cracking his knuckles, "we're here."

Chapter

6

ONE NIGHT, AFTER we had made love, my third wife asked me how many women I'd slept with, and I laughed and said she didn't want to know. Turning in fury, slamming the pillow, she insisted. She was in the stage of our marriage when she was demanding some abstraction called intimacy, the most favored word that year of women's magazines and the self-help industry. "If you don't tell me," she hissed, "I'll never *ever* know you." Rose had a genius for making small talk seem like a stickup. I reached for a cigarette and sighed and started to calculate. But my long pause filled her with the grief she must have been seeking; she sobbed, she cursed, she pulled a pillow over her head. And I tried to remember all those faces, the blurred flesh of three decades and five continents, blond hair and brown, pale skin and olive, bodies thin and thick. Furious, she got up, slamming the door on her way to the bathroom, and was gone a long time, and when she came back, I said I thought the number was around twelve hundred. But then, I added, I couldn't be expected to remember everything. She fell back as if wounded and lay in a theatrical state of trembling shock. I knew almost immediately that I should have lied; some truths are always unacceptable. To say that she had asked for this information—had *demanded* it—wasn't sufficient excuse. Actually *telling* her was cruel, even stupid. So then I lied. In the name of peace. I told her that I was only kidding, that I'd slept with only twenty-odd women, including wives, and none were as good as Rose was in bed and she smiled through tears and looked grateful and in an hour was talking about Elizabeth Taylor's diet. But as I lay beside her in the dark,

and then made love to her again (another lie), with my brain
flooding with the images of other women, I remembered the first.
The woman I'd seen so briefly on a bus. The woman named Eden
Santana. And tonight, close to the Gulf again, I am full of the aching
loneliness I felt the first time I thought I had lost her forever. Eden
Santana.

We had arrived in Pensacola at last, the bright sun hurting my
eyes. There was no bus station. The Greyhound pulled up at a curb
and I saw signs telling me I was on the corner of Garden Street and
North Palafox. "Pensacola, folks," the driver said, and there was
a wheeze of doors opening and then people were pulling luggage
from racks. Turner went ahead. I stopped and talked to the driver.

"There was a woman sitting beside me," I said. "Got on in
Atlanta, got off somewhere between there and here."

"White woman?"

"Yeah."

"I remember. Yeah. Pretty woman. Got off with some cullid
folks in, oh, hell, musta been Palatka."

"Where's that?"

"Oh, fipty mile back. She figget somethin?"

"No. Nothing. I was just . . . "

He smiled. "She was a looker, awright."

"Yeah."

That was all. I'd met her, felt her body against mine, was sure
somehow that she had touched me in the night, felt all other women
vanish from me, felt all things to be possible; and she was gone. In
some place called Palatka. I got off and saw Turner drinking from
a water fountain shoved against a wall in the shade. It was marked
"White." The water dribbled steadily into a white ceramic dish. A
pipe ran five feet from the white fountain to the right, connecting
to a smaller fountain labeled "Colored." None of the Negroes used
their fountain.

"Taste like seawater," Turner said, pulling a face. "Maybe
they're tryin to get us feelin at home."

"Should I try it?"

"Seawater drives you crazy, sailor."

"I guess I'll wait."

"You can watch a while and see if I go crazy."

"By then I'll be dead of thirst."

The local buses were around the corner of Palafox, engines

idling in the sun. A group of sailors waited in single file to board a bus marked Mainside. The Greyhound driver came around the corner with a bundle of copies of the *Atlanta Constitution* and dropped them in the lobby of a movie theater called the Rex. *The Glass Menagerie* was on the marquee, but the doors were locked, the box office dark.

"Well, I'll see you, Devlin," Turner said. "There must be another bus goes to Ellyson. I gotta jump this one to Mainside."

I told him I would see him around and we shook hands and said good-bye. I felt strange. I'd heard about the man's wives on the long ride. I'd drunk his whiskey. Now he was vanishing. Just like that. And I thought that as I went around in the world more and more people were like characters in movies: You saw them on the screen, you got to know them, and then they were gone. Turner was like that. And the woman with the curly hair. All the guys from boot camp. The guys I knew in high school. Buddies to the death. And then gone. At the door of the Mainside bus, Turner shook my hand, nodded good-bye, then turned on the steps and said, "Happy New Year."

I waved, and the Mainside bus pulled away from the curb and moved out of sight. I stood there alone for a long while. Tonight, arriving here for the first time in more than thirty years, I drove into the center of Pensacola again, to get my bearings, and found that exact spot. I was thrown instantly back into that first day-bright arrival when I was some other person. Neat careful rows of palm trees seemed to be at parade rest all the way up the broad sloping street. About four blocks up, I could see three churches plugging the avenue, staring down at the town in a gloomy stone-faced way. They gave me a chilly moment, pebbling my skin; in 1953, churches always seemed to be saying *No*. So I turned my back on them that morning and looked around the empty sunbaked corner. There was a hotel called the San Carlos across the street, and as I waited for the Ellyson bus I counted floors. I did the same thing again tonight, gazing up at the shuttered hotel, its boarded doors and begrimed windows. Nine stories, including the ground floor. Tonight a wino slept where a Negro doorman in a white uniform once stood on the steps. There was a bar and restaurant on either side of the entrance; the polished glass of both were now hidden behind sheets of plywood. A thick-bodied man in a sleeveless undershirt stared out a third-floor window that first day, and though back then there were few other signs of life, tonight there were none at all. That first day in Pensacola, I thought the usual guests must all be home for the holidays, sleeping off hangovers, getting laid. Tonight I thought they must all be dead.

To the right of the San Carlos there was (and is) a small red-brick building, and beside that a cream-colored church whose cross and steeple were level with the hotel's sixth floor. The brick building must be the rectory, I thought. And the church bore a cross, so it must be Catholic. Looks Spanish, too, I thought. Or Mexican. Like pictures of churches in *National Geographic* in places where the sun was hot and clear and blinding. And I remembered the brief lines in the encyclopedia, about Pensacola being called "The City of Five Flags." The book said it had changed hands thirteen times in twenty years. Obviously, the name itself must be Spanish. Pensa-cola. Cola-cola. Pepsi-Cola. *Nickel-nickel, ta-rootie-da-dot-tah.* . . .

I was sweating hard and could smell my own stink rising out of the thick wool winter uniform that I'd worn from the North. Thinking then (as I would later, with other women) that maybe that was why she'd left. The odor of my body, unwashed for two long days, glazed by other men's cigarette smoke and farts and whiskey breaths: it must have driven her out of the seat and then out of the bus. Maybe she thought all sailors smelled like me. For all I knew, maybe they *did.* Maybe she had been nauseated by the possibility that Pensacola would be a whole town full of stinking sailors and she would rather get off in Palatka with a bunch of colored people than keep on going. Or perhaps there was some other reason. Something more mysterious, scary, female.

Then a battered gray bus pulled around the corner from Garden Street and stopped in front of the Rex theater. A piece of cardboard was jammed between the windshield and the dashboard. *Ellyson Field,* it said, hand-lettered in a tight, awkward way. The door opened. A civilian driver got out and stretched.

"This go to Ellyson Field?" I said.

"What's the sign say, sailor? Brownsville, Texas?"

I got on and sat in a front seat, feeling stupider than ever. Where was Brownsville, Texas, anyway? And why didn't I say anything back to the man? I wished I could react like the bus driver did. Quickly. Sarcastically. And then thought *I never learned her goddamned name.* I shifted around, as if expecting her to step off some other bus, maybe the local from Palatka, and saw three sailors in

soiled whites hurrying around the side of the San Carlos hotel.
They were waving frantically at the bus, mouthing words I couldn't
hear. The driver was behind the wheel now, and looked at them
in a blank disgusted way. Then two civilians came down the street,
carrying lunch in paper bags. They all got on the bus. The sailors
were in their late twenties. I could see from their shoulder patches
that one of them was a gunner's mate, another a second-class radio-
man, the third a machinist. They were cursing and laughing, bleary
from a long night's drinking. They went all the way to the rear and
sat down hard. The civilians eased into a seat across the aisle from
me. They said nothing, as if by their silence they were issuing a
judgment of the drunk sailors in the rear. As for me, a hairless kid
in dress blues, I didn't exist. The driver came back and glanced at
his watch and then looked at me.

"What's the fare?" I said.

"No charge in uniform," the driver said. "You jest comin
aboard, boy?"

"Yeah."

"Be careful when you get to Ellyson. The excitement's libel to
kill ya."

Then he slid in behind the wheel, put the bus in gear, closed the
door and moved up Palafox Street. This route was to become a
permanent part of my life, one of those templates that are engraved
on the mind forever. I've lost all traces of offices where I've
worked, houses where I've lived with women, the terrain of battle-
fields where my life came close to ending. I've never forgotten the
road to Ellyson Field. I saw a luncheonette, a clothing store, a
jeweler's; then a large United States Courthouse, a restaurant called
the Driftwood, a deli. The names were different when I cruised the
block tonight, but the basic structures remained the same. There
were the three churches, which on that day long ago revealed
themselves to be Lutheran, Baptist, a Masonic temple. In the New
Year's Day sunlight, while snow choked the northern cities, people
stood outside each of the churches, keeping to themselves. There
were men in dark suits, looking hot and alien in the brightness, and
a lot of what at the time I called older women, at least in their
thirties, wearing long dresses and straw hats and white gloves and
low-heeled sensible shoes. All were carrying Bibles. I looked at the
women, searching for my lost night woman with the curly hair,
thinking that her hair would be wild in the heat, that she might have

exchanged her jeans and turtleneck for a yellow summer dress. But she wasn't there; they were all strangers. Not one of them knew me. *She called me child.*

We moved into a rougher area. One-story buildings made of raw concrete blocks. Jumbled scrapyards full of rusting, anonymous iron. Auto-repair shops with greasy sidewalks out front. A few cheap luncheonettes, closed for New Year's. There were telegraph poles everywhere. And still no people. The light here was less intense than it had been on Palafox. Across the aisle, the civilians sat like statues. But I could hear mumbling and sudden laughter from the sailors in the back, as if they were recalling what had happened during the night. I wished I could tell someone what had happened to *me* during the night. *O curly-haired woman without a name.*

Then we were out of the ugly district, moving into open country. The fields along the highway were ruled into neat rows of vegetables, and there were more Negroes walking along the edge of the road and more churches: smaller, made of wood or concrete blocks, with white steeples on the larger ones, signs calling to sinners: CHRIST IS RISEN NOW IT'S YOUR TURN and CHRIST IS ON THE WAY and WHAT DOTH IT PROFIT A MAN?

The bus slowed as we passed a row of honky-tonks on both sides of the road, flat-roofed one-story buildings with cars parked outside. The Circle O and Good Times and Jack's Port 'o' Call and The Palms Away and The Fleet's Inn. Some had signs in the windows saying PACKAGE STORE or FISH FRY or BURGERS. The bus stopped at a red light. Cars darted out of the side street. Then a sailor in dress whites came hurrying from a place called The Anchor Inn. The driver opened the door. The man climbed in, a machinist's mate, third class, breathing hard, his eyes runny and sore. He needed a shave. The sailors in the back all started applauding. One of them shouted: "You didn't get the clap this time, Roscoe, you oughtta shoot yisself in the foot!"

"Fuck you bastards," he said.

"You now got yisself the only discharge you'll ever see!"

He laughed and went past me to join the others in the back. From the open door of The Anchor Inn I heard a fragment of music from the jukebox. Guitars. A woman's sad and wounded voice. It could have been in another language. At home, when I heard pieces of music, the whole song would play through my head. But this was hillbilly music, music out of the South, and I didn't know any of it. The tavern door closed. I realized it had been days since I'd heard any music at all. Just "Auld Lang Syne" on the Greyhound bus. Today, every time I hear it I remember that New Year's night on the bus. And when I hear country music, I'm back in the South, moving along those roads.

The driver turned right at a cross street, and there ahead of me was a long avenue, with unkempt fields on each side and small stunted palm trees planted along the shoulders. Eight-foot barbed-wire fences bordered the empty fields. Then I could see a brick building getting larger as we came closer and a sign that said HTU-I ELLYSON FIELD and Marines with tan uniforms and white belts and pistols on their hips, watching the approach of the bus. And beyond them I could see this place where I was going to live for a long time: hangars, a lone helicopter the size of an insect rising from a hidden landing strip, and then barracks, white and silent, on green lawns off to the left. Ellyson Field. Where they trained helicopter pilots for the Navy and the Marines, men who went from here to Korea and picked fliers right out of the sea after they'd been shot down. I knew nobody. Nobody at all. I was very hungry and my stomach tingled and then turned uneasy and I wondered who was here to try to break me and who wished me harm. I took out my packet of orders and got my ID card ready and then wondered why I was there at all.

The bus made a slow half turn and stopped parallel to the gate. I was the only passenger with a sea bag, so I waited for the others to get off, then stepped out and saw the others presenting their ID cards to a Marine sergeant. The civilians nodded to the Marines, the sailors saluted. I went up to the sergeant.

"Airman apprentice Michael Devlin reporting for duty, sir," I said and saluted. The Marine's face was a formal grid. He looked at the papers and the ID card and then at me. He returned the salute.

"Welcome aboard, sailor," he said.

Chapter

7

WITH THE SEA BAG on my shoulder, I walked down the main
street of the base, following the Marine's directions to the barracks.
I tried to walk in what I thought was a rolling, sea-duty gait, just
in case anyone was watching, an affectation so heavily practiced
then that it became in fact my adult walk. In the years that followed,
women sometimes laughed at it, and so did I, but it is now too late
to make a change. Sometimes you actually become what you want
to become. But on the first day of 1953 I was not yet formed as a
man, and was still anxiously trying on the various styles of the
world. Perhaps that's why I still see myself so clearly, walking for
the first time into Ellyson Field. Anxiety sure does sharpen focus.

I know that I turned left into a street without sidewalks. And I
remember how the grass came right down to the curbs, as precisely
cut as my boot-camp crewcut, uniformly green and flat and perfect.
A rich, creamy earth smell rose from the grass and little jewels of
water sparkled among the blades. That odor is one of the memories
I can never reclaim in the way buildings can be revisited, and
streets; my senses have been blunted by too many cigarettes. Everywhere I go, the American air is now stained with the fumes of
gasoline and chemicals. That day I inhaled the fresh wet air and
thought: *I'm in Florida, goddamnit, and nobody I ever knew has been here
before me.*

Three raked gravel paths were cut through the grass from the
street to the barracks doors. I stood there for a moment, wondering
which door to choose, hearing the chirring sound of insects in the
close, drowsy air. The Bachelor's Enlisted Men's Quarters were in

a wooden building almost a block long, painted a shiny white. Birds clung to the peak of the tar-papered roof. I couldn't see through the screened windows. The entire building was three feet off the ground, on concrete blocks the color of mice.

I turned and looked around at my new slice of the world. Most of the base was blocked from my view by the low white building right across the street. My pulse quickened when I saw a sign saying *Supply Department.* That's where I'd be working. And I felt as if I'd put something over on the Navy Department. I could sleep late and still make muster in less than a minute. *Right across the street.* Beautiful.

From where I stood, the building seemed to be divided in two. There was a door in the center, and through the windows on the left of it I could see the rough wood of packing crates. Nothing was clear through the screened windows on the right. *That's where they must work,* I thought, *and all the gear must be stored in the section on the left.* I was standing there for what seemed a long moment, trying to imagine what might happen to me on the other side of those doors, when I heard from a great distance the sound of a saxophone.

He was playing the blues. A slow, mournful tune, drifting from somewhere on the empty base. Long sad lines. And then a pause. And then more long lines. A tenor, probably. Little phrases breaking and curling around themselves and then a longer line, and then a pause again. Sounding as lonesome as I was. Like a broken heart. Or hunger. Or jail.

Then it stopped. I waited and listened. But there was no other sound except the insects and the muffled engine of a lone helicopter: *chumpchump chumpchump chumpchump.*

I lifted the sea bag and started up the path to the barracks, my feet crunching on the gravel. I opened the screen door, and went through into a cool gray room with a picture of Harry Truman on the wall. He was still president; Eisenhower had been elected the previous November, but wouldn't take office until January. To the right was a corkboard covered with Navy bulletins; a small wooden table and chair were shoved against the wall. Through an archway, I could see double-decker bunks divided down the center by a row of high metal lockers. The floor was scrubbed almost white. Sunlight knifed through the windows, making glaring patterns on the floor. I laid the sea bag down and stepped into the room. There wasn't a single person in sight. I remember feeling like a burglar.

"Hello?" I said. "Anybody home?"

There was no answer.

Then I heard a toilet flushing at the far end of the row of bunks and walked toward the sound. Names were stenciled on some of the lockers. Each bunk was made up like the next, the mattress covers pulled taut and rough Navy blankets folded at the foot. I heard water running, then stopping. And then someone whistling: "Cry." By Johnnie Ray. A big hit in '51. Even if you hated the singer or the song, there was no way to avoid the words, because for most of a year you heard it everywhere:

> *If your sweetheart*
> *Sends a letter of good-bye . . .*

A man in faded blue dungarees suddenly walked out of the head, whistling the tune. He stopped and smiled. Lank brown hair, freckled skin, crooked smile.

"Hey, whatta ya say?" the man said.

I fell into the response: "Airman apprentice Michael Devlin reporting for—"

"Jack Waleski," he said, shaking my hand. "You just get assigned here?"

"Yeah."

"What did you do wrong?"

"Well, I didn't ask for it," I said. I didn't mention Port Lyautey; that might truly sound weird. "They—"

"Yeah, nobody ever *asks* for Pensacola."

He took out a pack of Chesterfields, laughing to himself. He offered me one and I turned it down. He lit a cigarette.

"The thing to know," he said, "is that about the time you realize this *is* the asshole of the earth, it gets worse."

He laughed in a wheezy way. I asked him how bad it could be, and he shook his head.

"Look, I got the watch here today," he said, cupping the cigarette to keep the ashes from falling on the floor, "but I'll tell you what: Get out of those blues and into a shower. Then pick yourself a rack. When you're settled, come down to the office and I'll give you the gouge on Pensacola."

"It didn't look too bad coming in."

"Pal, It makes Shit City look like Paris."

I smiled as he walked away. Okay. This guy was okay. The place was gonna be okay. Waleski stopped and shouted:

"I was you, I'd get in that shower real fast, sailor. You're a little ripe."

"I sure am," I said, and thought about the woman with the curly hair.

Away off, I could hear the saxophone again, playing the blues.

Chapter

8

I PICKED AN EMPTY top rack on the shady side of the lockers. I unlocked my sea bag and found a pair of whites. Then I stripped off the gummy woolen blues and for the first time felt the hot damp air of the Gulf on my skin. The horn player's sadness drifted through the screened windows of the barracks. He was playing "Boulevard of Broken Dreams," in a jazzy, middle-of-the night way. I wiggled my hot sore feet into rubber thongs, humming: *I walk along the street of sorrows . . .*

In an empty locker opposite the bunk, I hung up the pea jacket, then stacked my skivvies, T-shirts, socks, dungarees. The locker was narrow but deep. I turned my blues inside out to let them dry and laid them across the striped uncovered mattress. I still had my ditty bag from boot camp, lumpy with shaving gear, Pepsodent, deodorant, and I laid that on the rack too, along with a standard-issue Navy towel.

At the bottom of the sea bag were three books, and I took them out, too. One was *The Bluejackets' Manual,* navy blue and compact; it was a kind of catechism for sailors, full of rules and regulations. The second was a book my Aunt Margaret had given me for Christmas. She was my mother's sister and was married to an undertaker and lived in Manhattan. She was always giving me books. This one was called *A Treasury of Art Masterpieces.* It had been put together by someone named Thomas Craven. On the cover, there was a beautiful yellow-haired woman rising naked from the sea, one hand covering a breast, the other holding the long hair over her crotch. The third was The Blue Notebook. I slipped it inside the art book and put the books deep into the back of the locker.

Waleski came back with a blanket, a pillow and a mattress cover. "They say every man in this man's Navy is guaranteed three squares a day and a dry fartsack," he said. "Here's the fartsack."

As he turned to leave, I asked him who the horn player was. Waleski cocked his head, listening. "You mean Bobby Bolden? He's a bad ass, a war hero, a prick, and a whoremaster. But he sure can play the saxophone, can't he?"

"Sure can."

"Want some advice? Stay away from him."

I remember shaving for the first time in the deserted head with its shallow sinks and small mirrors, urinals and doorless toilet stalls. In a corner there was a metal trashcan fitted with a large white laundry sack. A hand-lettered sign said: LUCKY BAG. In the Navy, that was where you threw stray or worn-out clothing, and you were free to take anything that you might use. I glanced at it and thought: *She smoked Luckies.* She was out there somewhere. Probably with a man. A man who knew what he was doing. Who didn't have a kid's smooth face or have to submit to the discipline of the Navy. She was out there. In Palatka. A breeze lifted the palm fronds outside the screened window, rattling them against one another. And I thought: *Until this day I've never seen palm trees. Except in movies and comics and* National Geographic. *And here I am, shaving at a sink, and they're right outside the window. I can hear them rattle. I can hear them sigh. I could walk outside and touch them. In Florida.* Pen-sa-co-la. *I'm here. I've come a long way from Brooklyn to this special place. I've done it. She smoked Luckies with her left hand.*

In the shower, I turned the hot-water knob as high as I could, hoping the hurting water would wash away the long trip, the three different buses and drivers, perhaps even the fragile memory of the woman with the curly hair. I didn't want to leave the scalding luxury of the shower. Until I went into the Navy, I'd never showered alone. To stand under a shower alone, your hair squeaking and your skin pink and red: paradise. I felt that then; I believe it now, and to hell with the Freudian interpretations. I remember confessing this once to a guy in boot camp. Told him I'd never taken a shower alone. And he didn't believe me. He had grown up in a house, not a railroad flat in Brooklyn. I couldn't explain about our flat, with its L-shaped bathroom—the tub crammed into one arm of the L, the toilet in the other, with a sink in between. In the years

since, I've tried to explain it to women who wanted to know why
I spent so long in the shower, telling them how there was barely
room to turn around and the water pipes were scalding hot in all
seasons so you could never relax and lean against them, and the
roaches fattened in the dampness and the single window was sealed
by generations of paint. Women didn't get it. Nobody gets it. And
on that first day in Ellyson Field, even I was sick of the images of
my old life. *Hey, man* (I said to my young self): *Stop this! You're here.
You made it. You're in Florida, and it's snowing in New York.*

I was drying myself with a towel when I heard Bobby Bolden
playing again. A quick jump tune. The words moved through my
head: *Jumpin with my boy Sid in the city. He's the pres-i-dent of the deejay
committee . . .* Lester Young wrote it and King Pleasure sang it. For
Symphony Sid's radio show on WEVD, the ethnic radio station. I
used to listen at night, fall asleep, and wake up to a lot of singing
Hungarians. The weirdest station in New York. They had a Hungarian hour and a Russian hour and an Irish hour and a Lithuanian
hour. And every night at midnight, Sid showed up to play jazz. I
was then so young that I actually cared about being hip or square,
and I knew that Sid was hip. I was also sure that Bobby Bolden was
hip, even though I'd never met him. And I thought: *I gotta meet this
guy.* I finished drying myself, wrapped a towel around my waist and
wriggled into the shower shoes. I picked up the ditty bag and soiled
skivvies and flip-flopped back to the bunk

I paused in the archway. An older sailor was standing at my bunk,
a billy club attached to his wrist with a leather thong. He was
tapping it gently on his thigh. A first-class gunner's mate. In dress
whites. He was shorter than I was, but his back was very straight
and muscles rippled under his tight jumper. There were three hash
marks on his sleeve, each standing for a four-year hitch. He looked
like a battering ram. And I felt suddenly afraid. Not of the hard
body. Or the billy club. It was his face. Pale red sideburns. The
white hat precisely two fingers above where his brows should have
been. Except that he had no eyebrows. And no eyelashes. His eyes
were a slushy pale blue and he didn't blink. His mouth was a slice.
Lipless. Without color. Bracketed by two lines that seemed etched
into his cheeks. The skin on his face was shiny. Like plastic. This
was my first sight of Red Cannon.

He moved a few feet to his left and stood beside the locker I'd
chosen. His eyes never left me. He didn't speak a word. For a

moment, I felt as if I were looking down from the ceiling at the two of us. I saw the empty barracks, the palm trees outside, and felt the breeze coming through the windows. And the young man facing the Old Salt. We locked eyes for a long time. Two seconds or an hour. Even now I can remember the feeling, the knowledge that if I broke the stare I was doomed. Fear entered my belly like a piece of ice.

Finally, without taking my eyes off him, I said: "Excuse me."

I reached for the locker but the gunner's mate didn't move. I would have to go though him to get to the locker.

"That's my locker," I said.

Something like a smile showed on his face. But he didn't move. For a moment his eyes clouded, as if a drop of milk had been added to the slushy blue. And then they were diving deep into me, probing for weakness or softness like a knife. And I broke it off. I turned to the side and fiddled with my towel and groped in the ditty bag for something I didn't want. I felt humiliated. The gunner's mate had faced me down. And I'd quit to him like a dog. In this strange and alien place. On New Year's Day. A long way from home.

"What's your name, boy?" the man whispered.

"Michael Devlin."

"Your *Navy* name, boy."

"464 0267."

"464 0267, *what?*"

"464 0267, sir."

There was a long, silent moment. He stared at me, and I tried to smile in a casual way to cover up my fear.

"Open it," he said, stepping aside from the locker. His short arms were hanging at his sides. "Let's see what y' *got* heah, boy."

I turned the combination lock. Six, for the month I was born. Twenty-four, for the day. Thirty-five, for the year. I unhooked the lock and lifted the latch and opened the locker door. The gunner's mate stared into it. Then, with his free hand, he grabbed the edge of the door and slammed it hard. The sound was explosive. He did it again. And again, the metallic sound caroming through the barracks. And then he did it once more.

"*First* off, boy, this ain't *your* locker, heah?"

He snarled the words and then banged the door with the billy club.

"This heah locker is the property of the Yew-Nited States *Navy.*"

He banged it again. "Second of all, you aint s'posed even be *near* this lockuh 'thout my p'mission. You unna*stand* me?"

He slammed the door again. His mouth was quivering but the glossy skin on his face didn't move. Then he looked inside. He reached to the back of one shelf and pulled out everything: work shirts, dress whites, skivvies, socks. He cleaned out the second shelf. Then he dropped my pea coat on top of the pile on the floor.

"Now, heah this, boy. I am the M A A on this base. The Master at Arms, case you don't know what I'm saying to you. *I* assign the racks in these barracks. *Me!* Nobody else. You got that? *Me!* First-class gunner's mate Wendell Cannon, U.S.N."

"Sir, I was told—"

"I don't give a rat's ass *what* you was told, boy. *I'm* tellin you now. You don't pick a locker, you don't pick a rack, you don't pick your goddamn nose, less I give you p'mission. You got me?"

His eyes fell to the clothes, then wandered back to the locker. "What in the *fuck*?"

He lifted out the oversized art book with the long-haired Botticelli blonde on the cover. He blinked as he read the title. Then he turned to me.

"*A Treasury of* Art *Masterpieces?*"

"Yes, sir. I—"

"*A Treasury of* Art *Masterpieces?*" he screamed. He shook the book in my face. "What are you, some kind of gahdam *faggot*?" His voice rose another decibel. "What in the fuck is *this* doing in a locker in *this man's Navy?*"

He whirled and heaved the book the length of the barracks. I saw it bounce off an empty rack and skid across the floor. The Blue Notebook fell out, but Cannon didn't seem to notice. He was looking at me. Waiting. I stepped forward. A red film fell over everything. My body was bursting. I wanted to swing out and destroy him, but when my hands came up, the towel fell. I was naked before him. He had his jaw clamped shut, breathing hard through his nose. His eyes widened. I stepped forward. An inch from his face. The blue eyes didn't blink.

"You thinkin of *doing* somethin, boy?" he said quietly. "Standing there with yo' pecker hangin out? Huh? You want to *do* something?"

I didn't say anything.

"Well, I'll tell you what you *bettah* do, boy," Cannon said. He smiled thinly. I stepped back, still looking at him. His face didn't move, didn't sweat. I picked up the towel and covered myself. "You better get all your gear together and go down there to locker 211. Y'heah me? And then move your fartsack and your ass down to that rack there. You see the one I mean? Yeah, that one. Next to the head. Be perfect for you, boy. There's lots of light all night long, f' you to read about your *art* masterpieces. Easy for you too, ef you hafta shit your pants. Like you're doin now. Save a lot of wear and tear on this good U.S. Navy beddin."

He seemed cooler then, almost cold.

"And tonight," he said, "I think you oughtta go out and stand watch at post three. At midnight. A good midnight to four, that'll give you lots of time to think about your *art* masterpieces, boy."

With that, Cannon turned abruptly and walked the length of the barracks to the far door, his polished shoes clacking on the hardwood floor. The screen door slammed loudly behind him.

I stood there for a long moment. On the Outside (as we called civilian life), I would have beaten his brains out. Or gone down trying. On the Outside, I would have made him eat the book. For sure, I'd have put some damage on his plastic face and made the son of a bitch sweat. But there in the Navy, if I did any of those things, I'd be sent to the brig. "Shit," I said out loud. And then shuddered. The man had punked me out. Like that. With his sweatless face and slushy eyes and the three hash marks on his sleeve. That was all it took. No punches. Just authority. And I was there because I asked to be there. I signed the papers. I joined the Navy. And this was the deal. For a moment I felt like crying, thinking of myself free on the streets of a city. And then I twisted and threw a punch at the locker door, slamming it one final time.

Chapter

9

From The Blue Notebook

ACQUILINE. AQUALINE.

I love the sound of a pen on paper. I'm writing these words with a Sheaffer fountain pen. It leaks and stains my fingers, but I love the skoosh *sound it makes. I know that professional cartoonists all use steel crow-quill nibs, but I can't seem to make them work. The nibs always break. Maybe my hand is too heavy. Maybe I don't hold them right. I tried a Parker 51 once in a department store. It was beautiful. So smooth, and the nib was flexible, so I could get the thicks and thins I need for drawing. But it cost $20. One of these days, maybe I'll be able to afford one. But not now. Not soon, the way the Navy pays.*

I need to make some drawings, but I can't right now. I don't have my stuff, and anyway this guy C. would probably have me courtmartialed if he caught me drawing. I can just hear him saying it: Only a Gah-dam faggot would draw pictures like that.

QUALITIES OF A GOOD NAVY MAN. *Be loyal. Obey orders. Show initiative. Be a fighter. Be reliable. Keep a clean record. Be fair. Be honest. Be cheerful. Be neat.*

—The Bluejackets' Manual

Maybe we're just something God dreamed. Or is still dreaming. If there even is a God. I used to believe in God, too. Like everybody else in the world. I prayed to him and worshiped him. Right up to the day my mother died.

Then I said, What kind of God could this be who lets a good woman like that die?

Once I started thinking that way, I couldn't stop. What kind of God lets Hiroshima happen? What kind of God lets six million Jews die in the concentration camps? What kind of God lets people be poor? Back home in Brooklyn, there were crooked cops and murderers and sleazeball politicians. How could God let them live while my mother dies? How could he put up with a guy that throws an art book against a wall? If there's a God, then he's responsible for art, too. He must of said once, Okay, now let there be art. *But if He did, why put guys like C. on the earth to hate art? It doesn't make any sense. And it's nothing new. There were all those vandals in history, the Visigoths and guys like that, always sacking Rome. They destroyed all sorts of beautiful things, while killing and raping thousands of people. How could they be part of God's plan? Unless He's having a bad dream.*

Or maybe it's something else. Something simpler. Maybe God's a mean bastard. Maybe that's it. Maybe He's just a mean bastard who likes to see people suffer.

Agnostic. *One who holds that the ultimate cause (God) and the essential nature of things are unknown and unknowable, or that human knowledge is limited to experience. (That's me).*

Aquiline.

Chapter

10

AT TWENTY TO twelve that night I wandered out along a dirt road beside the fence and relieved a small Oriental kid named Freddie Harada at post three. He handed me a dummy Springfield rifle and an adjustable cartridge belt without bullets. In a thin singsong voice he told me to forget about sleeping on the post. Red Cannon or the goddamn Marines came around every half hour in a jeep. Then he hurried away into the darkness.

I was supposed to be guarding a dumpster, one of those metal bins that was filled over the course of a week with garbage and junk and then lifted onto a truck and taken away and emptied. It was big enough to hold a car. I'd seen them in boot camp, but even in that land of total chickenshit I was never asked to guard one. I walked around it, feeling foolish with my rifle that didn't shoot.

There was a barbed-wire fence just past the dumpster and empty black fields beyond and away off lights moving on the highway. Obviously, I thought, feeling hipper than Cannon or the task before me, the Russians weren't about to steal a giant garbage can. So this watch was really about staying awake. They called it Building Discipline. Usually that meant you did something useless just because someone commanded you to do it. You stayed up all night, watching for a patrol to come around in a jeep, and the patrol came around in the jeep just to make sure you stayed up all night. The Navy. The goddamned Navy.

But after a while I realized it took too much energy to stay pissed off. I started feeling good out there in the open, with the steady drone of insects coming from the fields and silvery clouds moving across the stars. The darkness smelled of the sea and was so humid I thought I could grab it and shape it, pack it like a snowball, throw it at the stars. There was no purpose to my being there, but in all the years since, as I've stayed up through the night working with purpose, developing film, making love, arranging tickets and passports and visas for my next stop, I've sometimes longed for those nights without meaning under the stars of Pensacola, when I was solitary and young.

I remember my eyes adjusting to the darkness and how I began to see the varieties of the color black. A green black beyond the barbed wire. The pale black of wild grass. The blacker black of tree trunks. I tried to imagine the way Roy Crane would draw it. All grays and blacks. He would probably add some palms to show it was Florida, even though there were no palms out here. Along the edge of the barracks, the trees were all pine. But I knew that an artist could change things to make them better or truer; in fact, it was probably his *duty* to make such changes. I was sure Crane always did. And so did Caniff: They made pictures that were truer than photographs. They made a lot of things neater than life. The world was a mess, and all the things they taught us in school were lies. But when an artist shaped the world, things always worked out better. An artist would have that curly-haired woman stay on the bus and take the young sailor home with her and make love to him and stay with him forever.

I opened the door to the dumpster. A foul odor rose from it. I stepped closer and objects began to reveal themselves: automobile tires, broken pieces of metal, a lot of paper torn in strips, dry palm fronds. But there was a wet jumble of other stuff that I couldn't make out. The smells were suddenly more distinct: rusting iron, burnt paper, rubber, decay. Not city odors. But they didn't make me feel I was in the country either. And I thought: *It's a Navy smell. I'll only smell this in the Navy. I'll remember this mixture of smells all my life.* And I did.

Then I saw lights bobbing in the darkness on the far side of the field. They moved left, then stopped. I picked up the rifle. The lights moved again, stopped, then were moving again and getting larger. I could hear a car engine now, and then the lights were very bright and the jeep was fixing me with its high beams, stopping a dozen feet away. I held the rifle at the ready and tried to look tough.

"Who goes there?" I said. Like in a bad movie.

No answer. A man stepped out of the car on the passenger side, but I couldn't see him clearly in the glare of the lights. He came forward. It was Cannon. Carrying a clipboard.

"You'd be dead by now, boy," he said. He came very close, fixing me with those lashless eyes. "You sposed to ask for a password, boy, and if it ain't forthcomin, you shoot."

"Nobody gave me a password. Sir."

"Then whyn hell didn't you *ask* for one, boy?"

"I just got to this base. *Sir.* I don't know the routine. *Sir.* I was—"

"Don't explain, boy. *Admit.*"

"Admit what?"

"Admit you done fucked up, shitbird! You are tellin me you went to a United States military post, on *duty,* without askin anyone what you was sposed to do. You didn't get a password. You didn't do your *duty,* boy, cause you never did find out what it *was.*"

I said, "If you were a Russian, I couldn't do my duty anyway. This goddamned rifle doesn't shoot! So what's the big deal?"

Cannon blinked. Then he turned to the driver of the jeep, still out of sight behind the glare of the headlights.

"You hear that, Infantino? You hear what this shitf'brains just said?"

"No, sir."

"He said, 'What's the big deal?' "

I could see veins pulsing in Cannon's neck.

"So it looks like we got us another wiseass punk from New York, don't it, Infantino?"

Infantino didn't answer.

"And when you scratch a New York wise guy, whatta you find trying to get out? You find a New York big shot. And all we need is some seaman deuce thinks he's a big shot. Isn't that right, Mister Infantino?" Then he got angry at Infantino's silence. "Are you *deaf,* boy? Do you *hear* me, boy?"

"Yes, sir, I hear you."

"Well, what should we do with this big shot, this Mister Wiseass Brooklyn New York?"

I'd never told him I was from Brooklyn, so I knew he'd examined my papers.

"That's obviously up to you, sir," Infantino said from behind the brights. His voice was raspy, familiar.

"I tell you what I'd *like* to do," Cannon said. "I'd like to shitcan him right out of this man's Navy. Couple years in the brig, a D.D., and gone." He sighed. "But this new damned Navy, you can't do it like that anymore."

He handed me the clipboard and a ballpoint pen. "Sign here," he said, and pointed to a box on a ruled sheet of paper. The form listed the various posts on the base and the times. Each of the other guys on duty had signed in a box on the right. I did the same. Cannon's fingernails were neatly trimmed and polished.

"At ease," he said. I relaxed. Then he squinted at me and changed his tone and barked: "Tain-SHUN!" I snapped to attention, the rifle on my shoulder. "Now you stay like that till yore relieved, wiseass," he said. "You even *dream* about takin a rest, I'll put you on report."

He turned on his heel, walked quickly to the jeep and got in. They moved off quickly. Briefly, I glimpsed the other sailor: dark-haired and ruddy-faced. In dungarees.

It was much darker after the jeep left. I stood at attention until the lights of the jeep merged with the lights of the main gate, then I squatted beside the dumpster with the rifle on my lap. Fuck you, Cannon. I didn't sleep, but I wasn't awake either; my anger was like an extra pulse. I tried something I did back home when the furies got to me. I made my mind blank. Like a blackboard after it's washed. I saw Cannon, the dumpster, even *The Bluejackets' Manual* on the slate. Then I pulled a wet cloth across it. Twice. And they were gone. I stared at the empty slate. It was blank and pure, like peace.

Then I came suddenly awake. The lights of the jeep were moving again. I stood up and brushed off my dungarees. I snapped to attention, the rifle on my shoulder. My heart thumped. Maybe they had those field glasses that let you see in the dark. Maybe they had photographs of me goofing off. Then the jeep arrived with a squeal of brakes. Infantino jumped from behind the wheel without shutting off the engine. He came right up to me and handed me two doughnuts in a napkin and a cardboard cup of coffee.

"Fuck *him*," he said, and then hurried back to the jeep without a word and drove away.

Chapter

11

IT IS MORNING on the Gulf and I'm at the window in a bathrobe I bought in Tokyo, staring out at the gray ocean. A storm is coming. There are some young people on the beach, spreading a blanket in defiance of the message from the sky. One is a girl in a flowery bikini, with long legs and beautiful breasts. A boy makes a fuss over her. I am sure he wants her to stay with him forever. But they each have a half century ahead of them now, full of perils and temptations. To survive at all is difficult enough. To run the course together will require a miracle. When they are my age I will be dead, and I wish I could go down there and tell them one sentence that they could carry as a talisman. Words so clean and perfect that they would protect those kids from all danger. But nothing comes. One couple runs into the surf. The girl in the bikini touches the boy's face and he moves forward clumsily to kiss her cheek. It's the morning of their lives. And then the sentence forms itself: *Watch it.*

I dress slowly, and move again into that first morning at Ellyson Field, when I awoke feeling drugged, my mouth sour, my bones rubbery after two hours sleep. I hear the sounds of all Navy mornings: shouts of *reveille, reveille,* groans of protest, and *drop yore cocks and grab yore socks.* And over and over, the slamming of those locker doors.

Then I was up, nodding at strangers, saying nothing, stretching and squatting to force some bone or muscle into my body. I showered and dried myself, the floor of the head wet and slippery and men at the sinks scraping at beards. They rubbed their faces, their skin, their bellies as if they were mad at their own flesh. Some hummed tunes, others grumbled in solitude. Some were tattooed. Many were matted with hair. I am sure I dressed in the uniform of the day: dungarees, black shoes, white hat. I am sure I made my bed, and felt ready for the challenge of the morning.

Then a short sunburnt muscle-bound man came over. His nose was peeling and he grinned in a crooked way.

"You're from New York, I hear."

"Yeah. Brooklyn."

"I'm Max Pilsner. The East Side. You goin' to chow?"

It was as easy as that. A hello in the morning and I had a friend. I don't make new friends anymore. There have been too many fakers, too many disappointments, and too many real friends have died. Max Pilsner was my friend, and it is a measure of how far we've traveled that I no longer know if he is dead or alive. That morning, Max stepped out before me into the steamy Florida air. His arms hung straight from his shoulders. His waist was narrow. And he walked in a series of rolling movements, like gears shifting. He made walking seem like a brilliant performance. All around us, sailors hurried along in the half darkness, their cigarettes bobbing like fireflies. We walked beyond the Supply Shack to the chow hall, where the smell of toast and hash filled the air. Max told me he was a mechanic in Hangar Three, and had come here straight from mechanics school in Memphis and he was hoping for sea duty, anything, to get out of Ellyson Field.

"I'd even join the Fleet Marines," he said. "And they're fighting in Korea. The medics, anyway . . ."

The only good thing about Ellyson was that there were some decent guys here, he said, New Yorkers *and* shitkickers. "They're all nuts." He was telling me this as we waited on line under the eaves along the side of the chow hall. We passed a single piece of graffiti: *Find it hard getting up in the morning? Slam a window on it.* Through the window, I could see Waleski sitting with other sailors at one of the long wooden tables. Freddie Harada was with two other Orientals. The morning sounds were louder now: metal trays, silverware clattering against metal, cups clunking, coffee urns hissing, guys on KP yelling at one another in the steam, all mixed up with the sound of helicopters beating their way through the morning air.

"Who's this Bobby Bolden?"

"The best," Max said. "Greatest horn player in the Navy. Maybe in the whole friggin South. Now that's a guy that was in the Fleet Marines. A medic. He got wounded, too, in Korea. Won a bunch of medals. Know what's great about him? He doesn't give a shit. Nobody can scare him. Nobody. So nobody bothers him. Bobby Bolden . . ."

He showed me the apartment above the mess hall, where Bobby Bolden lived with all the other Negro sailors, most of them mess cooks. And he pointed out a chief petty officer named Francis Xavier McDaid, standing near the door in starched suntans. Red Cannon was bad enough, Max said, one of those Old Salts who remembered when men were men and ships were wood, but McDaid was Red's boss and infinitely worse. We had our trays full of scrambled eggs and bacon now. I looked at the chief. He had a broad flat face and a deep tan. He seemed to be staring right at me. I wondered whether Red Cannon had told him about me. Put me in some New York Wise Guy category. We sat down. I turned to look at the door. And saw a black man coming in, powerfully built, with coffee-colored skin. Even from the distance, I could see that he had green eyes. Max told me that this was Bobby Bolden.

"He's only got one major problem," he said. "Pussy."

"Isn't that everybody's problem?"

"White pussy."

I was eating quickly now. Max looked at me.

"That bother you?" Max said.

"I don't know," I said. "I never thought about it before."

"Down here, they lynch colored guys for it. Maybe that'll help you think about it."

"Come on, they don't lynch people anymore, do they?"

"Only when they catch them."

Bobby Bolden passed through the line like some visiting prince. The black mess cooks cracked wise with him, heaped his tray with food. Then Bolden walked past us down the aisle, nodding at Max, and sat among a group of whites, without saying a word to any of them.

"See what I mean? There's empty tables all over, but he sits with the worst rednecks on the base. Just to break their balls. Now watch."

Without finishing their breakfasts, five men got up and left the table. Three of them moved to other tables. Two walked right out of the chow hall. Bobby Bolden showed no emotion. He just sat there eating.

"Does he have *one* white girl? Or a bunch of them?"

"I don't know," Max said, "I don't follow him around. I'm allergic to gunshots." He smiled. "But there's a Wave who works out at Mainside, I know he's got *her*. A real good broad, very funny. Not my type, understand? But truly tremendous tits."

I laughed. "I guess you can't blame him then."

"I can blame him for being stupid," Max said. "Down here, they kill colored guys for *lookin'* at white broads."

I sipped my coffee. It tasted brackish. I said, "You tell him that?"

"Hey, how you gonna tell him? What do I do? Go up to the guy and say, 'Hey, Bobby, you're a *nigger,* you know? And they have *segregation* down here. So it ain't *safe* for you to be screwing a white broad.' I mean, Bobby Bolden was a hero in Korea, two Purple Hearts, two Bronze Stars, a whole shitload of other medals. How am I gonna tell *him* what to do?" He glanced around the hall. "Besides, he just don't give a shit."

I looked down at Bobby Bolden again, remembering the sound of the horn. A human being playing the blues on a bright lonesome New Year's afternoon. Telling everybody who'd listen about the boulevard of broken dreams. He ate slowly and deliberately, in what seemed to be permanent solitude.

Chapter

12

SOMEWHERE IN THE South, the woman from the bus was walking along a street or driving a car or shopping in a market. She was naked in a shower. She was lighting a Lucky and smoking it quickly, holding the butt in her left hand. She didn't know how desperately I wanted her. How I wanted her promise of female darkness and secret things in the night. How I wanted to know what she knew. But I was in the Navy. The Navy brought me South. Because of the Navy, I was on that bus. And before I could get to her, before I could start my search for her (locating mysterious Palatka on a map and going toward it the way desperate men once searched for El Dorado) I would have to deal with the Navy. And that turned out to be not very hard.

After breakfast, I walked into the Supply Shack and waiting for me at the counter was a first-class airman storekeeper named Donnie Ray Bradford. Not Donald. Or Don. *Donnie Ray.* He was a thin-lipped man in crisp tailor-made dungarees. His eyes were watery, with a wounded look in them. I told him who I was and he said "Welcome aboard" and then I joined a dozen other sailors at 0800 for the formal morning muster. This was to be the routine of every Pensacola morning, and it is built into me now; no matter where I am or who I sleep with, if I fall asleep at five A.M., I still rise to make the eight o'clock muster. On this first morning, Donnie Ray called each of our names, checked them off a muster sheet, then nodded in a generalized way at the group, dismissing us. It was very loose and casual and, I thought, grown up. A few shook my hand and welcomed me aboard, then quickly dispersed to various parts of the building. Some left to take a truck to Mainside. I remember all of them now, and will carry them with me to the grave, but that first morning, I still couldn't match names to faces.

Donnie Ray took me on a tour of the Supply Shack. As I thought, the storeroom was in the rear, with crates stacked almost to the ceiling and narrow aisles running between them. A Hi-Lo was parked near the door. Inside the crates there were rotor blades, Donnie Ray told me, and engines and pontoons. They were all up on pallets to make it easier for the prongs of the Hi-Lo to lift them and also to guard against flooding. Sometimes the Gulf was hit with hurricanes. He explained the parts numbering system and told me twice that it was important to account for every piece. "If you forget something," he said, "they go nuts in Washington."

He showed me my desk, which was the last in a row of five desks set at right angles to the wall. There were neat trays of requisition forms, a dictionary, a telephone. "All yours," Donnie Ray said. "The complete aviation storekeeper's kit." And then someone called his name and told him he had a phone call and he hurried away. I sat down at the desk. It wasn't the same as operating twin .50s on a destroyer in the South China Sea. But it was mine. The place where I would work for a long time. I sat back, engulfed by the aroma of cut grass, the fronds of the palm trees clattering in the soft breeze, the sprinklers whirring. Even inside the Supply Shack, the air seemed thick and sensual. A picture of my lost woman scribbled across my mind, then vanished.

Through the screened window, I could see sailors in white hats walking in pairs in the distance, and more white-painted wooden buildings, and then the main administration building, all brick with white trim, rising three stories out of a plaza, a control tower on top, its wide windows made of green-tinted glass. Thinking: *I'm here. On the first morning of a new life. This* is. *New York* was. I found myself breathing the thick air as if it were food.

Donnie Ray Bradford came back. His face looked troubled but he said nothing and began to explain what I would be doing. Filling out requisitions for re-supply. Servicing the mechanics and electronics' mates and even an occasional pilot. "We call them customers," he said, "though they don't pay for a damned thing." They came here to the Supply Shack for their parts or for new tools. And they would wait to be served at the long wide counter at the front of the building. Usually they would have their requisition slips

filled out, approved by a superior. "But they might not always have
the numbers right," Donnie Ray said. "So you'll have to double-
check the numbers in the book." It wasn't all tedious detail; there
were housekeeping chores too. The storekeepers cleaned the Supply Shack once a day, swabbing it down on a rotating basis. And
we weren't imprisoned in this building; sometimes we had to go to
Mainside on a truck to pick up new supplies. A bunch of the crew
was over there now.

"You gotta watch this weather, too," he said. "You think 'cause
it's Florida it's always hot, like yesterday, today. But it sometimes
gets goddamned cold. These big storms come down from Canada
and take half of damned Alabama with them. Most of the time it's
too hot. All the time it's too damp. So you gotta keep parts dry and
clean. Otherwise they end up little blobs of rust. And get all the
numbers right on the forms. You get one digit wrong, you end up
with a jeep instead of a screwdriver . . ."

His voice was soft, but there was an edge underneath. It was as
if he was reciting a set speech and had something else on his mind.
He said other things; I didn't really hear them all. I felt blurred.
Ready for the sleep I'd missed while guarding my dumpster.

"You got a driver's license, right?" he said.

"No, I don't, Donnie Ray."

"Really? How come?"

"I don't know how to drive."

He looked surprised. "You don't know how to *drive*?"

"Never learned."

"Hell, *everybody* knows how to drive."

"We didn't have a car in our family," I said, already tired of the
old explanation. "Nobody had cars where I grew up. So there was
nobody to learn from."

Besides, I wanted to say, but didn't: I'm the oldest son. My father
was born in Ireland and my mother's dead and I'm the first American. I had to learn the American things first. Baseball and football.
Sugar Ray Robinson. And *Batman* and *The Spirit* and *Sheena, Queen
of the Jungle.* And Charlie Parker late at night on *Symphony Sid.* I
guess I'll have to learn to drive, too, I wanted to say, but didn't.

"Well," Donnie Ray Bradford said, "you can load and unload
till you get a license." He glanced out a window at a lone sailor,
then back to me. "Someone around here'll teach you."

He said all this in a quiet, even tone. No redneck bullying. None of Red Cannon's malignant style. He talked to me as if I were a man, not a slave, not an inferior, not a boy. He ended by repeating, "Welcome aboard, sailor." I liked him for that. I liked him a lot. He went off to use the phone again. Then another sailor came over. His name was stenciled above the pocket of his shirt: Harold R. Jones. A second-class storekeeper on his second hitch. He had lank blond hair that lay flat on his skull. Wary eyes. Dungarees so heavily starched they looked as if they'd crack when he walked. He was holding a requisition slip.

"Gimme a hand," he said casually.

"Sure."

We went into the back room together, and he led the way to a long flat crate that contained a rotor blade.

"Donnie Ray looks nervous," I said. "He always that way?"

"Yeah, he's a bit of a nellie," Jones said. "But he's extra nervous today. We got a missing sailor. Jimmy Boswell didn't make muster. He's Donnie Ray's big buddy."

"You mean he's AWOL?"

"Who knows? I'm sure Donnie Ray didn't report him yet. He just don't know what the skinny is on Ole Boz. The man likes his whiskey, so maybe he got himself in a nice little car wreck somewhere. Nobody knows. Donnie Ray called the hospitals. But nothin turned up yet. Here, grab that end . . ."

I was surprised at how light the crate was. We lifted it and laid it on a dolly. Jones looked at my shoes.

"You better do something about those shoes," he said.

My black shoes looked dull, but they weren't dirty. Jones was wearing shoes brought to a high gloss.

"Man that won't shine his shoes, won't wipe his ass," Jones said, as we moved the rotor blade to the front room. *A man that won't shine his shoes won't wipe his ass?* The wisdom of the ages, a certain entry for The Blue Notebook. At the counter, Jones showed me how to fill out the forms and had a mechanic sign for the rotor blade. Jones went back to his desk and I started for mine when I met another second class. He was coming out of the head. His name was Jean Becket.

"The shithouse looks like Poirl Harbuh t'day," he said.

"You from New York?" I asked.

"New Awlins. Why?"

I tried to explain that in New York, particularly in Brooklyn, people said "poirl" for "pearl" and "terlit" for "toilet." They could say things like "I dropped my poirls down the terlit." If Waite Hoyt was pitching for the Dodgers, and something happened to him, they'd say, "Hert's hoit." They could also tell you that the men's room looked like Poirl Harbuh.

"Just like New Awlins," he said. He had a wide gap-toothed grin and eyebrows that touched, making him look wicked. "What's your name again?"

It was that easy. Becket showed me the metal bins where smaller parts—tools, nuts and bolts—were stored. Donnie Ray gave me a new Navy coffee cup. The phones were ringing and traffic was heavy at the counter. I watched Jones and Becket work and then I handled a few requisitions myself, and during a lull I took a walk down to the coffee urn.

A bony man with a pinched face stood beside the urn, a cup in his hand. His shirt told me his name was J. T. Harrelson. He groaned softly, then again. I poured myself a cup. Harrelson stared bleakly at the empty morning. His hands trembled.

"You okay?" I said.

"Ah'll never be okay again," he said. "That gah-dam white lightnin eats you gah-dam guts out."

"Maybe you need somethin to eat."

"Ah'd rather swallow a can of worms."

Harrelson looked at me, squinting. I must've been smiling.

"Who in the hell *are* you?"

I told him and started to shake his hand. But he was using both hands for his cup.

"And where you *from,* boy?"

I said the fatal words: New York.

"Gah-dam. Yawl got anybody *left* in New York? More gah-dam New Yorkers in this man's Navy now than I seen in *thirteen years.*"

"Ah, well," I said and walked away. I didn't like the hint of coldness about Harrelson, the curl to his lip when he mentioned New York. I went back to my desk and studied the parts catalogs. The coffee cooled and tasted sour.

Suddenly the side door slammed open. A gangly sailor in dirty dress whites lurched into the room. Everything stopped. Donnie Ray looked up from the telephone, at once alarmed and relieved. The sailor was in his twenties and was wearing a third-class AK's V-stripe. His eyes were wild and red. His big hands waved in the air, jerking, twisting, as if detached from his arms. His shoes were dirty and scuffed. The missing Boswell.

"Hank's dead!" he screamed.

Donnie Ray came on a run. Becket emerged from the back room and hurried over, with Jones behind him.

Donnie Ray said, "Gah-dammit, Boz, I been looking all over for—"

"Hank's dead!"

Donnie Ray took his arm but Boswell shook him off.

"Hank's dead, gah-damnit! Hank is fuckin *dead!*"

"What are you—"

"Hank *Williams!* Hank Williams died, *Donnieray!* They found him *dead* in some car in West Virgin ia! Just dead. Dead in the back of a *Cadillac!*"

I'd never heard of Hank Williams. I thought: *Why is Boswell so upset? What's going on here?* Then Harrelson was there, his face ashen. He said: "Hank Williams is *dead?*"

"*Dead.* He's fuckin dead."

Boswell's eyes closed, then widened.

"Dead!" he screamed and sat down hard on the concrete floor. "It's on the radio. In the fuckin newspapers. Hank's *dead*. On New Year's fuckin Day."

Harrelson hurried to his desk, took out a small radio and started turning the dials. There were three sailors waiting at the counter now, staring down the hundred-foot length of the Supply Shack, watching us. Donnie Ray leaned over Boswell.

"Boz, you gotta go somewhere, get cleaned up," he said. "How'd you get on the damned base anyway?"

"The back," Boswell mumbled. "You know, the hole in the fence . . ."

Jones and Becket grabbed him under the arms and started to lift his dead weight off the floor. Donnie Ray nodded at me to help. I grabbed Boswell's waist and together we got him to his feet. Donnie Ray glanced at the people waiting for parts. About five of them now. Boswell started sobbing. "Poor fuckin Hank. Poor skinny redneck bastard. Poor drunk sonuvabitch . . ." As if describing himself. Then he passed out in our arms.

Donnie Ray said, "Can't even get him in a shower in this shape. Can't lay him out in the barracks, or McDaid'll find him." He glanced around, then said: "Put him on a pallet."

He walked quickly away to the front counter. We carried Boswell into the storeroom, with Becket leading the way through the rough wood tunnels formed by stacked crates. In an empty area against the far wall there were a half dozen pallets neatly piled on top of one another. We moved toward them and then Boswell was suddenly awake.

"What the hell you doin?" he said. "Where you *takin* me?"

"You're drunk as a skunk, Boz," Becket said. "We're gonna let you sleep it off."

Boswell looked angry and trapped. "You gonna *make* me?"

"Not if we don't have to," Becket said.

There was a pause, as if he were trying to remember something that was very important. Then his eyes widened again.

"Hank's *dead.*"

"Yeah, we know that, Boz. It's a terrible thing. But to be poifectly frank, it aint our business today. We got other things to do."

Suddenly Boswell shook us off and kicked Becket hard in the stomach. He whirled and punched Jones in the chest with a wild right aimed at his face. Then he turned to me, blinking. He started another roundhouse right and I bent at the knees, went under the punch, and ripped a hook to his belly. He went *hooooo.* And sat down. He blinked again and then keeled over.

Becket looked at me: "Jesus. Where you loirn to do that?"

"I used to work out," I said.

"You boxed?" Jones said.

We were lifting Boswell onto a pallet. "A little. I wasn't very good."

I didn't say anything else. I was as astonished as they were at the way Boswell went out from one punch to the body. Anything I said would sound like bragging. Boswell was stretched on a pallet now, and Becket built a little fence of them to hide him. Then Jones laid Boswell's white hat on his chest.

"Will you look at this man's shoes?" Jones said.

Chapter

13

THERE ARE ENTIRE years of my life I can't remember at all, and days that are as dense in memory as granite. That first day on the job at Ellyson Field was one of those. First, I learned about Hank Williams—which is to say, I learned about the American South. I knew only a few things about this vast region of my own country: In the 1860s, the North had fought a bitter, brutal war against the Confederacy, a war that we were taught was about slavery; colored people still were not complete citizens there; southern politicians were figures of fun on radio shows. Good baseball players came from the South and they played a lot of football. But I didn't know anything about the people; my ignorance extended even to the lies, for I was probably the only person left in America who had not even seen *Gone With the Wind.* That day I learned that the South of Hank Williams was not the South of Clark Gable and Vivien Leigh. On the day Hank Williams died, the air itself seemed charged with emotion, packed with loneliness and loss, as the radio stations played the man's songs over and over, the deejays sounding hushed, tearful, even reverent. At first I thought this was comical; I even turned away to smile as the corn-pone voices grieved on the radio. But then, as the words and voices accumulated, I knew they must be serious.

On the news shows, everything else was forgotten. Instead, we heard the governors of Florida and Alabama and Georgia, Mississippi and Louisiana, all saying what a great tragedy the death of Hank Williams was for the South, for America, for the human race. This all sounded ludicrous then; more than thirty years later, I think they were probably right. The radio reporters interviewed other hillbilly singers, and though their names meant nothing to me, there was something genuine about their heartbreak. We heard too from sobbing people in the streets of a dozen southern cities. By late afternoon, at least two women were claiming to be the true wives of Hank Williams and were described as shocked and in tears. I felt as if I'd arrived in a country where the king had just died and I didn't even know his name.

At one point, an announcer said that a grand farewell to Hank Williams was being planned at the Municipal Auditorium in Montgomery, and Harrelson shouted: "Ah'm *goin*!" He slammed the desk with the flat of his hand. "Ah don't care whether Ah got duty or *not*—Ah'm goin!"

And the details began to come in, too. A cop named Jamey was on the radio, explaining that he found Mister Hank Williams dead in the back of a Cadillac in Glen Burdette's 24 Hour Pure Oil Service Station on Main Street in Oak Hill. That was in West Virginia, at five-thirty in the morning. There were two men with Mister Williams, the cop said. One of them was the driver of the Cadillac, the other a friend. They were taking him to Canton, Ohio, where he was supposed to sing in a concert that night. The weather was so bad they couldn't risk a plane. "That's it!" Harrelson shouted. "*They* killed him! The driver and that so-called friend. They killed him cause he was *too damned good to live*!" The cause of death, a coroner said, was probably heart failure. "But we'll have to wait for an autopsy." Harrelson didn't have to wait: "They gave him some kinda shot, you wait an see. They *killed* him." Hank Williams was twenty-nine. Only twelve years older than me. "Shit," Harrelson said. "Shit."

As the music played, Harrelson moved around in a distracted way, singing along with Hank Williams in a low, tuneless voice. *She warned me once, She warned me twice. But I don't take no one's advice . . .* Becket knew the words too, but only his lips moved, and he kept working, hurrying from desk to counter to storeroom, sometimes enlisting my help. He didn't try to explain the spreading sorrow. That was another thing I learned: I wasn't one of them, maybe never could be one of them, because the things that were deep in me didn't exist for them, and the things that were deep in the southerners didn't mean anything to me. I could be quiet, that was all. I could respect them. But I couldn't truly feel what they felt. I was an outsider here, as they would be in the gardens of Brooklyn.

The customers were all talking about Hank Williams too. *Musta been the whiskey,* they'd say. A shake of the head: *All them women.* Then a glance out at the airfield and heads cocked as they heard the lonesome voice from the radio. *The honky-tonks got ole Hank at last.*

Then I heard a Hank Williams song I actually knew. *I tried so hard, my dear, to show / That you're my every dream . . .* The tempo was different, the accents broader. But I knew that one. *You're afraid each thing I do / Is just some evil scheme.* Backed by strings, sounding like South Brooklyn, Tony Bennett sang it all through the fall of '5 1, his voice aching the way my heart did then, as I tried to convince a girl named Maureen I loved her. *A mem'ry from your lonesome past / Keeps us so far apart . . .* Until I met her in the back room of the Caton Inn on a Saturday night, held her close, whispered the usual lies into her hair. On a night of bitter wind. *Why can't I free your doubtful mind? / And melt your cold, cold heart?*

That was when the death of Hank Williams finally touched me too. Hearing "Cold, Cold Heart." After that, I listened more closely, imagining that the whole South must be full of men who remembered women they held in their arms, while Hank Williams sang from the jukebox or the radio. The man's voice was so goddamned lonesome and hurt that I felt sure nothing could have saved him. He had six Cadillacs and a mansion in Nashville (the radio said) and a couple of kids and those two wives. But here he was: dead at twenty-nine. So I listened to all the rest of it, as Harrelson turned up the volume, and a crowd of customers began to gather at the counter. To me it was like the day Roosevelt died, when everybody in the neighborhood listened to radios and some cried and others wondered who the hell this Harry Truman was; later, when Jack Kennedy was killed and Martin Luther King and Robert Kennedy and Malcolm X and John Lennon, all the great public killings of my time, I was always working, professionally numb as I chased the faces of disaster. As a photographer, I was paid to focus deeply on the moment, but late at night, exhausted in a motel room in Dallas or Memphis or Los Angeles, I would remember the death of Hank Williams. I was seventeen again and looking over at the side of the counter in the Supply Shack in Pensacola, where a mechanic with grease-blackened hands was sobbing openly and another man was trying to console him. I'd never seen a man cry like that before. "Come on, now, Jimmy," his friend was saying to the mechanic. "Don't you cry, boy. Don't you cry." And then someone brought in a copy of the *Pensacola News* and there was a picture of Hank Williams on page one, and they all looked at it in silence, as if the picture and the print and the paper finally and irrevocably had confirmed what they'd heard on the radio but didn't fully believe. Another man left in tears.

Suddenly the door slammed hard. Everybody stopped and turned. Chief McDaid was standing there, with Red Cannon beside him. All we could hear was the radio.

> *"I'm free and ready*
> *So we can go steady*
> *How's about time for me . . ."*

"Shut that goddamned thing off," McDaid said.

Harrelson switched off the radio. It was quiet, except for one of the customers, who was blowing his nose.

"What in the hell is going *on* here?" McDaid said. Cannon searched our faces and his eyes narrowed. Nobody answered. I noticed for the first time that Donnie Ray wasn't with us. He was the senior man. He should have been there to answer Chief McDaid.

McDaid took a few steps closer to the center of the counter, still on the other side. The customers eased away to give him room.

"This some kind of a *prayer* meeting?" he said. His voice was round and deep, like the voice of a radio announcer. "Is this a *circle* jerk? *What is this?*"

Finally Harrelson said softly: "Hank Williams died, Chief."

McDaid and Cannon exchanged a weary look that said: See what we have to put up with? Then McDaid pushed through the swinging door that separated our work area from the service area. One mechanic started to walk away, but Cannon blocked him.

"Mister Cannon, what would you do with a lot like this?" McDaid said.

"A little extra duty'd sure help, Chief," Cannon said.

"How about a firing squad?"

"That'd probably help the most."

McDaid stepped in among us, looking at our faces, uniforms, shoes. I hoped he wouldn't go in the back and find Boswell. When he got to me, McDaid stopped.

"You're new here, aren't you, boy?"

"Yes, sir. Came on board yesterday."

"You crying for Hank Williams too?"

"No, sir."

"Why not?"

"I don't know his music, sir."

"You don't know his music." McDaid paused. "Why not?"

"I'm not from the South, sir."

"And where, pray tell, are you *from*?"

Cannon interrupted. "He's from New York."

"I see," McDaid said. He looked at the stenciled name on my shirt pocket, then at me. The tan was perfect. I could smell after-shave lotion. "Are you a New York wise guy, Mister Devlin?"

"I'm a sailor in the United States Navy," I said.

"You didn't answer my question, boy."

"No, sir. I'm not a wise guy."

"Good," McDaid said. "You'd better not be."

Then he turned to the others.

"Where's Donnie Ray Bradford?"

"Out at the hangars, Chief," Jones said.

"You tell him to call me as soon as he gets back."

"Yes, Chief," Jones said.

McDaid separated himself from us and then coiled tightly and addressed us and the customers.

"Now all you sorry-ass son-of-bitches get back to work," he said. "This is the United States Navy, not an amusement park. If the *President* of the *United* States dies, you still must perform your duties. You *certainly* don't stop your work because some banjo player dies. I hope you understand me clearly."

With that he strode ahead through the swinging door and out into the morning light, with Cannon behind him. Everybody at the counter breathed hard in disgust and started mumbling.

"Fuck you, pal," I said.

"Forget it," Becket said. "Dat's da way he is."

"Hey, the man's right," Jones said casually. "We don't get paid to hang around and listen to the radio."

Becket gave him a look. "You know, sometimes, Jonesie, you are a real sorry son of a bitch."

He walked away and Jones shrugged. Away off, I could hear Bobby Bolden playing his horn.

"Cold, Cold Heart."

A slow blues.

Chapter

14

JUST BEFORE LUNCH that day, three more storekeepers returned from the Mainside run. One was a big, blond, muscle-bound guy named Larry Parsons, who always seemed to be two beats behind the rest of the world. He came in and shouted: "Did you hear about Hank Williams?" And didn't understand why everyone laughed. The second was Charlie Dunbar. He was a small, precise man whose clothes were nattily tailored and perfectly faded to make him look more of an Old Salt. He had a quick smile, white teeth, a tanned face. He was the first man I'd ever met who'd actually gone to college and the only Republican. We didn't see much of either breed in Brooklyn. Later, he told me that he only had one ambition: to become president of the United States.

The third man was Miles Rayfield, and he would become my closest friend, although I didn't know it then. His face was blocky, with a long upper lip, thick, black-rimmed eyeglasses, deep lines around his mouth. His head was too large for his body and his fingers looked like tubes. He groaned, sweated, cursed as Becket and I helped him, Dunbar and Parsons move some heavy crates into the back room. We all stopped to looked down at the unconscious Boswell.

"Do you think we should take his pulse?" Miles said.

"Hell, no," Becket said. "He might be alive."

When we were finished, they scattered to the head, the gedunk, the barracks and I went to my desk. After a while, Miles came over. He told me his name and said he was twenty-three years old and from Marietta, Georgia and he didn't know why he joined the Navy, so I shouldn't ask.

"That's the essential Navy intro, isn't it?" he said. "I also have to say that I truly don't give a flying fiddler's fabulous fuck about Hank Williams either." He smiled. "Welcome to *Anus Mundi,* the asshole of the earth."

I laughed and told him my name and where I was from, saying New York instead of Brooklyn. His desk was directly in front of mine and he moved papers around in a busy way and opened his window to let in the breeze.

"They're going absolutely completely apeshit over at Mainside about this Hank Williams," he said. "Mencken is right. The South is the Sahara of the Bozart. You can see what passes for art down here: the cheapest, most maudlin, most sickeningly disgusting sentimental crap."

I wasn't sure what some of the words meant. I certainly didn't know who Mencken was or even how to spell a Bozart. But I got the drift.

"You got in last night?" he said.

"Yesterday afternoon. I was on the midnight to four last night. Post three."

"The *dumpster!*" Miles laughed. "So you must have met that great American intellectual, Wendell the Red Cannon. He sends everyone out to that dumpster the first night. I think he must have a former wife in there, chopped into bits."

"What's his problem, anyway?" I said.

"His problem is that he's a reptile. A cretin. A disgusting red-necked toad. With the brains of an oyster. He's a pig sticker and a turd, an arrogant simple-minded ignorant little lowlife despicable son of a bitch bastard." He ran out of breath and paused. "In other words, he's a Navy lifer."

He sat down at his desk and gazed out the window. His large hands seemed to be operating on their own, lifting pencils, playing with paper clips.

"How do I handle him?" I said.

"Just tell yourself he's got bubonic plague and act accordingly." He rolled a sheet of blank blue paper into his Royal typewriter. He typed one word. Then turned to me. "But you know something? If Wendell Cannon ever *did* get bubonic plague, he'd probably *thrive.*" I rolled a sheet of paper into my Royal. Miles said: "Maybe we could turn him in to the McCarthy committee. If anybody on this base is converting people to the Communist cause, it's Red Cannon."

I'd never heard anyone talk like this, with all the sentences perfectly formed, and words rolling around in a rich crazy obscene way. Miles had a southern accent, too, a softness in the vowels that made the consonants sound even harder when he started firing his sentences like bullets. He looked at me through the thick glasses. Deadpan all the way.

"You think I'm kidding, don't you, Devlin?" he said. "Well, I'm not. I'm just stating a fact that's as obvious as a tit on a cow."

Harrelson switched on the radio again. Hank Williams began to sing. Miles turned to the music and then to me.

"Let's get some lunch," he said. "If that's what you can call that vile slop at the mess hall . . . "

As we got up to leave, I glanced at the sheet of paper in his typewriter. The single word was *Help.*

"Let's scrape this disgusting crap into a garbage can and go to the gedunk for some tea," Miles said. He looked down at the gnawed remains of his hamburger steak and mashed potatoes. I had eaten most of mine. "Why not?" I said.

On the way out, I saw Bobby Bolden. He was just ahead of us, scraping his tray into a can and shoving it at the faceless sets of arms and hands on the other side of the slot. When we went outside, I called his name and he turned. His hands were jammed in his pockets. Miles kept walking. Bolden looked at me warily.

"Hey, I loved the way you played 'Cold, Cold Heart,' " I said. "This morning . . . "

"Do I know you?" he said.

"No, I just got here." I told him my name and offered my hand, but he ignored it. "I heard you playing all day yesterday. 'Jumping with Symphony Sid,' that was great. I used to listen to Sid every night back home in New York. WEVD. Is that an alto or tenor you're playing?"

"Tenor."

"I thought so. You dig Charlie Parker?"

"He's an alto player."

"I know, but—"

"Whatta you *want,* man?"

"Hey, don't get *pissed,* pal. I was trying to tell you I *liked* what you do. I thought maybe I could come over and talk to you about *music.* I wasn't trying to ruin your day. So why don't you go fuck yourself?"

I started to leave. He grabbed my arm. I turned, ready to slip a punch. Those green eyes narrowed, then he released his grip.

"Thanks," he said. And walked away.

Chapter

15

Lonesome. *Adj.* 1 Depressed or sad because of the lack of friends, companionship, etc.; lonely; to feel lonesome. 2 Attended with or causing such a state of feeling. 3 Lonely in situation; remote, desolate, or isolated; a lonesome road.

One thing that separates me from most of the other guys here is music. They grew up with Hank Williams and I didn't. As simple as that. And music is one of the ways I think we figure out time. Not with watches and calendars. With music. Music is time. They talk about 4/4 time and three-quarter time (a waltz). But also music freezes the time in the world, puts a given period of time into your head so you can't ever get it out. So I remember the war whenever I hear the big bands. And it works the other way around too: I think of a year, and I remember the songs. If you say "1950" to me, I hear the Andrews Sisters singing "I Can Dream, Can't I?" Or junk by Theresa Brewer, Eileen Barton, and Phil Harris. While guys were getting killed in Korea that summer, we were standing on corners trying to sound like Frankie Laine singing "Mule Train" and "That Lucky Old Sun." I sometimes wonder what they were singing in Korea.

I hear the music, and I think of myself in the kitchen trying to draw and the young kids yelling and how much we all missed my mother that first summer after she died. The junk is stuck in my head. Patti Page. The Weavers. Joni James. Mario Lanza. The Four Aces. Les Paul and Mary Ford, Nat Cole and Rosemary Clooney. All lies with music, and I'm carrying them around. In the fall of '51, Tony Bennett showed up with

"Because of You." We heard it everywhere—in all the bars, at parties. The older guys were going to Korea then, and there were a lot of going-away parties and it was always "Because of You." And right after that, "Cold, Cold Heart." That's what I shared with these guys in Pensacola. That song.

When I went to boot camp, the big song was "You Belong to Me." Jo Stafford. All the guys knew it, guys from all over the country. We sang it in the barracks late at night. Maybe it was junk too, but I thought it was written exactly for me. So did everybody else. To me, that's a great song, if it says what you feel. "See the ocean when it's wet with rain . . ."

I sure did listen to a lot of junk (not even choosing to hear it, just being there in bars and other places when it was playing). But I also listened to Symphony Sid, Charlie Parker, Dizzy, Max, Horace Silver, Ben Webster—I know they are better musicians than the hokey mellow crap on WNEW. They seem to know they are doing something important, trying to make the music sound like something nobody ever did before. But they are never on the jukeboxes. They weren't even on the radio in New York, except for Sid. Maybe if they were, I wouldn't feel so bad now when I hear those other songs. Maybe I'd have all the notes of "A Night in Tunisia" (by Diz) in my head, instead of "You Belong to Me." It didn't work that way. And now I hear all the crap and I'm afraid I'll never get rid of it. Because I hear those lousy songs now. All the time.

> "Fly the ocean in a silver plane,
> See the jungle when it's wet with rain
> Just remember when you're home again . . . "

Who is Menkin? What's a Bozart? (Listening to Miles Rayfield.)

Palatka is 46 miles away.

Steve Canyon is back home, working at some university. I like him better when he's in the Himalayas with Princess Snowflower.

Chapter

16

THAT EVENING I waited for Max Pilsner and Sal Infantino outside the locker club on the corner of Washington Avenue and Jefferson Davis Highway. We were going into town, and they were inside, changing into civvies. I was in dress whites, wearing the two green stripes of the lowly airman deuce. I'd have to wait until payday to buy civvies or until my father could figure out how to send me a box of clothes in the mail. The line of palms leading to the base looked stately in the fading late-afternoon light. The weeds, pines and palmettos in the fields seemed more lush. Across the highway there was a place called Billy's, with a sign in the window offering a *Happy Hour From Five to Seven Ladies Welcome.* There was a flag outside at half-mast (mourning Hank Williams, I supposed) and about a dozen cars nuzzled against the front wall. The town was down the highway to the left. About a hundred yards away, back in the pine trees, I could see the white spire of a church.

I watched the traffic. A few cars. A big truck. And then I saw a woman in a yellow T-shirt and dungaree shorts pedaling a blue bicycle. Her legs were lean and cabled with muscle and I thought vaguely about drawing them. She had a baseball cap pulled tight on her head and she was wearing sunglasses.

And I realized it was her.

The woman from the bus.

Here.

In Pensacola.

I was frozen for a few seconds and then started toward the highway. A garbage truck roared past me.

"Hey!" I yelled. "Hey, miss . . ."

But almost as quickly as I'd seen her, she was gone. Around the bend of the highway, past the church and out of sight.

And then Max and Sal were there, Max in a tight-fitting T-shirt and starched jeans, Sal in a flowered rayon shirt, busy with palm trees and surf and beaches. I glanced at the highway again, tense and anxious but somehow feeling better. I wanted to chase after the woman in the yellow T-shirt, call a taxi, get on a bus. Too late. But at least now I knew she wasn't in far-off Palatka. She was here. In Pensacola. Where I could find her.

"You must of gone for a pump, Max," Sal said. He hit Max on the shoulder with the heel of his hand. "Your muscles got a hard-on."

"Up yours, Sal."

"Max works out," Sal said to me, as we started across the high-way, waiting for a break in traffic. I wanted to move fast, to get on a bus, to catch a glimpse of the woman, *my* woman. They moved too casually. "They got a gym on the base so small you can't get three pairs of sneakers in it at the same time. Somehow Max gets in there and lifts dumbbells. When he wears a T-shirt, like tonight, he always goes for an extra pump."

"Pump this," Max said.

"Hey, Max, I know a girl that wants to suck your lats."

Max growled as we hurried behind a slow truck to the far side of the highway, then said, "Hey, I'm so horny, I'd pay a dog to lick my hand."

Sal and Max told me to stay out of Billy's. It was the Old Salt's bar, the headquarters for Red Cannon and his friends. We walked past the joint to a bus stop just short of the Baptist church. A painted billboard said: WHAT IS MISSING FROM JES S? U R. A smaller sign under the billboard advertised square dances every Friday night. I couldn't remember what day it was. Thrown off by the holiday. I didn't ask, afraid of their laughter. Devlin: So hip he doesn't know what day it is. I looked at another sign, above a small white cross: GOD BLESS YOU HANK.

Sal pointed at the sign.

"You know what's missing in Jesus, Max? *You* are."

Max turned to me and shook his head. "It's the water they got up in The Bronx."

Sal said, "Now these are the *real* goyim." He saw the notice for the square dance. "I gotta take you there some Friday night . . ."

"Not me," Max said. "I hear they commit ritual murder in there."

"Absolutely true," Sal said. "But only on Jews and spades. They take you in back, tie you up, and check to see if you're, one, circumcised or, two, can balance a basketball on your dick. You can do either, that's enough, a sign from God. Then they beat you to death with Bibles wrapped in argyle socks. Whatever's left, they sell as bait out in the Gulf. . . . So we'd have to disguise you as an Irishman. Teach you the words to 'Danny Boy.' Get you a plastic foreskin . . . "

The bus arrived and we got on. Max and Sal sat together and I took the seat behind them. All the way into town I looked for the woman in the yellow T-shirt and baseball cap, pedaling a blue bicycle. I didn't see her. But I was certain I would find her.

Chapter

17

DIXIE SHAFER WAS just inside the door of the Dirt Bar when we arrived. She wasn't very tall, but great piles of silky red hair rose off her face and made her seem gigantic. Her mouth and nose were small, and her skin was creamy, but she must have weighed three hundred pounds. A lot of that weight was in her breasts, which were round, full, straining against a flowered off-the-shoulder gypsy blouse. A gold cross on a chain lay between the breasts, sometimes turning on its side and flattening between them when she moved. Her eyes were blue behind oversized red harlequin glasses. Gold hoops hung from her ears and every one of her fingers was adorned with rings. I'd never seen anyone like her in my life.

"New man!" Sal yelled. "Mike Devlin!"

"First one's on me!" Dixie shouted, jamming those huge tits against me and hugging me. "After that, you pay!"

"She means it," Sal said, raising his eyebrows at me as Dixie moved behind the bar. He explained that Dixie had built the bar a year before on this empty lot on O Street. Land was cheap and Dixie saw something; she grabbed the plot, bought some concrete blocks from a chief ordnance man who robbed them from Mainside, and had the roof up in a week. A moonlighting shipwright built the bar and she moved in the jukebox and the shuffleboard machine and then ran out of money. She didn't have a dime left for the floor. The sailors started coming, and she realized that sailors could get along without a floor—understood that Sal and some of the others actually *loved* the dirt—and that sailors could get along without almost everything except a bar and a jukebox, cold beer and warm pussy. So Dixie saved the money that should have gone for the floor and used it to build an extension: a place in the back, where she lived. And she did her best to give all her young men what they needed most. Beer and pussy. Pussy and beer.

"If heaven ain't like Dixie's Dirt Bar," Sal said, "I don't want to go."

Dixie shoved three Jax beers at us, and we pooled single dollars on the bar and I could see other faces from the base in the smoky room and heard Hank Williams from the juke. *"Jambalaya and a crawfish pie / And a filé gumbo. . . ."* There were four men in civvies playing a shuffleboard machine and the door opened and two more came in to join the dozen at the bar. *"Son of a gun, we'll have big fun, on the bayouuuu."* The beer was full of little slivers of ice and I watched Dixie's breasts move as she hurried around behind the bar, jerking tops off bottles with a church key and making change from a tray beside the icebox. I wondered what it would feel like to push my face between those creamy breasts.

"Hank ain't dead!" Sal suddenly yelled, shaking both fists in the air like a Holy Roller. "Oh lord, no, *Hank ain't dead!*" The shuffleboard players paused. Dixie gave him a look. "Don't be telling *me* Hank Williams done died!" He was talking like a preacher now, with a little bit of Senator Claghorn too. "Just listen, brothers an' sisters! You *hear* him? Do you hear poor Hank, poor Luke the Driftuh hisself? He lives, brothers and sisters! Right *there* on that jukebox! An' I tell you, he's gonna be there the rest of our *lives*!"

"Amen, brother," one of the shuffleboard players said solemnly. "Amen, amen . . ."

"The *Lord* put him among us an' the *Lord* done took him away, but brothers and sisters, we will be with him again in Paradise! I *tell* you! An' right here, tonight, in *this* place, among us *poor* sinners, he is with us, because there ain't a man among us who can't say it loud and clear: *Hank lives!* Just shout it *out,* brothers."

Two sailors at the bar yelled, "Hank lives! Yeah. Hank *lives!*"

"No, you gotta *shout* it! You gotta shout so the *Lord* kin hear ya! Do you *know* what I'm saying?"

I couldn't tell if Sal was serious or what, but in seconds he had all of us chanting, shouting, pounding the bar, yelling *Hank lives! Hank lives! Hank lives!* While Sal threw his head back, chug-a-lugged the beer and then clunked the bottle down hard. While the words came from the juke: *"Another love before my time. Made your heart sad and blue . . ."*

Max said, "Sal, we can't keep up with you like this."

"You have to, mah man, mah Hebrew brother, cuz *Hank* would've *wanted* it this way."

We chug-a-lugged together, in a kind of ritual, Sal moving us with the almost religious fervor of his sarcasm; Max let out an enormous belch, while Dixie opened three fresh bottles and Hank Williams sang "Ramblin' Man." Three more sailors came in, all wearing civvies, and the place was packed and full of smoke, with the bubbling lights racing through the columns of the great Wurlitzer against the concrete wall. I didn't chug-a-lug the second beer, but I did manage a fat gassy belch as a kind of punctuation. Sal slapped me on the back and yelled for Dixie, who brought three more bottles. Her breasts were beautiful. They weren't actually breasts at all, I thought, full of distinctions; they were *tits*. Real-life beautiful *tits*. Everybody was talking at once, with Sal roaring over them all and the talk was all Hank Williams.

"Hank ain't dead," Sal said, and finished a beer. "Hank *lives*!"

He had set the refrain for the night. *Hank would've wanted it this way.* Sal was making fun, I guess; I don't think he truly felt very bad about Hank Williams. But, in his loud wild way, he was consoling the others, and maybe pitying them a little, too. So the night became a series of fragments: beer and new faces and change on the bar and bottles being smashed in a garbage can and Dixie's creamy bigness, all of it held together by a poor lonesome dead man. *Hank would've wanted it that way.*

At one point, Dixie came up beside me and said, "You're a quiet one, ain't you?" And moved away. While Hank Williams sang:

> *"Did you ever see a robin weep*
> *When leaves begin to die?*
> *That means he's lost the will to live*
> *I'm so lonesome I could cry. . . . "*

In the blur I tried to sort out the members of what they all called The Gang. Brian Maher from Hartford. Pale Irish skin untouched by the Gulf sun. Slick hair as black as India ink. A yeoman so good Sal said he could take stenography like a pro. Brian drank his beer very fast and belched almost demurely, and talked to me in a soft secretive way about ice skating on the Merrimac River when he was a boy and how no other women in the whole world had such round firm eatable asses as the girls on that winter river. Beside him, Don

Carter from Newark. His accent harder than any New Yorker's. Long-nosed, gap-toothed, with big hands, a deep tan, working at Ellyson as a parachute rigger (and Sal yelling at him over the words of "Mind Your Own Business": What are you going to do with PARACHUTE RIGGING on The Outside? Carter glancing at me, shrugging, pulling at his long nose, staring into the top of the Jax beer bottle: *I don't know, the rigging school was in Lakehurst, near home, and I just wanted to be near my girl.* And Sal slammed the bar and shouted: And where in the FUCKING FUCK is the girl NOW, Carter? Carter whispered: *Gone.* Sal blinked, and said: Drink up, asshole. Hank would've wanted it that way.)

And here was Boswell arriving, bouncing off the shuffleboard, hearing "Jambalaya," and bursting into tears. While Waleski turned to me, saying he liked the way New York looked in the movies and he liked New Yorkers, but Chicago was the real place, the great place, the best city. Hey, New York couldn't have anything like Pulaski Boulevard on the Near West Side or a bridge named after Kosciusko (and I said, Hey, no, man, we got a Kosciusko Bridge too, and Waleski said, No *shit?*) and anyway, you couldn't drive at night from New York to Calumet City, the way you could from Chicago, to see the guy named The Human Prick ("What's that?" said Dixie), a guy they dressed up in a prick costume, who would then proceed to eat himself on the stage ("Did he look like Red Cannon?" I said) and in New York there wasn't no place like Madison Street in Calumet, either. Five Bucks A Fuck. Black and White All Night ("You mean you fucked a colored girl?" I said, walking into it, and Waleski said, "I thought I fucked a colored girl until I saw a colored guy fuck a colored girl") and slower now, staring at the beer, he told me how hard it was that year before he joined the Navy, getting up in the dark to drive to work at Inland Steel in Gary and his girl Sherry ragging his ass at night 'cause he could never get the black stuff out of his fingernails and so she would never let him play with her glory hole, and then I said: Where is this Sherry now? And Waleski said, as we all said, every last one of us: *Gone.*

We'd gone off first, of course. That was the worst thing. All of us knew it. We signed up for the messes we made of our lives. We went off to join the Navy because they needed us in Korea, or because we didn't want to go in the infantry, or because our brothers were in the Navy in the last war, or because we heard Kate

Smith sing "God Bless America" or we saw a movie called *The Fighting Sullivans* when we were kids, or *They Were Expendable.* Maybe we wanted a uniform. Maybe we just wanted to prove we were men. Whatever it was, we went, and the girls watched our backs, and they said to themselves, as we said later (watching their backs): *Gone.* There were going-away parties. There were feverish good-byes. Some of the guys got engaged to the girls. Some even got married, standing with the new wives while the photographers took their pictures in downtown studios, the guys in their rented tuxes, the girls in white gowns, the rented cars double-parked outside. They carried those pictures in their wallets and their sea bags, took them to boot camp, and to the training schools in Memphis and Jacksonville and Norman, Oklahoma, took them across oceans, looking at the pictures and trying to remember the feel of flesh, the sound of their woman's laugh. And learned too late that all the girls were gone. They'd found other guys who were always around on a Saturday night, flesh-and-blood men of bone and cock, not addresses on envelopes; young men who could dance with them and drink with them and lie with them.

That's what I heard in the smoke and noise and broken pieces of the night, in those murmured stories held together by the voice of a poor dead lonesome hillbilly singer. And I felt for the first time since leaving home that I was not alone. That I'd never been alone. That I too was part of this huge secret society of loss, and here in Dixie's Dirt Bar I was attending a meeting of the Pensacola chapter.

Around ten, as they did every night, the whores arrived. "Look at em, God's truest angels," Sal said. Max shook his head and whispered about the clap, but Sal just laughed and grabbed a skinny girl and danced with her to "Cold, Cold Heart." The other guys grabbed for female arms and waists and asses, and the girls were all weepy over Hank and buried their heads on Navy shoulders and some of them kicked off their shoes to feel the damp dirt of the Dirt Bar's floor. "Go ahead, honey," Dixie said, and I danced with a skinny gap-toothed girl from the bayous of what she called Luziana, washed up here in Pensacola four years before while trying to get to Miami. She called me "mate" and said she sure felt bad for Hank and asked me if I wanted to go out to the van and I said I was broke and she said it was only four dollars and I said maybe next time, and she said, Well, okay sailor, fair enough and when the tune ended, she went to Max and took him to the dance floor and after awhile they went outside.

Soon it was all sailors and whores, dancing on the hard-packed red dirt. There was a tattooed girl and a toothless girl and some rough girls with coarse skin and hillbilly accents. They called us "mate" or "sailor," and I thought that must have been part of what they did. They couldn't possibly remember the names of all the guys they fucked, so they called us mate or sailor or sport. Maybe they didn't want to remember. I danced with some of them, but mostly I watched, trying to sort out the faces, thinking that I would like to draw them, that maybe I could make them more beautiful than they were and that would make them happy. For they were not happy, not one of them. And I realized then that I was at a wake. The corpse had been found in a Cadillac in West Virginia, but they were mourning other things: people forgotten and lost, lovers gone, broken promises, the past. Still, no matter what its object, it was a proper wake, like any other back home. And when the whores laughed when Sal yelled or grabbed their asses they were just doing that night what the Irish always did on other nights in Brooklyn. They'd even done it when my mother died. They started out weeping and mournful. Then got formal. And then drunk and singing the old songs. It was what the Irish had instead of the blues.

By midnight the place was a steady thumping roar, Hank Williams and beer and some white lightnin that Boswell brought in from outside, and then the door burst open and two jolly fat girls came waddling in, bellowing "yee-HAW" at the crowd. Sal yelled *"Tons of Fun!"* And went running at them, yelling "Hee-Fuckin-HAW!" And leaped, as the women, whose names were Betty and Freddie, made a cat's cradle with their hands and caught him in the air, like a turn in a circus, like something they'd rehearsed. They began rubbing their breasts in Sal's face, and Freddie grabbed his crotch and massaged it, while Sal screamed in mock panic: "Get me a priest! Get me a fuckin *priest*!"

I looked at Dixie and she shook her head at me. *No.* A sign. A message. *No.* Did they have the clap? *No.* And then Freddie and Betty let go of Sal and he fell to the dirt floor with his feet straight up in the air like the last panel in *Mutt and Jeff* and the whole bar cheered and more beers came slamming down on the bar and Sal grabbed my arm and said, "Come and meet my *Fee-ahn-says . . .*"

. . . And the girls were beside us at the bar, rubbing, pressing,

Boswell sticking a tongue in Betty's ear, Sal faking exhaustion, Maher paralyzed. And Freddie swore that she once sucked Hank's dick and Betty said that was the truth and Freddie said that Hank had a tiny little dick and was built like a weed and Betty said, No lie, and Freddie said that when she heard the news she wished it had been her instead of Hank Williams and how bad he musta felt all his life about that itty-bitty pecker and how he never did get to use it all that much, what with the drinkin and everything. She poured some cold Jax down her throat without ever touching the bottle to her lips, which made Sal holler in delight. While Betty played with me. And Dixie Shafer shook her head again, No, saying with her look, Don't dare, saying, Absolutely not. Saying *No*.

Until they all were gone, sailors and whores, Sal leaving with Betty and Freddie, shouting "Hank would want it this way!" And the others paired off or left alone, while the floor rolled under me like an ocean swell and the walls advanced and receded and the jukebox went silent at last. Dixie Shafer looked at me across the bar and then glanced at the corridor leading to the back room. There were no lights down there. She took off the harlequin glasses and slid them between her breasts, then reached across the bar and took my hand in hers.

"First one is on the house," she said.

Chapter

18

What Dixie Told Me

I'M FROM KENTUCKY, *originally. Breathitt County. Ever hear of hit? All mountains and forests and then the mines later on. My daddy was a Hardshell Baptist and in that little pineboard church of theirs, hit was real strict, I tell you. Women on one side the aisle, men on the other, and a lot of singin and tambourines but nothin you could call fun. There was a preacher came when I was eight year old, a Reverent Woodford, and he was somethin. That's when they started the footwashin and the snake handlin. The footwashin warnt nothin, really, all of us there watchin, as theyd get down and wash each others feet.*

But the snakehandlin, that was a different matter haltogether. They always did the snakes at night and I remember seeing everybody coming through the woods with lanterns and big shadows everywhere until we got to that little board church, just a sign in hit saying "Jesus is Comin" and a potbelly stove and kerosene lamps on the walls. The women almost all wore gingham in them days. And the men—by that time they uz miners—they hung their helmets on nails and got in the aisles and waited for the snakes.

The Reverent Woodford would start hit, holdin a rattler in his hands, and prayin to the Lord, and soon people started wailin, beatin them tambourines, speakin in tongues, and the Reverent uz tellin them that if they uz without sin the Lord would protect them and if they warn't then they uz in big trouble. Well, my daddy never would do hit and my momma said that uz proof he uz sinnin, he must have him some woman down the hollow, he must be drinkin liquor in the damn mines. But he said, No, he warnt gonna do hit, no snakes for him. And he stuck by his guns, until one night,

I uz about twelve, we were there, and Momma uz pressin him, and the music got to playin louder and louder, and someone shouted, and I uz up shoutin, cause they called that The Shouts, hit just come right out of you. And then all of a suddint, Momma had a rattler in her hands, in front of all of them, and Daddy uz a bit shamed, and they were shoutin louder, and then Daddy uz up there too, I guess to get rid of his shame, or maybe to keep Momma, and the shoutin got to be real powerful, and I got real excited, and then pow! *I tell you, boy, I know now what happen to me. I* came. *I just plumb* came. *Without no cock in me. Without no help at all. I just* came, *boy!*

I uz something else, then, boy. Not what I am now. Boys thunk I uz a lovely girl. And I uz risin again and Daddy had that four-foot rattler in his hands and I felt hit comin again, felt the explosion comin up in me. And then the rattler bit Daddy. First rattled. Then bit him right in the neck. Rattled. Bit him again. And Daddy dropped the rattler and backed up and he had this look in his eyes like he jest seed the Devil and then he fell back and the chapel become quiet and Momma just stood up, she dint cry, she dint run to him. I did. I dint care where the rattler went, I went to my Daddy. I cried at him, Daddy. I cried Oh Daddy get up. Oh Daddy, I love ya Daddy. But hit dint do no good. We buried Daddy two days later with the wind howlin down the hollows and Reverent Woodford singin and all of them lookin at me, and I could tell they uz thinkin, Poor child, her Daddy uz a sinner.

Momma kept on keepin on. She could weave. She knew how to shear a sheep and card the wool and spin hit into yarn. Then she sold the weavins to someone who brung them down someplace to the river and sold them. We lived in a little ole shambly place, a shack really, but hit had a good stone fireplace, and there uz always enough pumpkin and sorghum, gravy and onions, cornbread and shucky beans. Most days I watched the least-uns, while Momma worked the loom. She never did mention Daddy and his sin. She dint mention him at all.

And then one night I come home from the woods at night and hit gettin to be real dark cause we had no electrick in them days, not even radios, nothin up in them hills at all. And then I saw the Reverent Woodford in the clearin out back of the shack and hit warnt snakes he was handlin, hit was Momma's titties. I stayed all night alone in the woods, cryin mostly for my Daddy, and began to thinkin about goin out to the world.

I knew there had to be a world out there, cause I seen hit in the Montgomery Ward catalogs. I couldn't read the words, but Cousin Frances could. And I near memorized the names of the things you could get out in the world. *Dr. Scott's Electric Hairbrush, good for headache and dandruff. Don't laugh, boy! And stuff called Mum and Kotex and Listerine and Odorono. Cuticura soap and perfume called Wild Rose and Shandon Bells and Ylang Ylang and Dr. Fuller's Bust Developer and Food (I sure never did need that stuff). Most of all I wanted a gown called Moonlight Sonata. I remember what hit said in the catalog: "You, winsome and desirable in clouds of rayon net, your tiny waist sashed with whispering rayon taffeta." For three ninety-eight. Oh, how I wanted to be winsome and desirable. Down there in the world.*

I also knew about the world from Uncle Fred that was married to Aunt Mildred. He'd been down to the world. Actually seen hit, lived in hit, and told me all about hit. How people lived in brick houses and had roads with tar on them and stores with gowns in them better than in the Montgomery Ward catalogs and how everybody went to school and workin people owned cars. I made him tell me over an over about the gowns. And the jewlry. And he could really speak, Uncle Fred, so he made me see all the beautiful stuff of the world.

Then, I met Robert. I uz talkin to him a long time, and then he got to be laying with me crost a bed. Not doin nothin. Jest touchin. But we decided to get married. I said, Okay Momma, but I don't want that Reverent Woodford to do no service, and she said Why, and I said, Because. So we got us a preacher from over the ridge. He come to the house and did a big praying service for us and later we had a big shivaree and then we moved into the hayloft. Robert war a big strong boy, a woodcutter by trade, but he had him a pindling little dick. That uz so sad. Momma gave me a poke o' wheat to help me have babies, but hit dint do no good. Hit jest warnt to be. Poor Robert was so worried bout the size of his dick, he couldn't get hit hard. So he moped all the time and drunk a lot.

He got worse when I started goin to the new school. This got to be round the time Roosevelt sent them teachers into the hills and there was a young man from up North, from Pennsylvania, from out in the world. Eli. He was a Jewboy. Like that boy Max comes in the Dirt Bar. Eli come among us and got us to put up the school. Just a plain board buildin with a tin roof and a stove and no electrick. The girls had to go to the outhouse four at a time to keep them boys out of there. But kids come six, eight mile to that school, and even ef I uz too old, I wanted to learn me something about the world, so I went to that young man from up North and I said I wanted to learn how to read and I'd help with the least-uns if he'd teach me. And he said yes.

Well, you couldn't learn some of them boys nothin with a pistol in yore hands, but he did his best. Eli. The Jewboy. When there got to be snow on the ground, the kids dint come. When the creeks were up, they stayed home too. But Eli taught us, he showed us words, he had us make poetry, he showed us a great big map of the world. And I'd get all het up and go home and tell Robert. And soon he was sure I was layin for Eli, which I warnt. Robert dint believe me and one night he went down and burnt that school to the ground.

So Eli left and I walked around the hills for two days callin his name, trying to get him to stay. Them hills used to be so thick and beautiful. But then the loggin people come and they started cutting down the trees. They rolled them down to the creeks and floated them off to the mills where they were cut into lumber, and soon the hills were naked. But even in the naked hills, Eli warnt to be seen. And I thought: there's nothin left for me in this valley.

So I went away. I jest left Robert and went to the town, walkin for days, waitin to see the place with the brick houses and the tar streets and the Moonlight Sonata gowns in the store windows that'd make me feel, you know, winsome and desirable. I couldn't find hit. Cause that place never did exist except in my foolish damned schoolgirl head. But I did find Hazard and got me a job in a tool store, wearing shoes cause the streets was all mud. And I met some other girls in town and we started goin to these barns, jenny barns they called them, where people drank Cream of Kentucky whiskey out of Coca-Cola glasses and there uz gamblin in the back rooms, and I met other girls that worked in these places, that dint just come for the dancin, girls that were stayin there for the winter, followin the carnivals in the summer. The jenny barns was wild, with music playin and men from all over, down from the hills, comin to the towns, like the hills uz emptyin out. Which they was.

And one day the store I worked in closed from the Depression, which was all over the world by then. So I went to work in the jenny barns and I just dint care. The first time I uz scared and started cryin, sure I'd be slain by the Lord for my terrible sin. But I hadn't et for three days and the Lord dint hear my prayers so I did what I did to live. After the first time, I dint care. Fact is, I liked hit. Those boys was crazy and wild and drunk and lonesome, but they was all better'n poor Robert. And they sure did love my titties. Trouble is, that's when I started getting large. There was some shacks back in the woods and I'd go there with them, for three dollars apiece, which was good money in them days. I give the man that run the jenny barn a dollar but hit was all right. I dint care long's I dint get the old rale, or a good dose, and I was lucky, I never did. I specialized in the other thing anyway. I guess after a while, I was knowed all over for hit.

*And then one night, who comes in but Eli. My Jewboy. He couldn't stand
what I uz doin, and asked me to come away with him, and so I did. He
uz organizin for the National Miners' Union now, trying to get everybody
to band together against the operators in Harlan County. He was a Communist, my Jewboy, and he lived stricter than some Hardshell Baptist. He only
et once a day, so he was all skin an bones, jest pathetic, and he went around
makin his speeches, usin a bicycle until someone came in from up North with
a Ford car. The only place he warnt strict uz in bed. He got to be the hottest
man I ever seed in bed. I even got skinny again. And I'm tellin you, you
never heard anything like this boy when he was speechifyin. All about how
we should own the fruits of our labor and how the bosses was usin our work
to make themselves rich while men was dying in the bottom of coal mines
and kids warnt learnin how to read an write. When he talked about readin
and writing the tears come to his eyes and to tell the truth, they come to my
eyes too, and to everybody that could hear his voice.*

*And soon they was a war right there in Harlan County. My Jewboy
brung down a bunch of big writers from the North to see what was happenin
and all the men come from around the hills, living in the streets of the town,
in the mud, making tents, houses out of Coca-Cola signs, good men, hurt
men, men that had families starvin, men that wanted their kids to learn
how to read. It was so goddamned excitin, I tell you. They was guns
everywhere. Rifles and pistols. And the women were the hardest, the women
warnt so beaten down, and we got together and we war making speeches
in the square when the sheriff locked us all up. Sixteen women in all. We
sat in jail, singin all the songs that was written at the time. And we saw
that the companies really did run the sheriff, jest like Eli said, the company
men jest walked in and gave the sheriff his orders, we seed it, they brung
in gangsters from someplace and made them all deputies. And then they let
us out, cause they was so many bad stories in the newspapers, and there was
another big meetin.*

*This time they got my Jewboy. They beat him vicious on the head with
blackjacks and I seed them carryin him off and I was screamin at them,
cause his face was all blood, and when I screamed they bashed him again
and then grabbed me and dragged me off. So they took my Jewboy out to the
county line and they dumped him in a ditch. Some of the men found him
and got him to a hospital but hit war too damn late. Two days later he
died. When someone asked the sheriff why they arrested poor Eli, the sheriff
jest smiled and said quote unquote resistin assault. Some joke. They said too
that Eli had run away, he escaped and that uz why he war in that ditch,
and nobody got locked up for it, even though everybody in the county knew
it was murder, plain and simple.*

That was hit for me. I left then. Forever. I dint want nothin to do no more with no politics or with them damn hills. I found my way to New Orleans. I had my specialty. I married a man for a while, but nothin come of hit. I made some money in the war. Workin down by the Higgins shipyard. And I thought: I don't ever want to need nobody ever again. Specially no man. And here I am, boy. You lookin at a free woman. You uz a virgin boy, warnt you? I could tell. Well, it jest got to be time. Get used to hit, boy. You gonna have lots more, all the rest of your days and nights.

Chapter
19

DIXIE DROVE ME back to Ellyson Field in her 1950 Plymouth in the gray chilly dawn. We had the windows up and I could smell her perfume. She didn't say anything. I felt strange. I looked for a woman on a blue bicycle, with a yellow T-shirt and a baseball cap, but she was nowhere in sight. Dixie stopped a hundred feet from the main gate. I opened the door and thanked her for the ride. She looked at me and nodded.

"You're a nice boy," she said.

And then pulled away.

PART
TWO

Chapter

20

THEN SUDDENLY IT was winter. The wind came howling down from Canada, and when we woke up the blankets weren't warm enough and the showers were cold and we couldn't tell the time of day from the morning light. We closed all windows tightly and changed white hats to watchcaps. The sky at noon was the color of slate, and thousands of gulls came in from the Gulf to huddle close to the earth. The helicopters were grounded. Gigantic gray clouds rose in the sky. And then one afternoon it began to snow.

We did cartwheels in the snow and threw snowballs at one another, while Becket took pictures with a little box Brownie. Liberty was canceled and we were handed shovels and put on work details to clear the streets of the base and the landing strips beyond the hangars. Out at the hangars, shoveling snow with Sal and Max and a dozen others, I saw the pilots up close, smoking, playing gin rummy, posing for photographs. They were all lean men in loose baggy flight suits. Sal pointed out a Marine who had just come back from Korea, where he'd flown 151 helicopter missions, 86 behind enemy lines, picking up the wounded or the dead. When I looked at his eyes they didn't seem dashing and cocky, the way Clark Gable's eyes looked in the old movies; they just looked sad and tired.

Most of the pilots wore patches on their flight suits, showing a goggled grasshopper with a rotor blade above its head and a figure eight below it. And as we scraped the snow off the landing strips I realized I was standing on a huge painted figure eight within a painted square. Max explained that this was a basic part of the training routine, the pilots learning to maneuver with precision, to hover, to land right on a mark. They called the helicopters pin-wheels, whirlybirds, or eggbeaters, and they hated flying them because the center of gravity was so low that they turned over too easily. And after flying jets, said Sal, who would want to play with these toys?

We cleaned the snow away and then the wind rose and blew more snow across the strips and covered them again and Max laughed and said, "Well, that's the Navy." I saw a Spanish-looking guy in a flight suit, his features clean, with a neat moustache and high cheekbones standing on the runway taking pictures, and he motioned to us to join him. His name was Tony Mercado, a pilot with the Mexican Air Force, taking copter training in the States. He handed me the camera and asked me to photograph him in the falling snow.

It was a Leica, the first real camera I'd ever held. Heavy, solid, somehow mysteriously beautiful and scary. In all the years since, whenever I pick up a new camera in a store, or heft one of my own for the first time after waking in the morning, I remember that snowy day beside the hangars of Ellyson Field. I'd never felt any-thing like it before: a piece of machinery that made pictures.

Mercado told me what to do and I looked through the viewfinder and saw him posing before the half-open hangar doors, his smile bright, looking dashing, the snow blowing around him. He had me cock the camera again and then posed squatting, coffee cup casually in his hand, and I realized that he looked more like Clark Gable than any of the pilots who had been to the war. He thanked me in an accented voice and strolled away and I wanted to get the camera back from him and take pictures of the windsock flying straight out in the wind and the snow gathering at the base of the palm trees and Red Cannon hurrying over from the administration building with his plastic face all flushed and Sal loping away to the head. But I said nothing. Max leaned on his shovel and said, "You're a photographer now." And of course he was right, but I didn't know it for a long long time.

The next day the snow was gone. The sun burned its way back, high and dim in the clear cold sky, but it wasn't strong enough to rid us of the bitter cold. Liberty was restored. I wanted to go to town and search for the curly-haired woman, but after the night at the Dirt Bar I had no money, and it was three more days until payday. Still, Dixie Shafer had erased my shameful secret and I felt triumphant and powerful except for the money. Harrelson and Boswell left for Montgomery and the big service for Hank Williams. When they came back two days later, full of details and white lightning, we were all tired of Hank Williams and nobody wanted to hear about it. I walked through the Panhandle afternoons, listening for Bobby Bolden. But all the windows were still closed against the cold. I thought about going up to see him, but I was afraid he'd play some game in front of the other blacks and tell me to get lost. I wouldn't let him do that.

We worked long days, with the helicopters flying from 0500 until sunset, thirty of them in the air at once, catching up on lost time. Somewhere in those few days I started to know the difference between push-pull rods and irreversibles, swash plates and wobble plates, cuff and trunion assemblies. I wasn't sure what a gimbal ring was, but when Sal came to get one, he said that for shit sure it wasn't available at Macy's.

All Navy nights resembled one another. Broke, confined, we sat around on the bunks and read the newspapers or listened to the radio. We exchanged what was called "the gouge," another word for lore, or "scuttlebutt," which was rumor and gossip. I learned how to spit-shine my shoes. My hair grew longer. I pulled another midnight-to-four, learning the password first, and signed the clipboard once more for Red Cannon. I learned that the best place for tailor-made uniforms was Anchor Tailors on South Baylen Street. The manager's name was Marie. But I didn't want tailor-mades. I wanted civvies. I wanted to be able to go into town in normal clothes, with some money in my pocket, and find that woman with the curly hair.

But I needed money for clothes and a locker. As an airman apprentice in pay scale E-2, just above the bottom, I would get a check for $80.90 after the taxes were taken out. A fortune. Finally we lined up one morning at 1020 in Hangar Two to get our paychecks. Everybody else got paid, but there was nothing for me. Maher was the duty yeoman and he said he was sorry, that this sometimes happened to new sailors while the paperwork was being sent back and forth to BuPers in Washington. He'd look into it and let me know. Sal, Max and Miles Rayfield offered to loan me some money; I said I'd wait.

I stayed on the base for more than two weeks, waiting for the paycheck. Sal and Max went out most nights. Miles remained on board, but went off most evenings to some destination on the base itself, saying nothing. The image of the woman began to fade. I was sure she was with a guy now, perhaps a husband, some Navy lover. The weather stayed cold, but there was no more snow. I read the art book, my head filling with Rembrandt and Goya, Leonardo and Botticelli. At the Supply Shack, I got better at my work each day, and the mechanics now knew my name. I heard other hillbilly singers on the radio, Webb Pierce and Lefty Frizzell, and began to know the words. If Bobby Bolden was playing his horn, nobody on the base could hear him except the mess cooks. One chilly night I was in the barracks reading the *Pensacola Journal.* Miles and Jones were there. A story on page one said that 40,000 American servicemen had deserted since the beginning of the Korean War and 36,000 had been recaptured. That was astonishing. "Who the hell *blames* them?" Miles said acidly. "What's that goddamned war *about* anyway?" Jones bristled, said it wasn't a war, it was a police action, and Miles said you couldn't tell that to the dead, and Jones said that if we didn't fight the Communists in Korea we'd have to fight them in San Diego, and at that, Miles laughed and shook his head. "Jonesie," he said, "that's the hoariest cliché of the decade so far." Jones bristled again, said there'd always be cowards in any war, men who'd rather run away. Miles said: "We're talking about two complete *divisions* of deserters, Jonesie. Doesn't that tell you something? "Yeah," Jonesie said. "It tells me this country's getting soft." And he walked away.

Miles and I were quiet for a while, and then he looked up at me and said, "Do you ever think of doing it?"

"Going over the hill?"

"Yeah."

"No," I said, and meant it. "I made a deal. I have to keep up my end, even if I don't like it."

He stared at his hands.

"What about you?" I said.

He took off his glasses and rubbed his eyes. "I think about it all the time."

One frigid afternoon, Miles showed me the base library, up one flight of wooden stairs to room 912, above the post office. "It's actually not too bad," he said, in an amazed way. "They've got some magazines and a few good books." He was right. I remember the first time I went up those stairs. A middle-aged yeoman in a pea jacket was sleeping at a desk. He came suddenly awake, blinked at me with the sore eyes of a rummy, saw I was just a kid sailor and went back to sleep. The place was a kind of refuge from the Navy, with five aisles of books, a magazine rack, and a long table where you could write letters or just look out the three screened windows at the base.

I picked up *Life* magazine. On the cover, a model with blurry features peered through a beaded curtain. I remember that issue so clearly. It was the first *Life* I'd ever read, and it was full of marvels. I studied an advertisement for Philco television sets, equipped with the Golden Grid Tuner. A woman who looked like Joan Fontaine was turning the knob of a huge set. She was perfectly groomed, wearing earrings and a filmy dress.

We didn't have TV at home yet, and in our neighborhood none of the women looked like Joan Fontaine. But that winter everybody I knew was buying television sets. They had already begun to change everything, something I noticed the summer before I went away. At night, there were just not as many people on the streets as there used to be. When you looked up, you could see a blue glow in more and more windows. They were in all the bars, too, and men now stood quietly, staring at the black-and-white images, while the bartenders made endless adjustments. I thought that when I sold my first cartoons, I'd get my father a set. Maybe he'd enjoy the Dodger games. The kids could look at cartoons and Westerns. But I just couldn't picture myself sitting there with them.

I examined the magazine as if it were a papyrus discovered in some pharaoh's tomb. There seemed to be a woman in every ad: standing cheek to cheek with a guy in the Chlorodent toothpaste ad, holding her head in the Anacin ad, dressed as a bride in the Kingston sewing machine ad, scrubbing the floor in the ad for Flor-Ever vinyl flooring and a smaller shot of a woman with a sheet wrapped around her, shoulders bare, as a nurse noted her weight on a scale. She was selling lemons as a diet aid. She didn't look fat to me.

In the news part of the magazine, there were photographs of some quintuplets from Argentina and a lot of pictures of Republicans taking over the House of Representatives from the Democrats.

Harry Truman was still president, and they showed him sitting with some senator named Johnson, who had big ears and was smoking a cigarette, his hair sleeked back. The pictures made me think of Tony Mercado's camera, and I tried to imagine the photographers looking through their cameras at these events. How did they know where to go to take pictures? Did someone send them or call them? And did they take the film to a drugstore or develop it in some mysterious way themselves? Another story said that 1952 was the first year since 1882 without a lynching of a Negro in the United States, and that made me think of Bobby Bolden. How would he feel reading this news? Would he feel better? I didn't think so. If I was colored, I'd want to go out and lynch someone back.

I stopped at a full-page ad for Kotex. There was a woman in a tailored suit the color of oatmeal, with dark brown shoes, reddish gloves, a hat and earrings. In her right hand she was holding a leather-trimmed bag. She touched her throat nervously with her gloved left hand. In the distance, a man in a business suit was waving to her with his hat; he had a briefcase and raincoat under his arm. Behind him was a small two-engine airplane. I wasn't quite sure how Kotex worked, although I knew it had to do with a woman's period. The ad didn't exactly expand my knowledge. "Not A Shadow Of A Doubt With Kotex" said the headline. But the rest of the copy promised Protection, and Absorbency, and a Fresh, Dainty Feeling. What did all of this mean? And what did they mean by "no revealing outline"? Most of all I wondered about the nervous woman in the ad. Since this was a Kotex ad, she must have her period. But was this some secret she was keeping from the guy coming off the plane? If so, why? He looked like a husband, she looked like a wife. But she was wearing gloves, so I couldn't check for a wedding ring. Was she somebody *else's* wife? And had she made a date with this guy, only to discover that she had her period and wouldn't be able to sleep with him? Life was full of mysteries.

A few pages later, I saw a woman on skis, soaring through the air up in the mountains. She was wearing ski pants and boots but no shirt. *"I dreamed I went skiing in my Maidenform Bra . . ."* A blonde. Tinted glasses. Good teeth. I imagined her coming into a small dark room to meet me, the heavy boots making a clumping sound, her tits shoved up by the satiny bra. She ran the tip of her tongue over her lips, and sat down on the edge of my bed. I put my hand on her back, the flesh soft, and pulled her close. The hard breasts pushed up against my bare chest, the bra making a satiny noise as her tits touched me . . . Without working at it, I had another hopeless hard-on.

I looked over at the yeoman, who was still asleep. But I tried to distract myself from the loveliest sight on the dreamscape. Through the window, I could see Captain Pritchett and two other officers walking slowly down the paths. The captain was looking at the lawns. They were browned from the snow and the cold. He squatted and ran his hand across the top of the grass, then plunged his fingers into the dirt. He stood up and shook his head sadly, like a man about to cry. I closed *Life,* and watched Captain Pritchett walk away, his body sagging. At that moment I liked him very much. No matter what else he might be, he was a man who loved something.

Eisenhower was sworn in, but there was still no sign of my paycheck. "Maybe Truman stole it," Dunbar said. "Put it in a deep freeze. Put a down payment on a vicuña coat." The *Journal* said that more than 10,000 people crowded into two inaugural balls, paying $12 apiece, and they were so crowded nobody could dance. Back home, Republicans were a separate nationality. But at least now, for sure, the war would end. Eisenhower had gone to Korea between the election and the inauguration. He was a general. He would end it. One way or another. Maybe it wouldn't be like the last war. No celebrations, no V-J Day, with everybody running wild in the streets and block parties everywhere in the neighborhood and sailors kissing girls in Times Square. Korea was different. Nobody knew what Korea was about. But at least, if it ended, the men would stop dying, would stop being wounded, would stop being lost behind enemy lines. And that meant that there would be no need to train any more helicopter pilots. The Navy could close Ellyson Field. I could go to sea.

The weather turned warmer, but it was still not the hot weather of the day I arrived. During those weeks, I took seven trips to Mainside. Becket promised to teach me to drive. Most days, Sal and Max came to the Supply Shack, telling me that Dixie Shafer was asking for me at the Dirt Bar. I told them again that I wasn't going anywhere until I got paid. They offered to try to smuggle her onto the base some night, disguised as a case of pontoons. I donated a pint of blood to the Bloodmobile and later Captain Pritchett sent

around a notice congratulating everybody on the eighty percent
donation rate, adding up to 478 pints of blood. Walking back from
the library one afternoon, I saw Bobby Bolden and nodded. He
said hello.

"I miss hearing you," I said. "Maybe you could play some night
at the EM club."

"I don't think so."

"Why not?"

"Too many crackers."

"Ah, they won't bother you."

"They won't serve a black man there. Why should a black man
play for them?"

"You'd be playing for us, not for them." I thought about the
lynchings, and masked men from the Ku Klux Klan dragging
Negroes out of their homes. "Most of us are from the North."

"Forget it."

I wanted to keep talking to him, wanted to get to know him. I
thought that maybe Navy small talk was the best way. I gazed off
at the helicopters, trying to be casual.

"You give blood yesterday?" I said.

"Are you a fool or what?" he said. "They won't *take* our blood."

"You're kidding me."

"Wise up, chump. This is the Navy. You can't integrate *blood* in
the United States Navy. Spose one of them crackers learned he had
a black man's blood in him?"

"What would he care if it saved his life?"

"He'd rather fucking die."

"I don't believe it."

"You better learn, chump. This is America. They got *laws* down
here."

I felt awkward, but also pleased. At least Bolden was talking to
me. I mentioned musicians I'd heard on the radio, Max Roach and
Kenny Clarke, Roy Eldridge and Milt Jackson. He liked them all,
talked about their best work, then said, "You're pretty hip for an
ofay motherfucker." And laughed. It was as if he'd pinned a medal
on my chest. I said I'd like to come visit him and hear him play. He
said he'd think about it.

"I'm waiting to get paid," I said. "If the Navy ever finds the
check, maybe we could go out and spend a day at the beach."

He made a blubbering sound with his lips. "Don't you understand *nothin,* man? This is *Florida.* These beaches are segregated."

"You mean you can't go to any beach in Florida?"

"I can swim with the other niggers. That's all."

"You won a bunch of medals. Doesn't that matter?"

"Not a goddamned bit." He turned his head. "See yuh."

On the comics page, there was then a beautifully drawn sequence of Buz Sawyer's dumb brother, Lucky, walking into a Latin American revolution. Crane at his best. One of the Latin officers looked like Mercado, and I wondered if Mercado was learning to fly helicopters to fight in some future revolution. If so, I envied him. At least a revolution would be clear, not some blurry mess like Korea. But if there were a new revolution in Mexico, which side would Mercado be on? He would have to choose. And he would probably choose the side of the people who owned Leicas. Here, we never had to choose. Or so I thought then, at seventeen, and ignorant of most things.

Then one morning, the winter was gone. The sun came closer to the earth. We didn't need peajackets to go to the chow hall. Windows were opened all over the base. I heard Bobby Bolden playing "It Might As Well Be Spring" and started humming the words. *Starry eyed . . . vaguely discontented . . . like a nightingale without a song to sing . . .* I was picked for the Mainside run and stood in the back of the truck. Becket was driving and said we had to go to the waterfront first, to pick up a crate. We moved slowly into town through the morning traffic, heading down South Palafox to the piers.

Then, as we passed Trader Jon's, I saw the woman.

She was walking quickly toward Garden Street, her head down, dressed in dark maroon slacks, penny loafers, and a starched white blouse. Her face was masked with sunglasses, but I knew it was her from the curly hair.

"Hey, *miss*!" I shouted, as we rolled by.

She looked up, but there was no expression on her face.

"Remember me?" I yelled, pointing at my chest.

She looked up for a moment as Becket drove me away from her. Then she lowered her head and hurried across the street. I waved at her, like a desperate signalman semaphoring for help. At the door of Woolworth's she looked up again and saw me waving. She paused, waved back and then ducked into the store.

Chapter

21

From The Blue Notebook

Segregate: *v.* 1 To separate or set apart from others or from the main body or group. 2 Isolate. 3 To require, often with force, the separation of a specific racial, religious, or other group from the general body of society; to practice, require, or enforce segregation, esp. racial segregation. Also, maintaining separate facilities for members of different, esp. racially different groups. Segregated education, segregated buses.

Is this country nuts? A guy wins all kinds of medals in Korea and he can't swim on a beach in Florida? A white draft dodger, a white murderer on parole, the head of the Mafia, a white hooker with the syph—they can all swim on the beach, but Bobby Bolden can't? What is this all about? How can Eisenhower and these people make all those speeches about freedom and how important it is to fight the godless Communists and then tell Bobby Bolden he can't swim on a beach with white people? They sure didn't teach us any of this in school. The amazing thing is that any Negro would ever fight for this country at all. And the white people that pass these laws—what are they afraid of?

The goyim are everybody else in the world who is (are?) not Jewish. I know that from the old rabbi on 14th Street in Brooklyn, that year when I was the Shabbas goy. So I'm one of the goyim and so is Charlie Parker and Eisenhower and William Holden and June Allyson. Sal is always breaking Max's balls about the power of the goyim, but Max doesn't seem to mind. Max is the first Jew I ever met that is my own age, but he never talks about some of the things that must drive him crazy. Like Hitler and the concentration camps. It was only eight years ago when all that happened. I mean, back home my father's friends still sing songs about the Irish Famine, and that was in the 1840s or something. It's hard to imagine that the thing with the Jews really happened. When I was ten years old and reading Captain America. *Hard to believe that people could put other people in ovens and burn them alive or gas them. Not just a couple of people. But millions of them. Just for being a Jew. The newspapers say that six million Jews died. The weird thing is that there are people who still say things like: Hitler didn't kill enough of them. Boy, there are some sick bastards in this world. I don't understand how any Jew could believe in God after what happened. Any more than I can believe Bobby Bolden could pledge allegiance to the flag when he can't sit where he wants in a bus or swim on any beach in the country or eat in any restaurant or go to any school.*

I keep hearing the word gone. *Over and over. My girl is gone. The guy's wife is gone. But it isn't just ordinary people that are gone. It's everybody. They show up and you get to know them and then they're gone. Roosevelt is gone. His picture was on the kitchen wall because my mother tore it out of the* Daily News *magazine. Then he died, and then she died, and after she died, my father took it down. I guess it reminded him of her. Or maybe he never did like Roosevelt. Anyway they're* gone. *There was that Henry Wallace, who was vice president and then after the war—1948—he started his own party and ran for president against Truman and Dewey and some guy from the South, the shitkicker that started the Dixiecrats. Everybody was against Wallace. They said he was a Communist, even if he did use to be vice president of the United States, and he's gone now, too. And so is La Guardia and Pete Reiser and DiMaggio and Dixie Walker.* Gone. *How does that happen? Why can't these people just stay there? Why do things always change?*

Sometimes I think about America (after looking at Life *or* The Saturday Evening Post*) and it's like a foreign country. I never went to* any *of these American things: sock hops, drive-in movies, homecoming games, pajama parties. I might as well be reading* National Geographic *about Brazil. I never saw a cheerleader with pompons on her ass. I never got laid in a car. I used to look at* Archie *comics like they were science fiction. Archie and Jughead, Betty and Veronica, with those oxford shoes and school letters* *on short-sleeved sweaters: Where did all those kind of people live? Not where I lived. Not even where I live now, at HTU-1 Ellyson Field.*

Becket told me that the word Dixie came from New Orleans. The French word for ten was dix. *And they had a ten-dollar (or franc?) bill with the word* dix *written on it and all those crazy men who worked on the Mississippi river would get drunk and say, "Got to get down to New Awlins and get me some of them* Dixies." *I wonder if Dixie Shafer knows she's named after money? I think it would make her happy.*

Sal's greatest ambition when he goes to town: to get screwed, blued, and tattooed.

Words for Jew: kike, yid, hebe. Hitler probably used them all.

Chapter

22

ONE MORNING, MAHER called me at the Supply Shack and told me my check had finally arrived. All these years later I remember the great bright lightness of the moment, a kind of fierce exuberance, the sense that I'd just been released from jail. Donnie Ray told me to go cash it and take the rest of the day off, since I'd suffered enough for my country. Coming back from the yeoman's office with the money in my pocket, I ran into Sal.

"For Chrissakes, get *decent* clothes," he said. "And we'll meet you tonight in the Dirt Bar."

"Yeah," I said. "Maybe."

And went back to the barracks with a signed Liberty Pass in my hands and got dressed in a hurry.

All the way into town on the bus, I tried to recover the image of the woman. For three weeks, I'd deliberately shoved her out of my mind; what I couldn't have, I didn't want to imagine. Now I wanted her back, the true goal beyond the pursuit of civilian clothes or a cold beer. But as I gazed out at the passing streets, the drowsing bars and forbidding churches, I found the process of recovery harder than it should have been. The woman had become like an out-of-focus snapshot. This alone confused me; how could I have a grand passion for a woman I could barely remember? So I looked for the woman as if seeing her would be the only way I could remember her clearly, or prove that she had existed at all. And I thought that maybe all I wanted was the feeling she aroused in me, and not the woman herself. The words of a song drifted through me: *"Falling in love with love, is falling for make believe . . ."*

I saw women of all sizes, shapes and ages, but not the woman of the New Year's Eve bus. I knew she was in Pensacola; I'd seen her on South Palafox Street, walking into a store. She had waved at me as the truck rolled to the piers. But I started to erode that vision with doubt. Maybe I only *thought* I'd seen the woman that day. The woman I'd seen wore different clothes, hair tied up in a different way, eyes masked with sunglasses. Maybe my longing had created a mirage, a promise of lush green in a harsh desert. Maybe I'd waved to a total stranger. I wouldn't know until I saw her. And there was some chance I'd never see her again.

I got off at Garden and Palafox. The sun was high and not very hot and a salty breeze was blowing in from the waterfront. I stared into the window of a men's store on the ground floor of the Blount Building, across the street from the San Carlos Hotel. The clothes there were too expensive. I looked across the street at the hotel, thinking I'd like to walk around the lobby. Then, like a scene in some old movie, Tony Mercado, the Mexican pilot, came out on the steps. He had a blonde woman with him. He kissed her on the cheek and she disappeared in a taxi. The tall colored doorman in his white uniform said something; Mercado smiled and then another colored man drove up in a shiny blue convertible. He got out and backed up a step. Mercado handed him what must have been a tip, slipped behind the wheel and drove away. It was all done with ease and command and I envied him. I wondered what it would be like to spend a night with a woman in a big hotel. On silk sheets. With drinks in a bucket beside the bed. And enough money to order food brought to the room. Just like in the movies.

"Hey, sailor."

Two Shore Patrol were standing there, each holding a club, each with a pistol strapped to his hip. One was tall, with square shoulders, dark sideburns. The other was short and compact.

"Let's see your Liberty Pass, sailor," the tall one said.

I gave it to him, and he studied it in a suspicious way, making me nervous. I knew what it said. I'd practically memorized it. Armed Forces Liberty Pass. With the name of the service, the date, my name, my service number, the card number, my rate and the name of the organization. Signed by Donnie Ray. I was here legally. But still, the SPs made me nervous. The tall one nodded to the shorter one and then handed me back the pass.

"Just checkin," he said.

I asked them where I could buy civvies at a decent price and they directed me to Sears, down on South Palafox. I saluted and walked away. When I glanced back, they were strolling into the lobby of the San Carlos. Maybe they had some women stashed there too.

Sears was a long, narrow, badly lit store with signs everywhere advertising bargains. The men's department was just inside the door. I bought a ghastly green Hawaiian shirt that wasn't as loud as Sal's but still made me feel as if I were in Florida. It cost $2.50. A pair of chinos went for six bucks. I told the man at the counter that I wanted to wear them out of the store and he showed me a dressing room. I took off the uniform and folded it neatly. Then, dressed in civvies at last, I brought the uniform back and asked the salesman to wrap it for me. The man nodded silently; his face looked permanently unhappy.

On the way out, I saw an area that displayed art supplies. I went over and looked at the pads, hefted some of the heavy tubes of oil paint, examined various chalks and pencils. I thought that on the long dead days and in the slow evenings I could start to draw again. Maybe I'd buy a sketchbook. Some pencils. I looked for a salesman and my eyes wandered and then, five aisles away, I saw her.

The woman from the bus.

She was behind the counter in the lingerie department. Right there. Across the room. She was wearing a gray Sears jacket over her street clothes and her hair was pulled back tightly in a bun. It was her all right. I hadn't imagined her that day. When I rolled past on the truck, she must have been going to work. She was talking to a fat woman in a blue dress. The fat woman had a pair of panties in her hands, and as I drifted closer (my heart beating faster, my face damp), I could see my woman stretch the silken garment at the crotch, explaining its wonders.

I drifted closer, looking blindly at other counters, glancing at her as she waited on the fat woman. *When she's finished and the fat woman's gone,* I thought, *I'll just go over and say hello. Casual. Without showing that I care too much.* Suddenly, a black man in his forties came up to me and asked if I worked there. No, I said, I didn't. Damn, he said, looking frustrated, glancing at a cheap wristwatch. What's the problem? I said. I got to get me some thread over by that notions countuh, he said. There was a thin pale woman behind the counter. I said, why don't you just ask that salesgirl? You *crazy,* man? he said. That woman's *white.* I must have looked like some dumb immigrant, just off the boat. The black man explained, No white woman's 'lowed to wait on no cullid in *this* town. He walked away, looking for a white man who could wait on him. I thought: *Jesus Christ.*

I couldn't wait any longer, and ambled over to the lingerie counter. I went to the right of the fat lady, my head down, stealing glances at the woman in the Sears jacket. A nameplate was pinned above the swell of her breasts. *Eden Santana.* A name. Her name. The name that would work its way into me for the rest of my life. Eden. Like a promise of paradise. The overhead fluorescent lights made her hair look darker, the highlights tinged with green. She had thick black eyebrows. And that aquiline nose, with a small bump in the middle, was the way I'd remembered it. Her upper lip was thin, but the lower lip was thick and pouty. She smiled at the fat woman as she handed her a bag and change and I saw dimples in her cheeks. In the harsh overhead light, she looked at least twenty-eight. Maybe even thirty. I wasn't even old enough to drink in New York. And then she touched her face and I saw a wedding band on her left hand. Plain. Gold. And I thought: *aw, shit.* For a moment, I wanted the fat woman to come back, get involved in some complicated transaction, give me time to slip away.

"Can I help you—?"

It was too late for flight.

"Hi," I said. "I'm the guy from the bus."

"The what?"

"Remember? New Year's Eve? You got off in Palatka."

She squinted at me, and then smiled. That beautiful smile. "Oh, the *bus.* And you *are* the guy, awnt you? Sure enough. I didn't recognize you in the Harry Truman shirt."

"Just got it," I said. "Right here in Sears."

"And you got a bit more hair, too."

I kept trying to sort out words in my head, to say things that were quick and witty and what was the word? *Charming.* And I wanted to do more than make brilliant remarks. For just a second, I wanted to reach over the counter and kiss her hard on the mouth and then lay her among the slips and panties. Just like that. Just *do* it. And be quick and witty and charming later.

"What can I do for you, child?" she said.

I turned my head. A few counters away, a heavy-set, balding white man was waiting on the Negro. I couldn't tell this woman, this Eden Santana, that I'd gone on certain evenings to the highway near Ellyson Field hoping to see her pedal by. I couldn't explain how hard I'd worked to erase her face from my mind. *Child. She called me child.*

"Well, I uh, well—" *Get to it, just get to it.* "I was wondering if you wanted to, well, go for a cup of coffee after work? You know, should auld acquaintance be forgot, and all that. Maybe we could even catch a movie at the Rex . . ."

And thought: *Please don't laugh.*

Eden Santana looked at me and smiled in a warm sad way.

"Sure," she said. "That'd be nice."

Chapter

23

WHEN SHE WALKED out of Sears that evening, the church bells of the entire town were tolling seven and for a long moment I just stood there looking at her. All afternoon I had rehearsed words, actions, scenarios: if she said this, I would say that. I wanted to be with her immediately and wondered what she was doing at precisely this moment or that. But I also was riddled with fear and trembling; I wished for some great sudden disaster, an earthquake or a hurricane, anything that might postpone our appointment.

I had a paper sack in my hand, and inside were pencils, chalks and a sketchbook. I didn't even remember buying them. The blur was total. But I sat down by the waterfront, made sketches of the blackened stumps of some piers that had burned the year before and threw them away. I counted seagulls. I wandered streets where old Victorian houses were sealed against the day, all of them large and grand and facing the sea. I said her name, over and over again: *Eden Santana.* Like decades of the Rosary. *Eden Santana.* Like music. It didn't seem possible that she was there, in Pensacola, and that she had agreed to meet me after work; at the same time, she filled me with dread. Perhaps she would make fun of me, toy with me, stand me up as her friends watched.

And then, suddenly, she *was* there, in the fading gray Gulf light. She was smiling at me. And then beside me, holding the strap of her bag with both hands, seeming almost shy. I don't know what I said to her, the first words, the initial greetings: Hello and how are you?, I suppose. But I remember how she looked: about five six, with thin arms and a yellow blouse and legs hidden by slacks.

I must have stammered out my name. She must have suggested The
Greek's. I remember looking at our reflections in a window, as we
walked to Garden Street. I was taller than she was. She looked
beautiful. As we crossed Garden Street, she took my arm. My
muscles tensed.

Then we were holding menus and facing each other in a booth
along the wall in a bright side room of The Greek's. A dumpy
waitress waited with her pencil poised. I said, You must be hungry,
and Eden said, Damn sure. I read the menu from right to left, from
prices to food, and decided on a hamburger. Eden said she'd have
a bacon-and-tomato sandwich and a Coke, and the dumpy woman
wrote down the order and went away. Eden Santana looked at me
and smiled.

"Dutch treat, okay?" she said. "You can't be makin' all that
much in the Navy."

"No, no," I said. "I got paid today. It's on me." I smiled. "I
mean, *I* asked *you.*"

I glanced away from her, trying to look casual. The two Shore
Patrol men sat together on stools at the counter. A guy in a Jax beer
jacket was two stools away from them. Four teenagers on a double
date were drinking ice-cream sodas in a booth. Apart from them,
The Greek's was empty.

"They'll go broke in here if this is all they get for customers,"
Eden said, looking around.

"Everybody's probably waiting to get paid," I said.

She fumbled in her purse, took out the Luckies. She pulled a
match from one of those "Draw Me" packs of book matches. I took
it from her, struck the match. She leaned in and sucked on the
flame.

"I thought I'd never find you," I said. Like that. Blurting out
some of the words I'd rehearsed all afternoon.

She exhaled, then smiled. "You don't even *know* me, child."

"I know I saw you on that bus and I know you were beautiful
and I know I wanted to see you again," I said. "I know how bad
I felt when I woke up and you were gone."

I couldn't look directly at her after saying the words, afraid she
would laugh. She didn't. "Had to get off," she said in a flat voice.
"I—well, I wasn't feelin' too good." Then I looked up. Her color
deepened and she opened her mouth as if to say something else,
then bit her lower lip.

"You should've woke me up," I said. "I'd've stayed with you. I'd've gotten off the bus if you needed me."

She looked at me in an amazed way. "You know, I think you just might've done that."

The food came and she asked me what base I was at and I told her and she said that she lived out past there a few miles, out past Ellyson Field, you know, over the bridge, by the bayou. She asked me why I joined the Navy and I said, Oh, you know, to see the world. So you could have a girl in every port? No, I really wanted to see what was out here. There's people out here'd like to see what you saw every day. Brooklyn? Sure, New York, all those buildings, Broadway. She ate quickly, but in a dainty way, cutting up the sandwich with knife and fork and using the fork to pick up the sections. And she asked me questions: Where was I from and did I have a girl and how many were in my family and what did I do in the Navy and what did I want to do with my life. I've heard these same questions from many women since then, the diligent and wary assembling of a profile; but Eden Santana was the first to ask me such things. She said all this in her low voice with its hoarse burr, eating as I was talking, never speaking with food in her mouth. She kept her left hand in her lap.

And at her urging, I talked too. Didn't talk, *rolled,* great tides of nouns and verbs flowing out of me, in combinations that surprised me, phrases I hadn't rehearsed in my wandering afternoon. I tried to explain about Brooklyn, how I loved it and missed it and sometimes longed for it but hated it too, hated the stupidity of some of the people, the insistence on conformity, the worship of the ordinary, the surrender of themselves to the Church: telling the truth because if I tried to fake it, I'd never be able to remember the lies later. I told about Prospect Park and the Dodgers and my father (but left out my mother's long and painful dying); asked her if she'd ever heard of Charlie Parker and when she hadn't, I said I'd try to get her one of his records and then talked about Hank Williams as if I'd grown up listening to him. No, I told her, I didn't have a girl. Well, I had one, I said, but that was before I went in the Navy, that was long ago, that was last summer, and besides, she's gone. And then (quickly, smiling, tentative) said I wanted to be an artist. Really? Yeah, when I get out. Why wait? Well, I didn't want to be an *artist,* I wanted to write and draw a comic strip, be a comic-strip artist, telling stories and drawing pictures; I wanted to live in Paris or Rome or somewhere like that, using all those foreign places as backgrounds to the story. Oh, like *Terry and the Pirates?* Yeah, exactly. Maybe you can make me into the Dragon Lady. I was thinking exactly that. You're lyin, now, child. Telling all this, I hoped she wouldn't laugh.

She didn't laugh. She looked at me, her brow furrowed, as I talked, saying things that made sense (and knowing *Terry and the Pirates,* knowing the Dragon Lady) and she seemed to be thinking: *You're a strange young man.*

"Do you draw real people too?" she said.

"Sure."

"I mean, could you draw, say, that guy in the Jax Beer shirt?"

"I could try."

I took out the sketchbook and the pencils, and my hands went damp with nerves. Nobody'd ever asked me before to perform with a pencil (and surely this was a performance); I felt the way I used to feel when my mother was alive and we'd go visiting on Sundays and all the cousins would be called to the living room and each of us would be forced to sing. I was always afraid that if I forgot the words—to "Danny Boy" or "The Green Glens of Antrim" or that other cherished Irish tune, "The Marine Corps Hymn"—I would fail my mother in some terrible, final way or give my father the satisfaction of calling me stupid. I'd talked on and on about being an artist; if my hand went dead with clumsiness, if I botched the drawing, she would think I was just another talker. And maybe that's why she asked: to give me a test, to see if what I said could be matched by what I did. So I had no choice. I looked at the man in the Jax Beer shirt and started to draw. The bulky shape of his body. The pouchy face. Trying to imagine how Caniff would draw him. The first few marks were gray and tentative and then I started drawing with a heavier line, smashing in great patches of black for shadows, seeing the man come off the page, working very fast, adding details (an ear, the hair in the nostrils) and then, at the end, lettering the words Jax Beer in a more delicate way across his back. When I was finished, I handed her the sketchbook.

"Now *that* is damn good, child," Eden said. "You really *do* have some talent. I mean, you have a *lot* of talent."

I mumbled something and she touched my hand.

"You're blushing," she said.

"Well, it's, uh—"

"I hope I didn't make you feel embarrassed."

"Nah," I said. "It's just, you know . . . drawing is something I usually do alone. It's funny, doing it in front of somebody."

"Well, you did it," she said, and looked again at the drawing and then at the man in the Jax Beer shirt.

"Now you've got to sign it," she said. "And put the date."

I signed it and tore it out of the sketchbook and handed it to her: gift, souvenir, elaborate hello: she rolled it and slipped it into her purse. "Someday, when you're rich and famous," she said, "that'll be worth a lot of money. I can always say I knew you when."

That chilled me. Was she making fun? Or was such a thing really possible? The waitress brought two coffees and cleared away the plates. Eden Santana rested her chin on the heel of her hand and stared at me for a long moment.

"Why'd you really ask me to come here?" she said.

"Because you're so damned beautiful," I said, then leaned forward to sip my coffee. She kept staring at me.

"You're serious, awn't you, child?"

"Yeah."

"It's not some damn line."

"No."

She took out the Luckies, fumbled with the matches. I took them from her again and struck a match for her. As she inhaled, I examined the cover: *Draw Me,* it said. I could draw this woman on the matchbook with my left hand. Maybe that's what I should do, send it in, see if I could win the free correspondence course. Didn't Roy Crane learn from a correspondence course? But wait: I was in the Navy. Would they send the lessons to me here? And where would I work at the drawings? All this in a fraction of a second, and then I looked up at her. Something had changed in her face: she was more open, somehow younger, not quite as sure of herself, giving up some of her command.

"I haven't felt beautiful in a long, long time," she said.

"That's hard to believe."

"It's the truth."

"Come on—all you have to do is look in the mirror."

She turned away and watched two sailors in civvies come in the door as the Shore Patrolmen went out. She was blushing again. Then she poked at her coffee with a spoon and took a drag from the cigarette.

"Well, I guess we better go down to that movie," she said. And I noticed that she wasn't wearing the wedding ring.

The movie was *Seminole* with Rock Hudson, all about a brave white man building a farm out in the wilds of Florida, until the Seminole War began and everything went to pot. I think Rock was a West Point graduate too, which made him an officer and made me root for the Indians. But in truth, I wasn't paying much attention and had trouble following the story. We sat downstairs with a bag of popcorn she insisted on buying. When we finished the popcorn, she handed me a napkin and I wiped my fingers, and sat there, with my hands loose on my knees. And then when some Indians came crashing through a door to slaughter some white woman, she grabbed my hand and held it for the rest of the movie.

Her nails were short and the skin on her fingers was coarse. But there was a damp soft center in her palm and she wrapped her hand around my thumb, holding it snug in the damp core. After a while, she leaned her head against my shoulder and her hair smelled clean and there was a faint flowery odor to her too, soap or perfume, and I wondered what it would be like to kiss her neck and her back, and then I felt her breast against my arm, firm, slippery under the blouse from the silky material of a bra. Was the bra white or black? Did the straps leave marks in her skin? My cock was hard for most of the movie. But I felt something else, sitting there with Eden Santana: it was if we had known each other for a very long time.

Then the movie ended and the lights came on.

"Those poor damned Seminoles," she said, separating herself from me, smoothing her hair. "All they ever did was let escaped slaves come to Florida to be free and the damned white man came down to get 'em and killed everything in sight."

"I didn't know that's what happened."

"Sure," she said. "Read the history, child."

Then I looked toward the exit and saw Turner leaving. He was in a sports shirt. Beside him was another sailor, also in sports shirt and slacks. Red Cannon.

"You okay?" she said.

"Uh, yeah. There's a sailor there, you see him, going out? He's from my base. A real jerk, name of Red Cannon. Let's wait a minute, till he goes."

She looked at me in a puzzled way. "You afraid of that man?"

"No. I just don't want a hassle."

We waited a bit and then went out. She took my hand and held it, and then we were in the lobby. Outside, standing on the corner, were Turner and Cannon. I hesitated for a moment, thinking: *Go back inside, go to the john, let them wander away, avoid seeing them, keep them from seeing you with this woman* and then, afraid that Eden would think I was a coward went on out. They turned to look at us.

"Hey, sailor," Turner said, with a big grin. "See you settled in."

"How are you, Jack?" I said. I didn't introduce Eden Santana. I looked at Cannon, and nodded a hello. His eyes were slushy again. "I'll call you next time I'm at Mainside," I said to Turner. "Or if you get out to Ellyson, come round to the Supply Shack."

I started to leave, and Cannon said: "Guess they don't teach no manners in New York."

I stopped and looked at him. His eyes were without emotion, staring at me, challenging me, judging me too, judging the whole North, coming on with some smirking kind of southern superiority that I didn't understand. I didn't care what Cannon thought, but I wanted Turner's good opinion.

"Oh, sure," I said. "This is my friend, Eden. Eden, this is Jack Turner. Wendell Cannon. Both sailors."

She shook their hands in a formal way and there was a lot of pleased-to-meet-you and a knowing, admiring glance from Turner to me that said: *You're doin' okay, sailor . . .*

"Didn't I see you over at the San Carlos bar last week?" Cannon said to Eden. "With that Mexican flyboy?"

"Not me, mister," Eden said, and tugged my hand and started away.

"I could swear it was you," Cannon said. "You got a twin sister?"

She didn't answer. She led the way to the corner and turned left on Garden Street, away from the lights of Palafox. There were a few blocks of shops and then houses with white porches and swings and she was still walking, still holding my hand, silent until they were far behind us.

"That son of a bitch," she said after a while.

"Now you know why I didn't want to see him," I said.

"With his plastic face and his dead eyes."

"It ain't his eyes that're dead. It's his heart."

"Not dead enough," she said.

We slowed and there was a little park, dark and deserted, with streetlights burning off in the distance through the trees. We sat on a bench. She smoked a cigarette, breathing hard. Saying nothing.

"I'm sorry," I said.

"For what?"

"For you having to hear that crap about the bar at the San Carlos."

"It wasn't crap. I was there."

"With Tony Mercado?"

"Yes."

She flipped the half-smoked cigarette into the darkness, where it glowed for a moment and then died. I looked at her, feeling her sudden bitterness and regret rising like an odor, and saw that her eyes were filling with tears. I put my arm around her shoulder and pulled her to me, trying to comfort her. Or trying to comfort myself, holding her to me, to fend off the feeling that she was going away from me without ever having arrived. She pulled away.

"Men," she said. The word hung in the dark air. I remember seeing myself suddenly like a character in a comic strip. A thought balloon hovered over my head as I sat on a bench beside a woman who was plunged into despair. Inside the balloon were words: "What does she mean by that? *Men.* Did she sleep with Mercado, the way that blonde obviously did this afternoon? Did she do it for money? Or does she love Mercado? And if she does love Mercado, what does that do to me? How could I compete with him? His looks, his skills, his officer's bars, his age, his money? His Leica." *Men.*

"Well, I'd better go get my bike," she said.

The balloon dissolved.

"You're gonna pedal all the way home?"

"No, I take the bus to Ellyson Field, and bicycle the rest of the way."

She was up now, and I was walking beside her, back to Garden Street. For more than three hours she had been sweet, warm, intimate; she made me try to define myself and my life; she took a drawing that I'd made and rolled it up and put it in her purse; she held my hand in the dark. Now she was going away.

"You want to talk about this?" I said.

"No."

Then she turned and looked at me. "Hey, listen, child. This's got nothing to do with *you.* You're *nice.* It's not you, if that's what you're thinkin."

"But I want to see you again."

We were crossing the street, going toward Sears.

"I don't think that's a good idea," she said.

"I do."

"You're eighteen years old, child. I'm thirty-one."

"I don't care."

"I got two kids."

"So what?"

"With you, I'm just rockin the cradle."

"I don't think so."

She turned into an alley beside the Sears store and unlocked her bicycle.

"I want to draw you," I said.

"There must be hundreds of girls your age, you could draw them," she said, wheeling the bike out of the alley. "That's what you need. Not an old beat-up lady like me."

I put my hand around her waist and held her close and kissed her hard on the mouth. She didn't move. I touched the side of her face and then she shuddered and let the bicycle fall against the wall and she put her hands behind my neck and shoved her belly against mine.

"You silly damn boy," she said.

Chapter

24

I SIT HERE IN the car, the engine running, the radio silent. I am parked in an abandoned gas station, the pumps hauled away, a CLOSED sign hanging at an odd angle in the window. Down the wide street to the right is the entrance to Ellyson Field. Once this morning, I drove slowly along the familiar road and even more slowly back, but when I started for the motel, I couldn't go on. I pulled over, to pause on the broken concrete slabs that once were a wilderness of palmetto weeds and scrub and seem certain to be so again. Billy's old bar is gone. The locker club is gone. And so too is the airfield. The place is an industrial park now, and there is a school for truckdrivers out on the landing strips. I drove in and saw weeds breaking through the cracks in the tarmac. There was stunted summer-baked grass where the barracks once stood and the mess hall has been gutted and converted to a warehouse. The sky is empty and silent.

And I remember waking the day after my first evening with Eden Santana, hurrying into the gray mess-hall morning, wanting to tell everybody about her. There have been many women since then, but none who made me feel that way, made me want to trumpet the news of their amazing existence. I remember that as a Tuesday morning. She had agreed to see me again on Saturday night: a parenthesis in time, but a stretch of almost endless hours if you were not yet eighteen.

In the chow hall, I sat with Miles Rayfield. I'm sure we were both eating Rice Krispies because just as surely the hot dish was creamed chipped beef on toast, popularly known as SOS, or shit on a shingle. Sure, because I remember him turning to me and saying Snap,

Krackle, Pop, you goddamned swabby reprobate. And then he
went back to reading a letter. He said it was from his wife. I must
have looked surprised (he'd never mentioned her existence), because he chattered away almost desperately about how women
never knew what they wanted and his woman knew less than all the
others. Now she wanted to be an actress. She wanted to move to
Hollywood. She had given up ceramics and was studying Stanislav-
ski from a book. She wanted to meet James Dean. She wanted to
work with Kazan. Miles just shook his head. But when I suggested
that he have her move to Pensacola, where they could get an
apartment and he would pick up extra money from the Navy—they
called it comrats—he just shook his head again and said, Ah, well
. . . And mumbled about the terrors of taking a pretty woman to
a Navy town. Then he said, Hollywood. Hissed it: *Hollywood.*

After a while, they all came drifting in: Max and Sal, Waleski and
Maher, Harrelson and Boswell and the others, hung over, noisy,
laughing. Max came over and told me they were going to the
Baptist church on Friday night, to investigate ritual murders for the
Anti-Defamation League, and Miles laughed, and Sal said that the
two of us had to go with them, to protect Max from the insane
Baptists and sinister Masons who infested the place. Miles just
smiled and nodded until they moved on to another table, joking
and grab-assing.

As always, Miles was holding a Pall Mall with his wrist bent,
pressing the butt to his mouth in an almost dainty way. That didn't
matter much to me; Miles was Miles. I wanted to talk to him about
Eden Santana, ask him whether I should try hard to find out if she
was really married, if she really had two kids, and where the kids
were. Or should I ignore all that? Should I press her to find out
what happened in the San Carlos bar with Mercado? Was it wrong
to feel jealous one minute, elated the next? Miles was twenty-three.
He would know about such matters. But I didn't say anything at all
because I realized that I didn't really know *him.* I was afraid he
would use all those words of his, his scorn and contempt, to make
fun of me. He was probably my friend, but I wasn't really sure. I
wouldn't know until we'd been in some trouble together. I didn't
know yet if any of them were my friends.

Then Harrelson came down the aisle behind Miles. He was
holding a coffee cup. He ran a finger across the back of Miles's neck
and swiveled his hips.

"Morning, Milesetta," he said.

"Fuck you, redneck," Miles snapped.

Harrelson walked on, as if he hadn't heard Miles reply, and wiggled his ass again before sitting down. I looked at Miles and thought: *If I were truly Miles's friend, I'd smack Harrelson in the mouth. The stupid son of a bitch.* But I said nothing.

"That redneck swine," Miles said. A vein throbbed in his temple. He took a deep drag on his cigarette.

"Sticks and stones, and all that," I said. "Don't waste your energy."

"I know, I know," he said. But when I looked at him again, there were tears in his eyes behind the thick glasses.

"I've got work to do," he said, and stood up abruptly, grabbed his tray and hurried out.

The morning seemed endless. The weather was warm, the hangars heavy with traffic. I handed out engine parts, filled in forms, entered requisition slips in logs. Harrelson hurried around, looking busy, whistling Hank Williams tunes. In front of me, Miles sat at his desk, typing grimly, speaking quickly on the phone, doodling with a thick black Ebony pencil. Late in the morning, he was sent on a run to Mainside. I got up and stretched and had started for the coffee pot when I glanced at Miles's doodle. He had made a beautiful drawing of Becket. I called Becket over and showed it to him. "Well, I'll be damned," Becket said. "We got us an artist here." He wanted to take the drawing, but I said maybe he should wait and ask Miles and he said, Yeah, sure, of course, you're right, Miles is sensitive about some things. He laughed.

"Too many things sometimes," Becket said. "I wonder about him."

Jonesie came over and said he thought my shoes looked better. The newspaper arrived and on the front page Eisenhower's new Secretary of State, a guy named Dulles, said we wanted peace but didn't want to be encircled by the Russians and their allies. The big problem, Dulles said, was in Asia, where the Communists were trying to take over Indochina. I wasn't even sure where Indochina was. The newspaper (and Dulles) said that the Communists had pinned down the French in Indochina and pinned down the United States in Korea, and they'd managed all this without losing even a single Russian soldier. He didn't say what we should do about it, but his speech didn't sound like the world was about to turn wonderful.

Just before lunch, I looked up from the paper and saw Mercado at the counter. I went over to wait on him. He smiled. My stomach flopped over. He was so fucking handsome I couldn't believe Eden would choose me over him.

"Hey, how are you doing, fella?" he said.

"Just great," I said.

He needed a swash plate and had the forms all filled out, neatly hand-lettered. I went to get the part and saw Becket again. He shook his head and said, "You know something? I'm fum New Awlins, but if I hear 'Jambalaya' one more time, I'm gonna throw something." I came back to the counter. Mercado was reading the newspaper.

"Where you from anyway, Lieutenant?" I said, knowing the answer, but wondering what he'd say.

"Mexico City," he said. "You ever been there?"

"Nah, this is the farthest south I've ever been. I'm from New York."

"Ah, New York. I love New York. Well, if you're from New York, you will *love* Mexico." He pronounced it May-hee-koe. "It's a beautiful city with many tall buildings, you know, the skyscrapers. Well, the truth is, not as *tall* as New York, not as many people. We have beautiful mountains all around the city, with snow on the top, volcanoes, and many beautiful women, and it's like spring all year. You should come. You look me up and I show you around."

"Sounds great."

He signed for the swash plate. "I mean it. You come to Mexico, you look for me."

He left and I thought: *This is probably an okay guy. Open, decent, free of all the officer bullshit you get with the Americans.* So why did the sight of him mess me up? I knew why. I'd seen him come out of the San Carlos with a blonde; but I really wanted to know what he'd done there with Eden Santana. I tried not to think about it, pushed back the details that ran through my mind, thinking: *Forget it, you'll go nuts.* Two mechanics came in and asked for tools and bolts, and I went to get them. *Isn't Santana a Latin name?* I thought. Yes, it was, of course it was. So maybe *she* was Latin, too. Even with that slurred southern accent. Maybe that was what would give him an edge over me. That and his age and his money and his looks. Maybe she loved him and he didn't love her back. Yeah: I would see her Saturday. But who would she see tonight? Or tomorrow night? Or the night after that? Maybe he would offer to take her to Mexico with him. May-hee-koe. The country where all those American outlaws went, racing across the Rio Grande to freedom, a hundred yards ahead of the sheriff's posse. Maybe Mercado was going to take her there. And here he was, only a few minutes ago, telling me to visit him. In a city where it was always spring and where there were many beautiful women. Mexico.

"Hey, stargazer."

I looked around and saw Donnie Ray. I handed the supplies to the mechanics. The men signed their requisition forms and left.

"You look like you just left earth," Donnie Ray said.

"Musta been the chow working on me," I said.

Donnie Ray smiled and tapped the desk softly. "Listen, when Rayfield gets back from Mainside, grab some swabs and give the deck a good cleanin. It's Miles's turn. And yours."

"Sure."

Just after four, Miles and I went into the head and filled some large iron-wheeled pails in the sink. We poured in soap and extra pine scent. Each pail had a roller attached to the top. We wheeled the pails the length of the storeroom, to start at the counter and work our way back to the head. Everybody was gone now except Jonesie, who was the duty storekeeper, there for emergencies. I soaked my mop in the soapy water, then pulled it through the rollers until it was flat. Miles was in the next aisle, doing the same thing.

"Uck," he said. "Filthy. Disgusting. Just the *feel* of this slimy thing in your hands. A billion microbes per ounce. Cholera. Polio."

"All you have to do with it is wash the floor, Miles," I said. "You don't have to fuck it."

"I know, but Jesus Christ . . ."

I mopped in wide broad strokes, covering the floor of my aisle in one stroke. I remember actually liking this job. It was dumb and simple, but it made me feel like a sailor. Miles was grumbling and I peered through the shelving between us and understood: He couldn't move his body with any grace. None at all. He had his feet together, and was pushing the mop at the floor in small stabbing strokes, whimpering with each push. The mop looked oddly obscene in his hands.

"Miles," I said, peering past a tray of ballpeen hammers, "you're doing it wrong."

"There's no way to do this *right*!"

I leaned my mop against the shelves and came around to Miles's side. "Here, watch," I said, taking his mop. I didn't know much about anything, but I certainly knew how to mop a floor. "First thing you do, spread your legs."

"I *beg* your pardon."

"Don't be a wiseass. Spread your legs and plant them, see? Like a baseball player at bat. Then—"

"I hate baseball."

I paused. "You hate baseball?" I was amazed. "How could anybody hate *baseball*?"

"Bunch of grown men standing around in knickers trying to hit a little white ball with a stick."

Then I understood. "You never played ball when you were a kid, did you?"

Miles assumed the batter's stance, then grabbed the mop and started swabbing the deck.

"You never played baseball."

"Fuck off."

"You must be some kind of a Communist, Miles. A secret agent."

He looked at me in a timid way. "So I never played baseball. So *what*?"

"Miles, that's the saddest thing I ever heard."

He started to get into the rhythm of the mopping. I went back to my aisle, swabbing in broad quick steps. Then Miles said through the shelving: "Baseball isn't everything, you know!"

"No, and neither is air. But you need it to *live,* man."

"I don't."

"Well, learn about baseball, and learn to swab the decks," I said. "Then you can explain it all to your wife. When you move to Hollywood . . ."

He laughed. "You've got a fresh mouth on you, boy."

I swung the mop almost fiercely now, the moves punctuated by Miles grunting in the next aisle. A screen door slammed. I turned and saw Becket.

"Hey, Miles" he said. "That picture of me. Can I have it? I'd like to send—"

"*What* picture of you?" Miles said.

I glanced at his desk. It was bare.

"The picture you drew this morning. I saw it on your desk."

"Not me," Miles said. "I didn't draw any picture of you."

He was lying. Flat out lying. I'd seen the drawing. So had Becket. A good drawing. A *beautiful* drawing.

"Well, then, who—"

"Maybe someone was visiting," Miles said. "It wasn't me."

Chapter

25

I STAYED ON THE base for the rest of the week, reading books and magazines, saving my money for Saturday night and Eden Santana. One evening after dinner I went up to the barracks where the blacks lived, looking for Bobby Bolden. An older messcook met me at the door, blocking my way, and told me that Bobby wasn't there. He looked at me as if I were a cop. "Okay," I said, "just tell him Devlin, from the Supply Shack, came around to talk." The man nodded in a way that might have been saying: *Don't bother.* I went away, thinking: *What's with these goddamned Negroes* anyway? Most evenings, I dozed. I wished I had a radio. I thought about New York. And on another evening, Red Cannon caught me asleep on my bunk with my shoes on. He smacked me on the soles with the club.

"Listen, shitbird," he said, "what makes you think you can sleep wearing *shoes* on that fartsack?"

"They're clean, sir."

"They're *clean*? You walkin around in *shit* all day, on *dirt,* on *gas*oline, you say they're *clean*?"

I sat up and looked at my shoes. Slowly and deliberately.

"Jesus Christ," I said.

Cannon placed a hand on the overhead rack and leaned close to me. An odor of whiskey seeped from his body, though his breath smelled of toothpaste.

"What'd you say, boy?" he whispered.

"I said, 'Jesus Christ,' sir," I said, standing now and looking him directly in the eyes.

"That's what I thought you said," Cannon said, his voice rising. "Maybe that fine dark pussy in town's rottin your brain, boy."

"I said, 'Jesus Christ', sir. I didn't mention women."

"You got yo'sef a mouth on you, boy."

I was taller than Red Cannon by a couple of inches, but he looked like a puncher. So I turned sideways to him, ready to block anything he threw at me. Or try to. But I knew now I couldn't back away from him. It was too late. The barracks were empty and this was between us. Just us. Without witnesses. If he tried to hit me, I'd hit him back. I must have wanted him to try. Just to get it over with.

"Tell me what you plan to *do* about it, *sir,*" I said. "Have me executed, *sir?* Call a General Court Martial under the Uniform Code of Military Justice, *sir?* For saying 'Jesus Christ' on my own time, and placing the heel of my shoe on a U.S. Navy fartsack? *Sir?*"

That was it. A direct challenge. And Cannon knew it. I pulled my mouth tight over my teeth in a tough guy's mask, but my heart was pounding and I felt trapped in the old cycle. Challenge and reply, hurt, then retaliate. Right off the streets of Brooklyn. I didn't like it back there either. But it was the way you lived: If you're pushed, push back. That was the code. If you're hurt, hurt back. When you're leaned on, lean back, and I'd just leaned back.

Cannon glared at me. "Get that fartsack washed tonight, boy." He stepped back. "And remember, I'll be watchin you."

With that he turned on his heel and walked out of the barracks. When the screen door slammed behind him, I exhaled loudly. My heart kept fluttering for a long time after that.

Then I saw Miles coming around from the other side of the row of lockers. He'd obviously been there all along. His face was beaming.

"Magnificent!" he said. "Glorious!"

He came forward as if to embrace me, then turned and grabbed a bunk and shook it.

"*You faced down Red Cannon!*" he said. "The jackass champion of the world!"

"Hey, I—"

"I'm going to call the *Pensacola Journal. This* should be on page one."

"Come on—"

"Let's get some tea at the gedunk."

·   ·   ·

On Thursday night, I was back at the dumpster. But I didn't really mind. If Red Cannon wanted to be the King of Chickenshit, I wasn't going to let him know he got to me. Whatever chickenshit he threw at me, I would take; it was heavy shit that I wouldn't. Besides, Donnie Ray let the guys on twelve-to-fours have the afternoon off the next day; so it all evened up in the end. Donnie Ray didn't like Red Cannon any more than the rest of us did. Now I see myself standing out there under the stars, thinking about Eden Santana, and I want to hug that boy I used to be. He was nervous all week, but at the dumpster he couldn't drive her out of his mind by reading a book. So he thought all the worst things: that maybe she wouldn't show up or maybe she was just playing some joke or maybe she was going to meet him while holding hands with her husband, if she had a husband, or with her kids, if she really had those kids. I let all these maybes flower in my imagination, like a baseball fan trying to imagine some disastrous ninth inning or a kid rolling off a cliff.

The problem was simple; I didn't know very much about her. Sitting with her in The Greek's, I'd done most of the talking. She'd asked all the questions and I'd tried to answer, tried to sound older than I was, a more experienced man, a man of the world. But while I was answering her questions, she wasn't telling me anything. Sure, I knew she worked at Sears, but I didn't know where she *lived,* and I didn't know where she *came* from. I didn't know why she'd ended up on a Greyhound bus on a New Year's Eve either, and most of all, I didn't know why she'd agreed to see me this Saturday night. I was afraid to know. She was beautiful, as beautiful as any woman I'd ever seen. But because she was beautiful, I was scared. She could have all those other guys, veterans, guys with cars and money to spend, officers. *Mercado.* That was why I couldn't tell anyone about her. Suppose I told them I had a date with this woman from Sears? The next thing I knew, Max and Sal and the others would probably go to Sears and find her and tell her I had the clap or something. Or they'd wait across the street when I showed up for my big date and if she didn't come to meet me, they'd see me standing there like a goddamned fool, and I'd never hear the end of it. It would be back to the Dirt Bar and Dixie's immensities. So I said nothing. The eerie thing was that after Mercado, only one other man on the base had seen her. And that was Red Cannon. Jesus Christ.

·   ·   ·

On Friday, the mail arrived just before noon and there was a
pale-blue letter for me. My name, rank, serial number and address
were written in the sharp Palmer method script the nuns taught all
their young ladies. The serifs of the Rs and Ms were hooked and
barbed like thorns protecting roses. Donnie Ray gave me my afternoon off and I went over to the barracks after lunch and took off
my shoes and lay down on the bunk to read the letter. A few guys
came in and out at the tail end of lunch, slamming locker doors. I
read:

Dear Michael
   Well I got your letter and I'm sorry I took so long to answer but
it was busy here after the holiday's as you can imagine. It was good
to here from you. You must be settleing in their by now and everybody here wishes they were there in sunny Fla.
   Just after you left, we had to go in on our vacation and get our
pictures done for the yearbook. They wont be ready for a while but
we'll have them before graduation, so I'll have to wait a while until
I can send you one. That way I'll look halfway descent not like a
snapshot.
   Its real cold here, lot's of snow since you left. Its all turned to slush
tho so its really rotten out and very bad for walking. Everybodys
been staying home most of the time. I went down Stevens Lun-
chanette the other day just to have a coke with Betty K. but none
of the crowd was there. Almost everybody in the Army or Navy now
and Mike Fishetti went in the Marine's. Even the Sander's or the
Prospect on a Fr. or Sat. night are half empty. Nobody is sure why
they are still joining up because it says in the paper's that as soon as
Eisenhower has a chance, then the war is over. Everybody hope's so.
But its strange they are still joining up, the guys, I mean.
   I heard they are going to name an American legion post for
Buddy Tiernan. His mother is still a wreck. She just cant believe he
got killed in Korea and she holds Truman and the other communists
responsable. She says she think's hes a prisoner over their, in China
maybe, and they will fined him when the war is over. She look's like
a zombie. And Carol Wells is even worse. You know, she was
suppose to marry Buddy when he got back but now most people
think it will never happen.
   Micahel I hope you understand everything now. I didn't want to
hurt you you know that. I just wanted to go out with you not go
steady. I guess its my fault because I didn't make myself clear. And
I was worried you wouldnt respect me for all the other things. So

I stayed with you until you went away. But were too young to get all tied up with each other in a perminent way. I read your letter over and over and it made me cry. You say some thing's so beautiful sometimes, like a poet almost. But some of the thing's you said like about Paris and all that I dont know what to say about that. I never thought about thing's like that before I met you and I dont know what I'm suppose to feel. Anyway your their and I'm here and theres nothing to be done about it for now is there?

I just don't want you to think bad about me. I know you think I cheated on you when I went out with Charlie Templeton but Michael I never would do what we did with anyone else believe me and also I never said I was going steady with you so how could I be cheating on you? We had a thing that was special but maybe it was a mistake. I think of you as a good friend and I hope you know that. Charlie is a freind too but not like we were and were not going Steady (me and Charlie) no matter what you here from the rotten gossips. I always try and think of the good time's and hope you do too.

I hope your happy down there in sunny Fla. Maybe the best thing that could happen is that you find a real nice girl down their. And we could always be good friends right?

Love,
Maureen

PS Eddie Terrell got married out in Calif. and is going to stay there with his bride when he get's out of the Marine's.

I lay back on the bunk and closed my eyes and for the first time in weeks, I was back in Brooklyn. I saw myself on a summer evening leaving the tenement on Seventh Avenue to walk to Maureen's house on the far side of the hill. I walked past the red brick hulk of The Factory, where my father worked, and then past the bar Maureen's father owned. I crossed the avenue at 14th Street and walked under the marquee of the Minerva (where *Drums* was always playing on a double bill with *Four Feathers*) and up along the brick ramparts of the 14th Regiment Armory and the synagogue on the other side of the street (where I'd served as the Shabbas goy one year). I passed the Syrian grocery store and walked under the trees along the street that ended at the park. I stopped there, dazed by the lights of the Sanders movie house, the crowded bars of Bartel Pritchard Square, the clanging of the trolley cars, the shouts of the men selling the *News* and *Mirror,* two cents each, and looked

at all the crowded benches along the side of the park and felt the
arctic blast of the air conditioning from the movie house, the cold-
est in all the world. The sight of this place always gave me a thrill.

For an hour, I'd stand there with my friends, joking, stalling,
shadowboxing, hanging out. And then I'd move off, walking more
quickly down the parkside to the other end of The Neighborhood
(a separate neighborhood, really), where the houses were solid and
safe and there were no tenements to block the sky or the breeze or
change the light on summer afternoons. I went there in the uniform
of Seventh Avenue, where I came from: pegged pants and thick-
soled Flagg Bros. shoes. The way I dressed had nothing to do with
Maureen's neighborhood, its trimmed gardens and fancy curtains
and polished cars parked in driveways. I certainly wasn't one of
them. Her family made that clear the first time they saw me. Her
mother looked at my clothes, and retreated upstairs. And her father's face said the rest: stony, blue-eyed, deeply lined, no humor
in the eyes, no understanding, no passion. Only suspicion and
contempt. It was the face of a man who might have worked for the
English in Dublin, one of the people my mother used to call the
Castle Irish. That first night, he studied me like a judge, knowing
from my clothes and my posture that I came from the poor Irish of
Seventh Avenue. On all later nights I would go up there to see his
daughter with anger as strong in my heart as love.

And so the boy I was then, dozing in the Pensacola afternoon,
her letter in hand, knew he would probably never take that long
summer walk again. Maureen had told him in this letter one more
time: What she felt for him was not what he felt for her.

And he thought: *Well, the hell with it and the hell with you. Until
your goddamned letter arrived, I hadn't even thought of you, girl, for a
couple of weeks. There's a woman here named Eden Santana. I mean a real
woman. More beautiful than you. So to hell with you, with your ignorant
writing and your rotten spelling and your stupid grammatical mistakes. I
don't want to hear any gossip about the neighborhood from you anymore.
Or this crap about friendship. I was in love with you. I didn't want to be
your goddamned* friend. *I have* friends. *I even have friends* here, *guys
you'll never know. I wanted to love you and for you to love me back
. . .* And then thought: *Okay, good-bye, so long. See you, girl. Someday
you'll be sorry.*

I must have slept then.

·   ·   ·

Until Sal shouted: "Hey, what's this! Get up!"

And saw Max and Sal looking down at me.

"That must've been some letter," Sal said. "Had you talking in your sleep."

I sat up, tucking the letter into my dungarees.

"Yeah," I said. "Nice letter."

"Get dressed," Sal said. "We're going to church."

Chapter

26

SAL LED THE way, words rushing from him in a torrent, Max and I behind him, carried along by the talk of God and blow jobs and beer and the Navy, words pulsing like blood. *Friday night: all right!* We left the locker club and crossed the highway, Sal's long legs striding ahead, his crew cut at attention, like nails banged into his skull, the sky a lavender wash, cars pulling up in front of Billy's, and Sal ignoring them, marching on down the highway, our fearless leader.

He turned right at the Baptist church, walking as if he'd been coming here all his life, pushing across a lumpy field to the unpaved driveway and past the white-painted church, until we could hear guitars and fiddles up ahead and a blurry voice on a bad microphone and we were following Sal across a lot to another low white wooden building: the Community Hall. A wide flight of stairs led to doors opening into the hall, the fiddle music louder as Sal led us closer, pointing at a sign saying SQUARE DANCE TONIGHT as if it were a caption to some exotic photograph. Off to the right were a dozen parked cars, a few pickup trucks, at least one hot rod. Behind the hall was a dense green wall of pine trees.

"Sal, I can't go in here," Max said. "I'm a Jew. It ain't—"

"Come on, they got the greatest-looking broads in all of Pensacola in here—*trust* me!"

At the top of the steps, two young women sat at a card table selling tickets. Looming behind them was a gaunt somber man in black somber clothes. Rimless glasses perched on his long knuckled nose. "Dig the preacher!" Sal whispered. "His nose looks like a *prick!*" The terrible thing was that it did, right down to its knobby tip, and we started giggling as Sal handed a ten-dollar bill to one of the girls and asked for three tickets. The preacher stepped forward. His extra prick quivered above his thin mouth.

"Excuse me, young man," he said, holding up a hand to the girls before they could tear any tickets off the roll. "I must warn you. This is a *Christian* affair. Neither liquor nor beer nor rowdy behavior will be tolerated."

"Reverend," Sal said, in a smooth, radio announcer voice, "do I look like a drinker? A *rowdy*? Why, I read in the *Pensacola Journal* about how you're helpin' all the young people with your wholesome dances and I tell, you, Reverend, the things that go on in the Navy, they just would turn your stomach. My friends here, they feel like me, they want a little goodness in their lives, somethin' truly wholesome and truly American."

The extra prick quivered again, as if sensing the presence of the wiles of Satan, but unable to prove anything.

"Well," the preacher said, "you've been warned."

He turned around and went into the hall. Sal then leaned down to the two young women. One was about fifteen, her hair tied back in a ponytail; her grin was crooked from trying to hide braces, but her breasts rose impressively beneath a dark-blue cotton dress; I had a tough time keeping my eyes off them. The other was a woman: maybe twenty-two, a strawberry blonde, thin, with a disappointed mouth and hungry eyes. "Well," Sal said to the younger one, switching to his Rhett Butler voice, "you sure are a dee-lahtful lookin' youngun." And then turned in a more courtly manner to the older one. "And you must be her *baby* sister." She struggled against a smile. "Can I have the honor of the fust dance with you, my darlin'?" She giggled and the younger girl flushed. "Ah do hope," Sal said, "that it will be a waltz . . . "

He took his three tickets, and turned to us. "Gentlemen," he said and led the way into the hall. The younger one said, "Yawl have fun, y'heah?" And the older one stared after Sal.

The hall was very crowded and there were more women than men. "Will you look at all the ginch in here?" Sal whispered. "Am I smart or am I smart?"

"Yeah, but listen to the music," Max said. "What do you dance to this music?"

"Don't worry about it," Sal said. "Because the broads don't care.

All their guys are off at the war someplace, and they're *here.* The guys write these stupid letters, all full of moony romantic bullshit from greeting cards, and the women are sittin' around, living with their mothers, or worse, the *guy's* mother, and so they go out . . . Looking . . . And how can they go to the Dirt Bar? Or Trader Jon's? Where can they go where the old man won't get pissed if he hears about it? So they go to *church.* I mean, just *look* at them: gettin' wet just seein' us walk in the door.''

"I still don't know what to dance to this music,'' Max said.

"It bothers you so much, don't even try,'' Sal said. "Just go out in the woods and fuck to it.''

We moved along the side of the crowded hall. The band was up on a raw pine stage, the musicians dressed in coveralls and flannel shirts and straw cowboy hats: two fiddlers, a bass guitar player, a balding man on piano. There was no drummer. I remembered reading in *Down Beat* that for centuries the drum was banned in the South because the old slave owners were afraid the slaves would use it to send messages. Messages like "Kill the fucking owners tonight.'' So for rhythm, hillbilly music depended on bass players and the strong left hands of piano players. This band was playing "Jambalaya,'' with the piano player handling the singing in a nasal Hank Williams twang; he couldn't sing, but he did have a hard left hand.

We walked casually along the side of the hall, studying the girls. They were all sizes and shapes, big and fat, tall and skinny, short and round, and some with big-titted narrow-waisted long-legged big-assed bodies right out of the movies. The tall girls wore flats and the short girls wore heels. None of them wore makeup, the devil's paint. They were clustered in small groups, their eyes darting in our direction, for a second locking into contact, then shying away, dissolving into giggles. And moving among their fleshiness, their hair and cheeks and breasts, their sweet milky odor, I thought about Eden Santana.

The following night I would be with her, but this was Friday, not Saturday, and there I was, out on the town with Sal and Max, looking at other women and aching for them. What was *wrong* with me? How could I feel the way I thought I felt about Eden and still want to take one of these horny Baptist women off to the dark woods? And then I thought: *Why* not? She could be out somewhere with Mercado: right then, as I stood alone in the crowded hall. And suppose she didn't show up on Saturday night? Suppose she treated me like some dumb kid? Another sailor, to laugh at. Anyway, I just had a *date* with her. I wasn't going *steady* with her, for Chrissakes. I wondered how she would look here at this dance and what I would think of her among all these young women. But that image just wouldn't come. She was from somewhere else in the world, not New York, but not here either. And then (not yet eighteen, not yet an ex-Catholic, a virgin except for Dixie Shafer's fleshy embrace) I felt oddly guilty, as if just being there was a kind of betrayal.

"Get'em while they're wet!" Sal whispered, and hurried to a group of girls, peeled off a small stocky blonde and led her to the dance floor. "He's nuts," Max said. "Committable." Sal was dancing with the blonde in a wild foot-stomping hee-hawing style that made the girl laugh and forced other dancers to clear some room. A brown-haired girl came over to Max. "Come on," she said, "we'll show your friend!" And then a tall redhead took my hand, and said, "Hi, I'm Evelyn" and we were all out on the floor, dancing and yelling, and following Sal's moves, mixing them with Lindy Hops and jitterbug and a little bit of mambo, cutting one another with sudden moves, putting on a New York street show (I thought proudly) until the number ended. Evelyn was breathless. "Well, than kyew," she said, and looked scared. I said, "A pleasure." And she hurried away. I wasn't sure whether it was my dancing or the word "pleasure" that scared her, but she vanished into the crowd.

I stood against the wall while another tune played, and Sal and Max exchanged girls; I wondered if this was the way people lived all over America, meeting in these places where nobody smoked or drank, where they all danced to corny music and drove home later or walked, where after a month or two they kissed and worked their way up to feels in parked cars before they got married and lived happily ever after. Maybe that was the way the whole goddamned American thing really worked. The scene made me feel sad, knowing that I *should* want it, like all good red-blooded Americans did, but also knowing that somehow I might never be a part of it, or even truly want it. I could spend my life the way I was on that night: standing there watching the women, with their excited eyes and their soft and succulent asses and tits, full of mystery and power, able to put out, as we said, or to withhold, while I tried so desperately to find the words or the moves that would unlock the mysteries between their thighs. And if that was my fate (I used such words then), I might end up as I was at that moment: alone.

Then, for the first time, I noticed the men. Maybe the same thoughts were moving through them; maybe they too were in thrall to the power of cunt and had no defense except to surrender to the power of God. If you had a fever in the blood, you could console yourself with life after death by postponing your life; heaven or hell might cool the flood. Gazing at them, I started drawing them in my head. They would be easy to draw, with their bony angular faces, no fat to disguise cheekbones or blur the jaws. Their mouths were mostly slits, turned down in resentment—of me and Sal and Max, maybe, or the Communists who were subverting America, or of women: women who'd gone off, women who'd said no, women who'd taken their money or their hearts: and if not women, maybe the resentment came from life itself. Drawing their eyes would be harder. Most of them were squinty, but the eyes themselves were hidden behind the squint, and I'd read somewhere that eyes were the windows of the soul; how could I draw them right? But as I looked closer I did find eyes buried in the squints, and saw coldness, anger, above all *certainty,* as if something had given them a faith I'd never found in New York; and that would be harder to get right. I watched them until they looked at me and then I shifted my eyes to the door, where more people were still arriving. The older ticket seller was now dancing with Sal. And then I saw a young woman across the hall and I wanted her.

She was standing alone, wearing a yellow dress, her hands entwined in front of her. Her hair was dark brown, her oval face very white and she seemed lonelier than anyone else in the hall. Except possibly me. I moved toward her, edging my way around the side of the hall. I tried to look casual, didn't want her to see my interest, didn't want to give her the power to say no. I wanted her to think I was as cool, say, as Clifford Brown, without the shades (knowing that she had never heard of Clifford Brown or his golden trumpet, but not knowing who she thought was cool). I would be—what was the word?—*aloof.* Hell, I was a man from the biggest city in America. And she was from Pensacola, Florida.

As I drew closer, I saw that she was one of the few women at the dance who was wearing makeup and the reason was obvious: beneath the powder, her skin was pitted with acne scars. The band rose into a Western swing groove, and she shifted her eyes to look at the musicians. And then turned back directly to me. Her eyes seemed to say: *Please ask me to dance. Please. You've come across the room*

and if you see my skin and walk away, I'll be humiliated. Dance with me.
Please.

"Dance?" I said.

"Sure."

Aloof.

I started doing a Lindy, but she was awkward, not knowing what to do with her hands, trying to keep up, watching my feet. But then the music changed again, this time to a ballad: "I Can't Help It If I'm Still in Love with You." The girl's hands were damp and she used them to keep me at a distance, not pushing me off, but holding me back from her. I glanced down and saw that she had full round breasts.

"Sure was a shame about Hank Williams," I said.

"That's the truth," she said. "He just didn't live right, I reckon."

"I reckon not," I said.

"Hope he got himse'f straight with the Lord."

"Yeah."

I told her my name was Michael (and glanced again at her breasts) and she said her name was Sue Ellen. I tried to press closer, just to feel the edge of those tits against my chest, and failed, and she looked up at me in a doubtful way. When I returned her look (thinking: *her face, not her tits, look at her* face) she averted her eyes. When I tried again to move her closer to me, she gave a few inches until I could feel the warmth of her flesh; she said nothing, but her hands were wet. I couldn't see Sal or Max now on the crowded floor. The piano player was trying hard to sing like Hank Williams.

"This is some sad song," I said.

"Yeah, it is. 'Course old Buddy Jackson up there, he ain't no Hank Williams."

"No, but he's doin' his best," I said, trying to get into a southern rhythm. What did I call her? Sue? Ellen? Swellen? "You live around here?"

"Up the road a piece," she said. She took a deep breath, as if trying to get up courage. "You in the Navy?"

"Yeah," I said. "Navy man, that's me."

"My daddy'd kill me, he knew I was dancin' with a sailor."

"That so?"

"Same with all the other girls here," she said. "Sailors ain't too popular in these parts. Hope I don't hurt your feelin's, but I reckon you know that anyways."

"No," I said, "I guess sailors aren't ever too popular. Except when they're dying in some war."

It was shameless bullshit. But she looked at me and frowned.

"I'm not sayin' *I* feel that way, Michael. I'm saying' *some* folks, well, they—"

"I'm not just a sailor, Sue Ellen. I was a regular human being until I joined up."

"Yeah, well, I guess people *should* keep an open mind."

"And I won't be a sailor all my life either," I said. Thinking: *Come on, man, be cooler than that. Leave it alone. Go for the pussy. Don't lay this Navy crap on too thick. The tips of her tits are brushing your chest.*

"No, I reckon that's the truth, Michael. Still, you're a sailor *right now* and if my daddy walked in this minute he'd have me whupped."

"No!"

"He sure would."

"Can't believe he'd whup someone pretty as you," I said. "A grown-up woman."

She paused, then her eyes examined me, a puzzled furrow on her brow. Maybe *grown-up woman* was the password. She was about five four, and when I glanced down at her, I could see her breasts heave anxiously as she hit me with the big question.

"You a Christian?"

I smiled. Cool. The man from New York. Experienced. A traveler. Aloof. "Well, not really," I said. "I mean, I was raised as a Catholic, but—"

"You were raised as a Catholic?"

Fucked.

She backed up, as if I'd told her I had the mange. "Yeah," I said, "anything wrong with that?"

"Uh, well, I don't *know.* Yeah. I mean, uh—I never did meet a *Catholic* before."

I'd fumbled, then tried to recover. The band played harder now. I heard nothing, saw nothing; I needed words.

"Well," I started to say, "I was raised one, but I don't think I'm one anymore. You a Baptist?"

"Methodist."

"See, I can't tell the difference," I said. "Baptists, Methodists, Presbyterians, Anglicans, First Reformed, Second Reformed . . ."

I suppose I was trying to give the impression that none of these distinctions mattered to me, and the only distinction being made was by her. "It's all a little nutty to me . . ."

She stopped dancing and squinted at me, her eyes vanishing the way they did in the slits of the men.

"What'd you say?"

"I said it all seems a little nutty to me. You know, religion."

"*Religion* seems nutty to you?"

"To tell the truth: yeah."

"Well, I never—"

We were near one of the poles along the edge of the dance floor. I had seen people say *Well, I never* in comic strips and heard the words on the radio; but she was the first live human who ever said them to me. *Well, I never*— I thought the next word I'd hear was "pshaw." She looked flustered, and that made me feel like an even bigger man of the world. Something I'd said had actually made her react to me. She'd think I was sophisticated, fearless, a rebel. And instead of shutting up, or telling lies, bending my knee to Jesus the better to see up her dress, I went on talking.

"I mean, here's this Jewish carpenter, Jesus, who died two thousand years ago, and all over the world people are still arguing about what he said, and *killing* one another over it. Does that make any *sense*? And—"

"You better mind what you're saying."

"They're all *Christians,* aren't they? So why are they all split into a hundred different groups? It's *nuts.* Jesus—"

"You said he was a *Jew*! You said the *Lord* was a Jew!"

"Well, he *was.* He was born in Nazareth, he went to the synagogue, he—"

"He wunt no *Jew*! The Lord wunt no damned *Jew*! The Lord was a *Christian*!!"

She turned abruptly away from me, pushing people aside, heading toward the front of the hall. I went after her, sorry I'd talked so much, saying: "Hey, I didn't mean to hurt your *feelings,* Sue Ellen!"

Then I saw that some faces were turning to examine me or gaze after Sue Ellen. A few dancers stopped. I saw them talking, nodding at me, and wondered where Sal and Max had gone. Then I saw a heavyset man in a tight shiny blue gabardine suit go to Sue Ellen. I came closer, still hoping to recover my lost moment, take back the words, try to find my way to those luscious hidden tits. He took her hand, as if about to bow and kiss it. Then he turned to face me. He had small abrupt features bunched together in a large round face. Staring at me, he said to her: "What's the problem, Sue Ellen?"

"Buster," she said, "this sailor said the Lord was Jew!"

"Now, hold it," I said. "What I said was—"

Buster said to me, "You said the Lord God, our Savior and Redeemer, was a *Jew?*" Then louder, as he dropped her hand: "A *Jew?*"

I tried to smile and turned slightly, keeping Buster in my sight, and saw Sal coming through the crowd. The band was playing loudly now. Then I saw Max coming over too. I relaxed (or grew braver, knowing I wasn't alone). And then saw that Buster was no longer on his own, either. Two, six, then a dozen young men were assembling behind Buster and Sue Ellen. In this sudden formation, they looked like some odd football team where the quarterback had big tits and a pockmarked face; she looked at me now as if possessed, suddenly realizing that she could call the signals. Ah, the power of cunt.

"What's going on?" Sal said in a flat even voice.

"A little theology discussion," I said, performing my cool part as much for him as for the others. "I was explaining that Jesus was a Jew. And—"

"See?" Sue Ellen said, as if I'd just snapped the ball from center. "He said it *again!*"

Then Max stepped in and raised his hands with the palms out, like a referee separating fighters.

"Please, please, folks, *please,*" he said. They waited, looking at him in a puzzled way. "I happen to be an expert on this subject. And I have to say that my friend Devlin here is right. It's a fact of history, beyond any question, that Jesus *was* a Jew. I know. Because *I'm a Jew myself.*"

A stunned moment, and then Buster said: "You're a *Jew?!*"

"Born and bred, my friend. A card-carrying New York Jew."

Suddenly the preacher was there, pushing through Sue Ellen's brawny backfield, his face ashen, and I thought: *Holy Christ,* his nose has a hard-on!

"What is this *all* about?" he said.

At that point, we could have bowed, shook hands and gone off to the Dirt Bar. But Sue Ellen then changed the terms of the debate. She pointed at Max, her eyes wide.

"This boy . . . this boy's a *Jew!*"

Her face was all snarled up now, her eyes indignant.

"And *this* one, that I made the mistake of *dancing* with, this one says that the *Lord* was a Jew!"

The preacher turned to me, his erect nose throbbing. But before he could say anything, Sal stepped in. He began to speak in a British accent, even drawing on some secret supply of phlegm.

"Reverend, reverend, with all due respect, dear boy, I think I'd better explain some of the theological ramifications and deep secular philosophical roots of the discussion between this barbaric young man and this lovely Christian lady."

He touched the side of his nose, as if raising spectacles. Everyone looked at him.

"You see, it wasn't, ahem, a discussion of phenomenology or epistemology they were engaged in, old chap."

He cleared his throat. "Nor were they involved in the historical roots of the Hebraic-Christian traditions and the shared tenets of all Mediterranean civilization including Christianity." He pursed his lips. "You see, dear reverend, what they were actually discussing was—" a pause—"*pussy.*"

For one long moment, nobody moved. Buster's jaw dropped. The preacher's nose wilted. Sue Ellen widened her stance, as if trying not to swoon.

And then Sal turned, grabbing Max and me with each of his hands, and we were running and laughing through the hall, with Buster and the football team after us. Chairs went flying, a table toppled over with a crash, there were shouts and screams while the band blasted harder than ever. We burst into the cool night air, Sal laughing and leaping, and Max turning, raising both muscled arms at the sky, shouting at the doors of the hall: *"I'm a Jew, I'm a Jew, I'm a Jew Jew Jew!"*

And then we were running and I could feel my blood pulsing and the muscles bunching in my legs and pain spearing my side as we raced for the highway. We could see the bus pulling around from the base to the bus stop and Sal started yelling for it to stop, as we went over a low fence and across a lumpy field. We could make it! We'd get on board and ride away to town and finish our night at the Dirt Bar, with Tons of Fun arriving in the van and Dixie Shafer telling me tales of the vanished hills. Yeah. Simple. And then I turned and saw Max fall and four of the rednecks coming over the fence, Buster leading the pack.

"Max! Come on, man! We can make this goddamned bus!" Sal shouted.

But Max got up and turned to the oncoming rednecks and planted his feet. It was as if he were saying, to us and to the world, that he was a tough proud Jew and he just wasn't going to run. Not from these morons. Not from anyone. So we stopped running and let the bus leave and joined Max. The first man came in a rush and Max bent low, twisted, let the right hand fly and the man went down. A second one came at me, a guy who looked like an auto engine in a shirt, and I threw the right hand hard and straight and felt the impact all the way up in my shoulder and the man's face seemed to explode in blood and he fell to his knees. I kicked him over on his side.

But then Buster was there, his rage ferocious, and I wasn't so lucky this time. I threw a punch and it glanced off Buster's head and then I was slammed, and lifted, suddenly without breath or bone or strength, and then was on my back. Time stopped. And sound. I saw the sky. Black, with pinwheeling stars. And thought: *I'm knocked out. He knocked me out.*

And then sound came rushing back in and I heard grunting and then a *phwocking* sound and a man's wordless high-pitched voice yelping in pain. And started to get up, and saw Sal on my left, swinging a gnarled tree branch like a club, hitting Buster on the arms and elbows and hips, while Max grappled with a fourth man, and still another came on a run, to leap on Max's back.

I got up, my heart pounding wildly, and dived for the man on Max. I grabbed his jacket, which tore down the middle, and then I stepped to the side and punched as hard as I could to the man's ear. He let go of Max's neck, holding his ear in pain, and staggered away. I bent him in half with a kick in the balls and then Sal came up, slowly and deliberately, Buster now on his face in the dirt, and hit the big man with the three-branch club and finished him off. We looked at Max. He had another man above his head now, like a strong man at a circus. And he ran forward and rammed the man against a tree.

It was over.

We stood there, panting, dirty, battered, and looked at what we'd done. Five huge men were unconscious on the dark field.

"Jesus Christ," I said.

"Don't start," Sal said.

We could hear the sounds of insects again, filling the night, and the band still playing a way off. Nobody seemed to have left the hall; the preacher must have held them back. And there was no sign of Sue Ellen.

Max said, "You know something? These guys might be dead."

Sal looked at him and then at the tree branch in his own hand. His eyes were still wild, as if he wanted more, and I thought for a moment that he looked like Alley Oop. He swung the branch like a bat and hurled it into the trees and then began to laugh wildly.

We hurried back across the highway to the locker club and were changing clothes when we heard the distant sound of a siren. "Jesus, it's just like the movies," Sal said. "The killer's in the building and he hears the cops coming, the sirens and all, and he starts to yell down at them—at Charles Bickford, who always has the fuckin bullhorn—and he says, 'Up your hole with a Mell-o-roll, coppers, you *ain't takin' me alive*!' " Max laughed, pulling on his whites, and said, "Why do they *do* that in the movies anyway? To warn the bad guys? The cops must be amazing schmucks . . ." I said it might just be an ambulance out there. "Those guys are pretty fucked up," I said. And Max said again that they might even be dead. Sal didn't want to wait around to find out. "Come on," he said, and with Sal leading the way, we slipped out of the locker club in our dress whites. The sirens went past the locker club toward the church, but we were out back, walking in the shadows of the palm trees to the main gate of Ellyson Field. Then a car pulled into Copter Road and Sal jumped out and waved at it.

"Hey, we need a *ride,* man."

The car stopped. A shiny new red Mercury. Max and I hurried over. Mercado was alone behind the wheel. He looked at us and smiled.

"Get in," he said.

Chapter

27

I N THE EARLY sixties, after my first wife died, I went out for a while with a red-haired stripper who loved to see me fight. She did an act at the Hudson Theater, undressing herself in a giant wineglass filled with dirty pink water. She believed in Rosicrucianism and lived like the guy in the Rosicrucian ads, who slept each night on the edge of a cliff. To her, danger was a religious experience. Wherever we went she caused trouble, giving various men the eye, then getting indignant when they came on to her, and stepping back to watch me fight for her outraged honor. I got so mad at her one night on the East River Drive, my hands raw and my suit ruined, that I pulled the steering wheel right off its shaft while screaming at her and had to grab the naked top of the shaft with both hands to keep from dying. As I sat there panting, she just laughed and then started to play with me. That was the last time I saw her and I heard later that she'd been shot to death by a female lover in a hotel room in Baltimore. There are women like that, and when I look back, I realize that little Sue Ellen was surely one of them.

All through the next day I hung out in the barracks, expecting the imminent arrival of the Shore Patrol. They would take me off to the Pensacola jail and little Sue Ellen, prim and clean, would breathe hard, making all the cops look at her breasts, and pick me out as the man who said that Jesus was a Jew. Then she would leave for Buster's funeral and I would spend the rest of my adult life in Portsmouth Naval Prison, or take a shorter trip to the Florida gas chamber.

But the Shore Patrol never came for me, and on Saturday evening I went out and changed clothes at the locker club and took the bus to town, slouching low as we passed the Baptist Church. It was too early for my date with Eden Santana, but I didn't want to be late, so I sat for almost an hour on a bench on Garden Street. I was uneasy: I didn't know where I would take her or what we would do; she'd just smiled and told me she would meet me. I said her name out loud: *Eden Santana.* Then whispered it: *Eden. San. Tana.* A beautiful name, I thought, shuddering at the hard ending of the first name and its promise of paradise. The second name was made of all those female vowels (for surely consonants are male) and rolled in a wave when you said it, like the name Pensacola itself. I wished I had a hundred dollars to spend without care for tomorrow or next week or the rest of the Navy month. Then, if I could sort out the words, I'd ask her to go with me to the San Carlos. To sleep with me between silk sheets. I'd whisper her name at midnight. First name and last, paradise and vowels. *Eden Santana, Eden Santana.* Like a decade of a wicked rosary.

She was due to finish work at six and ten minutes before the hour I got up and crossed Garden Street and walked slowly down the street toward Sears. I stopped at the alley and felt a sudden attack of hopelessness. Her bicycle wasn't there. And if her bicycle wasn't there, she probably wasn't there either. I dawdled past the store and glanced through the windows, as casually as possible. I didn't see her inside. *Maybe she's gone,* I thought, feeling lost and alone in a town that wasn't mine. Maybe she'd realized it was ridiculous to be seeing a kid like me on a Saturday night in a town full of men. Men with money. Fliers. *Officers.* Men who'd been around the world and back, flown combat missions, faced death. Men like Mercado. Down the street I saw the neon blinking on outside Trader Jon's, but in my mind, I imagined her waking up on Saturday morning, thinking, "Oh, that damned kid," and lying there deciding to call in sick so she wouldn't have to see me. Maybe there was a guy lying in bed beside her. Smoking a cigarette, while she phoned in her lie. Speaking to her in Spanish later. She touched his face and smiled, saying, "I can't go to town today." Then lighting a cigarette. Then adding, "I have to stay here." And the man did not protest because the man, of course, did not want to leave her. He reached out, touched her nipples, whispered her name.

I stopped at the corner just past Sears, and leaned on a lamppost, looking up and down the street. I hoped none of the gang would see me. I didn't want them asking me what I was doing standing on an empty street in Pensacola. They'd think I was a degenerate or something. Or they'd drag me down the street to Trader Jon's, or out to the Dirt Bar. And I didn't want to go to either place; this little hour belonged to me. Most of all, I couldn't tell them the truth. "I'm waiting for a woman named Eden Santana." I couldn't say that, admitting with my tone that I cared for the woman and was disappointed in her absence. We were sailors. *Ah remember the days* (the Old Salt said) *when men were men and women were carpets and all the ships was wood.* Anchors Aweigh, my boys. Bell-bottom trousers, suit of Navy blue, I love a sailor boy and— No. I couldn't say anything to them.

The clock on the Blount Building said it was ten after six. And I thought: *I'll wait five more minutes. If she's not here in five minutes, then she's not coming.* Maybe the whole thing was stupid. She was telling me something. I should take the hint. Just get out of here. Hell, I'm freshly shaved and smell good and have money in my pocket. I don't have to wait here like a goddamned fool.

A car horn honked. Once. Then again.

I looked across the street at the sound. Eden Santana was behind the wheel of an old dark-green car, smiling at me and waving. I felt like doing cartwheels, shouting, punching street signs. I went around to the passenger side and she leaned across and opened the door.

"Get in," she said. "You want to drive?"

"No, no," I said. Closing the door, trying not to slam it, to show I was anxious. "You drive."

She started driving again, making a left into a side street.

"I'm sorry I'm so damned late," she said. "Every girl in that place had a damned date tonight and the ladies' room looked like a football stadium. Then I had to go get the car, out in the back, and all the streets go the wrong way, and . . . How are you, child?"

"Great," I said. "Just great."

I could smell her now, all flowers, fields in the spring. She had done something to her hair; it was a controlled pile of a million curls. She was wearing a lavender dress and stockings with a seam down the back and high-heeled white shoes, which I watched as she shifted gears and pushed the car down dark streets.

"So, what d'you think?" she said.

"You look amazing," I said. "I love the dress. And your hair. And—"

"Not me! The *car!*"

"It's—"

"Cost me seventy-five bucks, up at Bargainville on West Cervantes. A 1940 Ford. Runs pretty good for a thirteen-year-old, don't you think?"

"It sounds good," I said (thinking: *When this car was new, I was four and she was nineteen*). And then glanced at her, as she turned the wheel, straightened out, went down another street. "But you know something? I gotta tell you the truth."

"You hate Fords."

"Worse. I don't know how to drive Fords or anything else."

"Say what?"

"I can't drive a car."

"Well, I'll be damned."

I explained why, and she listened and nodded and then reached for her purse and her Luckies.

"Anyway," I said, "I feel dumb about it."

"Don't feel dumb," she said. "You got good reasons. Up in the country, folks all learn to drive young 'cause it's so far from one place to another. Still see people walkin' everyplace they need to go, and once in a while you see an old cart, like in the old days, a cart with a horse. Now they mostly got them cars. Have to. But you didn't need to do that. So don't feel dumb."

She was talking very quickly, and it never occurred to me that night that she was throwing the words at me because she was nervous, too. I couldn't imagine Eden Santana being nervous. Not over me. She put a cigarette in her mouth, but couldn't strike a match without taking her hands off the wheel. I took the matches and tried to do it for her. The breeze blew out two matches and then she handed me the cigarette.

"Light it up for me, will you, Michael?"

The smoke tasted sour as I inhaled and handed the cigarette back to her.

"And hey, what the hell," she said, pausing to take a deep drag. "I can teach you how to drive. I used to—I'm a pretty fair driver, and I could teach you."

"I'd love that."

Thinking: *I'll be sure then to see you again. During the week and on weekends, too, maybe. You'll explain gears and shifts, gas pedal and accelerator. You'll place my hands on the wheel. I'll smell your hair, hear you laugh. This night is not the end. We begin.* There was water on my right, all the way to the horizon, and lights on small boats and a lighthouse away off. The sea was black.

"Where we going?" I said.

"The beach," she said. "Out the causeway to Santa Rosa Island. There's a little shrimp place there I found the other day. Just shrimp and beer. Nothin' else. And cheap too. All you can eat for a dollar."

"You're kidding?"

"You better like shrimp."

"All I can eat."

Then we were on the causeway, a long, narrow two-lane bridge out over the water. The breeze was cooler off the sea and I looked at Eden Santana, her brow furrowed slightly in concentration, her hair blowing, the lavender dress lifting and settling on her tan legs. And thought: *My life right now, at this moment, with this woman beside me and the breeze blowing, riding over the sea, is truly beautiful.* And I was right.

We ate great mounds of boiled shrimp: dozens hundreds millions of them, sitting at a metal table beside screened windows overlooking the dark beach. We filled a bowl with the shells and drank Jax beer while I looked at her and she asked questions and I tried to answer. The lipstick came off her mouth. The sea air made her hair frizzier than ever. People came in and sat down and ate and left and we were still there. I drew pictures on napkins, and signed and dated them and wrote "Pop's Shrimp Place" beneath the dates: pictures of a chief gunnery officer in uniform and a fat lady with a thin bearded man and a grizzled guy who looked like a fisherman. Then we ordered more shrimp and went on eating. When we were finished, Eden leaned back, a grin on her face, and rubbed her stomach.

"Gotta walk some of this off, child," she said.

I stood up, smothered a belch, and left a dollar tip, wondering if that was too much, and she would think I was showing off. But she took my hand and led the way out through the door to the beach. She took her shoes off and held them in one hand. Then she took my hand, lacing her fingers between mine, and we started to walk. The sand was very white, and the surf a long way off. Eden gazed up at the bunched thick stars. We left the lights of the shrimp place behind and soon were alone in a great emptiness.

Then she saw a piece of driftwood, huge as a tree but bone white, and we sat on its trunk while she smoked a cigarette.

"You said you had a husband," I said, then wished I hadn't.

"Yes," she said, without turning to me.

"What happened to him?"

"He's home."

"But you're not," I said, trying to be light.

She turned to me. "No, I'm not. I'm here, child. With you. Or didn't you notice?"

"I don't mean to pry."

"Then don't."

"It's just . . . well, you said to me the other night that I didn't know you. And that was true. That *is* true."

"The details, they don't matter, do they? This is me. Right here, sitting on this piece of driftwood. Nothing else *to* me. Just what's here."

"I've told you all about me," I said.

"Maybe there's less to tell," she said curtly.

I was quiet then. She was right: I had less to tell. For a simple reason: I was a kid and she wasn't. When I was two years old, she was sixteen. She was ready to fuck guys when I was learning to walk. She might even have been married then. At sixteen. Just a year younger than I was when I went in the Navy. They married younger than that down south. Yeah, she had a lot more to tell.

She squeezed my hand.

"Did I hurt your feelings, child?" she said softly.

"No, no—"

"I did, didn't I? Well, I'm sorry. I didn't mean to. I hope you know that. Just, I got me some bad habits. Someone says somethin' hard to me, I want to answer back. I wasn't always like that. I was a nice quiet little girl for a long long time. But then it got so I had to answer back."

"To him? The husband?"

She smiled in a knowing way. "Maybe someday I'll tell you all about that. Not tonight. Not now. It's just too damned beautiful out here for that."

She stood up and looked at the moon and the stars, and then said, "Don't look now. Don't watch me."

I stared at the sea and heard her moving behind me. And then she came up beside me and handed me her stockings.

"Couldn't stand them one more minute," she said.

The stockings were silky and feminine in my hands and I rubbed them slightly as we walked, thinking that they'd been where I'd never been. For a second, I wanted to put them in my mouth. And then rolled them and slipped them in my pocket.

"Look, you can see the sea oats, up on the dune. See? The dark stuff? That's what holds the dune together. They got deep wide roots, and they move under the sand, like steel in concrete, you know?" She led me over to look at the dark clusters in the light of the moon. "You ever see anyone pullin' them up, you give 'em a good quick hop in the butt, hear? Lose them sea oats, you lose the whole damned beach."

"I've never seen them before."

"You have a beach in New York, don't you?"

"Yeah, a bunch of them. Coney Island and Rockaway and Jones Beach, a bunch of others."

"Well, if they don't have sea oats, you're gonna lose them."

We climbed the dune. The island was all dark, the nearest lights a mere glow across the bay in the town, and the wind was rising and she looked up at the stars.

"There's something I'm gonna do. Something I wanted to do all my life," she said out loud, as much to the night or the wind as to me. "Gonna do it."

She turned her back and reached up under the dress and peeled off her panties. She looked at me as she stepped out of them, then smiled faintly, and handed them to me.

"I want to feel the wind," she whispered.

And faced the sea, lifting her dress, her legs spread and planted to the ankles in the sand. She threw her head back and closed her eyes and shivered. The wind moved between her thighs and I could see her dark roundness and then she shivered again. And then again. The wind was sighing and a buoy was *ting-tinging* away off and a moaning sound rose from her throat.

I held her panties to my face. They smelled of salt and the dark sea.

Chapter

28

SHE DROVE ME back to Ellyson Field.

"I'd rather go home with you," I said.

"No," she said. "I don't want to fool you."

"I don't think you'd do that."

"I might."

"Just tell me the truth," I said. "Even if it hurts."

"That's a deal. If I can't tell you the truth, I won't say anything at all."

"Deal."

We moved past bars and car lots and churches. I felt the lump of her rolled stockings in my pocket and slipped them out and laid them on the seat.

"You get awful quiet sometimes, child."

"Maybe I can't tell *you* the truth either."

"You better not bottle too much up. Lots of people do that, and it drives em crazy . . ."

The lazy drawl rose at the end, as if she had more to say. But she just shook her head in a rueful way. She was driving slowly now behind a fat squat truck. She looked out at the side, trying to see ahead, started to move once, suddenly darted back in lane as a car roared by in a blaze of light. "Gah-*damn*." Then she looked again and gave it the gas, biting her lower lip, and roared past the truck, honking her horn, half in anger, the rest a tease. Then another car was in front of us, lights very bright. She whipped into the right-hand lane, missing the other car by a foot. She laughed like a teenager and shook her head and then slowed again. I was beginning to love the way she did things: she was confident, sure, enjoying risk and escape. Who was she anyway? I turned to her.

"Can I ask you a question?" I said.

"Sure."

"Why did Red Cannon get you so upset last week? You know, about seeing you in the San Carlos bar with that Mexican pilot? That Tony Mercado?"

"You really want to know?"

"Yeah."

She took a deep breath.

"Okay . . . I went over there with a woman from work. A friend of mine, Roberta Stone. Just to have a drink. After work. That's all. Real innocent. Not to pick up men, hear? Just a drink on payday. I hadn't had a drink since I got to Pensacola, savin' my money for this car . . . We sat at a corner table. That fella Tony Mercado was standing at the bar and he saw us, and sent over a drink, and smiled at us. Roberta thought he was cute. She thought more than that, the truth be told . . . Well, maybe he saw it in her eyes. Anyway, he came over. The trouble was, he started makin' moves on me, not Roberta. And she got all upset and drank too much and though she was comin' on strong, this Tony Mercado backed away. Anyway, he had a key on him. A room key. For upstairs there in the San Carlos. And he slipped *me* the key. Well, I hadn't been with a man . . . It's been a long time. For good reasons . . ." She lit a cigarette with a small Zippo lighter, let the smoke drift out the window into the cool air. "But I didn't want him. I didn't like the idea, guy comin' over, slippin' you a room key. And besides, Roberta more or less staked her claim. I wasn't gonna do that to *her.* I mean, the guy *was* handsome, and *was* charming. But just like *that?* Picked up in a *bar?* No thanks. There were a lot of sailors and Marines in there, including, I guess, your Mister Cannon. So I gave Tony Mercado back his key and said, No thanks. You know, slipped it to him under the table. Well, he smiled in that charming way, real polite, and then turned to Roberta." She took a deep drag, let it out slowly. "Roberta took the key and then he left and then she left to go upstairs and then I left."

She flipped the cigarette out onto the highway. The locker club was less than a mile away.

"So that's the whole story. Pretty damned long-winded answer to your question, wasn't it? Why'd I get so upset? Cause that redheaded sailor with the dead face—he acted like I was some whore who works the bars. And I'm not."

"You don't even have to say that."

"But Roberta isn't either. Some women do for loneliness what they'd never do for money."

"Is she a blonde?"

"Why, yes . . . A real bright blonde."

"He's still seeing her."

"You'd make a good cop, child."

"I wasn't looking for her *or* for him, Eden. It was sheer luck."

"Well, here's the locker club."

She pulled into the lot. I gazed around, hoping Buster and his friends weren't waiting in ambush. There was nobody in sight.

"I want to see you again," I said.

She looked away, out at the highway and the traffic.

"When?"

"Tomorrow."

"Can't tomorrow."

"The next day."

A pause.

"Okay."

"Maybe we'll go to another movie."

"No. I want you to draw me."

"Serious?"

"Like artists do in the movies. I never done that before."

When I reached my locker, I had her panties in my pocket. Once more I held them to my face.

Chapter

29

I FEEL THAT TIME of my life in fragments now; then I stand back and glibly impose narrative upon it to give it sense. I am driving tentatively through side streets off the highway, feeling as if the next left turn might lead me deep into the past, the right into some scary bleak future. If I can remember that time without the gauzy editing of memory, maybe I can make sense of all the years that followed, the stupid deaths I later saw and recorded, the friends I lost, the women I loved too carelessly or too well. But memory does not exist in any orderly progression, following the clean planes of logic. That's the scary part: If there is no logic, no sense, what meaning could it possibly have?

I remember clearly the day after she told me she wanted me to draw her, the day after she opened her naked cunt to the breeze of the midnight Gulf. It makes me tremble even now. All that morning, I was like a bundle of jumbled wires. I needed to get to an art supply store, to buy a pad and some chalks. Eden Santana had challenged me, as if she could forgive my youth, my stumbling uncertainties, my awkward poses only if I had talent. So I wanted real tools: chalk, good paper. But I couldn't go to Sears, couldn't slide into their art supply section without Eden seeing me. If she saw me buying supplies only for this occasion, she might think I was a fake. Or a dumb boy. Or spying on her. There had to be another place that sold art supplies. In the Pensacola phone book, I found one: Art Land on West Cervantes. I called the store and a woman with a cracker voice told me she closed at five. There was no way I could get there in time. I wasn't even certain where West Cervantes was. I knew the downtown streets and I could find O Street, but the rest of the city was a blur.

Then Becket came over.

"Take a run to Mainside?" he said.

And I wanted to hug him.

Becket double-parked while I ran into Art Land. The chalks, paints and pens were in drawers behind the counter.

"Kin ah hey-elp yew?" a woman said, coming from behind an aisle. She had a dusty face and weak blue eyes and a disappointed look on her face. A sailor. In dungarees. What could *he* want?

"Yes, yes," I said, trying to remember the names of the materials. "I need some charcoal and some of that stuff, you know, the harder stuff, it's brown or reddish brown?"

"Conté," she said, bumping around behind the counter.

"And a pad," I said.

"They're behind you, right they-uh," she said. The store was empty of customers and most of the lights were off. From inside, the street was a blinding sun-baked white. "Yew want charcoal paypuh o' newsprint?"

I didn't really know. But I looked at the pads, and the prices, and a large newsprint pad was seventy-nine cents and the charcoal paper was two dollars. I picked up the newsprint pad and took it to the counter. "I'll take this." She had boxes of Conté crayons and sticks of vine charcoal on the counter. The charcoal looked fragile. She also shoved at me a box of something called compressed charcoal. I picked them up, a stick at a time; the compressed charcoal was heavier and blacker.

"I'll take two of each," I said.

"Two of each?" she said.

"Please."

"Usually we sell them by the box."

"I know," I said, "but I don't really have enough cash on me. I'll come back and buy the rest of the box, I promise. But I need these right now."

She sighed in a disgusted way and picked out two each of the vine charcoal, the compressed charcoal and the brown Conté crayons, and made an elaborately sarcastic ceremony of wrapping them. I could hear Becket honking for me. She took her time filling out a bill, listing each item, and then slipped them all into a bag.

"I guess you don't have enough money for fixative?" she said.

"No," I said. I didn't even know what fixative was. The bill was $1.90. I gave her two dollars, waited for my dime and then rushed out to the truck.

"Maybe *you* drew my picture dat day," Becket said. "Not Miles."

"No," I said. "It was Miles."

He went roaring down West Cervantes, making up time on his way through midday traffic to Mainside.

"So you're an artist too?" Becket said.

"Well, sort of," I said. I explained about cartoons and comic strips, trying to make cartooning sound like an occupation for adults and not something for kids who stayed too long with the funny papers. Milton Caniff made more than a hundred thousand a year, and some guys earned even more. Becket listened and nodded.

"You know," he said, "you could prolly make some money around the barracks. I remember a guy in Norfolk, he could draw, and he started makin' pictures from photographs. Two bucks apiece. You know, of different guy's goirls. Or da guys themselves. And he made him some good money. Not no hundid-thousin a year. Dere wasn't dat much money in da whole state of Virginia. But good beer money."

"How'd he start?"

"I guess wit' one guy. Like da guy dat makes a better mousetrap. The woid gets around."

"I oughtta try that."

"Start with me, you want," he said, as we slowed at the approach to the Mainside gate. "I'll give you my goirl's picture later."

Two dollars a drawing. Until then it had never occurred to me that I could earn money making pictures; that was something for the scary future, when I was out of the Navy. Becket saw things in the present tense. My head teemed with visions of riches.

Late that afternoon, a grizzled mechanic came into the Supply Shack looking for a joy stick. Only Donnie Ray and Harrelson were still at work, filling out forms. I walked to the storeroom, past my desk (where my new art supplies lay flat in the top drawer) and went looking for the joy stick. The storeroom felt gloomy in the fading light. I moved aside pallets and boxes, and found a joy stick in a crate. I went for a dolly, lifted the crate, placed it on the dolly and started to leave. Then, through the new space in the wall of crates, I saw the easel.

There was a painting leaning on the easel, which stood in a tiny room made from improvised walls of stacked crates and boxes. A low crate served as a chair and a second was topped with a sheet of glass upon which were laid tubes of paint and tins of liquid. There were a dozen brushes in a jar and more paintings stacked against the wall. Someone had created a secret art studio here in the Supply Shack. I knew it must be Miles.

I felt as if I'd just entered Aladdin's cave, piled with treasure. I lifted another crate to fill the space of the one I'd taken and hurried back to the counter with the joy stick. *Miles is an artist.* I thought about that at my desk, with my own secrets in the drawer, wondering when Miles would be back—he was off to Mainside with Jones and Boswell—and why he had lied to me about the Becket drawing. I waited on a few more customers. Typed forms. Read specification books. All the while anxious to return to the back room, to verify what I'd seen (was this what they meant by a mirage?) and waiting for Donnie Ray to leave. Harrelson had the duty. And he could be a problem; I certainly didn't want him to discover the studio and invoke the fierce laws of Chickenshit. So at closing time I left, too, and went across the street to the barracks and stood inside the door until I saw Donnie Ray leave.

Then I crossed the street again and opened the middle door, closed it quietly and tiptoed into the back room. I found I could enter the "studio" by flattening myself against the wall and sliding between it and the packing crates. Inside, a single window was covered with a shade tacked to the sill. It was a kind of nest, sealed off, special, private. I felt oddly safe, the way I did when I was a kid hiding under a bush in the park. There was another feeling too: of being in an empty church. I didn't believe in God, but there was something about the hushed solitude of an afternoon church that always got me. That little cave of packing crates provoked the same awed mood.

The painting on the easel wasn't finished, but I could see the blocky outlines of a ruined house, a blasted tree, endless green fields moving to a distant blue horizon. It was painted on some kind of heavy board, smooth on the painted surface, coarse on the other. So were all the other paintings. There was a harlequin in a beaded multicolored suit, blue eyes peering from a mask, neither male nor female. Another showed an old woman at the end of a country lane, trees rising above her in a menacing way, her back to the painter. In a third, a man in navy jeans held his head in his hands while a giant orange crowded out everything in the room. The room had screened windows, like the barracks, but there were prison bars beyond the screens, and a small black mask hung from a peg on a wall. There were two pictures of a middle-aged woman with youthful eyes glistening from her sagging face. And a painting of four sailors in Lone Ranger masks standing at the end of a ruined pier with their backs to the sea. I'd never seen pictures like them before. They weren't like illustrations in *Cosmopolitan* or *McCall's* or like the drawings of Crane and Caniff.

There was a black sketchbook on the floor, and I looked through it, recognizing Becket and Harrelson and Boswell, and Chief McDaid and Red Cannon, all drawn very delicately with a pencil, the shading done with hundreds of tiny lines. They were not photographic likenesses; they seemed to go deeper than that, to express Becket's good nature and Harrelson's cruelty and Boswell's blurry drunkenness, and the malignant core of Red and McDaid. There were also drawings of women, nude, heavy-breasted, with faces like crones, a drawing of a black man wearing a jock, his skin glistening as if he'd been oiled. A detailed study of a tree. The wreck of an old car. Ruined piers like the one in the painting. Many careful but unfinished drawings of oranges. And detailed renderings of masks. They were wonderful drawings, but they made me uneasy. Not simply because I couldn't do them, but because of the subject matter. I'd always been the best artist in my class but I couldn't draw like this; worse, I couldn't *imagine* like this. My own drawings were usually of fights and brawls, the stuff of the comics; these were pictures you saw in museums and art books.

There were a few blank pages and then I stopped short. The next three drawings were of me. In one of them I was sitting at my desk, my back to the artist, my face in profile gazing out at the Florida day. My jaw was slack and I seemed lost in thought. In the second, I was swabbing the deck. My body was bent at a violent angle and I was wielding the huge mop as if it were a blunt instrument. The muscles of my back and arms were perfectly drawn, taut and charged with tension. The third was an unfinished portrait. Some tentative overlapping lines defined my cheekbones and jaw. The incomplete nose was gouged with erasures.

But the eyes were my eyes.

And they looked scared.

Suddenly I felt almost sick: the next day I was supposed to draw
Eden Santana, but these pictures showed me that I just wasn't good
enough. If this was indeed Miles's work, *Miles* should be drawing
her. She deserved a better artist than I was. And I felt ashamed and
envious too. Somehow, in spite of everything, in spite of all the
same kind of crap that I had to put up with, Miles found a way to
do his work. He even found time to draw me. He was *serious.* In
six weeks at Ellyson, I'd made a dozen drawings in a couple of
restaurants, showing off to a woman who must have seen me as an
amusing amateur; certainly if Eden Santana could see Miles's drawings, she would know how crude I truly was. I was wasting my life.
I was hopelessly behind and could never catch up.

I heard footsteps out in the supply room. Someone grunted and
a crate fell. I heard Boswell's voice. "Shit. Goddamn." Then another grunt. And then he was walking away. He and Miles were
back from Mainside. I heard Harrelson's voice in the distance, the
words unclear, and a door slamming. Boswell was finished for the
day.

I should have left then, but I was held by the things I saw and
afraid of being spotted sneaking out of the back room. So I waited.
Five minutes. Ten. Miles wasn't coming back. I could stay a while.
I felt the way I used to when I showed up early for a Mass and the
priest wasn't there and I touched all of his garments and the chalice
and the Hosts, running my hands over the forbidden holy objects.
Part of that was defiance; if God existed, then let Him show himself,
let Him strike me dead. Part of it was awe of the beauty of the
objects. I could play at being a priest. In the same mood, I picked
up the tubes of paint. The label said "casein." I opened one, sniffed
it. Almost no smell. Or rather, a milky smell of some kind. Once
I'd walked into the lobby of the Art Students League on 57th Street
to see if they had courses in cartooning and the smell of oil and
turpentine was all through the building. Casein didn't smell like
that. The tins were filled with water, so I knew it must be something
you diluted.

For a moment I thought about picking up a brush and leaving a
mark on the unfinished painting. Let Miles know that somewhere
in the building there was another artist who knew what he was
doing. *Just take one little section,* I thought, *paint a brick into the concrete
wall, make the sun begin to lift over the horizon.* Then thought: *No.*

Don't do that. Suppose someone did that to one of your pictures? And thought: *Go ahead.* I picked up the largest brush and hefted it, surprised at its weight.

And then heard a door clicked shut. Silence. Then footsteps treading lightly down one of the aisles. The footsteps stopped. A grunt. A shuffling sound. And there before me, shocked and a little scared, was Miles Rayfield.

"What in the *fuck* are you doing here?" he said, looking angry and invaded.

"I was wondering what *this* was doing here," I said, waving around the tiny studio. "I moved a crate and here it was."

Miles didn't budge from the narrow passageway beside the wall. His eyes glanced over the paints, pictures, easel. His voice dropped to a whisper:

"Did you tell anybody?"

"No. I replaced the crate to keep it hidden."

"The truth. I have to know."

"Why would I *tell* anybody?"

He stepped into the tiny room, seeming to fill it. He picked up a brush, tapped his thigh with it.

"I could really be in the shit if they found this," he said. "*Deep* shit."

"Only if they find it."

Miles sighed. "That's inevitable. One fine morning, some asshole like Harrelson or Boswell or Jones will move a crate and it'll be all over. They'll arrest me. Arrest the paintings. Send *me* to the goddamned brig and the *pictures* to that fucking *dumpster* you're always guarding . . ." He smiled in a trapped way, then looked at me. "Why *didn't* you tell anybody?"

I struggled to say the words. "Well, I'm kind of an artist, too."

Miles blinked. "We'd better take a walk."

We walked around the base in the fading light. I tried to explain about being a cartoonist and Miles said he thought that if I had any talent at all, that was the way to waste it. I told him I was going to meet a woman the following night and make some drawings and he said he'd like to see them and asked me if she was a nude model and I said I didn't know, she was a woman I knew and he said that was the worst kind of model, because you want to flatter them, make them pretty when they're not. He wished there was a life class somewhere in Pensacola, so he could draw from a model again, but there wasn't 'cause all these goddamned Baptists would raid the place, and I asked him why he didn't have his wife come down and the two of them could live off the base and he could paint in the apartment and use her as a model and he just shook his head and said, No, that wouldn't work.

"She's gone to Jesus," he said, as we headed for the mess hall. "The last thing the goddamned Christians will let you do is see their bodies."

"If she's your wife . . ."

"She'd sit there thinking of spending eternity in the depths of hell."

He shifted then, explaining that casein was make of milk products, and you did dilute it with water. He liked the way casein covered a surface, but it was nowhere as subtle or juicy as oil, and you had to treat the boards, which were called Masonite, with a white primer called gesso. Some artists mixed the primer with a little sand to give it a rough texture; Miles preferred it smooth, using the brush to create textures. He mumbled when I asked him what his picture meant, saying he wasn't really sure. The sailor in the room with the orange obviously thought he was in a jail, with Florida filling the room and crushing him. But he wasn't sure who the old woman was on that country road and didn't much care for the picture.

"It's too simple, too easy," he said. "Those goddamned trees are stolen right out of *Snow White.*"

"What'll you do with it?"

"Burn it," he said. "Or give it to Red Cannon. He'll think it's his mother and love it to death."

I told him I'd bought a newsprint pad and the chalks, and he said newsprint was all right for sketching, but the paper was so frail you couldn't work it, couldn't erase or manipulate the chalk very much. "You've got to be right the first time," he said, "and almost nobody is." We went into the mess hall and sat down with slabs of gray pot roast. "You see, you couldn't *draw* this piece of dead animal," Miles said. "You have to *paint* it. To get the revolting dead color exactly right. If a *man* had this color, you'd rush him to the hospital."

I laughed and he ate slowly, cutting the pieces small, and chewing with the front of his mouth. "Fuel," he murmured, "just think of it as fuel."

There were some books about art that I should read, and he could loan them to me, he said. But if I were *serious,* I had to draw every day. It didn't matter how many books I read or how many pictures I saw in museums. You learned to draw by drawing. Scribble drawings, doodle them, go off and make pictures. And look at everything. "You'd better *feel* something about what you see, too," he said. "If you don't feel anything about your drawings, they'll be as dead as this disgusting pot roast."

After a while, I said: "Could you show me how to make paintings?"

"Sure," Miles said, as I felt myself swelling with new ideas, images, ambitions, and the sense that I'd made a friend and met a master. "If you don't try to teach me about that fucking baseball."

Chapter

30

What Miles Told Me

I BECAME AN ARTIST to keep from going crazy. It was as simple as that. My father killed himself in 1930, leaving my mother to take care of me. I was fourteen months old. We lived in Marietta, Georgia, a boring little suburb just outside of Atlanta, and my father was in the furniture business. I don't remember anything about him. The son of a bitch. After he killed himself, Mother hid all the photographs of him, all his letters, the documents that made up his shitty little life. She put them away in an old steamer trunk that she'd never taken anywhere (poor Mother) and I didn't see them until I was what is laughingly called Grown Up. By then, I could have been looking at pictures of George Washington.

Mother did her best. I give her that. This was the Depression, and it was hard on everyone, I suppose, but even harder in the South. The furniture company was gone before Father died; that's why he died (or so Mother said, telling me about him later, in bits and pieces, and stopping always at the part where she found him in the chair with his thumb in the trigger guard of the shotgun and his face blown off, stopping there until the last time she started the story and then, saying it, telling me, she was rid of it and never told about it again). His relatives stayed away from Mother, afraid, I suppose, that they'd remind her of him, or she would ask for money, or maybe they blamed her in some way, the miserable shits. I just don't know why they stayed away and I don't give a goddamn. The fact is they treated us like lepers. I wish them painful deaths. There's a blur there somewhere. Even now. Mother and I lived in a house where some things were never said.

But we had that house, bought and paid for when Father was alive. He *left her that, paid for when he and the country were riding high. A great gabled house, with porticoes and parquet floors and a piano in the living room and bad pictures hanging everywhere. I always had my own room, and after I started drawing (I was seven and the pictures always showed me with a father and mother, O Sigmund Freud, please do not puke!). Mother outfitted one of the other rooms as a little studio. I had my own table and lots of paper and crayons and watercolors. I would sit up there and draw and listen to Mother downstairs, giving her goddamned piano lessons. When she played, the music was nice. When the others played, I hated it; they couldn't do it right; they were flat or off-key, and this made me draw in the same way, losing whatever it was that I had.*

Mother did more than give piano lessons. She had to, to survive, to feed us both, to heat the house, to keep from losing it to the tax collectors. So she took in sewing too, although I don't know where she went to get it. She certainly didn't pick it up in the neighborhood. Not Mother. She was too proud for that. Right through the Depression, she still had a colored woman come in once a week to clean. A thin bony woman named Mahalia, who would come to the house when Mother was out and play the colored stations on the radio and dance around. Thin as she was, she had the eyes of a fat woman. Just scared hell out of me. Maybe outside every thin woman there's a fat one trying to get in. Those damned eyes were greedy, defiant, alarming. You couldn't make our Mahalia do anything she didn't want to do and once when I used the word nigger to describe someone else, she slapped my face. Good and hard. I cried and cried, not knowing what I'd done, and then knowing, slowly, when our Mahalia said that she was a woman, a person, colored, but not some damned nigger. I was about ten then, and I didn't tell my mother 'cause I knew Mahalia was right. I didn't want Mother taking my side.

Mother kept saying the Depression would be over soon, and then we'd be all right again, but I still don't know what she meant. It didn't matter. The Depression never ended, and all she talked about was how hopeless it was, and how even Franklin Roosevelt and the New Deal couldn't end it. Finally, when I was oh, twelve, she took a job in a restaurant. With a pink uniform. Five nights a week. I knew she thought this was a comedown, but she never talked about it; it was as if the humiliation wouldn't be real if she didn't mention it. She supported us with the waitress job and the sewing and the piano lessons, although as the Depression went on and on, fewer and fewer little bastards came over to assault the piano. That was good news to me, but terrible for Mother. She even thought it was an aesthetic judgment of some goddamned kind.

She took that waitress job because of me. She was convinced that I had talent, thought I was the greatest artist since Leonardo, or at least since Norman Rockwell. She saved all my drawings and made me date them and framed some of them. She bought me supplies. Nothing was too good for her darling little Miles. And then she enrolled me at the Art Institute in Atlanta, in the kiddie class every Saturday morning. She had to come up with bus money and charcoal and paint money and lunch money. That's why she started waiting on tables, just telling them at the restaurant (which I never saw, another mystery to be imagined and not touched, smelled, felt or seen) that she could work any day except Saturday.

All through this time, I started to feel odd. Out of it. Weird. You know how I feel about baseball. Well, even then, a kid, I didn't care for the game, never learned it, never played it with the other kids. I don't know why. Maybe it was timing. The summer I got scarlet fever, I had to stay home while the other boys were learning and by the time I could go out to the street again, I was already behind. Also, I felt strange, ugly even, with this damned big head, and I couldn't throw right or something . . . So I decided I didn't like the game. But I knew I was ahead in at least one goddamned thing and that was drawing. I had that, and the others didn't. So when football season came around, I felt the same way as I did about baseball. The same for swimming, too. Mother kept telling me that all the public swimming pools were just filthy breeding grounds for polio, and in some ways she was right. And she warned me that if I played football, I could break my drawing hand, my arm, my shoulder. I wouldn't be able to do this . . . thing, this magic thing. This thing of putting marks on paper that made human beings and places and light come to life. She was afraid for me and I was afraid of her being afraid so I never learned any sport. I don't know how they're played or how I'm supposed to watch them. Maybe you're right. Maybe that's very sad. But I don't care. I don't miss sports at all. They're of no interest to me.

But I did grow up feeling very strange. No father. No sports. No friends. And this mother who lived to feed me and please me and guide me, this mother who kept a big drafty house just for the two of us.

That Saturday art class changed everything. For the first time I met people who were something like me. The school was a community of oddballs, loners, kids who stayed home to draw instead of throwing rocks at buses or putting pennies on railroad tracks like every American kid is supposed to do. They were from all over the city and some of them had parents who were divorced and one had a father who was dead and another a father who'd just disappeared. We began to feel that people who didn't make art or have screwed-up families were the real odd ones in this world.

*My mother slaved to help me. You know all those clichés about wearing
your fingers to the bone? They were true about Mother. The most expensive
things were art books. They still are. But our public library was truly rotten,
because good art books always have nudes in them and the goddamned
ignorant Baptist idiots wouldn't allow nudes to be shown in a public place.
Afraid the whole male population of Marietta would whack themselves into
a coma. So Mother bought the books for me. There was hardly a week when
she didn't come home with at least one book or an art magazine. Always
on payday. I used to get excited when I woke up on a Friday morning
wondering what she'd bring me that night. I suppose when most boys my
age were reading the sports pages or comic books, I was reading Walter Pater
and the journals of Eugène Delacroix and books about Rubens and Leonardo and Degas. I was copying pictures from these books, trying to discover
how they had done what they did. And I was drunk on books about
Bohemias. Dreaming about the Left Bank in Paris and Greenwich Village
in New York and garrets everywhere. I wanted to leave the town of
Marietta, the state of Georgia, the whole goddamned backward South, and
join the real artists in some country of art.*

*When I graduated from high school, I went right into the Art Institute.
By then, Mother had saved some money, don't ask me how. I guess the war
changed it. I guess the damned Japanese ended the Depression when they
bombed Pearl Harbor. During the war, Mother became the most unlikely
goddamned Rosie the Riveter in America, but she did it, working at the
Glenn L. Martin plant in Marietta, her hair tied up in a kerchief. When
the war ended she was hysterical for days. At first I thought it was just
panic, that she was terrified that she was going to lose her job and the
Depression would come back with all its goddamned horrors. But it wasn't
that at all. Mother had learned that the Enola Gay was built by Martin
and so she was sure she'd helped drop The Bomb on Hiroshima. It was as
if she'd killed every one of those people, just by slamming a rivet into a tail
section. She cried about taking blood money. She told me that now everything
would be different, that The Bomb was something new in the world. And
then she cried again.*

*But she saved a lot of the blood money, and when I was ready to go to
art school full time she had enough for all the extra expenses. I was doing
oils, tempera, learning about casein and gouache, and all of that cost a lot.
There were some amazing students there, and plenty of fakers, too. Abstract
Expressionism had just been given its name, with a big glossy spread in* Life
*magazine, and every second painter was talking about space and the picture
plane and trying to paint like Jackson Pollock or Franz Kline. I went my
own way. I liked faces, bodies, mood, weather, atmosphere. I loved drawing,*

not dripping. Maybe I was just afraid to take risks. But I kept going, doing it the older way. It was strange to be out of fashion at eighteen. Still, it was the South; they didn't really care about all this newfangled stuff from New York. So I had my first show in June of 1950, while I was a junior at the Institute. At a small gallery in Marietta. The pictures were still hanging when the war started in Korea. I was terrified. And furious. I'd grown up believing that World War II would be the last war in the history of the world. Or at least the last American war. I really believed all that crap. And here on this lovely summer day, with my whole life ahead of me, another war had started. In some goddamned place called Korea. Men were dying again, and soon it would be my turn too.

That changed everything, I knew it, and I cried myself to sleep that night in late June when the war began. I felt such a goddamned fool. I'd tried to plan my life. The Depression was over, the war was over, and now we'd have peace forever and live like human beings again. I had it all in the plan. I even wrote it down: art school, then Paris for a year or two, then on to Florence, to embrace the work of the Renaissance masters, learning their secrets. I'd get brown in the sun of Rome. Then, around 1962, I'd return in triumph to the Village and the New York galleries and see my pictures in the museums and the art magazines . . . I had a plan. Only a stupid romantic fool ever does that.

By winter, men were dying by the thousands and I was ready to be drafted. I started to think about the Navy. I'm not sure why. Probably from looking at all those paintings by Winslow Homer and Turner. Once the notion got into my head, I couldn't leave it alone. I would lie awake in Marietta, and hear my mother playing the piano (for herself now, the students gone, the money not a problem) and start creating seascapes in my mind. Out at sea, on the bridge of some sleek ship, I would examine the architecture of waves. I would memorize the tones and colors of the sky. Miles Rayfield: on the deck of a great ship.

But it wasn't just fear of the infantry and the Yalu that pushed me to the Navy. There were other things going on. Some trouble with people at school. And my wife. The details are none of your goddamned business. But one morning I joined the Navy, thinking that it was better than the infantry. Thinking it would get me out of the goddamned South. Thinking I would end up on the bridge of that great ship. It was the stupidest fucking thing I ever did. Now I paint like a pack rat. Hiding in a dark hole. I don't think I'll ever see the sun of Rome.

Chapter
31

ABOUT FOUR O'CLOCK that afternoon, it started to rain. The sky darkened, all helicopters were grounded. I wrapped my pad and the chalks in some butcher paper and sealed the package with masking tape, and then hitched a ride to the locker club with Larry Parsons. He was big and blond and friendless; he was married and lived off the base and seemed always to be about three beats behind everybody else.

"Where you going with the package?" he said.

"A friend's house."

"You have *friends* down here?"

"Sure, don't you?"

"Well, yeah, I guess I do," he said, in a puzzled way. "To tell the truth, my wife has more friends than I do. She's real active in the church, so there's always something doing. Baking contests and clambakes and stuff like that."

"Sounds great," I said, and hurried away from him when he stopped at the locker club. I changed clothes quickly and combed my hair in front of the mirror above the sink. I waited inside the door, watching the rain come in from the Gulf in great slanting sheets. Across the highway, Billy's neon sign seemed to sizzle. *Eden Santana.* I started rehearsing what I would say to her and what I would do. And then cut myself off. I couldn't come to her with a lot of rehearsed lines and moves. She'd know. She'd been around longer than I had and she was just too damned smart for me to play-act with her. I remember thinking then about drawing, and how it might make her just an object of my skill, and therefore less scary and unpredictable. I think Miles had shown me how to use the side of the chalk to create form and volume, how to lay out the figure. But I'm really not sure. Had he told me those things before I went to meet Eden? Or was it after? Now: years later: sitting in a parked car, watching the sky darken and older trees heaving and settling in a wet Gulf wind: am I remembering the feeling of that young man standing inside the locker club, or am I inventing him?

There was a sudden honk. Of that I'm certain. I peered out through the rain, and Eden Santana was waving at me through the steamy windows of the Ford. That sight of her still thrills me. She had kept her word. I held the pad close to my body and ran through the spattering mud.

"I didn't really expect you to be here," she said, smiling as she opened the door. "This kind of weather . . . But I decided to come on by anyways. No way to call you. No way for you to call me."

"I'm glad you came."

She drove up onto the highway, heading away from the city. It was hard to see. Out beyond the city limits there were no lights on the road and the car's high beams seemed to bounce off the rain. The Ford's engine coughed, stammered, but kept going. Eden was smoking hard, and in the gray light her face looked tired. She was wearing the black turtleneck she'd worn in the bus on New Year's Eve.

"My hair must look like I stuck a finger in an electric socket," she said, and glanced at me and smiled. When she smiled, she didn't look tired. Her hair was all wiry and curly.

"It looks great."

"I always wanted hair like that actress? Lizabeth Scott? Know her? Hair like that. But I guess I lost the hair lottery and there's nothing' I can do about it. And when it rains, this damned hair shoots all over the place. Doesn't matter if I cut it long or short. It just ups and shoots off my head."

She laughed (and now I hear the nervous trill in her).

"Dumbest damn thing," she said. *"Hair."*

We crossed a bridge over a dark river and then she made a right and the car started kicking up gravel and we were between trees on a one-lane road. The car jerked, rose, fell, slowed, spun its wheels, then moved again, Eden Santana setting her mouth grimly, her hands tight on the wheel. "Son of a bitch," she said. "Son of a goddamn bitch." Then glanced at me and said, "Sorry." And pulled into a cleared place, with tall trees rising high about us. "I'll get as close as I can," she said, pulling around to the left, then jerking gears, backing up. "This is the best we can do."

She turned off the engine, and I could see better now. We were in front of a long house trailer. The body of the trailer was blue, the trim silver. Flowers sprouted in pots out front, bending under the rain.

"Come on," she said, "we'll make a run for it."

She ran through the mud to the trailer, the Sears jacket over her head, stood on a step and unlocked the door. We went in, and she reached behind me to slam it shut, then turned the lock and flicked on a light.

"It's not much," she said, "but it's cozy."

There were flowers everywhere: in dirt-filled earthen pots, in ceramic jars, in glass milk bottles filled with water. They were on the counter beside the sink, and on top of the small regrigerator and on the window shelves, pressed against drawn blinds. There were geraniums in a jar on top of a small table that jutted out from the wall. The smell in the trailer was sweet and close, full of the rain.

"Some sailor bought the trailer after the war and then got sent to sea duty when Korea happened and he's been rentin' it out ever since," she said. "Only thirty-five dollars a month. They wanted more but I got it cheap 'cause this is, well, mostly a colored neighborhood out here." I felt thick, large, as I watched her take a hanger from a shallow closet, slip the wet Sears jacket on it, then carry it into a small john and hang it up to dry. I thought *If I try to help, if I dare to move, I will knock down a flowerpot and make a mess.*

"Hey, almost forgot . . ."

She turned a knob on the gas stove and moved a fat iron pot over the low flame.

"Made some gumbo for you last night," she said. "Thought you might be hungry for some good home cookin', after all that Navy stuff. Gumbo's always best the second night."

She looked at me awkwardly, and that relieved me; she was probably feeling as clumsy in her way as I was in mine. Then she excused herself and went into the bathroom. I stood there, waiting, uncertain; all I could hear was the rain drumming on the roof—a steady, lulling sound that was mixed with the drowsy odor of the flowers. I ran my hands through my hair, trying to make it stand up (I see that boy now, hair pasted to his skull, dripping, without

sideburns or a beard, entering for the first time this special world).
She came back from the bathroom and motioned me into a chair.
Then she went to the small refrigerator and took out lettuce, onions, and tomatoes and started making a salad, her hands quick and
strong, pulling the lettuce leaves apart, slicing the tomatoes, adding
oil, vinegar, salt. She popped two slices of whole-wheat bread into
a toaster. Her hands never stopped moving, and she talked briskly,
even nervously (thus relaxing me more), now tossing the salad,
then stirring the gumbo, while I looked at her bare feet.

She was smaller than I had first thought, and she had wide feet.
I felt vaguely aroused by the padding sound they made on the
linoleum floor. She fired questions at me, quickly, breathlessly,
making me talk. She wanted to know where I went to school and
what my parents were like and the names of my brothers; she was
sorry about my mother. She seemed pleased that I was brought up
a Catholic ("They sure do have beautiful music . . ."). She ladled
the gumbo into white bowls, and the aroma was pungent, strong,
thick with crab and shrimp and rice, and she pushed the toast down
into the toaster and brought the salad to me on a plate, then did
the same for herself. I waited until she sat down facing me and then
began to eat in a greedy way. "Don't use salt, child," she said.
"Everything's salted. And besides, I noticed you use too much salt
anyway."

She had been watching and found a flaw; *you use too much salt
anyway.* I'd never thought about salt before; I just used it, on eggs
and meat and salad. I slowed down, glancing at her, trying to match
her movements; I didn't know much about what was then called
etiquette. At home, it didn't matter how I used knives and forks;
in the Navy they had too many other rules and regulations to inflict
upon us first. So I decided to follow her lead. I watched the way
she ate the gumbo. I didn't touch the salt. Somehow a faint odor
of her perfume got mixed in with the fragrance of the soup, and
the trailer turned all female and closed and lovely, the flower scents
filling the air too and the rain hammering at the roof. She wanted
to know about New York, and whether there really was a chance
there for everybody to make good. I tried to answer, tried to sound
casual; I didn't tell her that I'd only been to two Broadway plays
in my life, that Brooklyn was different from Manhattan, and that I
didn't know what chance anybody had to make good, since it hadn't
happened to anyone I knew. Including me. Instead, I started talking

about the Paramount and the Metropolitan Museum and Lindy's and Toots Shor's, places I'd read about in Walter Winchell's column in the *Mirror* or heard about on the radio. She listened to my vaguely fraudulent answers and asked more questions, and all the time I was thinking about what would happen if she posed for me, and when I should begin the session by taking the drawing pad out of its wrapper. I wanted the meal to last for hours so I wouldn't have to deal with the next move and its astonishments.

"I guess New York has just about everything you'd ever want to see," I heard myself saying. "Everything."

"Well, not *everything,*" she said. "I'd like to see the pyramids in Egypt."

"Yeah?"

"Wouldn't you?" she said. "Imagine what it would be like to see where they found King Tut and all his treasures. See the Spinx." That's how she said it: The Spinx. She wiped her mouth with a napkin. "You know, I'd like to see *all* the Seven Wonders of the World. *All of them!*" She paused. "I guess that's pretty far-fetched. But I saw them in an encyclopedia once, all the Seven Wonders, and I couldn't even name them now. But I could read up on them again, make a list, and even if I never saw them, I sure would like to dream about them . . ."

Do I see the boy relaxing at last? Michael Devlin has eaten, he is full, he has avoided all additional use of salt. And listening to her he thinks: *She isn't that much older that I am, is she?* There she was in the trailer, talking *straight* to me, not performing on some date, not angling for some extravagant trip to a prom, certainly not trying to look like a movie star. She pushed her chair back, relaxed, crossed one leg over another, lit a cigarette.

And I had discovered I could hold my own with her in conversation. She was older than I was, but I was sure there were things I knew that she didn't. I couldn't name the Seven Wonders of the World either, but I felt as she talked about them that I was sitting with someone my own age, the two of us in awe at the unknowable mysteries of the world. She got up and made coffee and then I started feeling nervous again. She cleared the table, laid her cigarette in an ashtray and ran hot water over the dishes, her face very concentrated. She dried her hands on a dish towel and waited a long moment, her back to me, staring into the sink. Then she took a deep breath, exhaled, turned to me and smiled.

"Well, I guess I'd better get ready for the posing," she said.

"Good," I said, and reached for the package. "I have my stuff." Panicking. "But you know, if you're too tired or something, you don't—"

"I never done something like this in my life before," she said quietly. She turned and looked around the small crowded trailer, at the couchlike bed at the far end. "That's why I want to do it."

"Look," I said nervously, "if you don't want to—"

"You're more nervous than I am, ain't you, child?"

"Well, no, I just—"

"You ever done this before? The truth . . ."

"No."

"Then I guess we both better go ahead, huh?"

She turned then, padding on her wide bare feet into the bedroom area. She closed the drapes behind her. I took out the pad and chalks and laid them on top of the counter that separated the dining area from the sleeping quarters. I had to dry my hands on my trousers. The rain hammered down and the air felt wetter and thicker. I thought: *We're using all the oxygen, we should open a window.* Better: *We should leave. We might smother. I can do this some other time. Suppose I can't draw her? I could freeze, could lose what I think I can do, could botch it, could be exposed as a fraud. Before I even got to really know her,* she could find me out. *I certainly couldn't draw her the way Miles could. But then, what* does *she look like? If I. If she. What if.*

The curtain parted. She stepped out in an oversized man's shirt. Her hair was wild and electric. She looked at me and her face darkened into a blush. She covered one foot with the other, and suddenly seemed very young.

"What do you want me to do?" she murmured.

"Well, maybe—why don't you just sit there on the couch, and I'll move this stool over here, and—You want your cigarettes?"

"No, I don't want to smoke while I'm—how's this?"

She sat on the couch bed, and pulled a couple of pillows up beside her and leaned one arm on them.

"Great, yeah, that's it, nice and relaxed."

"Should I take this off?"

Cool, said Michael Devlin to himself. *You've gotta be cool. Like Doagie Hogan, like Canyon or Sawyer, like Charlie Parker. It's like drawing bottles or fruit or a mountain.* And answered, staring at the chalk, its blackness on his thumb and forefinger: "If you want."

She unbuttoned the shirt and wiggled out of the sleeves and let it fall behind her. *There it is, skin and tits, flesh and nipples and hair, her body before me.* She crossed her arms over her breasts for a moment, almost instinctively. Then she lifted one leg and let the other dangle off the edge of the bed and shrugged her shoulders as if loosening her muscles. "There," she said. *No panties bra garterbelts girdles no slip no dress no trousers just her before me in this small tight place and the rain and the flowers too.* "That should be okay."

I stopped breathing. I didn't want to exhale, to let her hear me reacting to her nakedness, her lush woman's body. O Catholic boy: as if it were all right to take pleasure as long as it was not expressed. This was no boyish angular body like that of the girls at home (touched smelled brushed against but never feasted upon), or the body of a fashion model in some magazine, with all her bones sticking out. *Womenflesh.* I started to draw almost frantically, blocking in the ripe breasts, the strong lean shoulders, trying to get the taut skin stretched properly across her belly. Her breasts and hips were much lighter than the rest of her body. Except, of course, for her nipples. Face skin and back skin and leg skin and arm skin had been glazed by the sun. But now I was seeing clearly what I'd only glimpsed that night on the beach: the lighter skin, the indoor skin. She had a thick mat of jet-black curly pubic hair, curlier than the hair on her head, glistening in the light as if it were wet. *Look boy look at her pussy her box her snatch her cunt.* I was trying desperately to keep from getting an erection. Seven heads, I told my hand. Get the head right and the proportions will follow. Don't make a big deal out of her breasts or she'll think you're obsessed with them. *Jesus Christ her tits right here right there.* Those full round breasts, with their dark-brown nipples. Get the legs right. Make it right. Make it beautiful. The arc of her instep. The long curving neck.

She was looking at me calmly now, the blush off her cheeks, watching me in a fascinated way. I used the vine charcoal for all the basics: the shape, the form, a thin outline. It broke three times in my hand, too frail for my ferocious pressure. Then I switched to the blacker charcoal, making her eyes, using the side of the chalk for shading, digging in for the black hair on her head and between her legs. I smoothed out the hard edges with my fingers, smeared her legs to try to get flesh tones, and then, looking at her, and looking at the drawing, I saw there was nothing more to add. One more mark and I would botch it. I tore the drawing off the pad and laid it on the kitchen counter.

"You can change positions," I said, trying to sound like a cool-

eyed professional. I was relieved that she didn't ask to see the first
drawing. She shifted, letting one leg fall flat, her back against the
wall of the trailer now. She shivered. "Damn wall's cold," she said.
"How's this?" She put her head back. I could see a thin scar about
three inches long under her jaw. White against her dark skin. There
was another scar just above the great black V, smaller but more raw
that the one on her jawbone. "Fine," I said, but thinking that this
time she was posing instead of being natural, as if remembering
pinups she'd seen somewhere; still, I was afraid that if I said I didn't
like the pose, she'd take it as criticism, the way I reacted to her line
about salt. Ah, the little lies . . . "Just swell," I said, and she closed
her eyes. I drew more carefully. She had very long lashes.

"What are you drawing now?" she whispered, her eyes still
closed.

"Your neck," I said.

She ran a hand down her neck as I was shading the same place
in my drawing.

"And now?"

"Your clavicle," I said. "You know, at the base of your neck?
Goes across from shoulder to shoulder."

She ran a single finger along the clavicle. Then paused.

She was breathing in a different way. Her eyes were still closed.

"What about now?" she whispered.

"Breasts."

She ran her hand around her breasts, from one to the other,
feeling their shape and form, caressing them as if they belonged to
someone else. Then she took both nipples gently between her
thumbs and forefingers. I tried to draw. Getting hard.

"And?"

"Belly."

Her hand moved over her belly, eyes closed tight, examining the
hard pads of muscle, the concave dip. And then she pressed the heel
of her hand above the blackness.

"You better get over here, child."

She guided me into the tight wet channel, the light off now, the
rain pounding down, arms around my back, squeezing my cock
inside her. "Don't move," she whispered. And squeezed again, as
if wanting to remember the feel of it, its size and thickness and
pulsing presence. I was afraid to move, and then she moved, press-

ing against me, and I moved, six, eight times, all the way into the tight emptiness, and once more, and then exploded, shuddering, a hoarse involuntary cry coming from me, with Eden Santana holding me tight and squeezing me, and pushing hard against me until I was done. I eased away from her, feeling the fool. A crude kid who couldn't hold it back. A boy who shot his load faster than a man ever would. But she held my head in her hands and kissed me on the mouth and whispered "You're so big." And told me "You're so strong." And kissed me again and then slipped away and went into the bathroom. Water ran. I couldn't believe I was there. This wasn't Dixie with her savage old eyes and hungry mouth. This was Eden Santana. Who was beautiful. And then she was back with a hot washcloth, bathing my cock and my balls, the hotness of the cloth like a second cunt. We lay there side by side for a long time, her arms around me, saying nothing, the flower smell very strong and the rain falling. And after a while she turned my head to hers and kissed me again and then I felt her hand lightly on my chest and she pinched my nipples, little stabbing pinpoints of pain, and she touched my flat belly and then my cock and I was hard again and the rain still falling. She lay on her side with one knee raised and delicately rubbed the head of my cock against the lips of her cunt, her breath coming in short quickening gasps, and then she whispered, "Now" and I was in her again and her body was convulsing and I drove into her and she moaned and I rammed harder and she groaned deeply and then her voice was rising with the rain still falling and she dug her fingers into my ass, kissing me wetly, rubbing her tongue on my face and eyes, making panting sounds and then a long high-pitched sound and still I kept going, driving away into her, her legs up high now, the wide feet flat against the low roof of the trailer and I kept going and going and going until everything in me exploded and convulsed and I could feel each part of myself bone muscle fiber blood plunging down and out of me and she screamed one last triumphant time while the rain still fell through the dark sky.

She dressed quietly, pulling on high rubber fishing boots and a yellow slicker. I looked at her, wishing I'd drawn more, knowing now what was beneath the clothes and thrilled by the private knowledge but wishing I had a record. I liked her in clothes too, tossing her hair, about to plunge again into the storm to drive me back to the locker club. She turned to me and smiled. *What do you think of me now woman tell the truth did I fuck you well or are you just being polite tell me tell me now tonight not tomorrow.* Her face seemed to glow in the soft light.

"We better hurry, child," she said hoarsely. "You'll be late."

She opened the door and the wind blew it shut again. I pushed against it, held it open. The rain was still falling in sheets, hurling itself loudly at the trees and echoing off unseen water. "That's a lake out there," she said, pointing at the darkness behind the trailer. "Little bitty lake, almost a pond, so small it don't have a name . . . Runs into the River Styx, if you could believe that name."

We dashed to the car, slamming the trailer door behind us. I got in on the passenger side and she slipped behind the wheel, dripping with rain. *Go ahead ask her how was it how was the fuck the second fuck not the first one ask ask.* She started the car.

"The River Styx?" I said (making talk instead of the real talk). "Isn't that the river of death?"

"In Egypt, maybe," she said, "Or Greece, but not in the god-damned Florida Panhandle. That's for damn sure. I figure they just didn't know how to spell sticks. S-t-i-c-k-s. That's the way they should of named it, cause this is where we are. Out in the damn *sticks.*"

She laughed hard and it was tough for me to imagine her doing all these things, running to the car, starting it, getting the wind-shields wiping, joking about the River Styx, after what we'd done in the trailer. She behaved as if we'd just left a movie. But I felt different. Not just in my teeming head. I felt as if my body was heavier and lighter at the same time, as if my skin had been stripped off and replaced, as if I was twenty years older and had just been born. All at once. There was no sign of any such extravagant change on her face, but in the tight, packed air of the car there was one difference and I couldn't define it.

"I smell like sex, don't I?" she said, and smiled. She must have sensed my awareness and how little I knew. Certainly she told me what it was in the car. "Haven't smelled this way in a long, long time."

And (Michael you dumbass kid you former virgin you schmuck) I thought: *Who made you smell this way last time? And where? And when? Husband lover sailor Mercado bus driver friend who?* But said: "It's a good beautiful smell."

And believed it.

"I'm glad you think so."

Now she was bumping up and down over the gravel road, the wheels spinning, the high beams trying to penetrate the driving rain. And then I saw a black man on the corner, before we turned out to the highway. He was under a tree, holding an umbrella. It was Bobby Bolden.

"Wait," I said. "Pull over. That's a guy from the base. Guy I know."

She paused, as if thinking this over. Then sighed: "Okay." And pulled across the highway onto the shoulder and waited. She rolled down the window. "He's gonna *know* what we been doin', child."

But it was too late. Bolden came over, slowly and carefully, looking at the car, peering at us. "Prob'ly thinks we're the damn Klan," she said. "Come *on,* man."

Then Bolden saw my face and nodded and began to fold the umbrella while I opened the back door.

"Thanks," he said, getting in.

"She's droppin' us at the locker club," I said. "After that, we're on our own."

"Just change your clothes fast, I'll drive to the gate," Eden said. "Otherwise you'll turn into pumpkins."

"Okay," Bobby said.

We drove to the locker club in silence, Eden Santana leaning over the wheel, squinting into the rain. She pulled around in front of the club and Bolden and I jumped out. In the club, I remembered: *I left the goddamned pad and the chalks in the trailer.* That meant I couldn't show the drawings to Miles. And thought: *Just as well.* They were probably terrible. And I didn't want anyone asking who the woman was. None of them. This was secret. Mine. Private. In the small tight trailer with the rain and the flowers. I pulled on my whites, hung up the civvies. Bolden was already waiting inside the door in uniform.

"Sure you want this?" he said.

"Want what?"

"Some fuckin' cracker jarhead libel to hassle our asses. Woman like that drivin' a black man home."

"Come on."

She drove us to the gate. Bolden got out first and hurried into the gatehouse. It was a minute to midnight.

"When can I see you again?" I said quickly.

"I don't know."

"What do you mean?"

"I gotta think about this, child. What happened tonight, well, it happened. But—"

"Saturday," I said. "Please. We can talk about it then. I got about a minute left and then I'm AWOL. Please . . ."

"Sunday," she said. There was doubt in her face but she squeezed my hand. "Ten in the morning. We'll have us a picnic."

I kissed her on the cheek and sprinted to the gate, showed my Liberty Pass to the guard. He glanced at the clock.

"Playin' it fine, ain't you, sailor?"

"Yeah," I said.

Bolden came over.

"The man's here, jarhead," he said. "He don't need no lectures from you."

He took my elbow and opened the umbrella and we hurried into the rain, heading for the barracks. I glanced back and saw Eden's taillights stopped at the highway. Going home. Bolden looked at me and shook his head.

"You are a sly motherfucker, boy," he said.

Chapter

32

THAT NIGHT, WITH the world sleeping under the Gulf rain, Bobby Bolden took me to the Negro barracks above the mess hall, the great long room that they all called the Kingdom of Darkness. At the near end, inside the door, there were tables and chairs and a four-burner gas stove, pots and pans and dishes and a refrigerator. The bunks and lockers were at the other end. The room was crowded with black sailors and a few Filipinos and loud with music. The close, humid air smelled of frying bacon. Bolden explained that the messcooks had keys to the galley and the food lockers and did their own cooking upstairs. "They work when everyone else eats," he said, "so they get to eat whenever they want to. Like now."

There were heavy blackout shades on all the windows and weather stripping on the doors to keep the sound from flying around the base. A big noisy air conditioner filled one window. ("They chipped in f'that," Bolden said. "Sounds like a C-47, don't it?") When I walked in, Freddie Harada looked up from a book and waved hello and went back to his reading (the Philippines only four years into independence and the Huks fighting in the mountains of Luzon while the Navy still treated them like colonial subjects, fit only to be messcooks or valets). Then Bobby Bolden introduced me to the others; there were a lot of oh-yeahs, heard-'bout-yous, so Bolden must have prepared them. I wondered what he'd said about me: The ofay that thinks he knows music, the white boy from New York, the storekeeper with the fresh mouth. But it couldn't have been too bad. They smiled as we shook hands and I tried to use a

mental shorthand, matching physical things against names so if I got
the names mixed up they wouldn't think I believed all Negroes
looked alike.

So here was Tampa (red hair, thin arms, a swell of belly) and
Lightnin' (lone gold tooth, short, muscular, trim) and Rhode Island
Freddie (big and fat with processed hair and a pencil moustache)
and Bumper (thin lips and horn-rimmed glasses) and Little Elroy
(bald, huge, a tattoo of a nude woman on his coffee-colored chest).
Others were sleeping, drifting around the bunks or out on the
town, but this was the basic crew in the Kingdom of Darkness. On
that night, as on all the others that followed, Rhode Island Freddie
was doing the cooking, his T-shirt very white against his skin, and
the others resembled football players in a locker room before a
game, jiving, shouting, saying terrible things about one another's
mothers and moving, consciously or not, and sometimes sitting
down, to the music. A singer named Lloyd Price was calling:

> *Lawdy lawdy lawdy*
> *Miz Clawdy . . .*

And they were singing the chorus with him while I was handed
a beer and a plate of bacon and eggs—I no longer felt gorged with
gumbo; emptied, in fact, by what happened after—and Freddie
Harada came down to me and asked how I was feeling and I said
great, great (the smell of sex on me too, but nobody here knew
except Bolden) and Rhode Island Freddie asked me did I ever go
to Minton's Playhouse in Harlem and I said no, never been there,
wasn't old enough, but I'd hung out on 52d Street, I'd heard Tatum
play piano through the open doors of the Club Ibis and saw Billie
Holiday once coming out of a limousine (with a white guy, but I
didn't say that) and then I looked up and Bobby Bolden was taking
his horn out of its case and Rhode Island Freddie said, *Here we go.*

Bolden blew honking comments on the Lloyd Price tune (which
they played again and then again), making dirty sounds in the lower
register, his tone fat and sweaty, everybody singing now, and
Bolden playing in and out of the words, *Lawdy lawdy lawdy, Miss
Clawdy* and the record falling again on the thick plug of a 45-rpm
player and I finished the beer and someone handed me another one
and then the music changed and it was Fats Domino singing *Goin
home tomorrow. Can't stand your evil ways . . . Goin home, tomorrow,*

Can't stand your evil ways . . . (no picture of him in my head, 'cause this was the time of Patti Page and Joni James and Jo Stafford and Johnnie Ray, the last year of Tin Pan Alley, the last year of white-bread American music, the last year before rock 'n' roll) and then the guy named Bumper said this was *some* song, black man up north working in some *factory,* tired of all the *bullshit,* wants to come home to the *South.* And Little Elroy laughed and said, "Shit, Bum-puh, I tho't this was about the muthafuckin *Navy!*"

While Bobby Bolden played on.

They kept drinking and eating and making a hundred little moves to the music. There was a record called "She Aint Got No Hair" by a group called Professor Longhair and the Shufflin Hungarians ("He puttin on the world, man," said Tampa. "Fess ain't no fuckin Hungarian, he just a nigger lak us") and a tune by Roy Brown and his Mighty Mighty Men called "Good Rockin' Tonight" and another one, same guy, "Cadillac Baby," and a sad, wailing, heartbroken song called "Trouble at Midnight." I remember feeling instantly changed, the way I'd felt with Eden in the trailer; I was one Michael Devlin before and another Michael Devlin afterward. I'd never heard this music before; it was all about balling, drinking and fucking up and it worked off a back beat of some kind, not 4/4 time or the kinds of mixed tempos the bebop-pers played on Symphony Sid. "Don't Roll Them Bloodshot Eyes at Me" another guy was shouting (Wynonie Harris, but I didn't know that then), while Bobby Bolden honked, and I opened another beer, feeling like I'd been granted a passport into a different world. Someone brought a steak to Bobby Bolden and he stopped playing. He saw me sitting on the edge of a bunk and came over. The music was thinner without his horn.

He watched Tampa doing a tight, intricate series of steps to an up-tempo honking shouter. I told him I liked the music.

"It sure ain't Ben Webster, but, you know, it's *alive,* man. Party music. Fuck music. Right outta the blues, with a little sound of the church in there too. You gotta hear it in a club. Like in Biloxi, or a place like Macon. Or the Dew Drop Inn over New Orleans . . . Go to some black joints. Drink some corn likker. Smoke some reefer. Then you really hear it. These records, they don't get it right. Sound like they playin' in a field. No bottom. No breath. No *feel* . . ."

He leaned back, looking drowsy and satisfied. Fats Domino was

playing again. I was trying to absorb what he was saying, to understand it, above all, to remember. And I felt cut off from other parts
of my life. Eden. The Navy.

"What'd Red Cannon do if he walked in here?"

"He don't come here."

"Why not?"

"Cause we'd eat the mothafucka."

He laughed.

"I'd pay to see that," I said.

"Don't take his shit," Bobby Bolden said.

"It's not his shit I worry about. It's the Navy's shit."

"Don't take that either."

He was finished eating. Then he faced me, while the music
pounded.

"How come you picked me up out there in the boondocks?"

"You were standing in the rain, man."

"So what? You in a car drove by a woman and you pick up a black
man . . . Could get yissef killed."

"From what I hear, you could get yourself killed any night of the
week."

He was suddenly suspicious. "Who you hear that from?"

"You know, the general gouge around the base."

"What they say, exactly?"

"I don't know exactly. Just Bobby Bolden got himself a white
woman . . ."

"You mean, that *nigger* Bobby Bolden got a white woman," he
said, his voice hardening.

"I didn't hear it put that way."

"Then you ain't hearin' too good, boy."

"Let's make a deal," I said with some heat. "You don't call *me*
boy and I won't call *you* boy."

He looked at me as if he were going to strike me. And then he
laughed.

"You got a mouth."

"That's what Red Cannon says."

"Okay, man. I hear you."

Chapter

33

What Bobby Bolden Told Me

I'M FROM NAPTOWN, *up north, Indianapolis, where we got all the seasons, includin winter. I grew up shoveling snow, sleighridin, slidin on trashcan covers down hills; just like a million other kids; just like you. But I love the South, spite of all the cracker bullshit, cause it's hot. In the summer here, it's so hot you can't breathe. You see snow here every forty years, they say, and that's all right with me. I don't even like seein* pictures *of snow, I don't even like ice in a drink anymore. I see snow now, I go to bed. When the snow's gone, I rise from the dead. And that goes back to Korea. Everything goes back to Korea.*

But shit, I'm gettin ahead of myself here. You want to know who I am and I talk about snow. Maybe Korea scrambled my brains. Maybe lots of things scramble your brains, though women do the best job of all.

Anyway, back home in Naptown we dint think much about color. Up to the war, the big *war, we lived pretty integrated. They was white kids on my street. I played with them, they played with me. Played in the school band with white kids too. Trumpet then. The attitude was, you got red hair, I got black skin, so what? Then it start to change. Dune the war, lots more black people start comin up from the South, to work in the war jobs. They just wasn't any new housin being built and black folks start doublin up in the black houses and then the whites start to move away. They never did say why, although my daddy said it was simple, that it was all right when they was more of them than they was of us, but when it started bein more of* us *than they was of* them, *they decided to move on outta there. And then the shit started. Little shit. Like we got our textbooks all marked up,* used *textbooks, while the white schools, they got them new. We cuddin get the streets fixed, the sewers, that kind of shit. Without even knowin how it happened, we ended up in a ghetto, except for a few real old white people that cuddin move.*

So I start to thinkin about going away. I was the oldest of the kids, seventeen and a senior in high school, but I had a cousin, Charlie Neal his name was. And he was messcookin in the Navy and I liked the way he looked on leave, all sharp and shit, and one night at a party, I toked to him about joinin up. This was just after the war, '47, '48, and I was listenin to all the players on the radio and thinkin, Hey, man, I could go to New York and try and play at Minton's with like, Bird and Dizzy, or I could go in the Navy and get the GI Bill and really learn the instrument, learn harmony and composition, become a great fuckin musician. I had to make up my mind. Just go for it, you know, go try to play with all these monsters in the Apple, which scairt me shitless. Or really prepare myself. Only way I could afford music school was the Bill. But when I thought about the Navy, I just dint like the idea of cookin for white folks for four fuckin years. Dint wanna be no messcook, no domestic in a uniform.

But there was another problem, you know what I'm sayin to you? At this same time, I got myself some trouble. A girl I knew got herself knocked up and her father and her brothers are lookin for me, comin around the block, lookin to shoot me or make me marry her. Either way, I'm dead. You see, I just dint love the girl. I felt sorry *for her but I dint think that was too good a reason to marry a woman. So after Charlie Neal left and I had some more time to think (a couple of hours to tell the truth) I went downtown and walked around the block and then toked to the guy, the recruiter, and he says, you know, the Navy is* different *now, it's* integrated, *you dont have to be a* messcook, *you could be a* musician. . . . *So I joined up.*

Trouble was when I get through boot camp, they tell me all the music rates are filled up, there's like a waitin list all the way to 1958, but if I dint want to go messcookin, hell, I could be a corpsman. Workin with *doctors . . . I figure, Hey, why not? At least I'd learn something I could use on the outside, in case the music thing dint work out. And I could practice, keep listenin to the new music, keep readin my* Down Beat *and* Metronome, *maybe play with some bands wherever I ended up. Yeah.*

So I go to corpsman school. I learn the job is the same as a nurse, but hey, what the hell, it's a start. I mean, wasn't Dexter Gordon's father a doctor? And Miles Davis, his old man was a dentist. Maybe there was some connection. . . . I work in Jacksonville. A year goes by. I see a little of Gitmo and those fine Cuban women and some great mambo bands, great horn players. And then Korea happens.

Bam.

Like that.

They assign me to the First Marines, cause they's a shortage of Marine corpsmen, they gettin the shit shot out of them, cause wherever there's a medic there's shooting and bleedin and dyin. By November, I'm the only sailor with this Marine company and we're climbin through the snow and ice in X Corps. Up by the Chosin Reservoir. All of us freezin, strung out over forty fuckin miles. We couldn't dig foxholes cause the ground was like iron. It was seventeen below zero in a place called Kato. And it got colder as we kept going, heading for the fuckin Yalu, heading for fuckin China for all we knew. I remember we come into a town called Yudan that the artillery wrecked, just blew the piss out of it. They was an old lady sitting there, cryin. Cryin and freezin and singing something in Korean, a gook blues, I reckon. And they was nothin we could do. We cuddin bring her with us, not where we were goin, and she cuddin go back. They was no back. So we just left her to die.

To fuckin die.

Alone in the cold.

We were wearin so much shit—long johns, hoods, parkas—that we'd sweat like hell, and when we stopped walkin the sweat froze. A few guys took they socks off and tore the skin away with them. In that cold, feet froze to boots. In that cold, if you touched the M-1 with your bare hands, the skin come off. Even the BARs froze. Some guys pissed on their guns to make them work and other guys started greasin them with Wildroot Cream Oil. Or Kreml. That fuckin Kreml was the best, all white and pearly and thick.

The night of the Big Cold, we're in the dark on Hill 403 when we start hearin the voices, short quick voices, know what I mean? Not Korean voices, we knew them by now. Chinese voices. And somebody says, they can't be Chinese, the Chinese ain't in this thing and we ain't in fuckin China. But a little after ten, they come at us. The Chinese. They lay down a mortar barrage and start blowing their fuckin bugles, all flat and out of tune, just blowing like crazy, and they was waves of them, all lumpy like, in their white clothes, comin through the fuckin snow. Comin over the ice. Comin at us.

The Marines shot them and shot them and shot them and they still kept comin. They was blood all over the snow and they still kept coming. One crazy fuckin Marine, his bolt froze and he stands up and throws the rifle at them and they shot him through the belly. And then they were on us, only nine of us left on that fuckin hill, and they wasn't time to help the wounded, all you could do was try to live. So we fight them with everything. Trenchin tools. Spades. Knives. Bayonets. Them frozen fuckin unshootable fuckin guns.

Then one of their bugles blows and they all start to leave. Like that. Whoever that fuckin horn player was, I loved his ass. They was wounded guys everywhere and I did what I cud. The morphine Syrettes was frozen. The fuckin plasma froze and then the plasma bottles started explodin from the cold. We had fifty-four guys wounded, and a bunch of other guys dead. We went to scavenge among the dead Chinese for weapons. I almost shit when I saw what they had. They were fightin us with 1903 Springfields. We had the latest guns and they froze in that cold. They were fightin us with the equal of a bow and arrow. And kickin ass. Right then and there, I wanted to run. We all did. Just get off that goddamned hill and go somewhere. But we cuddin go anywhere. The orders were to hold the hill to keep the road open, down below us in the valley. That was it. Wait for reinforcements.

So we drag the Chinese bodies over and make a wall out of them and we fill sleeping bags with snow and lay them out on the slopes. The wind was blowing hard and it was colder. And that night they came again with their bugles and we just kept shootin and shootin. We shot them while they were bayonetin the sleepin bags. And we shot them when they came close to overrunnin us again. We just kept shootin. I think I shot nineteen of them. I never did see one of their faces. And then, just like that, they went away again. And an hour later here comes some more Marines, fifty, a hundred of them, another outfit cut off and fightin its way out. They were as fucked up as we were. It gets lighter, day coming, the sky gray as steel. An air-drop comes over at dawn and drops ammo and food and drugs, all we need, and I shoot up the worst wounded with morphine and bandage the others.

The Chinese stayed away a whole day and I began to think: maybe I'm gonna live. *Cause for three fuckin days, I knew I was gonna die up there. Just knew it. And then I did die. Just let myself die. Knowing there was nothing to do about it. But now I got to thinking I was gonna live, and for the first time I got scared. Before I was just* doin. *Now I was* thinkin. *And I was afraid, I didn't want to die, didn't want to feel it, wanted to live and go home and play music and get laid. I didn't want to freeze in my own piss, or wait for the fuckin Chinese to come and kill me. I heard later that's what they did in their army. Fight two days, rest one. But we didn't know that up on that goddamned hill. We shivered. We ate crackers. We ate snow. We waited to hear the Chinese bugles.*

Then we hear we are leavin. A strategic withdrawal, they called it. Advancin in another direction, some Marine said later. But everyone knew it was a retreat. All up and down the line, the Chinese had beat the shit out of us and we were pullin out. We wunt going to the Yalu, we wunt going to fuckin China, no matter what MacArthur said. We were gettin the fuck out of there. And they was only one road, one way out, and we knew it and so did the Chinese. Somehow we buried the dead. Eighty-five of them. Still up there at Yudam. The men from Fox Company of the second Battalion of the Seventh Regiment. Still in Korea. Forever.

So we start out, with some trucks below us now on the road and more trucks comin and more and more fucked-up Marines staggerin outta the hills. We strap some of the worst wounded across the radiators of the trucks to keep them from freezin to death. Sometimes we cuddin tell who was dead and who was alive. You cuddin get a pulse, it was so fuckin cold. We cuddin change their dressins either. So right off, I learn that if the guy's eyes move, he's alive. If the eyes don't move, fuck him, leave him.

The guys who were walking had diarrhea and they eyes was crazy but they kept movin. They wanted to live. To fuckin live. *To get off the ice, to get to the warm, to go home. I cuddin feel my own feet. I just kept movin them. Tokin to them, sayin move, mothafucker, like Stepin fuckin Fetchit. Keep goin, feet, get me to the promised land, keep me alive. . . . We had some of the wounded on trucks on top of parachutes, tied on with primer cord. And we come to a bridge and start over and then the fuckin bridge collapsed. We all back up, but one truck went into the river. A half-frozen river, full of ice. And two of these crazy mothafuckin Marines dive into the river and rescued those guys. Cut em loose from the primer cord. Drug em up on the bank. Let them live. That's why nobody can tell me no shit about Marines, man. I mean, I don't take no crap from them, specially some rearguard asshole pullin guard duty in Florida. But I don't give them no shit either. They dive into frozen rivers, man.*

We got close to Hagaru on December third. That was a pretty good-size town. It was snowing like a bitch and we stop on a hill just outside the town. Then, through the snow, we see planes on a runway and an American flag and tents and trucks and so we know, shit, we fuckin made *it, we might actually fuckin* live. *And then those crazy mothafuckin Marines got in* drill *formation. All shot up and hurt and frozen. And they march into that town, countin fuckin* cadence. *One captain had most of his fuckin jaw shot off. He had so many bandages around his head he looked like a mummy. But he* walked, *man.* Marching. *In step. Proud. The crazy mothafuckin Marines.*

I dint even know I was shot till then. Frostbite, dehydration, shot in the left thigh, the hip. I don't remember nothin about how that happened. I for shitsure wunt trying to be no hero. I was just trying to live, even that real bad coldass night I was sure I died. Yeah, I killed some guys. I must of. I don't know how many. I dint take no names. I was just shooting, like every other poor mothafucka on the hill.

You think that changed me? Bet your sweet ofay ass it did. I come home knowin I wunt ever gonna take shit again. Never gonna be the white man's nigger. Even if that meant everybody makes me to be a troublemaker. I went to Korea. I did my so-called fuckin duty to America. Nobody gonna tell me how to live anymore. No cracker. No bowin an scrapin Uncle Tom black man. Nobody. Whether they like it or not, whether you *like it or not, I'm an American and I'm gonna start livin like one. I got six months to go in the Navy. In September I go to school somewhere, on the GI Bill, a free man. Music school.*

Somewhere warm.

Somewhere hot.

Chapter

34

THE RAIN WAS over when I went out into the night to find my way to the barracks. I felt gorged: with food and with Eden; with this newer, raunchier, dirtier, music; with the intimate opening into the lives of what I still called Negroes. I was full of images of the frozen dead in Korea too. And with the rich loamy smell of the wet earth.

I walked along the footpaths and as the clouds moved on, I could see the stars. Men my age had died because plasma froze in bottles, but I was alive. Men slept here in these barracks, wifeless and womanless, but I had found Eden Santana. I felt as if I could reach out and gather the stars in my hand, pack them loosely like some cosmic snowball and release them again into the universe.

"Come over here, sailor," a voice said.

A figure in officer's suntans was squatting down at the side of the gedunk. His back was to me, but I knew it was Captain Pritchett. He looked up.

"Give me a hand, here," he said.

"Yes, sir," I said, and wondered if I should salute and decided not to. He was digging in the earth around a bush. There was a large empty earthenware pot beside him. He handed me a small digging tool.

"Now dig on that side, see? But don't hit the roots. I'm gonna save this baby."

I started digging carefully in the dim light, feeling with my hand for the roots of the bush.

"This is oleander. The goddamned snowstorm practically killed her."

Then he started talking to the bush. "But I'm gonna save you, ain't I, honey? You been such a good girl. You been so *put* upon." His voice was crooning, as if directed at a baby. "We gonna get you up and into a pot and up to the control tower, where there's lots of sun. Give you lots of water to drink and keep your ass warm. You gonna *live,* honey. You ain't gonna die next to no brick wall."

We finished clearing the roots. He picked up a small paper bag and poured pebbles into the bottom of the pot.

"Now throw some of that dirt in there," he said, the voice abruptly full of authority. He went back to the bush.

"Yes, sir."

"And bring it over here, close to me. Yeah. That's it. Okay . . . Now, while I hold her up straight, pack some dirt in there. Not too *hard* now. Easy. The dirt from the top, the real black stuff, not that sandy clay crap at the bottom. Yeah. Okay, that's it. Good!"

He stepped back and gazed at the plant, looking happy. Then he was suddenly aware of me again, and fixed on my face.

"What's your name, sailor?" he said curtly.

I told him.

"Well, thank you, Devlin. What are you doing *out* anyway? After the base has been secured?"

"I was visiting with the messcooks, sir."

"Visiting with the *mess* cooks? You're *white,* sailor!"

"I know, sir."

"Well, what the hell you doin up there with that crazy bunch of galley slaves?"

"Listening to music, sir."

He looked suddenly interested. "No kidding? What are they playing these days? I bet it's not Glenn Miller or Bing Crosby anymore."

"No, sir."

"So what do they listen to?"

I smiled. "Well, there's a group called Professor Longhair and the Shuffling Hungarians, and a guy named—"

He guffawed. "Professor Longhair and the Shuffling *Armenians*?!"

"Hungarians, sir."

"Jesus Christ. What else?"

I told him the names of the other singers and groups, while he asked me to grab one side of the pot and help carry it to his office.

He repeated every name I gave him, as if memorizing them for a test. I told him about Bobby Bolden and how he should be given a band to play at the EM Club. He grunted, and repeated Bolden's name, as we carried the pot together up the three steps of the Administration Building, grunting and straining. A Marine private snapped to attention at the door.

"Open all those doors to my office, Private," Captain Pritchett said. The private led the way down a corridor to a corner office. He flicked on the lights, saluted again, and backed away as we entered the office with the plant. The room was very clean and sparsely furnished, except for the plants. They were everywhere. And I thought of all the flowers at Eden Santana's trailer.

"Over here in the corner, Devlin. We'll leave her until the morning and then I'll have her moved to the tower." We laid the plant down next to a window. He started crooning to it again. "Now you get a good night's sleep, you hear me? And tomorrow you're gonna live in the sunshine. Tomorrow, and for the rest of your life on this planet. You hear me, honey? You can bet on it."

I gazed around the office. There was a bookshelf with framed photographs of the captain on the deck of a ship, the captain with a woman, the woman alone, the captain and the woman coming under an arch of swords held by midshipmen. There were a couple of books: *The Ops Officers Manual, The Bluejackets' Manual,* various books of rules and regs from Bupers, *How to Win Friends and Influence People,* by Dale Carnegie. He glanced at the woman's picture.

"That's my wife," he said in a flat voice. "She died."

"Sorry to hear that, sir."

"I was in love with her from high school and we got married during the war and after all that, all that damned worrying and me being torpedoed and all the rest of it, she went and died on me."

He shook his head and turned to look again at the plant.

"She got me started on this stuff, the gardening," he said. "When I came home from the war, she had the goddamnedest garden waiting for me. So I guess maybe, in some way, if I keep these things living, then she's alive too. See that plant over there?" He pointed at a large green plant with leathery leaves. "That's from our garden in Sausalito. After I sold the house, I took it with me. I *know* she's alive in that one."

He looked at me as if suddenly aware that he had revealed

himself to me, that he was vulnerable. He saluted smartly. I returned the salute.

"Thank you, sailor," he said.

It was a dismissal.

"And, sailor? If you say a word about any of this to anyone, I'll
ship your ass to the Fleet Marines."

"I understand, sir."

I started to leave.

"Professor Longhair and the Shuffling Albanians," he said and
chuckled. "Jesus Christ . . ."

"Hungarians, sir," I said, and saluted again and went out into the
night.

PART

THREE

Chapter

35

THEN BEGAN THE time of my education. Miles Rayfield taught me the secrets of drawing. Bobby Bolden taught me about music. And Eden Santana taught me about everything else. Sitting here now, on a motel balcony facing the enormous Gulf evening, I try to reconstruct those hours, and although many have vanished into the blur, all seem accounted for, too. I know that I worked every day at the Supply Shack and stood my watches at the dumpster and was soon trusted with being the duty storekeeper. I know I did what I could to be a four-oh sailor and keep out of the way of Red Cannon. But I don't have a series of sharp pictures of all those moments: What I saw and what I did are still at war with the way I felt.

And most of those feelings are tangled up with the time of Eden Santana. All those Saturday nights and Sunday mornings. And some sweet and timeless Sunday afternoons. I was always with her on Tuesday and Thursday nights, too, unless I pulled duty at the Supply Shack, because Eden didn't work on those nights; even today, there is something oddly thrilling and poignant to me about meeting a woman on one of those weekday evenings. Eden worked late on Wednesdays and Saturdays, and though I could have spent each night with her, waiting at the trailer, she told me early on that it would be better if we didn't fall into too rigid a routine. "You're special, child," she said. "I don't want you ever to become ordinary." And then touched my face and added, "Or me to be ordinary for you."

That was never to happen. On some of those nights when I wasn't with her, I began to feel the presence of what I called The Boulder. The true word was jealousy, but I couldn't admit then that I could be shaken by a feeling that made me laugh when I saw it in movies or comics, or read about it in books. A real man wasn't supposed to feel jealous of a woman any more than he could admit to being afraid. But on some lonesome nights I could feel The Boulder pressing up out of my guts, or coming down upon me from outside, filling the room like the giant orange in Miles Rayfield's painting. I would hear a scrap of music, the rattle of the palms, smell the odor of the captain's flowers, and Eden would appear in my mind. I would wonder what she was doing at exactly that moment. Sometimes I wondered if she was seeing Mercado, leading him (or someone else) into the holy precincts of the trailer. I would get physically sick then: nauseated, pouring sweat. I saw myself scaling the fence, heading into the night, jerking open the trailer door, confronting the two of them, the pictures of all this as vivid as a front-page photo, while my guts coiled and knotted until I fell into exhausted sleep. Then it would be a Tuesday or a Thursday or a Saturday night or a Sunday morning, and I would see her again, and it would all go away.

One night I told her that I loved her, meaning it, blurting it out. And she smiled and said that was the sweetest thing anyone had said to her in a long long time. I said it again, expecting an echo, and again and again. But all through those first weeks and months, she wouldn't say that she loved me. She said everything else: You be good, child. You sleep nice, child. You sure are good to me, child. But never *I love you, child.* And I knew then that this was more complicated than it seemed, that it wasn't like Steve Canyon or a movie, where you said the words and the women said them back and you lived happily ever after, more or less. She was as close to me as skin to skin, but there were places inside her that I couldn't touch.

She wouldn't talk about her life in any detail. If I pressed her, trying to discover where the line was beyond which I could not press, I heard a few things. The most important I learned early on: there was a husband somewhere. She was still married to him, but she said that was just technical. I'm here with you, ain't I, child?, she said and smiled. But after she told me this, there would be times, even when I was with her, when The Boulder would push up and out of me, and I'd ask her why she didn't just divorce him, this man, this husband, and she'd say, "You can't divorce a ghost."

And I would think: *The ghost who walks. Like* The Phantom *in the Sunday* Journal-American. *Her husband is The Ghost That Walks, this mysterious husband, out there somewhere, haunting us, haunting me, able at any time to come back.* Because I could not see him, could not peer into his eyes (as I did with the photographs I now was copying in ink and wash for other sailors at two dollars each), he grew in importance and became more ominous, more of a threat. If I could look into his eyes, I could see whether there was fear there or uncertainty, swagger or evil. But in my mind he had no face and no eyes, and I was afraid of him.

The toughest times were when I was stuck on the base and the worst of all were when I was alone. Eventually I learned the trick of warding off fear with activity: If I just *did* something, if I got up off the bed or drew pictures in a fury, or ran slowly around the perimeter, I could drive away the phantoms. Sometimes I would simply walk over to the infirmary and hang out with Bobby Bolden or go up to see him in the evenings at the Kingdom of Darkness.

He loved talking about music; he did so with almost ferocious concentration, illustrating the complicated points on his horn. But it wasn't always just talking. Every week or so, on a night when Eden Santana was working, I'd go down with Bobby Bolden to the black joints around West Cervantes Street. Places with names like Patti's Bar and the Talk of the Town and the Two Spot and My Club and Mary Lou's Tavern. They were hot and packed and sweaty, their doors open to the street, ceiling fans churning lamely at the Gulf air, the black faces gleaming in the heat and eyes darting suddenly at me and then at Bobby Bolden and the messcooks who came with us. Almost always there would be a wary, frozen moment, then recognition, and then it would be all right. There were almost never any live bands, but there *were* jukeboxes. Immense monstrous jukes, the biggest I'd ever seen, with 45s falling steadily off spindles, and bubbles and lights careening through tubes up and down the sides and always some woman with a small waist and a big ass and sturdy legs staring at the lists and someone shouting, "Honey, play B-four."

"Watch these niggers move," Bobby Bolden said to me on one of those nights. "Least you might learn to *walk* better, white man. You aint *ever* gonna learn to dance."

The music pounded, the bass lines ramming into me, so that I'd

be moving to them the next day and through the night too, moving
even with Eden Santana to the dark and dirty song of Cervantes
Street. The jukes were loud with a few of the same singers I heard
in the Kingdom of Darkness: Lloyd Price, Professor Longhair, Roy
Brown. But there were others, too: big-voiced black men, shouters,
honkers, bluesmen: Lowell Fulsom, Percy Mayfield, Jimmy Wither-
spoon, Amos Milburn, Cleanhead Vinson. The names were all as
new to me as Hank Williams had been when I landed in Pensacola,
and yet I felt as if I now knew Hank Williams, had been drowned
in his songs, and now I had to learn about another whole platoon
of musicians. Back home, I thought I was hip. Hey, I listened to
Sid. I knew Bird from Dizzy. But I'd been suddenly dropped into
a world where I didn't know anything, a dark dense gleaming
world, where men at the bar first asked about New York and the
Dodgers before asking if I wanted some pussy; big black men,
grave men, surly men and sad men. All the while their music was
pounding, and I was looking at their women.

"Chick over there got eyes for you," Bobby Bolden said one
night, six of us packed together at the bar of the Two Spot, his nod
directed at a girl in a tight yellow dress at a table with two others.
"But if her ole man catch you wid her, he cut you *three* ways,
mothafucka: long, deep, and *con-tin-uously!*"

He laughed and slugged down some beer and I looked at the
woman and she looked at me. She had cinnamon skin and full lips,
an elegantly thin neck and squared shoulders, and I could see the
shape of her full breasts, undressing her with my eyes (taking small
short glances, not staring), drawing her in my head, wanting to
paint her, wanting to get the color right, wondering all the while
what her skin felt like, a black woman's skin, wondering what color
her nipples were and whether the hair on her pussy was straight or
kinky and whether she'd laugh at the size of my dick.

"Ever sleep with a colored girl?" Bobby Bolden said.

"No."

"Shit, you the first white man ever told me the truth on that one."

"I tell a lie in here, I'm dead," I said, sipping a beer, thinking
of Wajeski's line: *I thought I fucked a colored girl until I saw a colored
guy fuck a colored girl.* "And I try to do anything about it, I'd be dead
before I hit the sidewalk."

"Here she come."

The woman had to pass the length of the bar to get to the

jukebox. Louis Jordan was singing "Somebody Done Changed the Lock on My Door," while a half dozen couples danced in a small area behind the juke. The woman stood at the jukebox and slipped in a quarter and started punching tunes. Six of them. Thinking about each one. Standing on one high heel, curling the other foot around her ankle. She had beautiful tapered legs that came right off her ass. I wanted to draw her. No, that was a lie. I wanted to fuck her.

And then thought about Eden Santana. Where was she right then, at exactly that moment, while I stared at the ass of a strange woman? Home, I insisted. In the trailer. Alone. Maybe she was even thinking about me, imagining me in the barracks. She had no way of knowing where I was. And I thought: *If I went with this woman, I'd betray Eden.* I would be doing to her what I was always afraid Eden might be doing to me. That would be a betrayal. And then thought: *No. It wouldn't be a betrayal because there wasn't anything to betray. We didn't have a* deal, *did we?* I'd told Eden I loved her but she'd said nothing back. I was with her when I was with her: that's what *she* always said. What I did the rest of the time was *my* business, right? What she did was her business, too. That's what she said. But if she *knew,* what would she think? Probably the same thing I'd think, if *she* slept with a colored guy. Why was it such a big deal anyway? Skin is skin. White people and black people must have been doing it together for centuries in the South. Otherwise, where'd Bobby Bolden's green eyes come from? Not from Africa, for shit sure. And this girl at the jukebox, with her light skin: there was some goddamned *white* in there too.

She came back down the length of the packed bar, waved at a woman at one of the tables and then bumped into me.

"Uh, sorry, scuse me," she said in a furry small girl's voice. She was about my age. Maybe a little older. Maybe twenty.

"My fault," I said. "Blockin the way."

She looked at Bobby Bolden. "Whatchoo dune bringin this poor white boy here, Bobby Bolden?"

"To meet you, Little Mama."

"You such a bad ole boy," she said.

"What you drinkin?"

She asked for a rum and Coke and I looked at her face: curved nose, small hard nostrils, full lips. Her dress was cut low and her breasts looked solid and full. She was wearing perfume. Sweet perfume. Dark perfume. She asked me my name and I told her and she said her name was Winnie and where was I from and I said New York and she smiled and her eyes got brighter, and Bobby Bolden looked at the ceiling and the messcooks gave me a deadpan look and then laughed together. Winnie gave them a killer glare.

"Ahm jes trying to make the boy feel *welcome* and yawl ack like *chilrun.*"

"We jus admirin yo *style,* Winnie," Rhode Island Freddie said.

"Dats a lie," she said. "Yawl is thinkin I want to take this boy *home.*"

"It snow the *second* time this wintuh if you do," Bumper said. "White stuff in the chicken shack."

"See the lowlife yuh bring here, Bobby Bolden? You and the white boy and six dumbass zigaboos." She turned to me and shook my hand. "Well, please to met you, Michael. Come back sometahm, 'thout the lowlifes."

"Hey, Winnie," Bobby Bolden said. "Don't—"

But she walked away and went back to the table.

"Saved," Rhode Island Freddie said, draping a big hand on my shoulder.

And in a way I was. When Winnie walked away, I didn't have to choose to go with her or even to try. I didn't have to choose a betrayal.

Chapter

36

THE TRUTH WAS simple: after a few short weeks, Eden Santana had become a presence in almost everything I did. I filled pads with drawings of her. I sometimes had to stop myself in the middle of drawing the wives and girlfriends of sailors because I kept making them look like her: blondes, brunettes and redheads acquired her hair or her eyes or the mole on her cheekbone. When I read a novel from the base library, the women all resembled her, even Daisy Buchanan and Catherine Barkley. On those nights when I was the duty storekeeper, alone in the Supply Shack listening to dramas on Harrelson's radio, the women characters all appeared to me as Eden. I drew her so much, in so many different positions, that I could recall her body at will, sitting at my desk, doodling on scrap paper with an Ebony pencil, and had to keep hiding the drawings so the others wouldn't see her. They knew I had somebody out in that mysterious world called "off the base." But they didn't know who she was and I wouldn't tell them.

On three straight Sundays she took me out to the empty parking lot at the beach and taught me how to drive. "You just gotta relax," she said. "Just understand what you're doing and then *relax*. No white-knuckle jobs holdin that wheel, child." She sat beside me while I made circles around the lot, coming to abrupt stops, shifting gears, backing up in reverse, going forward again. "That's good, that's fine, just do that, watch what's behind you, don't look at the *road,* look up *ahead,* the distance, you'll see everything any-way . . ."

There was a small hill leading over the dunes to Fort Pickens and

I started up there on the second Sunday, brimming with confidence, when a truck came roaring over the rise, right at us, black, faceless. I panicked, and whipped the wheel around, driving it straight into the path of the truck, and then pulled it the other way, while Eden yelled "Right! *Right!*" We ended up stuck in the sand as the truck roared on. My hands shook. And I was so afraid I couldn't move: frightened of taking this ton of rubber and steel in my hands again and ending up mashed in the grille of another truck. Eden lit a cigarette and inhaled deeply. She said: "Better get back on the horse, child."

And I did. We got the car out of the sand, pushing and heaving until we got traction, Eden laughing through it and telling me I'd remember that moment all my days. And then I took the wheel again and went up over the rise, more slowly now, thinking *right,* go to the *right,* if someone comes barrel-assing down the road, *go fucking right.* But the road was empty and I shifted gears more smoothly and Eden laughed out loud and hit the dashboard with the palm of her hand. "Yeah! Good! *Go do it!*"

She let me drive back to the mainland across the causeway that day, and then switched seats with me for the ride home through traffic. "You got it, don't you worry now," she said. "You *got* it . . ."

I had some money from the drawings, and I said (trying to sound like a man) that I would pay for the food from now on (since that's what men did). After all, she did the cooking; and another thing: when we went off in the car for drives or lessons, I should pay for the gas. "It's only fair," I said, and she shook her head in an amused way and said, "If you say so."

Most of the time we went to Stop & Shop and picked up steaks at thirty-three cents a pound or shrimps for a quarter a pound and black-eyed peas for a nickel (ah, the fifties!) and with water, spices, salt and care, she'd turn these plain goods into food I'd never tasted before and have seldom tasted since. The process was as mysterious as art; casein wasn't art, it was something you used to make art; peas in her hands were the same. She prepared for meals the way a painter might prepare for a new canvas, first studying the newspaper, reading the ads for bargains and in her quest often expressing high moral outrage. Look, she'd say, at this A&P ad: round steak has gone up to fifty-nine cents a pound! That's a *damn shame!* And a five-pound bag of oranges is now thirty-seven cents (her voice rising). *In Florida!* But then she would see a twenty-eight-pound watermelon for $1.10 and Peter Pan peanut butter for thirty-five cents and her anger would ebb and we'd go off to the A&P, instead of Stop & Shop or Plee-Zing on T Street. She said she hoped I didn't think she was cheap. But she felt responsibility, she said, ever since I insisted on paying for the food. "People work hard for their money," she said, "they better spend it hard. Not easy." And when the food was back home, she would begin the magical process of changing it. Food had never been so sensual.

As the days grew longer and warmer, she moved some of the plants and flowers outside, making a small garden beside the trailer. She bought two folding chairs at Sears, and we'd sit outside sometimes and look at the small lake that fed the River Styx, with the trailer like a silver wall between us and the bumpy dirt road that ran through the colored district.

"I saw your friend, that Bobby Bolden, around here the other night," she said one Sunday afternoon. She was quiet for a long moment. "He's got a white woman in a house back there in the woods."

"That bother you?"

She gave me a funny look. "Well, I wonder about it."

"It's their business, I guess."

"Yeah. Till someone makes it *their* business."

"Like who?"

"Oh, hell, *any*body. . . . Some black lady jealous of a white woman. Some damned redneck. You never know . . ." She looked at me. "This is the South, you know."

"Yeah," I said. "I heard."

We didn't talk about it any longer that day.

In the spring she taught me the names of the world. She named the trees in the swamps, mostly cypress and tupelo, and the great hardwoods in the bottom land, oak and sweetgum, hickory, magnolia and red maple. I'd pluck leaves from each new tree, discovering that I could always draw a tree if I followed the basic structure of the leaf. In the higher land, she showed me the difference between slash pine and longleaf pine, and the dogwood and wax myrtle that grew at their base, and sometimes we would just sit there in the stillness and she'd point out warblers and woodpeckers and we'd close our eyes and hold each other and listen to the soughing of the wind through the longleaf pines.

One Sunday we drove west on route 98, hugging the sparse coast until we ran out of road. We moved inland then on a two-lane blacktop and parked the car under some live oaks hung with moss. We carried a picnic basket deep into the woods. When we were out of sight of the road, we heard a snapping sound and saw a white deer scamper away, and then Eden pointed out a possum and the tracks of a bobcat. "There's prob'ly some black bear in here too," she said. "Now *they* could kill ya . . . But not to worry, they been most hunted off."

The woods had a deep loamy smell that seemed to enter her, slowing her movements, making her more languorous, her voice more raw. She took my hand and made me bend under low-lying branches, then shoved me away from a pile of leaves ("Copperheads love them leaves") and made me walk around a fallen log ("That's where the cottonmouths live") and laughed at my city ways of walking and told me the names of the bugs: ticks and fire ants, chiggers and deer flies and black flies all mixed up with the mosquitoes and the no-see-ums. If you got a tick under your skin she said, patiently, quietly, you had to smother him, cover him with nail polish, force him to fight his way back out. Chiggers made a little tube under the skin and you had to scrape them away, tube and all, gouging them right off the surface. "Chiggers love the leaves too," she said. "Best thing you can say about a copperhead is they eat the chiggers . . ."

Just knowing the snakes were around made me feel creepy. But Eden talked about them in a casual way. "There's hardly any rattlers around here anymore," she said. "Nobody knows why. They just moved away, went someplace else. . . . Coral snakes could hurt you a little. They're tiny things, a real pretty color, but you'd have to be tryin to kiss one for it to do you any damage. The cottonmouth, well, you don't want to mess with him in any shape or fashion. He's big, color of gunmetal, fat and ugly with a head like a triangle. Stay away from that sumbitch." She smiled. "Mostly, snakes are harmless. Don't bother them, they don't bother you. Just cause the poor things ain't got legs, ain't no reason to kill em."

Then the darkness of the forest began to lift and bright yellow shafts of light cut through the trees; we suddenly saw a red wall, and she told me that was because the red buds had bloomed on the slash pines. And when we moved past them, we came to the river. It was about thirty feet wide, gurgling over smooth stones, and was the reddish color of tea. *A red river!* I thought, remembering the old Gene Autry song about remembering the Red River Valley. And she said it was that way because of the tannin in the cypress trees. Clean brown sand lined the river banks, and in the center of the river there was a wide flat boulder, the water coursing around it. The air was free of insects now, and I could see fish in the river, lolling in the eddies along the banks or moving without effort against the current. Catfish, she said, and bass and perch.

For a long while we stood there in the stillness along the bank, saying nothing, hushed by the solitude. Then we walked to the sand along the banks. Eden looked at me and put down the picnic basket and pulled her blouse out of her trousers. I did the same with my shirt. She wriggled out of her blouse and laid it flat across the top of the basket. She unzipped her jeans then, and I was undressing too; she laid the jeans and her panties across the basket and then breathed deeply and removed her brassiere.

"Come on, child," she whispered hoarsely.

We waded into the cold river. I held the basket and clothes above the water, my feet slipping on the stones. The water was up to her breasts and her skin was pebbled with the chill and her nipples hard, but she moved to the boulder, which lay like a dry, bone-colored island in the middle of the river. She slipped and almost went under and made a yelping sound and then giggled and righted herself as the swift water pushed against us. She reached the boulder first and pulled herself up, dripping and glistening, the muscles taut under her skin. She took the basket from me and I heaved myself up. We lay there side by side for a long time, her legs apart, her black V drying in the hot sun, the two of us engulfed by the sounds of unseen insects and animals and birds and the gurgling rush of the river. Only our hands touched. My cock felt thick and lazy. I let one hand trail in the cold river.

After a while, she sat up and looked at my face and ran her fingernails over my stomach and then leaned forward and took me in her hot tight mouth.

Chapter
37

ONE CHILLY WEDNESDAY evening in April, when Eden was
working late, Sal, Max and I waited outside the locker club for
Bobby Bolden. Traffic moved quickly down the highway. The lot
in front of Billy's was almost full.

"Can you imagine the balls on this guy?" Sal said. "Inviting us
to dinner at his *chick's* house?"

"He's got a death wish," Max said. "Or *we* do."

I saw a lot of Sal and Max around the base, but after meeting
Eden Santana, I'd only been back to the Dirt Bar twice. It wasn't
that I didn't like the drinking and the noise and the fun; I loved all
that, the recklessness of it, the lack of rules. I just wanted Eden
Santana more. To be with her, I had to have more money than I
made as a sailor, so I usually spent Monday and Wednesday nights
drawing my little ink portraits. Sal and Max (and most of the others)
knew I had a woman and kidded me about her, but I didn't care.
On this evening, Sal was insisting on a invitation to *my* girl's house
too, promising he would even wear socks for the occasion and use
a knife and fork. I was glad Eden was at work; we wouldn't see her
at the trailer on the way to the place in the woods where Bobby
Bolden lived with his white woman. I didn't want them to inspect
her; I didn't want her to think I was just another crazy kid sailor.

Then a blue '49 Mercury pulled into Billy's parking lot. Bobby
Bolden was behind the wheel. He honked and we hurried across
the highway. I glanced at Billy's window and saw Red Cannon and
Chief McDaid staring at us from beyond the neon sign. I got in the
car beside Bolden. Sal and Max slid into the back.

"What the hell are you doin with a lowlife good-for-nothing Mercury?" Sal said. "I thought spades only drove Buicks and Cadillacs."

"We use these when we gotta leave a body in the trunk," Bobby Bolden said in a dry way. "Don't wanna waste a good set of wheels on the dead." He was driving up the highway, away from town, toward the lumpy dirt road where Eden and I had picked him up in the rain.

"Should we lie on the floor?" Max asked.

"Won't help," Bobby Bolden said. "They kill black men aroun' here just for *leanin* on a Mercury."

"If they stop us," Max said to Sal, "start singing 'Mammy.' "

On cue, they started singing the old song, trying to sound like Al Jolson, and were up to the part about the sun shining east, the sun shining west, and them knowing where the sun shone best when we bumped over the gravel road and went under the live oaks and past the silver trailer. The evening light was fading now. The lake looked black. Bobby Bolden glanced at me. And I glanced to my right and felt The Boulder suddenly fill my stomach. This was Wednesday. Eden Santana was supposed to be working at Sears. But the car was parked in front of her trailer. She was home. With the lights out.

" 'Maaaaaaa-uh-uh-me, Maaaaaaaaaaa-uh-meeeeee . . .' "

"Now you gonna get us killed by the *niggers*," Bobby Bolden said.

"It's the Klan we don't want cutting up our ass."

"I wunt talkin about ya *color*," Bobby Bolden said. "I was talkin bout ya fuckin *singin*."

We all laughed, but I glanced back at the trailer as we followed the gravel road into the woods and I wasn't thinking about the Ku Klux Klan or anything else. *The car was there.* I imagined her in the half light with some man. Some *man*. Showing him my drawings. Laughing at his remarks. Through the woods I saw small unpainted houses, some with the doors wide open and lanterns inside on tables. Black kids moved around in the fading light, playing ball or running through bushes. There were no streets. *She's making him shrimp with the red sauce and a salad. She's bracing her feet against the roof of the trailer.* Bobby Bolden pulled the car through an opening in the bushes and down a narrow path and stopped in front of the house: one story with a front porch and a peaked roof. In the darkness, I could make out peeling traces of white paint. The shades were drawn and the front door closed. *She's got the door locked and his trousers are folded over a chair and there is ice clunking in a glass. They will whisper for a long time.* We got out of the car.

"Try to behave yourselves," Bobby Bolden said. "You in a civilized neighborhood now."

" 'The sun shines east, the sun shines west—' "

"Sal, you better shut yo mouf, boss," Bolden said, sounding like Rochester from *The Jack Benny Show.*

I realized then that Bolden was dressed entirely in black: shiny black shirt, black tapered trousers, high black shiny boots. He looked as if he'd painted himself in silhouette. The eyes seemed greener. He glanced behind us at the road, as if expecting someone. All he saw were a couple of black kids staring without visible emotion at the visiting white men. Then he led the way to the front door and knocked: one-two, one-two-three. Footsteps. Bolden said, "It's me." Two locks were turned and then Bobby Bolden's white woman was framed in the light. I couldn't see her face. She hugged Bolden warmly and then he casually introduced her as Catty Wolverton. She shook my hand, then stepped aside to let us in. She locked the door behind us.

"Ugliest group a strays I ever seen," she said.

"Saved them from a vagrancy arrest," Bolden said.

Catty was about twenty-five, with brown liquid eyes and a reddish tint in her hair. She had a short pert nose and an overbite that stopped just short of bucked teeth. Some people might think she was homely. But she had a dark smoky voice and heavy breasts above a narrow waist and a drowsy manner and a dirty laugh and I thought: *Yeah, I see.*

"Help yourself to the booze, guys," she said, and waved us toward some bottles, glasses and an ice bucket perched on top of a nearly empty bookcase. She went back to the stove. Inside, the house was very bright and clean, the walls painted white, but it was essentially one very large room that felt as if someone had just moved in or moved out.

A bed was shoved up against the far wall, with a braided rug beside it on the plank floor, flanked by two unmatched pinewood bureaus, and on one of them there was a phonograph and a stack of records. The kitchen was larger than the sleeping area; a wide round table was placed in the middle, covered with a red plastic tablecloth and set with dishes and silverware, and there was a new gas stove that contrasted with the plainness of the room. A small refrigerator huddled beside the range and next to it was a stainless-steel sink. There were no pictures on the walls and no flowers. *He will smell lilac and begonias and myrtle. He will stare out at the dark lake. He will hear insects droning on the River Styx.* Sal poured Jim Beam bourbon into three glasses, added ice, handed them to Max and me.

"So what are you three jackoffs up to?" Catty said, stirring something in a black iron pot. Smelled like gumbo.

"Chastity," Sal said. "Only thing that works every time."

"Not for Jews," Max said. "Go ye forth and multiply, saith the Lord."

Catty laughed in a dirty way and stirred the pot, then built a drink for herself and Bobby Bolden.

"Hell, chastity don't work for *anybody,*" Catty said.

Bobby stacked some records on the record player and a man with a deep throaty growl began to sing:

> *Keep your eyes off my lovin woman,*
> *Keep your eyes off that lovin woman,*
> *Stay away from that sweet lovin woman,*
> *'Cause that sweet little lovin woman,*
> *. . . She belongs to me. . . .*

Catty hummed along with the chorus, talking about the Navy and being stationed at Mainside (touching the small of Bobby's back) and her stupid son of a bitch of a chief yeoman (pinching his neck) and how as bad as he was, he wasn't as bad as that total butternut muffdiver out at Ellyson, Chief McDaid. She knew McDaid from Dago, she said. Son of a whoremaster (she said, brushing Bobby's ass). Then she picked up the bowls from the table and went to the stove and ladled out the gumbo. *Why lie to me, woman? Why say you're working when you're not? Hey, you got to reap just what you sow.* . . . The Boulder rose and expanded and then I was sipping the gumbo, made with chicken and vegetables, and it was good but not as good as the first gumbo I'd ever had, down the road, under the live oaks, facing the lake. Then as quickly as it had arrived, The Boulder began to fade.

"Great," Sal said. "The best. Redneck minestrone."

"I figured I shouldn't give you pussyhunters anything *too* solid," Catty said. "Ruin your routine."

"Is this chicken kosher?" Max said.

"Is Chief McDaid?" Bobby Bolden said.

"That cunt," Sal said. That was the first time I'd ever heard any man use the word in front of a woman, but Catty didn't react the way I thought she would.

"Sal," she said, "please don't demean a perfectly beautiful piece of human anatomy by using it to describe that prick McDaid."

"You mean that cunt is a *prick*?"

"You ofays sure talk dirty," said Bobby Bolden.

"This is strictly a discussion of nomenclature, Bobby," Sal said. "Catty says a cunt is a beautiful thing and obviously I agree. Nothing has brought me greater happiness in this vale of tears. But then she implies that *a prick* is bad and dirty. So I say, if you can't call McDaid a cunt then you can't call him a prick either."

"Is he circumcised?" Max said.

"Only from the ears up," Catty said, and slammed the table. The bowls of gumbo all bounced.

Sal turned to me and said, "Welcome to the Pensacola chapter of the Holy Name Society."

Bobby fixed himself another drink and Max went to the stove for more gumbo and the blues man sang again about his lovin woman. There was no inside bathroom. A rotting outhouse stood in the woods behind the building but it looked so bad that the first time we all had to piss we just stood on the back porch and let go.

"Ooooh, wow," Sal said. "This gotta be the closest man can ever get to God."

"Do it downwind, will ya, wop?" Bobby Bolden said.

"Mine aint big enough to feel the wind," Sal said. "Where's downwind?"

"Toward me," Max said, "so aim for the tomatoes."

"*Aaaaaahhhhhh,*" Sal said, shook himself vigorously, and zipped up.

The moon was out now, and through the trees we could see its silvery reflection on the lake.

"God, it's beautiful," Sal whispered.

"It sure is," I agreed.

"Twenty years from now, we'll all be old men and there'll be houses and supermarkets on the lake and a bunch of assholes flyin around in speedboats," Max said. "And we'll remember this night."

"They'll pave the road," Sal said.

"They'll get rid of the niggers." Bobby Bolden laughed.

"They ain't gonna wait twenty years for *that.*"

"They'll have to bring guns," Bobby Bolden said.

"They will," Max said.

"They got them," Sal said.

"So do we," Bobby Bolden murmured. "So do we."

Back inside, we drank some more and took turns dancing with Catty and played more records. Catty wanted to know why I was so quiet and I said it was because I was so full of good food and Sal said, no, it wasn't that, it was because I was in love, and then he shifted to a Stan Laurel voice and said, "You can tell by the silly sloppy grin on his face." And I laughed and wondered if he could really tell from my face. I poured another drink.

Then there was a sharp single knock on the door.

We all stopped talking and Bobby Bolden put his hand up to quiet us, reached under the bed and came up with a big .45 caliber automatic. His face completely changed. The looseness turned hard. The green eyes were wary. He tiptoed to the door, motioning all of us to get down low and away from the windows. Sal picked up a carving knife.

Then Bobby positioned himself to the side of the door, the gun ready. I put myself in front of Catty, crouched down near the sink. Max picked up a chair. My heart was pounding.

Bobby Bolden unlocked the lock, then flicked off the lights, squatted and jerked open the door.

There was nobody there.

We hurried through the woods and saw nobody and checked the car engine for bombs and went down to the edge of the lake to see if there were any boats speeding away in the moonlight. Whoever had knocked on the door was gone. But when it was time for Bobby to go back with us to the base, he wouldn't let Catty stay alone at the house. "*Some* mothafucka was out there," he said. "Maybe a kid. Maybe someone playin trickster. But maybe somebody else, too." So he locked up the house and we all crowded into the Mercury. He'd drop us off at the locker club, take Catty on to Mainside, where she could stay in the bachelor women's quarters. "Just can't take no chances."

For a moment, I thought maybe Bolden was putting us on, that he'd arranged for someone to knock on the door, just to let us know that he had the gun and was ready to use it. And to show off for his white woman. But that didn't make any sense; wouldn't he rather spend the night with Catty Wolverton? The whole thing felt unreal. What *was* real was the gun. Bolden slipped it under the front seat. I asked him what he'd do if the cops stopped us and found the gun and he said he'd tell them it was Sal's. "They believe anything about a wop," he said. Sal said, "Except that he had a gun in a car with a spade and didn't *use* it on him." Catty giggled. We pulled out onto the gravel road. Max said, "Hey, we never had dessert."

Bobby drove quickly past the silver trailer, throwing up gravel. And when I looked, the world tilted. Eden's car was gone.

Bolden dropped us in front of Billy's and drove on to Mainside. I suggested a nightcap. Sal said, "Why not?"

There were about a dozen men in the place being tended by a middle-aged blond barmaid. Seated on a stool in his dress whites was Red Cannon. McDaid was gone. Cannon's head turned when we came in, but his body didn't move. He stared at us, but we ignored him, laid our dollars on the bar and ordered beers.

"Jesus Christ, that was spooky," Sal said, turning his back to Red Cannon. "Someone knockin' on the door like that."

"The guy's nuts," Max said.

"She's worse," I said. "The *blacks* could do her in, the *rednecks* could—"

"What you say, boy?"

I turned and looked at Red Cannon. He was very drunk, but holding himself still.

"You call me a redneck?" he said in a surly way.

"I didn't say anything about you," I said.

"I heard you say redneck, boy."

"He wasn't talking *about* you," Sal said, "or *to* you. So cool it, Red."

"Don't tell *me* to cool it, sailor," Cannon said, sliding off the stool. The barmaid moved down to him. She didn't say anything, just touched his hand and stared. He turned to her. And never said another word.

"She must be a fuckin hypnotist," Max murmured.

"I hope she makes him forget our names," Sal said.

"He never knew them," I said. "All he knows is our numbers."

"That's all he needs."

Then Sal started doing his version of Senator Claghorn. If Cannon was going to listen to our conversations, Sal was going to give him something to hear. "Well, FRANKLY, I think the future of NATO is a question of STRATEGIC priorities. The Mediterranean must be CONVERTED into an AMERICAN LAKE. We can't allow the damn RUSSIANS to THREATEN OUR NATIONAL SECURITY!"

"No doubt about it," Max said.

"Make no MISTAKE! They are out for WORLD DOMINATION! They plan to CONQUER AMERICA and CLOSE THE BAPTIST CHURCHES! They will come in and make MISCEGENATION THE LAW OF THE LAND! Turn us into a NATION OF HALF-BREEDS! They will let the COLORED RACES go to school! There'll be NIGGERS IN THE ORCHESTRA OF THE REX THEATER! Mark my words!"

Max rolled his eyes at me. Red Cannon stared at the bottles behind the bar, then stood up, holding himself very erect, and with a kind of wordless dignity walked straight to the door and went out. We all got very drunk. At closing time we slipped through the back fence onto the base. We found Maher on duty at the dumpster. He was drunk, too.

Chapter

38

OH, CHILD, SHE said, what'd you let get in your head? I took the damned *bike* to work. When I come home last night, I needed to pick up some groceries; couldn't do that riding the bike, could I? So I took the car. Went all the way back down the road to Sham's and got some fresh milk and some bread for breakfast. Simple as that. You can't let that *crazy* stuff get in your head. You won't get me *close* to you that way, child. Just drive me off.

I'm sorry, I said.

Don't you be saying you're *sorry,* hear me? Just don't let some devil eat your brain. You're here *now,* with *me,* on a Thursday night in 1953. This ain't some damn movie. This is *us.* This is *here.* We got *this.* You and me. I never thought I'd have this and here it is. And we don't need to have evil stuff eating up brains. Not your brains. Not mine.

You're right.

So come over here.

I went where there were always new things to learn. Maybe the only things that mattered. We lay side by side in the cool evening, and she kissed my neck and then sucked on it and pinched my skin and then pressed gently on my head, moving me to her breasts. She pushed them against my cheeks and then I had the wet tip of my tongue against the dry tip of a nipple, the aureole pebbling as I flicked it. But she pressed again, moving me away, and I was at her navel, kissing it, pushing my tongue into it, and her whole body writhed, her breath changing, the inhaling high pitched, the exhaling deeper, the sound beyond her control, and then my head was between her legs. I wasn't sure what to do, so I thought if I was her what would *I* want me to do, and I kissed the inside of one thigh and came up to the great black hairiness, breathing on it, afraid, unsure, and then kissed the inside of the other thigh, nibbling at her skin with my teeth, my hands sliding under her bottom and squeezing. I was afraid of doing the wrong thing, of moving to the wrong place out of stupidity, and then she put both hands on my head and guided me to the crevice, and I inhaled the damp female smell, the earth smell, the tidal salt, and I placed my tongue in the center of it, and moved gently and uncertainly along the closed lips, down into the wetness and then lightly dragged my tongue gently upward until everything else opened like a dark flower. She made a deep moaning sound, a sound almost detached from her and yet most deeply from her, a pleasured sound but sad too, as if life itself were leaving for just that moment and I did it again, and felt for the first time in my life that hard hidden slippery little nipple under my tongue and she said *there* and I flicked it and she said *Right there* and I flicked it again and then again, and her voice dropped deeper than I'd ever heard it before, it came from some deep underwater canyon, and she said *Oh Gawwwwwwddddddddd there.* Her hands leaving my body now, and gripping the side of the narrow bed, while I eased the flat of my tongue along the tiny tit, very lightly, then suddenly darting it into her as deeply as I could. My tongue become a cock: I glanced up once and saw her kneading her breasts, pulling them up to a point, and then I pressed my mouth on her and sucked the little tit as if it were a tiny cock, sucked her cock the way she'd sucked mine, doing it over and over, until at last a high-pitched plea came from her, all full of fear and resistance, saying *do it, stop,* saying *don't stop,* followed by a trembling lost wordless sound, and I kept doing it in rhythm to her breathing and mine, to her sounds, to her deep flooding need, until she just came apart. Her legs shot out the length of the bed and locked and she grabbed my head with both hands and then pressed her muscled thighs together and started to scream, up and high and down and low, like a flamenco singer, all in one long uncontrolled sound, and she arched up from the bed and then slammed back down hard at the shoulders, doing it again and then more weakly and then one final quivering time. She rolled to one side, then the other, and then took my head and moved me up and kissed my face that was wet from her. Licking me. And crying. Just bawling. She cried as she guided my cock into her soaked center and cried some more as I pounded fiercely into her and cried when I came and cried until she fell asleep with my arms around her.

Chapter

39

BBGAVE ME *a book to read, by a guy named Richard Wright. The man is a Negro. There were things in the book that I'd never thought about before. For example:*

"Among the subjects that white men would not discuss with Negroes were the following: American white women; the Ku Klux Klan; France, and how Negro soldiers fared while there; French women: Jack Johnson; the entire northern part of the United States; the civil war, Abraham Lincoln; U.S. Grant; General Sherman; Catholics; the Pope; Jews; the Republican Party; Slavery; Social Equality; Communism; Socialism; the 12th, 14th, and 15th Amendments to the Constitution; or any topic calling for positive knowledge or manly self-assertion on the part of the Negro."

It made me think that I should discuss all this with the Negroes but I don't know much about any of it. It's like a lot of other stuff: I feel ignorant most of the time, *not just when I hang out with the Negroes. It's with everybody. The dumbest thing I ever did was dropping out of high school. I thought nobody from Brooklyn could ever get to college and now I meet guys like Dunbar and they tell me college isn't that hard, that I could go when I get out. But I can't wait that long to learn about everything. I keep thinking I should just read the whole damned encyclopedia from A to Z. In a way, that's what they really mean by "hip"—* knowing *everything.*

.   .   .

The Boulder. Do I really feel it? Or am I imagining it? And if I only imagine it, is it real? I know the feeling *is real but it makes me feel ashamed, like I can't control myself. I hate the way feelings just take over. But if I didn't feel* anything, *what would I be? A rock. A plant. There's gotta be some way to have both.*

Vagina. *The passage leading from the uterus to the vulva in certain female mammals. A sheathlike part or organ.*

Vulva. *The external female genitalia.*

Uterus. *The portion of the oviduct in which the fertilized ovum implants itself and develops or rests during prenatal development. The womb of certain mammals.*

Clitoris. *The erectile organ of the vulva, homologous to the penis of the male.*

(Where did all the street names come from? Cunt, pussy, snatch, box, furburger, muff, crack, quim, crevice, twat. The glory hole. The bearded clam. And cunt. Always cunt. Cunt and cunt and cunt.)

"But above all, the best thing is to draw men and women from the nude and thus fix in the memory by constant exercise the muscles of the torso, back, legs, arms, and knees, with the bones underneath. Then one may be sure that through much study attitudes in any position can be drawn by help of the imagination without one's having the living forms in view." —Vasari on technique. *(In the base library.)*

Why are so many goddamned countries run by old men? Eisenhower's already old and he just started the job, and there's Churchill in England and Adenauer in Germany and Chiang in Formosa and this prick Syngman Rhee in Korea. The papers say the war could be over by now, that we have a deal for this peace treaty, but Rhee won't sign. Our guys keep getting killed and Rhee doesn't give a rat's ass. He wants it his way. So he will keep the war going as long as there's enough Americans to do the fighting. We ought to shoot the old bastard. How do *they do it? How do they get people to* obey *them? They couldn't beat up* anyone *in a street fight. How do they make young people go places to* die?

I find myself reading more and more of the front *of the newspaper.
Now there's a new thing, the French in Indochina, and it seems like it's
getting worse. Dulles says it's all tied up with Korea, but from the papers
you see right away that the French shouldn't be there. The place is a
colony, and the Indochinese want the French the fuck out. The French
won't go, so the Indochinese are trying to shoot them out. When does this
shit* end? *They also say there is a Communist govt in Guatemala. At
least that's closer to home, though I'm not even sure where Guatemala is.
Gotta check the atlas.*

*(I also find myself forgetting about the comics sometimes, and I worry
about it. I still read* Sawyer *and* Canyon, *and I glance at* Li'l Abner
and Joe Palooka. *But I used to read* everything *on the comics page. I
told people who laughed at me,* Hey, *this is just like a lawyer reading* law
books. *Since I was eleven I wanted to write and draw a comic strip. But
suppose I'm losing the urge? I mean, suppose I don't* care *about comics
anymore?* Then *what happens to me? What can I* become?)

I checked the atlas. Guatemala is just south of Mexico.

From The Art Spirit *by Robert Henri (great book lent to me by MR):
"Find out what you really like if you can. Find out what is really
important to you. Then sing your song. You will have something to sing
about and your whole heart will be in the singing."
That's so true. Henri is talking about music in order to make a point
about art. But it's also true about singing. I listen to the blues guys singing
and the power comes from the fact they are singing about what's important
to them, even if it is* pain. *Henri also says:
". . . Most people go through their lives without ever doing one whole
thing they really want to do."
(My father: it's true of him. It was probably true of my mother. True
of most of the people I know back in the neighborhood, even most of the people
in the Navy.)
And Henri says:
"The self-educator judges his own course, judges advices, judges the
evidence about him. He realizes that he is no longer an infant. He is already
a man: has his own development in process. No one can lead him. Many
can give advices, but the greatest artist in the world cannot point his course*

for he is a new man. Just what he should know, just how he should proceed can only be guessed at."
   Jesus Christ.

When I say the word "I" what do I mean?

Chapter

40

ONE EVENING WE went to the empty beach facing Perdido Bay. I loved the name of the great wide bay because of the loud honking record of "Perdido" by Illinois Jacquet and Flip Phillips. They'd taken a simple tune by Duke Ellington and made something insane of it, a sound without control. The bay didn't look at all the way the record sounded, but I felt some kinship to it because I'd at least heard the foreign word. Eden told me *"perdido"* meant "lost" in Spanish.

"What does *Santana* mean?" I said.

"Big holy one," she said, and laughed sarcastically.

"You don't think you're holy?"

"No."

We walked along the beach and talked about the history of the whole area, the fleets of French and Spanish sailors who washed up on its shores, to die of strange new diseases or to stay too long and die of an aching loneliness. The histories at the base library were vague and sketchy, written for high school students. Which one of those men first called this bay "lost" and why? Eden squeezed my hand. I asked her when her family had come to the Gulf and how and why. She gazed out past the bay and said, "Centuries ago." Explaining nothing about the how and the why.

And then we stopped. Two men were walking barefoot on the beach far ahead of us, their trousers rolled to their knees. One was short, the other much taller. But even at this distance, I recognized them. The tall one was Miles Rayfield. The other was Freddie Harada.

"Let's walk back," I said.

She looked at me, puzzled. "How come?"

"I know those guys up ahead. I don't really want to have to talk to them."

"Okay," she said, "we'll go to the shrimp place."

Chapter

41

LATE ONE MORNING in March, Sal burst through the double doors into the Supply Shack, leaned forward on the counter and sobbed: *"Joe's dead!"* His laid his forehead flat on the counter, pounded with balled fists, said "First *Hank,* and now *Joe*! Long live the proletarian revolution!", then whirled and hurried out. That's how we learned that Stalin had died.

Harrelson got out the radio and Jonesie said, *Good, I hope the son of a bitch suffered,* and Becket said, *Gee, dat makes Choichill de only one left outta da Big Tree.* The news bulletins were somber, but not sad. The words were all virtually the same: Stalin, the ruler of the Soviet Union, ferocious dictator, killer of millions, once an ally and then our most implacable enemy, was dead. To which Donnie Ray shrugged and said *This is all fine, but we still gotta swab down at four.* After a while, he took a phone call at his desk, nodding, grave. He talked a long time. A Marine pilot at the counter said *Maybe now we can get the goddamned thing in Korea settled.*

"This is sho nuff big shit," Harrelson said. "The whole damn shootin match could fall apart."

"Or start," Jonesie said. "Goddamn Commie bastards."

Then we saw Captain Pritchett hurrying around outside in a jeep, with a Marine driving and Chief McDaid and Red Cannon in the back. Donnie Ray finally put down the telephone.

"That's it, boys," he said gravely. "We're on full alert. The base is being secured *right this minute.* All liberty and leave is canceled."

And all I could think, while a near-panic swirled around me and the telephones started ringing crazily, was: *How am I going to tell*

Eden? I'm sure now that men thought the same things at Pearl
Harbor and Hiroshima and the Battle of Hastings. She was supposed to pick me up at the locker club at six and we were going
to the Warrington Drive-In to see *Moulin Rouge.* Miles had described the movie as pure hokum, full of lies and mistakes and
stupidities about this French painter Toulouse-Lautrec, but even so,
it was still the best Hollywood movie ever made about an artist. I
wanted to see it badly, wondering if I was anything like Toulouse-
Lautrec; Eden said she wanted to check out this José Ferrer, find out
if he was anything like me. But now all leaves were canceled and
we'd have to wait. I was eighteen and I didn't *want* to wait. Besides,
there was no telephone at the trailer and no way to call her at Sears.
I hoped someone in the store's appliance department would turn
on a radio and she'd discover that all the bases in Pensacola were
secured, so we could hold off the expected assault of the vengeful
Russians. She would know that I was joining all the other brave
American boys who would protect the country from a dead man.

"Are they kidding?" I said to Donnie Ray.

"Fraid not. Our troops are on alert all over the world."

"But *why?* The guy's *dead.*"

"Maybe he was murdered, sailor. Maybe there are some guys
worse than him, want to blow up the damn *world.* Maybe they'll
blame us. Who knows?"

"You mean there's a bunch of guys in the Kremlin saying, 'Okay,
now's our chance. *We can get Ellyson Field.'*"

Donnie Ray laughed. "Could be."

All through the day we saw jets screaming high across the sky.
We heard that there were plans to move the American government
to Cuba if the Russians invaded. We heard that SAC bombers were
in the air over Europe so they couldn't be destroyed on the ground.
All of them were carrying hydrogen bombs. Everybody talked
about the death of Stalin. Uncle Joe, some of them called him.
Worse than Hitler, a few said. A monster. Becket said Stalin was
a Catlick who started out to be a priest and then saw the light and
became a bankrobber and a Bolshevik and someone else said he was
born in Georgia, and Harrelson said, Yeah, near Macon. We drank
a lot of coffee. Customers arrived in a stream because the sky was
dense with helicopters, and that meant that parts were breaking,
failing, wearing out. Becket said he was glad that Miles Rayfield
was off at Mainside with Dunbar because if he was at Ellyson when

the Russian bombs started dropping that would *really* piss him off.

"He'd prob'ly throw his skirt in the air," Harrelson said.

And I thought of Miles Rayfield and Freddie Harada walking alone on the beach beside Perdido Bay. And that made me think of Eden Santana.

At lunchtime, Bumper was serving at the messhall and Harrelson was behind me on line. Bumper looked at me, his eyes twinkling in his round black face, laid some extra French fries on my tray, then reached under the counter and found me a piece of coconut pie. Harrelson stared at Bumper.

"How bout some of that pie?"

"Last piece," Bumper said, deadpan.

"You sure of that?"

Bumper held up an empty pie plate.

We moved on.

"Gahdam uppity niggers," Harrelson said.

"Is there anybody you *like,* Harrelson?" I said.

"Yeah. *Americans.* "

We sat together at one of the tables. Boswell came over and joined us. He didn't have any pie either.

"Captain's runnin around like a duck without a dick," he said.

"Ducks have dicks?" I said.

"Sure," Boswell said, "but they ain't what they're *quacked up to be*!" He slammed the table and Harrelson laughed, shaking his head, and then Boswell said: "Where'd you get that fuckin pie?"

"Why you even ask, Bos?" Harrelson said. "The boy's a damn Yankee niggerlover and the niggers love him back."

"Ah, fuck you," I said.

"It's the truth, ain't it? You upstairs in the slave quarters every other day."

"Maybe he likes the *smell* up there," Boswell said.

"Or the spearchuckin music."

"You guys just take your asshole pills, or what?" I said.

"Maybe he goes to town with em to get some a that dark meat," Harrelson said. I thought of Winnie standing at the jukebox, one foot curled around the other.

"Nah, he got his *own* stuff," Boswell said. "Everybody knows that."

"She ain't stuff," I said.

"Shew," Boswell said, "you *touchy* today, ain't you, boy?"

"Just lay off," I said. I was poking at the pie, then slid the plate toward Boswell.

"Want some?" I said.

Boswell grinned. "Nah. I don't even *like* coconut pie."

Harrelson reached over with a fork and clipped off a piece of the pie. "I do."

"Taste like creosote to me," Boswell said.

"If it ain't got grits with it, Bos don't eat it," Harrelson said to me. "What we gone do after the alert's over, Bos?"

"Jackson, Mississippi," Boswell said.

Harrelson turned to me. "He bin tryin to get me to go to Jackson Mi'sippi since last September."

"Do the ducks have dicks there?" I said.

"Five fuckin hours in the car," Harrelson said.

"We *gotta* go there," Boswell said.

"Why Jackson, *Mississippi*?" I said.

Boswell's eyes brightened. " 'Cause *it's the insurance capital of the whole damn South*!"

The words hung there for a long moment.

"So?" I said.

"*Insurance* companies, boy," he said.

"Yeah?"

"What does that mean?" Boswell said.

"I don't have a fucking clue."

"*Secretaries,* boy!

I got up, shaking my head, while Harrelson laughed. I started for the disposal room and saw Bobby Bolden coming toward me. There was a slice of coconut pie on his tray.

"Too bad about Stalin, huh?" he said.

Miles Rayfield and Dunbar came back around three. Rayfield's eyes were wide and agitated in his pink sunburned face. Dunbar was smoking a cigarette in an amused way.

"You just can't believe *Mainside*!" Miles said. "They're running around like a pack of medieval lunatics with the *plague*! You'd think the Russians just landed in *Mobile*!"

"Haulin out anti-aircraft guns," Dunbar said.

"They're making sailors *march*!" Miles said. "With *guns*!"

"And officers are checking all IDs, case someone got a Communist Party membership card on 'im," Dunbar said. "Tell him, Miles."

"My wallet was in the truck!" Miles said. "Who carries around an ID?"

"They *asked* him for it," Dunbar said, shaking his head in mock sympathy.

"And *arrested* me!"

"Marched him to the parkin lot to *get* the damned thing."

"Under *arrest*!"

"They didn't believe it was a Navy wallet cause it didn't have a rubber in it."

"And Dunbar here, this son of a bitch, he told them he hardly knew me," Miles said. "One of the damned jarheads said I even *looked* Russian. And then the thick-headed dumb bastard started doing one of those scenes out of some rotten World War II propaganda movie. He started asking me about *baseball*!"

"Babe Luth, you die," Dunbar said.

"And I didn't know what he was *talking* about. Then he asked me about *football*! Or as he called it . . . foot*bowl*. And I knew even *less*."

"So they took him to security," Dunbar said, laughing.

"And *held* me there, trying to get Donnie Ray on the damned phone," Miles said. "And of course the damn *lines* were busy for two hours and then *everybody* went out to lunch except that damned Larry Parsons."

"Dumbest white man in the United States," Dunbar said.

"And he didn't know my *last* name!" Miles said. "I've been here a year and *he never learned my last name*!"

"So what did you do?" I said.

"What do you always do in the damned Navy? We *waited*."

"Watched the flyboys get ready for an air strike on downtown Palatka."

Miles was laughing now at the absurdity of the whole world, smothering the laugh with a sunburned hand.

"The Navy," he said. "The goddamned Navy . . ."

We were at our desks, filling out forms. And then Larry Parsons came back from a late lunch. His face was all tensed up, his eyes wide.

"Hey," he said, "did you hear about *Stalin*?"

Dunbar fell on the floor and groaned.

A half hour later, Miles suddenly turned in his chair and faced
me.

"Jesus Christ, I almost *forgot*!"

He took a letter from his jeans pocket.

"There was a woman out by the gate, waved us down as we were
coming in," he said. "Asked us to get this to you."

He handed me the letter. Blinked. Turned back to his typewriter,
pecking out numbers on a form. The letter had my name written
on it in a small careful hand. I opened it.

> Dear Michael,
> Something has come up and I can't see you tonight. One of my
> kids is sick and I have to go to see her in New Orleans. I know you'll
> understand. Please take care of yourself and I'll see you as soon as
> I get back.
>
> > Love,
> > Eden

That was all. There was no phone number for me to call her, and
no address. Even the city was something new. She's never mentioned it to me, never told me that her children lived there, and I'd
been afraid to ask. There were a million things she never said, and
that I never asked. So as I studied the note as if it were a sacred text,
I thought it was very much like Eden Santana, full of holes and
confusions. She didn't say how sick the child was, or with what; she
didn't mention how long she'd be gone or how she'd get in touch
with me when she got back. All I knew for sure was that she was
gone.

"You okay?" Miles Rayfield said.

"Yeah . . . Why?"

"You're the color of newsprint paper."

"No. I'm okay."

At least she'd signed the note "love." I got up and went to the
counter and waited on customers. Move, I thought. *Do* something.
That way you will not have to think.

After a while, Miles left with Becket and Dunbar for the hangars,
the three of them hauling an engine on a truck. I went looking for
a pontoon part in the back, taking my time, trying to imagine
Stalin's last hours, anything to push Eden's face from my mind, and

then slipped into Miles Rayfield's studio. On the easel, a deserted beach was taking shape on a piece of Masonite. The colors were muted, the colors of dusk. But there were only large rough forms, no details, no drawing. I picked up the sketchbook and leafed through it. Miles Rayfield had made many more drawings.

The last five were of Freddie Harada. His face was beautifully captured in pencil from two different angles; his features looking boyish and innocent, but there was something new in his eyes and the set of his mouth, an aspect I'd never seen before on my visits to the Kingdom of Darkness. He seemed to be flirting with me. Or with the artist. The other pictures were of Freddie standing, looking directly off the page. He was naked. Late in the afternoon, I strolled over to the hangars to see Sal and Max. They were working together on the electronic system of a big HUP. I looked around for Mercado but didn't see him.

"Trouble with these goddamn things," Sal said, "if you *use* them, they break."

"The guys that design them don't have to fly them," Max said. "That's why they're so lousy."

"You guys seen that Mercado around?" I said.

Sal looked up. "He's off for a week. Went home to Mexico."

Jesus. *She's* gone. *He's* gone. *At the same time.* Max and Sal tried to explain to me what they were doing, but I couldn't follow it.

Chapter

42

THAT NIGHT, I couldn't sleep. Around midnight I went outside and sat on the stairs, breathing in the warm air, looking out at the thick clusters of stars. Then I saw Miles Rayfield coming around the side of the Supply Shack, walking fast, his head down. He didn't see me until he reached the stairs.

"Oh," he said, surprised, his manner oddly stiff. "Oh, *hello*. What are you doing *here?*"

"Can't sleep. Nice night."

He relaxed and took out his Pall Malls and lit up. "I thought maybe you were waiting for Lavrenti Beria to take over the base."

"Who's he?"

He told me and I laughed (too hard) at his little joke and felt stupid again. There were at least five hundred names of people in this world that were known by everyone except me. My head was filled with useless knowledge. But I didn't know Lavrenti Beria was the head of the Russian secret police. I didn't know a lot of things. I asked Miles if he'd just finished painting. He hesitated, then went rushing ahead.

"Hell, no," he said. "If there was ever a day they'd catch me, it's today. Imagine getting caught doing something *secret* on the day Stalin died? Oh, hey, I wanted to show you something."

I followed him into the barracks. The racks were full of sleeping men. Miles Rayfield went to his locker and I met him in the head, where the lights were still burning. He handed me a folder crammed with reproductions of paintings torn from magazines. "Study these," he said. "Copy them if you want." A lot of the pictures were by his own favorite, a Japanese-American named Yasuo Kuniyoshi. At first (conditioned by Caniff and Noel Sickles and Crane) I thought the drawing was clumsy, the postures awkward, the heads too big or the hands too small. Sometimes Kuniyoshi's people seemed to be falling out of the picture. But standing with Miles in the head, looking at the pictures while Miles smoked, I began to see in a new way. There was one painting of a fat big-headed kid with crazy eyes holding a banana in one hand, reaching with the other for a peach in a white bowl. The table was a dark orange and tilted so that we saw it from the top. A window was open to an empty landscape: two buildings, two clouds, the view empty and scary like the desolate buildings I'd seen in Renaissance paintings.

"Look at that kid's eyes," Miles whispered, pointing at Kuniyoshi's fat boy. "He's a monster. All appetite, all need, all want. Look at the way his hair is parted down the middle. . . . And see, he's got a little sailor boy's *shirt* on, but it's not *blue*. It's the color of dried blood. And the blue walls, the blue dead sky, you know he's living in a cold bleak world and eats to make himself feel *alive*. . . ."

Suddenly a door behind us opened and closed. And Harrelson was there, drunk, his eyes small and glittery. He looked at Miles and then at me.

"Well, looka this."

"Fuck off, Harrelson," Miles said. "The Russians are coming."

"*Two* of you . . . in the shithouse. In the middle of the goddamn *night*. Ain't *that* cute."

I stepped forward. "What's *that* supposed to mean?"

"You and honeybunch here," he said and grinned. "Couple of the year."

I grabbed him by his jumper and slammed him against the wall. I came within an inch of his face, smelling the souring booze on his breath.

"You say another word," I whispered, "and I'll break your fuckin head."

Someone yelled from the darkness of the barracks. "Knock it off!" And another: "Go to fucking bed!"

I waited for them to be quiet and released my grip on Harrelson. I was trembling. Not in fear of Harrelson. I was afraid of my own sudden rage. I might punch myself into the brig.

"You're a real fresh boy," Harrelson said coldly.

"And you're a sick bastard," I said. "Make any more remarks, to me or Miles and I'll knock your dick stiff. He's my *friend,* got it? Friend."

Harrelson said, sarcastically, "Excuse me." He swished past me to the urinals and pissed for a long time, humming "I Can't Help It if You're Still in Love With Me." I almost laughed. He was such a relentless bastard. And the fury seeped out of me. Harrelson was mean, and I'd just slammed him around; but I had to love him for this. Hank Williams all the way. When he was finished, he looked at us in an offended way, and walked into the dark slumbering barracks. I exhaled a little too loudly. And then chuckled in a forced way. Miles Rayfield wasn't laughing.

"Thanks," he said, and walked quickly to his bunk.

Afterward it was even harder to sleep. Harrelson was now my enemy and I didn't want enemies. Not here. Not anywhere. I didn't want to have to watch my back. I didn't want anyone working against me in secret. I'd defended myself: yes. And I had defended Miles Rayfield. But suppose Harrelson was *right* about Miles? What did that mean about *me?* Miles was my friend. He didn't hoard what he knew about painting and drawing; he shared it with me, and nobody in the world had ever done that before. And he was pushing me to be better, to grow out of comics and childhood, to look at real art, to try it myself. His friendship was a challenge. He'd already showed me how to make money. In a way, he had turned me pro. But if I liked him and he was *queer,* did that make *me* queer too? It was so goddamned confusing.

I got up again and went back into the head and studied the other pictures in Miles's folder. Painters named Adolph Dehn and Aaron Bohrod, Anton Refrigier and Arnold Blanch. Maybe Miles had handed me his folder of painters whose first names started with A. None of them were in the same league with Kuniyoshi.

And then I saw Ben Shahn for the first time and I said out loud, *Jesus Christ.* These were pictures I understood. Ben Shahn. He had to come from the kind of places I came from. Here was a picture called *Handball*. A high handball court with four players in front of it, one of them a Negro wearing a hat. There were two men watching in the foreground. One in a cap, his hands jammed deep into his baggy trousers. The other's hands were folded. Beyond the handball court stood a row of tenements. I felt as if I'd played on that court, stood on that street. I was certain I knew the guy with the cap. In another Ben Shahn picture called *Vacant Lot* there was a boy in a sweater and knickers just like those I wore until I was eleven. A white shirt collar rose above the sweater and he was playing ball alone against a brick wall in a vacant lot. The boy was totally isolated. Sitting there in the john, in Pensacola, Florida, on the day Stalin died, I thought of long Saturday mornings in Brooklyn, up early to serve Mass at Holy Name and how it felt when Mass was finished and it was still early and the neighborhood was silent because the men weren't up yet and I would go down to the Ansonia Clock Factory and play ball alone against its dirty brick walls. I looked at the picture thinking: *This could be me.*

Then I heard a door open and slam and someone bouncing off a wall and a giggle and a new stirring in the barracks. I got up. It was Sal. He saw me and excused himself and went past me and pissed in the sink.

"Had to do that since I left the Dirt Bar," he said.

"I thought all leave and liberty was canceled," I said.

"Nah, just a rumor. Stalin's still dead."

"Where's Sam?"

"Blow job."

"What about you?"

"Too broke up about Joe," he said, and went off to bed. One of these nights, I thought, I have to really talk to Sal.

And I did.

Chapter

43

What Sal Told Me

MY FATHER IS a baker, I like to say: he bakes cars. He owns a body shop in the South Bronx and fixes cars from all over the borough. He never asks anyone for registration papers. A guy wants a black car painted pink? Why not? You want certain numbers filed off the engine block? Step right up. The old man does good work. He has a good eye for color, and he can do anything with his hands. He could've been a sculptor in another life. I guess when he was young he didn't have the choices a lot of people get in this world. Before he got the body shop he worked in a gas station, and before that he fought World War II.

But in a weird way I always thought that my father's father was my real father. He lived three blocks away from us, in a tiny apartment packed with books and magazines and old brown photographs. Their family was from Florence, in Tuscany, and they were always Reds. They didn't mean what we mean by a Red. Grandpa was some kind of socialist anarchist. He thought everything in the country should be shared by the people. Food, the ports, oil, big industry, every fucking thing. Nobody should starve. Nobody should be unemployed. Everybody should have a doctor. You know, real terrible disgusting stuff that would destroy the United States if we had it. But then Grandpa also felt that if there was a government, he was against it. "Ideas are wonderful," he would shout, in the apartment, with his books everywhere, pulling on his white beard, his arms flying around. "Abstractions are wonderful. Love is wonderful and justice is wonderful and the common good? Most wonderful of all. But the son of a bitching politicians will always sell you out or put you in the dungeon."

He married a woman from Siena. I don't remember her. She died in the early thirties, after my father was born. There were pictures of her around, though, and she seemed thin and a little afraid, standing in Coney Island or out at the Statue of Liberty, her eyes looking at you like she didn't know what the fuck she was doing in this country. Grandpa himself would never say exactly why he came to New York. There was some trouble in the Old Country, he'd say, that's all. I could never find out what it was, but it must've had something to do with him being a Red.

He had beautiful handwriting when he was young. They call it calligraphy now. Just beautiful, done with goose feathers, he said, and with special black inks he bought from some Chinaman on Chatham Square. When he and his wife first came here, he worked in a horse-and-buggy place during the day, and at night he would write these beautiful business cards for rich people—wedding invitations and diplomas, all that kind of thing. His wife was always mad at him because he spent all the extra money on books instead of clothes or things for the house. I've seen a few of them, on cardboard that's yellow now, ones he did for his sample case, that he'd take around to these mansions on Fifth Avenue, him with his lousy English, and they'd laugh and say hey, a Wop who can write!

Then he got hurt in an accident and his hand, the one he used to write with, was all smashed up and the doctors amputated his forefinger. It must of broke his fuckin heart. Just telling you this, it almost breaks mine. But when he told me about it, a half a century later almost, he just shrugged. It was meant to be, he said. If it wasn't one thing, it would have been another. I guess he was what they call a fatalist. But I didn't really believe him when he just shrugged it off. I used to see him sometimes in a corner of the apartment, just staring at the hand.

He worked in a garage during the twenties; I guess that's where my father got his thing for cars. But when the Depression came, Grandpa opened a grocery store in The Bronx, moved from the Lower East Side to Pleasant Avenue uptown and finally to the Bronx. "With the store, I knew we would always eat," he said. "In the Depression, nobody drove cars." After my grandmother died, the heart went out of him (everybody said) but he kept the store going. He lived upstairs and he always had something for me when I went over there, ice cream, tea, little pastries. And he would tell me about the books. Most of them were in Italian, but he told me I had to read them, that nobody who claimed to be civilized could live without these books: Dante, Machiavelli (The Discourses, he said, read them, the plans for a republic, and remember that The Prince was really a job application) and Leopardi and Manzoni and Guicciardini. He talked about these guys as if they were his personal friends. "Like Dante said once . . ." He knew Latin, and when I went to Cardinal Hayes he would get me to read Caesar and Cicero and Virgil out loud, telling me how to pronounce the words with passion, as if they were written by living breathing men, not dead guys, not professors. He made me love Latin. When it was my turn to read, the brothers and the priests didn't know what the fuck I was up to. They were used to Latin sounding like a chant from the mass and not like a language that people used for giving orders and fucking women. I was good at it but I could never get the hang of Tacitus. Even Grandpa bitched about the man's style.

He hated Mussolini with a passion and that is what caused all the trouble in the family. My father married a woman whose parents were from Sicily. The Siggies hated the old Garibaldi people, because when Garibaldi conquered Sicily he got rid of all the old fucks, the Mafia, the hustlers, the guys bleeding the poor, the landlords. My mother's family thought people from Firenze (that's what we always called Florence because that was its name) were snobs, faggots, commies. My other grandfather wouldn't speak to Grandfather Infantino.

The families barely talked. Me and my sister were like prizes, passed back and forth from one family to the other. My mother was one of nine kids, so her side of the family acted like my Grandfather Infantino was some kind of faggot for only having two kids. But nobody had a monopoly on common sense. Grandpa couldn't stand my mother either. I heard him call her "that Arab" once and didn't know what he meant until I read how the Arabs were in Sicily for hundreds of years. They were opposites, those families; the Florentines were very clear about most things, a little cold, able to talk about subjects besides themselves. The Sicilians were hot, silent, and devious; I always felt there was something else going on, always; and then there would be those sudden explosions, screaming, yelling, even flat-out violence. It was like once a week someone got punched out. For staying out late. For flirting with some bad guy. For fucking up the toast. Anything would do as an excuse. My Aunt Marie got her jaw busted for going out with an Irish cop. My Aunt Marie was beaten with a belt for saying she didn't believe in God—by the other grandfather, who didn't even go to church. They were nuts.

But all during the war, we ate good. I gotta say that. We had my grandfather's store and there were two of my uncles on my mother's side who came around sometimes with steaks. They wore striped suits and pinkie rings and when they were there everybody whispered. I guess they were connected. Wise guys. I don't know. Nobody ever explained. Even today, my mother just says, "They're in business." I know one thing: they didn't go off and fight in the war.

My father did. That's why I barely knew the guy. He was gone almost from the time I started remembering things. Then in '44 he was in a place called the Hurtgen Forest and had part of his leg blown away. He came back home in the spring of '45. He never told anyone he was on his way, just came home, two days after Easter, in uniform and on crutches. And when my mother went to the door to answer the knock and she saw him she started bawling. I didn't know who the fuck he was. My sister Fioretta started bawling too; she's three years older than me so she remembered him. They sent me over to get my grandfather and wow! That night! That night! There musta been two hundred people in the apartment, coming from all over, my mother's people too, with trays of spaghetti, lasagna, ravioli, sodas, beer, whiskey. One guy had an accordion and they all started singing in English and Italian and every once in a while my mother would start bawling again. She never left my father's side. Not once. The noise was beyond belief. I wanted it to go on forever, for a week, a month, a fucking year.

The next day, my father slept until three in the afternoon, like he was catching up on three years' worth of sleep. My mother brought him breakfast in bed, pancakes and bacon and cold milk. And then she led him to the bathroom for a hot bath and that's when I saw how he needed help, he needed to lean on her, he couldn't walk without a crutch. He didn't say anything to me or my sister. He didn't complain. He just said to my mother, Okay, it's okay, thanks, it's okay.

He'd put on weight while he was away and didn't fit into his civvies, so that first day we called Ralph the Tailor to come up the flat and he made measurements, all of them talking in Italian, and then the tailor went away and for the next four hours my father just sat by the window in the living room, in the big chair, dressed in a bathrobe, looking out at the street. He didn't say a word to me. Not a fucking sentence. I was only eleven but I knew he had gone through some bad shit. I went to see my grandfather, to find out what I did wrong, whether it was my fault my father didn't talk to me, and Grandpa said to me, "He will never be the same, so you better get used to it." Now I meet some of these bullshitters in bars who tell you how they won the fucking war and I always think of my father on that first day, staring out the window, and I want to punch someone out.

I was getting pretty angry myself then. I was the top student in my class in grammar school, but the fucking Irish priests and nuns never encouraged me to do anything more. I was some kind of freak to them. I was Italian, so I had two choices: the Sanitation Department or the rackets. Somehow, around that time, I discovered that if I hit people on the chin they went down. That's what got me some respect. Not that I could read Latin or I knew who Leopardi was, but that I could beat the shit out of somebody. My mother's family began to approve of me at last. Some of my cousins saw me belt out two Irish guys at Orchard Beach one day and thought I was the next Rocky Graziano. They wanted me to start going to the gym, go in the Gloves; the two wiseguy uncles said they would take care of everything. I started to feel I was hot shit.

Then in 1947, when I graduated from grammar school, my grandfather sold the grocery store to a Puerto Rican and took me on a trip to Italy. He must have seen that I was on my way to being just another guinea hoodlum. He told me the trip was a gift for my good grades, but I always thought it was to save me from myself. And it was also a gift to himself. He hadn't been back since 1900. More than half of his life. Part of it was, he wouldn't go there while Mussolini was in power, part, he didn't have the money, part, some kind of crazy pride (he wouldn't go there as poor as the day he left). Now he wanted to see the Old Country. Just one more time.

I loved that fucking trip to Italy. Jesus Christ, I loved that trip. We went on a ship called the **Genoa;** *it was all white and everybody spoke Italian and there were some war brides on board, and I thought they were the most beautiful women I ever saw in my life. Even the ones with the moustaches. I could understand most of what they were saying (from my father's Italian and the Latin) and they made me so horny I whacked off five times a day, at* least. *At night, I would go out on deck with my grandfather and we'd stand next to the lifeboats and look out at the Atlantic with the moon shining and the waves slapping the hull and a band playing somewhere and I guess that's where the Navy thing came from later.*

On that trip, I started to think that Grandpa knew everything. He talked about the Mediterranean as the place where civilization came from, and he woke me up and dragged me to see Gibraltar when we went by in the night and showed me where Africa was and pointed toward where the Alps were and explained about the way all the rivers of Europe came from them. When we came into Genoa, he started to cry. Home at last.

Florence was pretty much a mess that year. There'd been some fighting there during the war and Grandpa's old house on the Arno was gone. They were still repairing the bridges and the museums weren't open yet because they were trying to figure out what was hidden and what the Germans stole and what had been destroyed. Most of the people he knew were dead or off to America or Argentina, but he didn't seem to care. He showed me the house where my grandmother lived. It was a pension now, filled with students.

And he showed me the place where Savonarola was burned at the stake. We sat at a table in a outdoor café and had coffee with a slice of lemon and he looked out and said, Leonardo walked here, and Michelangelo and Machiavelli. He talked like they were there when he was young. He told me to look at the light, too, the way the shadows fell. Clarity, he said. Always clarity. The clear light of Firenze. That's why they painted that way he said, with passion. And he told me to look at the faces of the people. And he told me, no matter what anybody says, no matter what you feel when they call you Wop or Dago or Guinea, remember this day. Remember this place, remember where you came from.

We were back home three months when he died. And there ain't a day goes by I don't miss him. I graduated top of the class at Hayes and I wanted to go to college. But Korea broke out. We had no money (my mother blamed my grandfather for wasting the store money on the trip to Italy and my father wouldn't ask the wiseguy in-laws for a dime). I had a girl at the time, an Irish girl from Brook Park. Her father didn't approve of me, but at least I was white. She's still my girl, I guess, but it seems like a long time ago. I decided if I went into the service I could go to college on the Bill when I came out. Study history or Latin. Teach, maybe. I know you don't believe that, seeing me fuck around the way I do sometimes. But I mean it. Fucking around keeps me from going crazy. When I told my father I wanted to enlist, he said, Go in the Coast Guard, go in the Navy, go in the Air Force. Go anyplace, but don't go in the goddamned infantry. And I thought of those nights with my grandfather, standing on the deck looking at the moon over the Mediterranean, and it wasn't even a choice.

Maybe, when this Navy bit is finished, I'll make that trip to Italy. Sometimes, just before I go to sleep, I see myself coming down a gangplank and there are people from customs and signs telling you where to go and a band playing music and everybody crying and laughing, and there, right *down there in the crowd, waiting for me in Italy, is Grandpa.*

Yeah.

Chapter

44

THEY BURIED STALIN, and a fat little guy named Malenkov took over. He had a high unlined forehead with a spear of hair falling over his brow. After one look at him the whole country calmed down. Even the Navy. Liberty and leave were restored. Sal organized a Josef V. Stalin Memorial Service at the Dirt Bar and we all got drunk while he tried to teach us the words of the "Internationale." Even Dixie Shafer gave it a try. Joe McCarthy got on the radio to warn us that Malenkov was worse than Stalin and had agents everywhere in the United States. Nobody believed him. In the mornings on the base, Captain Pritchett supervised the flowers of spring. Business at the Supply Shack was brisk. In the late afternoons, Bobby Bolden played the blues again, with the shades up and the windows open in the Kingdom of Darkness. I did seven portraits of women I didn't know. And there was still no word from Eden Santana.

I started to write her a letter, telling her how much I missed her and how I couldn't sleep at night thinking about her and how I wanted her now and next month and for the rest of my life. But there was nowhere to send it and so I destroyed it without finishing it. One afternoon, I walked all the way to the lake. Nothing had changed; the car was still gone, the trailer still locked up. I sat on the front step for an hour, breathing in the jasmine and honeysuckle, sweet alyssum and magnolia, the aromas of our days together. When the no-see-ums arrived at dusk, I walked back.

On Friday, Miles Rayfield asked me if I wanted to go with him to the Rex to see *Moulin Rouge*. He wanted to see the movie again before it left Pensacola forever. I hesitated, mumbled about how

I was waiting for my girlfriend to come back, and Miles said: "When a movie leaves the Rex, they burn the prints." The truth was that I was a little afraid of going to a movie with Miles Rayfield. What if he put a hand on my leg during the show or something? He was my friend and I didn't want anything to ruin that friendship. But what if Harrelson was *right*? And what about those drawings of Freddie Harada and the way they walked along Perdido Beach. Then I thought: *Jesus, you are letting Harrelson do your thinking for you.* "Okay," I said, "let's go."

We took the bus downtown. I remember thinking the movie was amazing, with color that I'd never seen before, and lovely music and even a great performance by Zsa Zsa Gabor, who until then I'd thought was a joke. It turned out that I didn't have anything in common with Toulouse-Lautrec; but sitting there in the dark, I wanted to *live* the way he did, in a studio in Paris, prowling around the cafés and whorehouses and music halls at night, making drawings. But even that vision reminded me of Eden. After all, how could I spend the nights in whorehouses and bring Eden along? How could I live that way and still go home to her at night? I watched the movie while another movie played in my head. Until Zsa Zsa Gabor's shimmering white skin forced me to embrace her. *Good-bye, Henri,* she called to me. *I have a rendezvous with a Russian guard. . . .* While her breasts pushed up out of her silky gowns. When the picture ended, I felt like crying. Miles Rayfield, as they say, never laid a hand on me.

On the way to the Ellyson Field bus, I bought a copy of *Life* with Stalin and Malenkov on the cover. The story inside had a headline, FALSE GOD DIES, CRISIS IS BORN, with pictures of the Kremlin at night, snow on the ground, a few lights burning, Russia in darkness. A guy named Edward Crankshaw said in an article that Malenkov and Beria had overthrown the Politburo within twenty-four hours of Stalin's death. He didn't say how he knew this. He certainly wasn't there. I read a paragraph to Miles: *"The men who have carried out this revolution, Malenkov and Beria, now work together. But the very violence of their first joint action has set the tone for times to come. . . ."* In other words, the Russians would be worse enemies than ever.

"How do you figure they pull this shit *off*?" I said. "Do they go in the room with their guns out and say, *We're the boss now?*"

"Yeah," he said, "it's sort of like a primary in Mississippi . . ." And turned away and closed his eyes.

The bus moved slowly, past the honky-tonks and the churches.

I read a little story about a guy named Raymond who worked for the Voice of America, which was being investigated by Joe McCarthy. Nobody had accused him of being a Communist but he'd thrown himself in front of a bus in Cambridge, Massachusetts, leaving a note for his wife that said, "Once the dogs are set on you, everything you have done since the beginning of time is suspect."

Jesus Christ.

That poor bastard.

The driver stopped at the locker club and we got out, went in and changed clothes. Then we walked slowly down the road to the main gate. Miles was quiet for a long time.

"Back to Anus Mundi," he said at the gate.

Chapter

45

B Y SATURDAY AFTERNOON, there was still no message from Eden. I was trying to sleep when Bobby Bolden came to the barracks. He told me to get dressed. They were all going to a club that night to hear a blues singer named Champion Jack Dupree. Out in the boondocks somewhere.

"Catty loves this guy," he said. "So she's *your* date, if you get what I mean."

He didn't ask me if I wanted to go. He seemed to know that Eden wasn't back from New Orleans and that I was feeling lost or abandoned or wasted. So he *told* me to go with them. And at dusk I was driving Bobby's Mercury, with Catty beside me, Bobby next to the door, and Bumper, Rhode Island Freddie and Tampa crowded into the back seat. We drove northeast out of the city, along roads that Bobby Bolden knew, through a thousand acres of longleaf pine. He pointed out small clusters of unpainted houses, part of the turpentine camps where blacks had worked since slavery days. Tampa argued about the true name of the pine. His folks called it loblolly pine or sand pine, and Bumper said it didn't matter, did it? Tampa said it sure did, 'cause after the Civil War, most of the cotton plantations closed. "Didn't have no free labor no more," he said. "So they planted the land with loblolly and sold it to the timber men. So it *do* matter, don't it?"

"In Africa, they be callin it Mau Mau pine 'fore long," said Rhode Island Freddie, and they all laughed. Catty glanced at me.

"We should've checked these damn local Mau Maus for guns," she said to me. "Before we got in the car."

"Not guns, woman," Bobby Bolden said. "Knives. *Long* knives. As in the Night of the Long Knives . . ."

"It's the Night of the Long Dicks everybody's afraid of."

They all laughed and then Catty pointed out a hawk circling over the pine forests and Bobby Bolden said, "Now *that's* free. No guard duty. No salutin'. No racist bullshit. Free . . ."

The hawk suddenly dove out of our sight, and then Bobby Bolden directed me into a side road, through darker country, plunging across bogs where the odor was suddenly sweet and musky and we could see hundreds of shrubs blooming like white walls.

"Jesus, that's beautiful," Catty said. "What *is* that stuff, anyway?" Nobody knew the name of the shrubs, and I wished Eden was there, she would know, she knew *everything,* and Catty said she'd like to find a perfume that smelled like that, and then suddenly it was dark. I turned on the lights, and we were moving down a back road, unable to see much except the trunks of pines and a few black people walking slowly on the shoulder. Bobby Bolden leaned forward, peering into the darkness. He took Catty's hand.

And then we began to hear music. It was way off, a thumping bass line at first, and then the tinny distant sound of brass, and now there were cars on the road, red taillights ahead of us, and more people walking in groups of four and five, all dressed up, and then we could see the lights of the club.

"Up there," Bobby Bolden said. "Slow down. Real slow. *Crawl,* man. There's people everywhere. . . . You see that white post? Take a right just past that."

We pulled into a dirt field serving as a parking lot, and we all got out and stretched. Before us stood the Blackhawk. It was a long, two-story building with a neon sign glowing in the humid night, and music pounding from its open doors. And I realized that there were hundreds of black faces all around us in the dark, and black laughter floating on the night air, and the sibilant sound of black women shushing men and deeper voices answering with words I couldn't hear.

"Better hold her hand," Bobby Bolden said. "Never know who might be watchin from the woods."

I took Catty's damp hand, and Bobby Bolden led the way to the door, with Tampa, Bumper and Long Island Freddie behind us. I saw eyes fall upon us, looking at Catty and me, our white faces, then turning away, neither the men nor the women making eye contact with us, with the music louder and Bobby Bolden paying for us all at the door. A huge black man was taking the money, wearing a dark jacket and sunglasses, nodding as Bobby Bolden whispered something to him, then calling a thin light-skinned black man over, saying something to him. Catty's hand was sweating now, and I wondered if she saw this as the future, barred from white clubs, excused, introduced, explained in the black world. I thought: *No wonder your hands are wet. They might be wet for the rest of your life.*

The light-skinned man led us to the last empty table in the large smoky room, and we sat down, I to Catty's left, Bobby Bolden to her right. I glanced around and saw the silhouttes of men and women against a bar along the far wall. At the tables beside us, all the faces were black, some shiny with sweat, the men dressed in suits, the women wearing flowers in their hair and bright dresses, bottles and ice buckets in front of them, a few people turning to look at the white faces, then turning back to the music. On the bandstand in front of us, seated at a piano, was a small neat man. Champion Jack Dupree. Singing.

Now some people calls me a junker . . .

The crowd roared.

Cause I'm loaded all the time.

Another roar.

I just feel happy and feel good all the time . . .

Bobby Bolden laughed and said we wouldn't hear this on the radio, a song about being a junkie, and then told me to watch the way Champion Jack played the piano with the thumb tucked under the fingers of his left hand, to make the bass notes jump, told me the man was a legend back home in Naptown, where he'd played for years in the thirties, told me he came from the same New Orleans orphanage where Louis Armstrong lived as a kid, was a boxer during the Depression, later played at the Cotton Club. Bolden glanced at the door then and looked around sternly at the other black faces, as if saying to them, *Be cool, don't start any shit, these white folks is my guests.* And Dupree sang on: *Please write my mother, tell her the shape I'm in . . .*

Then Rhode Island Freddie waved in the direction of the door, while a waiter set up ice and a bottle and glasses for our table. I turned to look at the door and three black women were moving through the room, men looking up at them with greedy eyes, the

three women all round and their hair piled up high and their
dresses fitting them like tattoos. One of them was Winnie. In a
white dress.

"Yo, yawl," she said, and Bobby Bolden covered his mouth with
a finger and nodded toward Dupree. No talking, the move said,
until the man finishes. Winnie sat next to me, and leaned close, her
breasts pressing against my arm, and whispered in my ear. "Mem-
ber me? Ah'm Winnie." I said I sure did remember her and she
reached past me for the ice and the bottle.

I want you to pull up your blouse
Let down on your skirt
Get down so low that
You think you're in the dirt . . .

Dupree smiled widely as the crowd yelled, stomped, banged on
tables. Winnie squealed and then tried to introduce the other two
women, Velma and Cissy, and then Rhode Island Freddie was
moving on Cissy and I saw Bobby holding Catty's hand below the
table and Bumper had moved beside Velma. Champion Jack Dupree was finishing, the whole room cheering and standing, the little
man nodding and smiling and walking off in a hurry.

"Sure do love the way that man sing," Winnie said. "Whad you
think?"

"Great."

Her eyes were fixed on me as if I was the only man in the place.
She looked even darker in the dim light of the Blackhawk, her skin
offset by the white dress, and she wore a lot of black makeup around
her eyes. Her lips were thick and full, covered with glossy coral
lipstick. She asked me again about New York, while Dupree's
musicians left the stand and some burly men in T-shirts began to
set up for another act. I tried not to look at her too hard or to stare
at her breasts. I didn't want her to say, Ain't you never seen no
cullid girl before? Recorded music played on the sound system,
slower stuff, some of those records I'd heard up in the Kingdom
of Darkness. Lowell Fulsom. Roy Brown. The small dance floor was
immediately crowded. Rhode Island Freddie led Cissy away by the
hand and Bumper took hold of Velma and Tampa went away
somewhere and came back with a bony woman with scared eyes and
slipped past us into the dancing crowd. Winnie said, "Dance?" I
glanced at Bobby, thinking: *What is this? Is she some gift?* Bobby said,
"Why in the fuck not, man? Go *ahead* . . ."

Winnie led the way, holding my hand, and I felt strange, wondering if this was the way black men felt when they were in a place where everyone was white. I was sure everybody was looking at me or looking at Winnie, or both. Just waiting to see if I made a grab at one of their women. Just waiting for a sign of arrogance. So I held her hands in a formal way, hoping everybody would think I was polite, that I was a visitor, a friend of the girl and the guys at our table, just a guy passing through. But the floor was packed now, bodies jammed against bodies, and Winnie pulled me close and said, "Relax, man," and we began truly to dance. I could smell soap in her kinky hair and felt her breasts against my chest and her syrupy belly against my crotch and I thought about Dean Martin and Jerry Lewis, I thought about Robert Henri and John Foster Dulles, but nothing worked: I got a hard-on. Not a mild run-of-the-mill Saturday afternoon hard-on. Not the hard-on you get from the shaking of a bus or seeing some luscious pearly-skinned Zsa Zsa Gabor in a movie. Not some piddling venial sin of a hard-on. This was a throbbing mortal sin, iron hard, thrusting right out my shorts and pressing for release from my trousers. She felt it. She squeezed my hand. Her voice was a growl.

"Least you aint no queer," she said. "Least Ah know that."

"I—uh—"

"Hush, now," she said, grinding into it, the heat coming off her, while I tried to keep my back to the people at the tables, so nobody could see what had happened to me but feeling that everybody had seen it already, that it was like Pinocchio's nose, getting bigger and longer by the second.

"We should take a walk," she said.

"I can't walk now," I whispered.

She eased away from me an inch or two. "Nobody can see you. Look aroun. Yawl see any other mens?"

I could barely see the couple next to us in the hot warm darkness.

"Where to?" I said.

"We got us a borried car. Outside."

And I knew then that she wanted it as much as I did, that maybe I was the first white man she'd ever been that close to, that I was as new and strange and dangerous to her as she was to me. We started to leave. And then the room got brighter, and the dance floor started to clear, and there was someone on the PA system talking in a blurred voice. The hard-on vanished. "Later," I whispered. She looked annoyed, but said, "Aw right . . . later."

I had to piss and said I'd be right back and started walking toward the entrance. Over the microphone, I heard the word ". . . Upset-ters" and turned around and Rhode Island Freddie was right be-hind me.

"Don't wantchoo getting lost," he said, and smiled. He guided me away from the entrance and along the back wall and down a corridor. There were a couple of bare forty-watt bulbs hanging from electric wires strung along the ceiling. I could hear a roar from the main room. Then in front of me I saw Champion Jack Dupree arguing with the large black man with the sunglasses.

"Ah, juss wunt muh fuckin *money,* man. Tha's all."

"You play you second set, you get the green."

"Shit," the old man said, turning away. "Shit."

Freddie and I went into the john. There was a shallow trench along one wall, and we stood there and pissed into it.

"Po fuck cain't get his bread," Freddie said. He stuck a hand-rolled cigarette in his mouth. He lit up, finished pissing, took a deep drag, then passed it to me.

"Little reefuh?" he said.

"Nah. Hey, what's with this Winnie, man? How come none of *you* guys want her? I feel funny, you know—"

"Doan feel funny, feel *her.*"

Champion Jack Dupree walked in and went to the trench and pissed in silence.

"I still don't get it," I said.

"Her husbin's on the Midway," Rhode Island Freddie said with a sigh. "Mos' of us, we know the dude. Wouldn't be right, us *knowin* him and all. But it seem lak such a waste, hear? And *you* don't know the man. . . . Hey, Champion," he said to Dupree, "want a toke?"

Champion Jack Dupree zipped up his trousers and reached for the reefer. "You hear that fat mothafucka?" he said. He inhaled, held it, let the smoke out slowly. "If he still in the *county* when I finish the second set, itd be a fuckin miracle." He looked at me. "What the fuck are *you* dune in this shithouse?"

"Came to hear you," I said.

"Don't bullshit a bullshittuh, white boy," he said. "I hoid yiz talkin. You here for da fine brown pussy . . ."

Rhode Island Freddie giggled.

"Know what I'm saying to you?" Champion Jack Dupree said. "But ya better watch it, white boy. Pussy drive men into da valley of fuckin deat'."

He took another toke, then sang a few lazy bars:
See, see, rider, see what you have done
You made me love you, now your man done come . . .
We all laughed, and started back to the hall. The place was going crazy. Women were standing, screaming, shouting, and the men were shaking their heads, and laughing, and tugging at the women. And up on the stage was the craziest looking black man I'd ever seen. He wasn't very big, but his hair rose high over his head in a pompadour, all greasy and wild, and he had on a long draped baby-blue jacket and red shoes and he was standing up at the piano, banging hard while horns and saxes honked behind him and his eyes rolled around, out of control. I couldn't hear the words. But words didn't matter. He came to a crashing windup and whirled, and did a double split, stood up, and bowed. The crowd went wild, calling at him, shouting for him. He had the mike in his hand, gazing in a glassy-eyed way around the room, and then saw me about to sit down again next to Winnie, who was very sweaty now, with deep stains under her arms and down her back.

"Why, hello, Miss Thang!" he said, and pranced toward me, and raised his eyes as the room laughed, and then abruptly turned around, furrowed his brows, stared into the darkness and started another song:
Awop-Bop-a-Loo-Mop Alop-Bam-Boom . . .

Chapter

46

WINNIE HAD A room on the first-floor right of Miss Harper's Boarding House on East Dancer Street. We lay together on the small bed.

Where you learn to *do* such a thang? she said.

I said I just learned, but I didn't say where.

She said, No black man ever did that.

No?

She said, He just be worryin bout his own sweet self.

I said she was beautiful. But she knew that. Beautiful women always do.

She said, You do such a thang, word get *around,* black ladies be lining up side yo *house,* boy.

I said she must have men lined up at her house too.

Winnie said, No, they all know mah man. Caint do nothin round here. . . . That's why when Ah saw you, Ah said, *him,* Winnie, grab *him.*

I asked her if she'd ever slept with a white man before.

She said, Hell, no. . . . Not that these crackers don't come own to me. . . . Oh no, they come *own.* But Ah wunt sleep with one of them, if they paid me a hunndid dollahs.

She looked at me, her breast dark against my chest. Her hand was playing with me.

Winnie said, It ain't really *white* anyway, is it? More like *pink.* . . . Hey, what about you? You slepp with a black woman before?

No.

That's not whut Ah hear, boy, she said, and laughed in a dirty way. You damn sailors.

I said, Don't believe every thing you hear about sailors, Winnie. She sat up and dragged the tips of her breasts across my face. She said, Kin you do that thang again?

Chapter

47

ALL DAY SUNDAY, I ached with shame. Not guilt. This was old-fashioned shame, as raw and pulsing and systemic as a toothache. In a way, of course, making love to Winnie was a corporal work of mercy, as they called it in the Catholic catechism. She'd been alone too long, trapped in a neighborhood where everybody knew her and her husband, growing old every minute. Or so I told myself (a lie I would tell myself all my life). I had given her pleasure in the here and now, while Winnie was young, while she *needed* it. We hadn't hurt anyone. Her husband didn't know and probably never would, unless that winter Winnie presented him with a blue-eyed boy. And yet I was ashamed of myself. The shame wasn't about screwing the wife of another guy, a sailor I didn't know. Nor was it about sleeping with a black woman, becoming at last, for a couple of hours, what Harrelson called a "nigger lover." No, the shame was about something else. Out of weakness, in a moment of opportunity, I had betrayed Eden Santana.

Yes, she had gone away and I didn't know when she'd be back. Yes, we had no deal, no verbal or written contract. But I knew that I couldn't tell Eden what I'd done. I was ashamed of that. And I hadn't used a rubber. Suppose Winnie gave me the clap? Suppose she'd given me a good dose of something her husband picked up somewhere? I could give it to Eden. And what if Winnie *was* pregnant? Nine months from now, her husband would show up at the hospital and a nurse would bring out the baby, which would have my eyes and skin that was lighter than Winnie's and lighter than his and the smile would shift into rage. And if the child *was* mine, wasn't that *my* responsibility too? A son. A daughter . . . my flesh and blood. I couldn't go around and say to Winnie, I'll give the child my name, I'll send some money. If I did, the husband *would* cut me (in Bobby Bolden's phrase) long, deep, and *con*tinuously. But if Winnie did have a baby, and it was mine, then all my life I'd wonder how that kid was doing, my kid, raised black in the back end of a small town on the Gulf of Mexico. I couldn't tell Eden about that either. Or anyone else.

And the odor of my shame would cling to me all my days.

On Monday, I drifted into routine and the shame began to ease. Harrelson wasn't talking to me. Not since the night I'd slammed him into the wall. I always said hello when we passed each other, but he kept walking, his eyes not even seeing me. It was as if I were black. Sometimes he and Boswell would look across at me and Miles Rayfield and something would be said and they'd giggle. I asked Boswell about this once, and he said, "Aw, you know Harrelson. He's just a redneck. Don't take his boolshit too serious."

"*I* don't," I said. "But *he* does. He thinks Miles and I are queer or something."

"Shit, he thinks *Eisenhower's* queer. Don't let it bother you none."

At lunch time that day, I walked over to the hangars to see Sal and Max, and there was Mercado just inside the hangar, looking dashing in a flight suit. He held a cup of coffee and was staring at a large blackboard that listed pilots and flight times.

"How are you?" I said.

"Ah, Mister Devlin. *¿Como estas?*"

"How was your trip to Mexico?" I said.

"Ah, hell, I didn't go," he said. "The last minute, I hear there was a flight to New York. From Mainsi'. So I take that instead. But you know what? I end up in Philadelphia. I think I am the first Mexican in history to ever go to Philadelphia. I wait three hours for a plane, then at last I give up and got a bus to New York . . ."

"What did you think?"

"I was there before with my father, when I was twelve," he said. "So I have seen it before, New York. My father was then working for the Mexican government. It's a great city, no? Life! Energy! But now, it looks a little more bad. More dirty. More crowded. And expensive? *¡Ay, caray!*" He smiled. "I should have gone to Mexico."

My stomach was turning over. *He took her to New York!* That's all Eden ever wanted to see and *he took her*! Anger shoved my shame away. Anger at her, anger at myself for being such a goddamned jerk. Go ahead (I said). Ask him. Ask him *did he take her there*!

"You go alone?" I said (trying to be casual, gazing off at the list of flights and landing strips and aircraft numbers) . . .

"Yes, what a sin! You ever try to get a girl on a Navy plane? Easier to get a Russian to come with you. But there were plenty of girls there, oh, boy. They got some *beauties* in New York, no kidding." He laughed. "All giants, too. What the hell they feed those women in New York? All big, like lampposts, those girls. And one disgusting habit: they all chew gum."

" 'Meet me in New York some time," I said. "I'll introduce you to some short girls that don't chew gum."

"They got any medium size?" he said, and we both laughed.

I was near *giddy* as I walked to the mess hall. Captain Pritchett's flowers were rioting happily against the walls of all the buildings on the base, red, yellow, violet. Sprinklers played brightly on the lawns and the grass looked green and plump with spring.

"Hey, lover man."

Bobby Bolden came up beside me, the two of us moving toward the mess hall.

"I don't know what you did Saturday night, man, but that Winnie done gone crazy."

I was scared for a moment, then saw Bobby Bolden's dirty grin, and smiled in what I thought was a cool way. That was one of the moments in my life when I truly felt abruptly older, as if some ability of mine had been ratified and granted approval. And I felt somehow bigger. I said (trying to underplay it), "She's some woman."

He looked at me and shook his head. It might have been in pity.

In late afternoon, I wrote a letter to my father, telling him the usual bland lies about life in the Navy. I didn't tell him about Eden Santana; Red Cannon; Miles Rayfield and Freddie Harada; Kuniyoshi or Ben Shahn; Winnie; the Blackhawk Club; the Dirt Bar; Dixie Shafer; the Kingdom of Darkness; Captain Pritchett's lost wife; Mercado; Sal's grandfather; or the way to use vine charcoal. I told him the weather was nice and the food okay and the beaches beautiful. I sent him a picture of me under a palm tree with the snow coming down, taken by Becket. I asked my brothers to write me. I was sealing the letter when the telephone jangled on my desk. I picked it up and said hello.

"It's me," Eden Santana said. "I'm back."

Chapter
48

What Eden Santana Told Me (I)

Y OU'VE NEVER HAD a child, so you don't know. But I have two girls, real pretty, one fifteen, the other ten. But just saying it that way doesn't explain anything. I could be describing someone else's kids, I could be talking about dogs or canaries. You see, having children's different from anything else on this poor earth, and maybe you can't ever explain it to people that never have had them. But those girls come from me, from my body, I held them in me, I gave them life in blood and pain, and then nursed them and watched them learn to walk and say words and ask for more than food, hear me? You ain't ever had that, child, so you don't know why I up and went when I got the word. Maybe you'll never know. Maybe no man ever could.

Those girls been part of me for half my life, since when I was younger than you are now, the oldest one anyways. I never had a time after I was sixteen that I didn't have a little girl pulling on me, followin me from room to room, callin for me scared in the night. Never. Maybe that's part of why I'm here and not in New Orleans. To be free of that love, that need, for just a little while. That and James Robinson. Maybe you don't want to hear about James Robinson but I better tell you, child, because if you're talkin to me you're talkin to someone who is part of James Robinson. As James Robinson sure is part of me. There's no getting round it. He is there. In my life. Important as those little girl children.

I was fifteen when I met him, the summer of thirty-eight. He came walking down Burgundy Street in a white suit and white shoes and the sun was on him and he was more than six foot tall and I thought I was seein some kinda god that come rising up outta the swamps and the morning and *landed in New Orleans and came walkin right at me, so close I could reach out and touch him. He walked in a rollin way, on the balls of his feet, like he knew all kinds of things and had been everywhere and he looked at me and paused and then kept on walkin, headin for Esplanade and the Faubourg Marigny. At the corner, he stopped and looked back and he had me.*

I didn't know him and neither did anyone else. He just came from nowhere and then I was pregnant and then he married me, dressed in that damned white suit, and we set up housekeepin. My daddy didn't talk to me for three months after the wedding, cuz he didn't like James Robinson from the startup. I was a girl and Robinson was a man and my daddy saw things I didn't see, I guess. Robinson wouldn't tell me what he did, he said it wasn't women's business, but he brought home money, lots of it, and my family helped me with the furnishing and the cooking, cause he had no family and this was the Depression still and everybody was tight, even them that had. James Robinson would bring me flowers, and fancy hats, and pretty clothes, and once even a pink silk parasol to hold off the sun. But most days he went to work in the evening and slept late in the morning and when I said to him at last that I wanted a body beside me at night, when I said I wanted him to do with me what he wanted to do, when I said I wanted to do with him some things too, that I had urgings, that I had wife need in me, James Robinson just smiled and said, Yes, my dear. That was all: Yes, my dear.

So I followed him one evening, me all swollen up with the first girl, feelin fat and watery and ugly, afraid that he had some other woman, some life that I didn't have a part of. And he went into a club on Rampart Street, with men and women at the door, all of them nodding at him when he went in, some dark place where they all knew him and I felt a chill then in August, a cold breeze upon my heart, knowing that James Robinson must be a man who was living off women. Just like that, just watching him, I wondered too did he have *something, a disease or something, that made him scared to come to me in the night. And I was terrible afraid, not of that, not catchin something, but afraid that when the baby was born, he would take me to that place on Rampart Street and make me work for him.*

But knowing that, knowing where he went, I couldn't come to askin him about it. It was his secret and it was mine, but I never told him of my knowing of it. I didn't sleep with him for the rest of the time of the waiting. I felt the baby's life in me, the stretching and pushing, that other heartbeat, that new need for room that the baby wanted: and that was what I had instead of James Robinson. We called the first baby Nola after New Orleans

Louisiana. Nola Robinson. He thought she was the cutest thing and he held her in his arms and was sweet to her and brought her all silk and satin clothes, but he never did come to me in the night, not for months, saying to me I had to heal long after I was healed, saying it wunt a good thing to have too much of that too soon and then I got mad and asked him did he get what he needed in the house on Rampart Street and that was the first time he beat me.

He put the baby down and tore off my clothes and took a strap to me, puttin welts all over me. And when I was bent over on the floor, weeping and hurt and the baby cryin, he just dressed and went out the door and walked away. He come home that night and run his hands over the welts and heard me cryin and then he finally came to me. And finished quick, with me all achin and unfilled and everything in me all coiled up and ready to burst, but not bursting, ready to be lost but not losing, ready to die but not dying, and he said, Yes, my dear. Like that. Yes, my dear.

So I knew that was what it would always be like with him and I kept it secret. He would come to me only when he caused pain. He would beat me and hurt me and then come to me. So that I hated it, the bed part. I didn't want it, the loving part. I erased it, the wife part. I watched movies and when people kissed I thought Yes, my dear. And waited for the beating to begin. I'd read a novel, and when it got to the point where they would sleep together, I began to tremble, afraid for the person in the book, afraid for me, thinking, Yes, my dear and Yes, my dear and Yes, my dear. I put everything into Nola, I touched her, squeezed her, kept her too long at my breast. And James Robinson, with his long body like a god, with his fine wild eyes and white suits, he just kept leaving for Rampart Street.

My mother must have picked up the grieving, knew there was an emptiness, a thing not happening. She knew just about everything about me anyway, cause I'd come from her the way Nola came from me, I'd been her extra heartbeat. And she started visiting in the afternoons, after James Robinson rose from his bed, and she would look at me and then hold the baby, then look at me and change the sheets, then look at me and go to the garden, then look at me and touch my face and say, finally, the last time, tired of looking, tired of not saying what she wanted to say, held my hand and said, You a woman now. You got to get you a man.

And I knew she was right. I was a woman now. I'd had a child within me and a child at my breast. I had a right to have a man. But there was one big problem: I had made a holy vow. That promise meant something to me. The keeping of it. And there was another thing: I was afraid. Afraid that a new man would be just another James Robinson. Sometimes I would look at men, all lathered with sweat in the hot sun fixing the streets, or delivering ice, or sawing off limbs in trees full of Spanish moss and I would imagine how they'd feel beside me, on me, in me, and then stop: seeing in my mind James Robinson in white walking up the street like a god. And not trusting myself, I closed up, sealed myself. I didn't even cry anymore, didn't fall into grieving. My mother saw that too.

And then the war started and the army took James Robinson and I was happy. We closed the little house and I moved back home with Nola and my mother cooked and cleaned and I started to read. I read every kind of book from the library down on Burgundy Street. I read Gone With the Wind, but that didn't sucker me in; I knew what Rhett Butler was, I seen my Rhett Butler go into a house on Rampart Street. I read Anna Karenina by this Russian Tolstoy, and that was better. He knew something about people. I read poetry. And I read books on nature. I learned the names of all the trees and plants, the birds and the insects and the animals. Readin those books, I was suppose to be teachin Nola, but I was really teachin me. My father was workin at the Higgins Shipyard then, making torpedo boats, and the money was comin in for the first time in his life and he bought a car and taught me how to drive and then when we had paid the car he bought a house out by the Atchafalaya River, an old house and small, but with plenty of room for us because my brothers and my sister were all grown up and gone by then. So my mother and I made that sweet little house into something. We planed the wood clean, we changed the windows, we painted everything white, inside and out, and hung pictures that she bought in the old markets in the Quarter, we scraped down the wide plank floors and stained them dark and shellacked them and kept polishin them until they were nearly black. And I was glad bein there, sweatin at the work and seein Nola walk. I was happy. James Robinson was gone. I hoped he'd never come back.

Nola learned to talk in that little house beside the river, and we had a Victrola and she began to sing too, learnin all the words of some songs before she could even make full sentences. My father loved her. Probably more than he loved me. On weekends he would take her fishing in the bayou, givin her a line, and they'd come home with buckets of catfish and sometimes my sister would come out with her children and we'd eat all night and sing the old songs and Nola would sing what she learned from the phonograph, and I was happy. Sealed up, closed, manless and happy.

I expected to hear some news from James Robinson, but I sure wasn't eatin my heart out over him. The truth be told, I dreaded hearin from him, or seein him show up. There wasn't a letter from him, not a call, and then

I started hoping that one day someone from the army would come to the door, looking sad and proper, like all the scenes in the movies, and he would tell me that James Robinson had been killed in action. The truth be told, I came to want that. The truth be told, I wanted him dead. Every day, I read The Item *and* The Times-Picayune, *lookin at the list of casualties, hoping in a shameful way that he'd be there among them and then I'd be free. I'd be through with the holy vow. I could start another life. The real one.*

But the war ground on and there was no word about James Robinson, and Nola started school, and I didn't even think anymore about a man beside me in the night. And then the war ended. There was a big celebration in New Orleans and we drove in, and my father said, "Well, now we see if the Depression's really over," and my mother looked at him in a funny way and there were soldiers and sailors all drunk on Bourbon Street and brass bands and girls dancin and people makin love in public and noise like the greatest Mardi Gras in history and we cheered and shouted and then went home. I lay in bed thinkin of all those young men I'd seen in the Quarter and how I could have had all of them that night, in cars or hotels or backyards, and didn't want even one. And I couldn't sleep, thinkin of their young hard bodies and sad drunk eyes, and got up and went outside, where it was hot and buggy, August it was, and my father was alone out there on a white chair, just looking off toward the swamp. He couldn't sleep either. He said, I'll have to look for another job tomorrow. He said, They ain't gonna need no more torpedo boats. And, of course, he was right. The war was over and both of us were sadder than we'd ever been.

I was in the garden a few weeks later, with the first cool breeze of the autumn blowin and no sun under a haze, when I heard the car and looked through the loblolly pines and saw him. James Robinson. Walkin with a limp, dressed in an army uniform. I stood up. He saw me. I waited. I wasn't gonna run to him. I waited and waited and he came to me limping and reached out his hands and I could see that he was much older now and he was cryin. So I hugged him and he hugged me and my mother came out and saw us and then took my father's car to school to get Nola.

James Robinson cried and cried and said he was sorry for everything, for the way he used to treat me, for not writin, for being the way he used to be before the war. But he was different now, he said. The war had changed him. He'd almost died and knew when he didn't die that there were things in his life that meant something and now he was home, had been home for three days, had walked the streets lookin for me, askin where we'd gone, and now he'd found me and now everything was going to be okay, now everything was going to be real truly fine, now everything was goin to be the way it should have been in the first place.

My mother arrived with Nola, and the father and the daughter regarded each other like strangers. Until the girl just started bawlin and James Robinson did too, and they hugged each other and took a walk down by the water and talked for a long time and I thought, Maybe it's true, maybe it's gonna be real truly fine. He came back holdin Nola's hand, and then my mother said to Nola, well, we better go spread the word, girl, so your momma and your poppa can be alone.

Alone with me, he was desperate, comin at me like a crazy man, sobbin, apologizin, tellin me not to look at his leg, not to touch it, not to let that leg bother me. I laid with him, and he started saying the names of places, all in the Pacific, the names of strange islands and old battles, all the while askin for forgiveness. Until at last I gave him what he wanted. And renewed the vow, in the back bedroom where everything had for so long been sealed.

We moved out two weeks later, to another house in the country that he bought with cash. He said he won the money gamblin while he was in the Pacific and I believed him and maybe he told the truth. But he said he didn't want to go back to the city, that he had no more to do with that life, that he would never even look at the house on Rampart Street again. He had money from the government too, he said and that helped when we needed paint and shellac and furnishings, and he kept busy all winter cleanin and fixin the house and choppin trees to make a path to a bayou, saying here we'd be happy, here we'd be safe. He didn't much like goin to my momma's house. He said he didn't like people watchin him. Not even relatives. And maybe I should've known then. But I wanted to believe what he was, that he'd changed, that he was this new man, that he'd been made different by the war. Made good.

And soon I was carryin Jesse within me. I could feel her bumpin, and Nola came and laid her hand on my belly, her eyes fillin up with wonder, and she sung lullabies to the sister she couldn't even see. And then James Robinson got silent again. I asked and he didn't answer, just glared at me for the sin of askin. Soon he would say only what had to be said, little telegrams of words, and he would stare off at the road and if a boat came down the bayou he would hurry into the house or hide behind some trees. Once we were driving across the Huey Long Bridge, the back seat full of new clothes for Jesse, and he kept looking behind him in the rearview mirror, and then took a right into Algiers and went up and down side streets and pulled into an alley and just sat there breathin hard and never said a word. I asked what was the matter and he snapped at me, No woman's business. I held his hand to calm him, and he pulled it away.

I was thirty-seven hours in labor with Jesse, in more physical pain than ever before in my life, my insides tearin apart, my every pore teemin with blood it seemed, feelin split, turned inside out. James Robinson come to the bedside later, looking down at me, his eyes all funny. I told him he had another little girl and we'd call her Jesse after my grandmother, if that was okay with him. He just nodded and looked out the window. And I could feel his goin away. Right there in the room.

He stayed with me when I came home cause I was sick still and exhausted and sore all over. I slept for almost three days. There was blood still leakin from me too and it was on the sheets and he took the sheets off the bed in a disgusted way and burned them and went to New Orleans for more and came back late at night, lookin at me in a scared way. I thought it was the blood, that maybe it reminded him of the war, and what had happened to his leg. But when I said that, he slapped me hard across the face and knocked me down and I knew then that it was beginnin again. I wouldn't cry. I knew that if I cried that would set him on me, and I was still hurtin from Jesse. He kept hittin me and I started thinkin about escape.

He knew. He told me in the morning, You better not run, woman. I told him I was free, I could go where I wanted to go, and then he took a board and hit me with it. Right here, see? Under the chin. The scar. The blood was drippin off me and I was knocked to my knees. And that got him hot and he made me do something to him, with the new blood flowin off me and the blood from Jesse still leaking out of me, and I knew that was the end. When he had his way, he went out, leavin me there, and drove off some-where in the car. I was all alone with the new baby—Nola was at my mother's—tryin to fix myself; no phone, no car, my jaw hangin loose, broken so I couldn't even brush my teeth, couldn't rinse him away with water and salt, and the blood not stoppin and the baby at my breast, the blood mixin with milk and then I heard another car and it pulled in front of the house and it was the police.

The two of them came to the door and I yelled through that I was locked inside, and they smashed down the door and saw me there, ragged and beaten and bloodied, and the older cop said, Oh my god, and they took me out to the police car with Jesse in my arms and rushed me to the hospital and on the way they told me they were tryin to find James Robinson.

The doctors wired my jaw and called my mother and father and everybody came to the hospital and Nola saw me and cried because I looked like an eggplant, all bent and distorted and purple and yellow. And then I found out from Daddy that there had been no war, not for Mister James Robinson. I found out he'd been part of a robbin crowd that shot up a place while he was in the army, and he'd been shot up too, by the cops, all of this out in Texas, and they'd put him in the penitentiary, slammin him away for twenty-five years, because two cops were shot and another man killed. That's what happened to his leg. And he'd spent the war there in prison, not in the Pacific Ocean fightin for his country. And then had escaped, comin back to New Orleans, looking for me, for refuge, for hiding. Until they picked up a trail, a stickup here, another one there; they smelled him like a hunter in Africa smells a lion.

And I cried and cried, not for him, but for the children, for Nola and Jesse, because they carried his blood, they carried the wildness, the anger, the lies, the need to inflict pain, and I knew that for the rest of their lives there would be a contest in their blood between me and James Robinson. The truth be told, I felt like such a damned fool too. For listenin to him. For believin him. For lying with him after what I knew. For renewin the goddamned holy vow.

The police pursued him, catchin him at last in Memphis a year later. By then I was back home at the house beside the Atchafalaya. This time sealed for good. I went to church every day, prayin for strength, wanting to resist everything now, hopin I would last long enough to cage the blood of my children, and then, when they were grown and decent and had found their way, I could be released. To Paradise. Yeah. That's what I thought. My father died. My mother grew old. The girls grew up and played piano and spoke French and Spanish along with English, taught to them in the Catholic school. Last year, Momma died too. I thought: When will it be my turn?

I was alone in the old house beside the Atchafalaya one morning last November. I went down to the water, to look at the boats goin by, sittin on the little dock we had down there, feeling empty and content. And when I came back to the house James Robinson was sittin at a table in the kitchen. On the table he had a big .45 pistol. He was peelin an apple with a parin knife. He didn't say anything to me. Didn't even look up.

I backed up to go to the door and run. To just get away from there. From him. He picked up the gun and said if I ran he would shoot me down and then when the children came back he would shoot them too, because he didn't care anymore, he wasn't afraid of death, he'd just as soon go out that way as any. And I stopped then and he told me to lock the door and I did and he took me there on the floor, tearin at me, slappin at me because I was dry, because I wouldn't move, because I wouldn't cry or even speak. He did what he wanted for an hour. In every place and every way he could think. And then said he was going to be around again, that he was free of prison, that he would always be around for me, that he would come and have me whenever he wanted. And left.

I said nothing to the children. He stayed away for a week and then came again to me in the middle of the night with the girls sleepin and put that big gun on the table beside the bed. This time I was wet without wantin to be and hated myself for it and tried to laugh at him to stop him and he beat me again with the strap, exulted at my wetness, made me beg for more when I didn't want more, and then pushed me face down on the floor and hurt me bad, and then started to dress. Don't you come back, I whispered to him, or I'll call the police. He smiled at me and shoved the big gun into his belt and said, Yes, my dear. And left.

That night I packed up the children and their clothes and took my father's old car and drove to my sister's house and hid there. For two weeks, I never saw the day. All the while, the children were wanting to know what was happening and why they couldn't go home and my sister's husband went out with a gun on his hip to the house on the Atchafalaya to pack up more things, all the old and good and personal things, and stored them in his place of business, while I trembled when I saw a shadow at the window or heard a board creak or a tree branch brush against the eaves at night. And then I discovered I was pregnant.

This time I knew what I had to do, knew I couldn't pass on more of James Robinson's evil blood. My sister found me a doctor in Atlanta. And before Christmas, I went up there and had an abortion and made the doctor tie my tubes. It was terrible. But when it was over, the truth be told, I was happy. I knew that I'd never have to worry, ever again, about life risin in my womb. That's when I saw you, child. Comin back from Atlanta, on New Year's Eve. Or more accurate, comin away from Atlanta. Because I wasn't going home. Not with James Robinson roaming around free. My sister found a place in a Catholic boarding school for my daughters. She sees them every Saturday and I tried to explain to them that this was only for a while, that James Robinson was still out there, with his big gun and evil ways. The police were lookin for him. My sister's husband had some people lookin for him too. And I came here, to Pensacola, to hide, to start to live.

I wasn't even sure what that meant, child. To live. But I knew that I was tired of not feelin anything but fear. I was tired of not bein a woman. Of bein sealed up. Of bein alone. I have missed so many things in my life. And then I met you and you were sweet and you were like the boy I should have had, the boy that might have come down that block the next afternoon, instead of that man in the white suit that I thought looked like a god. You are so good to me. I want to be good to you. I want you to know what I know and for you to know it for the rest of your life.

So when I had to leave so sudden, I hoped you would understand. It wasn't planned. I had called my sister to ask after the children and she said she'd been tryin to find me for two days because Nola hurt herself at the school, fell off a horse, fractured her skull. My heart just fell into my stomach. I went there as quick as I could, thinking: She could've been dead and buried and I never would've known. So I had to go. There just wunt any choice. The blood called me. Nola was so happy to see me and the doctors said she had a close call but would be all right and I explained and explained to the girl about where I was and what I was doin and how it would only be for a while (which is the truth) and explained again (tryin to find the words and not scare her too much about the blood of James Robinson that was coursin through her own sweet veins) and she understood, she's smart, she said she would pray for me and have the nuns pray for me too. I stayed until she was up from the bed and all right, and spent the rest of the time with little Jesse. She doesn't understand in the same way. She was hurt the most. But I think in the end that she understood too. I hope so. I hope you do too. Somewhere out there, James Robinson is movin in the dark. But I'm with you, child. So please be good to me.

PART
FOUR

Chapter
49

S**HE'S BACK.** *I'm happy again.*

Actors I like: Brando, Bogart, Cagney, Astaire. But I don't get it about James Dean. Maybe the girls just like his red jacket. I see him in a movie and I ask myself: What kind of actor would this guy be if Marlon Brando never existed? He steals all of Marlon's moves, and mumbles like Marlon sometimes does, but because he looks different they think he's something new. I bet if he went up against Brando in a movie, Marlon would destroy him. (On the other hand, what would happen if Brando went up against Bogart or Cagney, or any of those guys that came out of the Depression? Maybe they would eat **Marlon** *alive). Edward G. Robinson is the best of all. He looked scary as shit in* **Key Largo**, *sitting in the bathtub in the heat, waiting for the hurricane.*

Just what does a movie director do? And what is a producer? Ask somebody.

I'm happy, yes. But also confused. She has so much more of a life to think about than I have. If I told her my story, it would be a couple of sentences long. She has everything: New Orleans, kids, guns, beatings. And I don't think she's even begun to tell me all of it. I want to teach her something, tell her stories, change her with the things I know. But what do I know? Not enough, maybe never enough. She will always have a head start on me. And there's nothing I can ever do about that.

One thing I can do is learn more about the world out there. She never reads newspapers and I always do. So I can tell her about what is going on, if she is interested. Maybe that will keep her from thinking too much about her kids or James Robinson or New Orleans. Maybe she won't think about leaving Pensacola either. Or leaving me.

Why did I feel sorry for Red Cannon the other night? I should hate his guts but . . . It's got something to do with the way he belched as he was going out the door.

The second time he raped her, she got wet. She said so herself. So she liked it. She must have. Last night, I kept picturing her face as he did it to her, hating it and loving it at the same time. I couldn't sleep.

They say that King Farouk is about to be kicked out of Egypt. There's a picture of him in a bathing suit, walking along the beach somewhere with slippers on, so he won't get sand on his royal feet. He looks disgusting. And I wonder again: How do these fucking shitheads end up running countries? Who would follow that fat turd into battle?

And I wonder too, reading the papers, just what Porfirio Rubirosa and Baby Pignatari do for a living. They are always described as "playboys," but the papers never tell you where these playboys get the money to play with. One thing is for sure: It's not from work.

E finally explained the difference between Kotex and Tampax.

Something hurt Red Cannon. Real bad. I'm sure of it. (But he's still a prick.)

No wonder E never answers me when I talk about the future. She has this whole thing, over in N.O., kids, a sister, a brother, a house, a past, and this crazy husband roaming around someplace. How could she ever go off with me into the unknown? But then, how could I go off without her?

I don't really get Marilyn Monroe, but I'd like to fuck her. If she'd promise to talk in a normal voice.

Chapter
50

THE NIGHT BEACH is empty now, and the terrace doors shudder with the wind rising off the sea. I look at the telephone on its table beside the bed. With this steel and plastic instrument, I can choose to hear a hundred voices of the present. But I don't want to hear them, for the same reason that I do not switch on the television set or go down and stand at the hotel bar.

I am hearing the voice of Eden Santana.

I am a boy trying to make sense of the world and of women and of love. I am feeling again the sense of shame and forgiveness, separation and reconciliation. I am learning to walk.

And I am once more in the warm Gulf spring, during the time when Eden and I were playing The Games. I work every day at Ellyson Field. I draw pictures for money. I see Sal and Max and Miles Rayfield and Bobby Bolden and the others, but I cannot say what we did or talked about together in that wet season. The reason is simple: I was too deep into The Games. Every evening in the months after she returned from New Orleans, I would go with Eden to the trailer. Sometimes we simply ate dinner and then made love and slept together a while before I returned to the base.

Sometimes.

Most times we played.

One evening she pulled up before the locker club and looked out through the car window at me in a funny way. Her eyes seemed to be boring a hole in me. I started to get into the car on the passenger side but she slid over. You drive, she said. She was wearing a raincoat and dark stockings and new red high-heeled shoes.

Sure, I said, a little surprised because Eden Santana loved driving that car. I pulled away. I knew she was staring at me but I didn't want to take my eyes off the road to return the stare.

What do you think of me, child? she said after a while.

I mumbled.

Tell me, she said. Tell me what you really think of me.

I couldn't find the right words. My head was too full of pieces of songs, scraps of dialogue from old movies. They canceled one another out.

I love you, I said finally. That's what I think of you.

I was heading west into the open country that stretched away to Mobile Bay. She just gazed into the dusky light of the countryside.

There's something I always wanted to do, she said.

I waited.

She said: But maybe if I do it you won't love me anymore.

I felt a tremor of fear. Did she want to tell me about some other lover? About Mercado? Some terrible news about her husband?

She said: Follow the railroad tracks.

The road was two lanes wide and moved along the side of the railroad cut. Off in the woods there were small houses, an occasional barn or gas station. The trees were in full leaf and I drove slowly under them. There were no other cars. After a few miles, the road dipped and the world was much darker. She touched my hand.

Slow down, she said.

The dip led to a crossroads. The other road went north under a trestle.

Quick, she said. Pull over and stop.

I did. We sat there for a few minutes in the dark. I didn't know what she was going to do. She didn't speak. She didn't touch me. I pushed my fingers lightly through her hair but she didn't react. Her body hardened, as if she were gathering herself into one huge muscle of determination. Then she was alert, hearing something that I didn't.

Watch this, she said. I want you to get out and watch.

She climbed up the embankment, holding her red high heels in her hand, with me after her. When we reached the top, she slipped the shoes back on. She motioned for me to stay low beside the tracks, out of sight. Then I heard what she'd heard: the train whistle, away off, clearing the track, warning cars and children and animals to get out of the way, sounding mournful at first and then arrogant and commanding as it came nearer. I could see the train now. The light on the engine was cutting through the darkness. A half mile away. A quarter. Then a few hundred yards, the wheels clacking on the polished iron tracks, the whistle snarling, urgent.

And then, in the full glare of the light, Eden dropped the trench-coat. She was completely naked, except for the dark stockings and the red shoes. She placed her hands on her hips, her weight on her right leg, the wind lifting her hair, and I could see her nipples sticking out. So could the men in the cabin of the engine. The whistle paused, the train seemed to slow. And then Eden took her breasts in her hands, offering them to the railroad men. Great clouds of steam billowed from the engine, Brakes screeched, iron trying to grab iron. She picked up her coat, turned her back to them and came running to me, laughing and whooping as we slid down the embankment.

Did it, did it, did it, did it, she said, flushed with excitement. *I did it!*

She slipped on the coat and got into the car beside me, and I raced north under the trestle and then took a right on the first dirt road I saw. She whooped. She laughed. She squealed in a very young voice. And I laughed too. It was as if we'd just robbed the biggest bank in Pensacola.

Ho *boy,* she said: exultant. And then pointed toward a dark stand of trees in the woods up ahead, empty and unfenced.

In there, she said. I can't stand it another four seconds.

She dropped the coat again, leaned against the rough bark of a sycamore tree and had me enter her standing up.

Tell me you love me, she said. Tell me. Tell me.

She always took those red high heels along on the days and nights when we played The Games. She never wore them for anything else. If they were on the table, or lying on the front seat of the car, it was a sign that we were going to play. Sometimes she would have me lie facedown, naked in a field, and slowly press a heel into my ass until I made sounds of pain. While she was doing this she would play with herself, and when she was about to come she would turn around, straddling me, rubbing her cunt frantically against the back of my neck while kissing the marks of her heels on my skin until she came. Sometimes, in movie houses, she would slip off the shoe in the dark and use the heel to play with my cock. Or while I was licking her she would flick the heels of the red shoes against her hard dark nipples.

One evening I came to the trailer and she looked at me in that odd drilling way. Neatly laid upon the bed were some women's clothes. They weren't hers. Or I had never seen them before. Certainly they were much larger than hers. A long flowered dress. Panties. A garter belt. A bra.

Put them on, she said.

I smiled, but I was very nervous. Miles Rayfield's face flashed before me.

I'm serious, she whispered.

Then she was undressing me and my cock was getting hard.

Start with the panties, she said. I want to see you put them on.

The panties felt silky and feminine against my skin and my cock protruded against them. The bra fit tightly against my chest, the rayon straps digging into me, and she stuffed it with Kleenex. Then I added the garter belt, and she helped me slip the dress over my head. She told me to sit on the edge of the bed, and then, with her breath quickening, she started painting my face. Cream. Powder. Rouge. Pushing my lips apart with her lipstick. She put kohl around my eyes. Then produced a straw hat and tied it under my chin, her breath coming more quickly now. She pointed at a pair of low-heeled women's shoes.

I'll be right back, she said, and slipped into the john. I glanced at a mirror and saw a handsome young woman who happened to be me.

I was thrilled.

Then the door to the john opened and a sailor in dress whites appeared.

Eden.

She was completely without makeup, her hair hidden under a white hat, her breasts somehow flattened under the jumper. The pants were tight against her crotch.

Come on, bitch, she said sharply, and grabbed my hand roughly. She led me to the door. I'm taking you for a fucking ride, you dumb cunt.

I laughed out loud.

Eden didn't laugh.

She drove very fast to Sham's, a supermarket on the edge of

town. We went inside together with me thinking: *If I see Red Cannon now, I'm fucked for life.* I was wearing the flat women's shoes, but it was still hard to walk. Eden made me push the shopping cart down the aisle. She barked orders at me in a deep rough Louis Armstrong voice.

All right, she said, don't fo'get the damn co'n flakes.

I thought I would laugh again but a heavy woman in jeans and a flowered shirt turned into the aisle. Eden reached past me and squeezed my tit so the woman could see and then I giggled in a girlish way and slapped her on the wrist.

Stop that, Horace, I said.

Eden grabbed my other tit.

Ah'll do what I want wif you, woman, she said, and then grabbed my ass.

The woman in the flowered shirt looked panicky. She turned around and hurried away. Eden laughed and grabbed my ass again until it hurt.

Out in the parking lot, as I loaded the groceries into the trunk of Eden's car, she pressed up against me from behind, pawing my tits and my cunt.

I thought: *Couldn't this goddamned sailor keep his hands off me in public? Couldn't he wait? Couldn't he behave like a* gentleman?

I pulled angrily away from her, saw some startled people watching us from behind parked cars, and told Eden to take me home. *Now.*

In the trailer, she came at me. I was washing my hands at the sink when she pushed up hard against me from behind, reaching up under my dress, until she had a hand on the top of my panties. She pulled them down and I could feel the garter belt digging into my skin. She was breathing hard and I heard her twist the top off an unseen jar. The breathing got harder, and I closed my eyes and then felt a stabbing pain as she entered me from behind. Her finger was all the way up inside me and she bit and chewed the back of my neck until I started to slide away from her to stop the pain. She took her finger out of me, and I went on all fours on the floor. Above and behind me, she dug the nail of her thumb into my ass and moved the other finger down, as if pressing at the back of my balls, and then slipped it into my ass again. She unzipped the back of the dress with her free hand. She pulled the dress up to my shoulders and I stretched out my arms and allowed her to pull it over my head. I felt naked in the bra and garter belt. She slid her finger out of me and I panted with relief. The pain had stopped. I gasped for air. Her breathing sounded choked. I started to turn, get up, and then I was spread wide open again by something cold and hard in my rectum. Still dressed in the sailor suit, she slid under me, and took my cock in her mouth, all the while pushing the cold smooth object in and out of my ass until I came.

Now, she said, sliding out from under me, holding a silver butter knife with a vaselined handle in her hand, standing above me as I tried to get myself back into the world.

Now you better eat me, honey.

One evening I met her down at Sears. We always met there when we planned to go to a drive-in or to the beach. This night she came out of the store chewing the inside of her mouth.

Let's hurry, she said, sliding behind the wheel.

What's the problem? I asked.

Roberta, she said.

Roberta was her blond friend from Sears, the woman I'd seen months ago leaving the San Carlos one morning with Mercado. Eden talked about her from time to time, relating episodes of the woman's life. Usually it sounded like a soap opera. The thing with Mercado hadn't worked out, of course; Mercado wanted sex and Roberta wanted marriage. So Mercado smiled, kissed her, said good night and went away. After Mercado she'd met an ensign named Larry. Since Larry was an officer and a gentlemen, and I was an enlisted man, the four of us never went out together. It was forbidden by the rules of the democratic Navy. Sometimes we would see them in a drive-in or at the shrimp place, and wave hello. I was introduced just once to Larry. We were both in civvies. He was tall and thin and looked at me as if I were a shoeshine boy. I never said another word to him. And I never really got to see Roberta, although Eden talked to her every day at Sears.

She says she's gonna kill herself tonight, Eden said, as she drove through the back streets.

Why, for God's sake?

Larry jilted her. But not for another woman. Turns out he already *had* another woman. Little wifey back home in Ohio. Turns out *Roberta* is the other woman. And she can't *stand* it.

Aw, hell.

I tried to *tell* her; I said, Roberta, no man is worth *killin* yourself for. Not one of them. No matter *how* much you think you love him.

I thought: *What about me? Would you kill yourself over me?* But I said nothing.

Gotta get her thinkin' right, Eden said. Gotta save her life.

She drove fast until we came into a middle-class white section just beyond Mainside. Roberta lived in a small complex of new apartments, two stories high with stucco walls and tile roofs and cars parked in the driveways. The stairways were on the outside of the buildings. Eden led the way to Roberta's apartment and rang the bell. No answer. Eden listened at the door.

God, I don't hear a sound, she said.

She rang the bell more urgently, and this time we heard shuffling footsteps coming to the door.

Roberta's voice asked us who we were.

Eden and Michael, 'Berta, honey. Better let us in.

Go away.

Eden said, If you don't let us in, honey, we gonna knock the damn door down.

There was a pause, then the lock turned and the door opened and Roberta was standing there. She was wearing a white flannel bathrobe and she looked terrible. Her hair was wild and matted. There were splotches of makeup on her face and dirt under her fingernails. Her eyes were sore from crying and her face was swollen.

I don't want to hear your damned sad story, girl, Eden said, taking Roberta's arm and leading her into the apartment. I closed the door behind us and locked it.

Ain't nothin to tell, Roberta said.

Sure there is, Eden said. All about a low-life lying conniving son of a bitch flyboy. Lots to tell about *him.* But we just don't wanna hear it tonight, girl. We gotta get you lookin *human.*

She led Roberta to the bedroom. I wasn't sure what to do. This was something that happened in the country of women and I didn't know how they acted there. I looked around. There were gin bottles everywhere, overflowing ashtrays, dirty plates and glasses, mounds of clothes on the floor. Eden saw them too. She turned to me at the door of the bedroom.

Maybe you can clear up this mess, she said, while I clean up Roberta.

I nodded and she closed the bedroom door. I moved quickly around the small apartment, putting the gin bottles in garbage bags, emptying the ashtrays, folding the clothes and setting them on an armchair. I opened the windows to let the sour hangover smell drift into the damp night air.

All the while I heard the shower running and wondered if Eden had been forced to climb in with Roberta just to hold her up. And as I straightened the chairs and the couch, the apartment changed its character. The dirt and disorder had made it Roberta's place; now it seemed to belong to nobody. There were no photographs of friends or relatives or lovers anywhere in sight. Like the place where Bobby Bolden stayed with Catty Wolverton, there were no books on the shelves and no pictures on the walls. It was an empty space. Maybe, I thought, Roberta made it her own with chaos. I'd made it look like a hotel room.

The water had stopped running in the shower, but I heard nothing from the bedroom. Navy jets raced through the sky. *Their sound must drive Roberta mad,* I thought. One of them could be Larry. I heard a radio playing a Tommy Edwards song:

Many a tear has to fall, but it's all . . .

The door opened. Eden was standing there with a towel wrapped around her and nothing under the towel.

Come on in, she said.

Roberta was still wearing the bathrobe, but her hair was brushed straight back now, and her skin was shiny and her fingernails clean. She smiled at me like a kid arriving at a surprise party. Then she went to the large bed and, still wearing the robe, slipped under the covers. All the while, she was looking at me.

I turned to Eden.

She nodded at the bed, and then went past me, turning off lights.

I undressed and got into the bed beside Roberta, engulfed by the odor of soap and fresh perfume. Roberta looked directly at me and touched my face. Her skin shimmered whitely in the dim light.

Hello, Roberta, I whispered.

Take my robe off, she said, in a small frightened voice. If *you* take it off, then it's all right.

I turned and saw Eden suddenly naked, getting into the bed on the other side of Roberta. She nodded at me. I untied the belt of the robe. Roberta sat up and I slipped the robe off her shoulders and saw her pink nipples and lush breasts and she shifted her weight and I slid the robe out from under her and dropped it on the floor.

I been so unhappy, she said, and suddenly began to cry.

I held her close to me, one of my hands reaching past her for Eden, for her arms and breasts and face. Roberta turned her face up to me and I kissed her and tasted salt. Eden sucked one of my fingers.

And so Eden and I began to make love to Roberta, trying to console and heal her, taking her out of Pensacola, far from flyboys and liars, away from her loneliness, into some place where things would happen that she might remember after everything else had faded. We kissed her mouth together, lips and tongues moving against each other, twirling in a single movement. Then I kissed and sucked one of Roberta's breasts, while Eden kissed and sucked the other and then I put my cock in her and Roberta groaned and Eden kissed her mouth and played with her nipples.

Roberta whispered, Don't come in me, Michael. Please don't come in me. . . . That's just for Eden. Don't come in me and it'll be okay.

I eased out of Roberta and entered Eden, trying not to come, not to end this until Roberta was consoled, and while I was in Eden, Roberta covered Eden's face with kisses and sucked her breasts and dark-brown nipples and said, Oh, honey, you are my own true friend. You and Michael. My only friends . . .

Then Roberta was behind me, pushing hard against my ass as I drove into Eden, our double weight flattening Eden against the bed, Roberta's breasts against my back, her hands under me kneading Eden's breasts until I could hold back no longer and exploded. I rose like a horse bucking and Roberta pulled on my hair and Eden moaned until we all fell back on the bed.

That wasn't the end. We dozed together, Roberta holding my limp cock, my hand on her pussy. Eden brought in large cold glasses full of Coke and ice. We listened to the night sounds. We hugged Roberta between us. We dozed again. When I came fully awake, Roberta was sucking my cock. Over on a chair, facing the bed, watching us, a hand between her legs, Eden was transported. I couldn't come right away. Eden could. She groaned loudly. Roberta came off my cock and turned to Eden.

She said, Come here.

Half bent over, still coming, Eden rolled off the chair to the bed and then Roberta plunged her blonde head between those dark thighs, offering her own pink ass to me, her cunt a thick gorged red, the blonde hairs almost invisible, the lips slippery and her asshole tiny and tight, with dozens of little lines vanishing into the hole. I wet myself in the cunt and then eased into the other hole and her body shuddered and rose and trembled and pulled away and then pushed back at me to take me into her while Eden's dark hands gripped her blonde head.

We slept for a few hours and when I woke up, Roberta was gazing at me.

Thank you, she said.

Eden woke at the sound of Roberta's voice and saw the look on her face and smiled.

I guess we better go, Eden said.

We started to dress, with Roberta watching us, the covers pulled tight to her chin. I felt strange, as if this all had happened to somebody else. Certainly nobody would believe me if I told them about it at Ellyson Field. But here I was, pulling on my shorts over a cock that was not soft and not quite hard. The room smelled of perfume and pussy. Eden went over and kissed Roberta gently on the brow.

No more crazy phone calls, okay? she said.

Okay.

You promise?

I promise.

We'll see you soon.

I hope, Roberta said softly.

We drove away. I was late, and would have to go through the fence. It didn't matter. I held Eden's hand, but neither of us spoke for a long time. Then I started to think about the things we'd done with Roberta and my cock got hard again. What we'd done was supposed to be wrong, was supposed to tell me that Eden was some kind of strange and perverted woman: a woman who goes with *women*? But I knew that I felt better and it wasn't just the sex: we'd helped a woman live who might have died. And Eden was here, with me, not with anyone else, man or woman. Flashes of Roberta's bedroom played in my mind. And they must have filled Eden's too, because after a while, she reached over and gripped my thigh.

I can't stand it, she said. We've got to pull over. Before you go back. Right up there. In the parking lot. Behind that church.

Chapter

51

T HAT WAS THE way it was with us, in the time of The Games, as spring moved into summer. If we could imagine something, we'd try to do it. In a way, she was more like someone my own age, or younger, than a woman fourteen years older than I, a mother with two children. Sometimes she would lead the way; sometimes I did; and soon we were doing things without plan, instantly joining in some new unscripted play. There was a strange innocence to it too; neither of us had done these things before, so we were discovering them as we did them. The past, her history, the chilly sermons of priests: all receded as we lived in the fierce present tense. The Games were ours, inventions of the imagination; and I remember even then thinking that in the distant future I would remember this as the season when I did most things for the first time. And I also knew that this fresh wildness might never happen to me again, with any other woman. And about that I was right.

But our time together wasn't always games, costumes, scenes. Sometimes Eden just wanted to be still, to lie beside me in the silent trailer, listening to the night sounds of the lake and the River Styx. Other times, she wanted to make love quickly and brutally, explaining later that she had thought about it all day and had exhausted all the preliminaries in her mind. In a choked voice, she would blurt out the hardest words she knew and make me say them to her: words as hard as my prick. And on some strange nights, usually on the weekend when time was no consideration, we engaged in a kind of dance, an erotic version of the Mass, with a familiar sense of slowness and ritual; I would hear Latin phrases like *ad Deum qui laetificat juventutum meum,* and hum them in that dead language whose coded words were ground into me, echoing around in my skull like a dream that always comes back. In those moments I felt engulfed by sin. I wasn't violating Eden; I was negating my own past, my Catholicism, my enforced subservience to a tyrannical code that was not of my own invention. Embracing sin, I ceased being a Catholic. Sweet sin. Sin, dark and unflowering and delicious.

Neither of us asked if what we were doing was right or wrong. We just did it. Music always seemed to be playing somewhere, even when the radio was off, even deep into the night when no sounds drifted across the lake; the music of sin, of crossing frontiers, of changing ourselves by what we imagined and what we did. We listened to that music and moved to it, invented to it, made love to it. I asked her to sit at the table, looking prim and reading a newspaper, a proper housewife, my little sweet Doris Day Blondie wifey, with Bing Crosby singing nice wholesome songs on the radio, and then I would get under the table and slide my head between her thighs until she lost all control. But music wasn't always there. We made love once in the trunk of the car, in the parking lot of the Federal courthouse, with her panties keeping the trunk from locking. Once we found a small Catholic church out in the Alabama wilds, a building seemingly abandoned in the Protestant sea; we whispered in the emptiness of the nave and then went behind the rotting velvet drapes of a confessional, where she took me in her mouth. That was sin. And yet it didn't seem wrong. Sin was made up of violation, license, the breaking of the rules; but with Eden it never felt wrong. It just *felt.*

Sometimes, of course, sin wasn't easy for me. I would glimpse my mother's face and her austere Sunday morning Catholic piety and I would pause. A small fight would break out in my head; the child accused the man: would you do this in front of your *mother?* Invariably the man would win, arguing with vehemence: she had *her* life and she's dead and gone and this is *my* life and I'll do with it what I want. But sometimes the child was the temporary winner. The first few times we made love to Roberta, I was more upset than I let on. I thought (or the child did): *Would I be doing this if Roberta was a man named Robert and we were both fucking Eden Santana? Suppose Mercado and I had Eden between us on this bed and came in her together? And what really was going on in Eden's mind? Why did she seem to* enjoy *it so much?* Going to Roberta's house was one of the few things we did more than once. She truly did make our visits seem like corporal works of mercy, the healing of the sick, where flesh, tongue, cock and come closed all psychic sores in a churning of flesh. But back in the barracks, surrounded by men to whom I could confide nothing, I would think: *Suppose Eden was some sort of a lesbian? How would I feel if she and Roberta made love when I* wasn't *there?*

But after we'd gone to Roberta's a few more times, all those questions disappeared. It began to seem natural for the three of us to slide together into that bed. Roberta was dumb, but I liked her; she was a woman born to be lavishly fucked until she got fat and swamped with kids and could then cast sex into the past. There was no way I could fall in love with her, and I was sure that Eden didn't love her either. For me, there wasn't any mystery; she was what she appeared to be, all good-natured flesh and a sad sweet smile.

But I loved seeing Eden's dark skin stretched against Roberta's shimmering whiteness and the paler areas of both bodies that had been covered with bathing suits. There were 150 million people in the United States and I was one of the few people who had seen those parts of their bodies. I never asked Eden or Roberta why they allowed me to do the things I did with them. We never used condoms, and sometimes I came in each of them, each holding my ass tight when I started to pull out, silently insisting that I should finish what I had started. I knew there were secret things they did to avoid getting pregnant but I didn't ask what they were. They just went separately to the bathroom and I would hear water running for a while and then we'd be dozing together in the cool Gulf dark until a hand touched a thigh and we'd begin again. I knew just one thing for sure: they felt safe with me and I felt safe with them.

They were not, however, mere interchangeable bodies that gave and took heart-stopping pleasure. I enjoyed Roberta's plump coarse whiteness, and the open way she let me use it. I got even hotter when she urged me on in that little girl's voice. But in my eighteen-year-old arrogance I was sure there was nothing to know about Roberta beyond that bed, the hot shower, the light-blue veins on her breasts. There were a million things yet to learn about Eden Santana. And the challenge of that mystery, that place in her without maps, that undiscovered country, was what love was about. I was sure of that. Loving her was the name I gave to the process of unraveling her secrets. And as we moved around from one evening place to another, with feverish stops at Roberta's, I began to tell Eden that I loved her.

How can you say you *love* me, child? she'd say. You don't even *know* me.

Maybe that's the point, I'd answer. Maybe I love you cause I *don't* know you. Maybe won't ever know all of you.

She'd shake her head and say, That's damfool talk.

No, it's *not,* I said one night. If I don't *know* you—*all* of you— maybe I can spend the rest of my life finding *out* about you.

She looked at me for a long time. Then she lit a cigarette, took a deep drag, and said (not to me, but to the room and the night and the past):

One thing I sure done learned about life. Don't plan on anything.

Chapter

52

LATE ONE AFTERNOON I decided to walk all the way from the locker club to the trailer. The day was ripe with early summer.

I was on the bridge over the River Styx when I saw the pickup truck: pale blue, with a toolbox across the back behind the cab, Alabama plates. It was parked in front of a bait shop that was built on a hummock of scrubby land overlooking the river. Behind the bait shop a path led through swamp grass down to a boat dock. Three men were standing beside the pickup, drinking beer. One of them looked familiar. I hadn't seen him since the great brawl outside the Baptist church during my first week in Pensacola.

It was the one called Buster.

For a moment, I was afraid. That January night had been quick and violent and for Buster and his friends, humiliating. But it was months ago (I told myself), hundreds of days behind both of us. I was living a different life now, centered on Eden. Buster couldn't possibly remember me. But then, tensing, nervous, I wondered if I remembered *him,* why wouldn't he remember *me?*

I paused, looked casually down at the river without seeing it, my back to the pickup and the bait shop and Buster. I glanced up and saw a hawk wheeling in the sky. And when I turned, Buster was coming across the road.

One of the others was reaching into the cab of the truck.

I froze.

"Hey, you!" Buster shouted. *"Sailor* boy!"

I started to run.

Back down the road to Ellyson Field.

"We gone git you Yankee ass!"

I was running flat out now along the shoulder of the empty road. I turned and saw the pickup backing away from the bait shop and Buster climbing on the running board like a guy in a gangster movie. I passed a small launderette, its doors already locked, and a closed shop advertising mufflers. I stared around for a weapon: a board, a brick, any goddamned thing to use against Buster and his boys.

And then I went down, falling forward, scraping my left hand as I tried to break the fall.

Brakes screeched. I rolled over and looked up, expecting Buster and a beating.

Buddy Bolden was there in the Merc. He pushed open one of the back doors.

"Get in!" he shouted. "Come *on,* man . . ."

I dove through the open door onto the floor. Bolden pushed me down and pulled the door closed.

"Stay down!"

I could hear him breathing in short pulls, a truck roaring by.

"They just went by," he said. "Don't know if they seen you. They're up higher in a truck so maybe they—*Shit*! They hangin' a U. *Fuck*! Hold on!"

He floored the accelerator, turned, then turned again, then went speeding down a smooth hardtop road, ripped suddenly to the right, passed under trees I could see from the floor, whipped around again, the road going from smooth to rough, stones and pebbles hammering at the bottom of the car.

"The gun's under the front seat. You can reach it from back there . . ."

The .45, cold and wrapped in oilcloth, was heavy in my hand.

"I don't *see* the mothafuckas any more but—"

The gun felt cool and solid. *I might have to use it.* That came to me then: *I might have to shoot these fucking guys.* I might have to blow this Buster's *head* off.

Jesus Christ.

Then I was hurled against the opposite door and twisted around, and then we were moving very fast.

Yeah, I *could* kill one of the bastards.

And hey (I thought but didn't say) *if it's Buster or me, it's gonna be* Buster.

I got a woman *to live for.*

Then we were in a damp cool place, the sky blocked by trees, moving slowly. Bolden stopped the car. I listened in silence for the pickup truck, and heard only insects chirring and the sound of startled birds. Bolden turned off the engine. I sat up.

"Gimme that thing," he said. "I think we lost them."

I handed him the gun. We were on the far side of the lake in a dense grove of magnolias. The smell was thick and sweet, almost sickening. Bolden was very still, listening to the evening sounds like a hunter, trying to sort out one from a million others.

"We're okay now," he said softly.

"Thanks, man. I mean it."

"Now you know why I have a car."

"Down here, we need tanks."

"Who *were* those mothafuckas?"

I gave him a short version of the dance back in January and what Sal and Max and I did to Buster and his friends and why. When I finished, he grunted.

"It's the *dancin* that did it," Bolden said. "When white folks try to *dance,* they's always trouble."

He got out of the car, still holding the gun, and I looked out across the lake to where he and Catty had their little house and Eden and I had our trailer.

"You can't go walkin on no roads *alone* no more," he said. "Not while you down here. No more than *I* can. You do, you go talking shit about this being a *free* country an all that shit, they gonna *grab* you some night and drop you in a fuckin swamp." A pause. "Max and Sal too." He wrapped the gun carefully in the oilcloth. "These cracker mothafuckas ain't dumb. Now they *know* you still around Pensacola, prob'ly right there in Ellyson Field, and so they gonna *watch* for you. Watch the roads. The bars. The base. So if you don't have no car to carry you where you going, *then don't go . . .*"

I pictured myself sneaking through the woods for the rest of my time in Pensacola. And then I got angry. Three of us had fought Buster and four of his friends and kicked the shit out of them. That should've been the end of it. I was so young that I still thought the world had rules, that men fought and someone won and someone lost and then it was over. And Bobby Bolden was saying it wasn't the end of it. That some things in this world didn't end until someone was dead. That down here, anyway, they'd come to you in the night, memory as fresh as morning, and take back the blood they shed. That year, Bobby Bolden knew this better than I did. He knew where we were.

In the South.

The goddamned South.

"They try that, we can do the same," I said, almost bitterly. "We can go chasing after *them* too, man."

He looked at me in a sad way. "Wise up, kid. This is *their* country. Not yours. *Definitely* not mine."

"Well, we'll see what happens," I said.

He shoved the gun in his belt. "You better hope nothin happens at all."

Chapter

53

T HE LIGHT WAS on behind the blinds when I finally reached the trailer. I knocked and heard Eden's muffled voice telling me to come in. She hadn't given me a key and never would. I pushed the door open and she was facing me, a faint smile on her face, her back to the sink. She had never looked so beautiful. Her hair was pulled straight back and her face was scrubbed clean of makeup. She was wearing a black turtleneck and a short white apron. Her legs were bare and she was wearing the red shoes. I locked the door behind me.

You're late, she said in a husky voice.

She was smoking and flicked ashes behind her into the sink without taking her eyes off me.

Had a little trouble, I told her, but I'll tell you about it later.

You look good, child.

So do you, I said.

This too was part of the dance: the soft words and compliments, all part of saying hello. Tonight was different. Her eyes were unfocused as if she were thinking four moves ahead of me. I started to get hard, and reached for her and pulled her to me, kissing her. I ran my unscraped hand down her body and discovered that, except for the turtleneck, all she was wearing was the apron.

Gotta surprise for you, she whispered hoarsely.

Yeah?

Hope you like it.

She dropped the cigarette in the sink, and then she pressed both hands on my shoulders, pushing me down. I kissed her breasts, taking each in my mouth with the cloth of the sweater between me and her nipples and breathed hotly on her. Her voice sounded choked and she pressed again more firmly and then I was on my knees in front of her and she lifted her apron delicately and there in front of me was the surprise.

She had shaved.

Every last hair was gone and I was facing her beautifully formed cunt, which was very pale, looking like those perfect pubic mounds I'd seen on the classical statues in the art books. Except that this wasn't art made by hand from marble, bronze or polished wood. This was packed with muscle and blood, and it was in front of me now as I kneeled before her, and I thought the word *cunt,* and saw the crevice clearly defined and tightly shut, thought *cunt* again, saw no evidence of clitoris or entry to the dark channel within and whispered loudly, like a prayer for mercy from the position of worship: *Cunt.*

Eden took a small step to the right, braced against the sink, gripped my head with both hands and pulled me to her.

It was as if I'd never been there before, the hairless lips suddenly parting, slippery under my tongue, the opening at once tighter and wetter. I put my brow against her pelvic bone and pushed hard, pressing her now against the cold metal sink, while playing delicately with my tongue in this new bald place. Almost from the start she was trembling and moving, her legs straight out, drawing up on the heels of those red shoes, the legs hardening and locking, then loosening, then hard again. She eased away, then squatted hard against my tongue, pulling fiercely on my hair, as if trying to suck me up into her, the nude wet cunt demanding more and more tongue, her voice rising and shuddering, until she was suddenly completely crazily coming: tearing away the apron with both hands, then yanking again at my hair, pumping forward, then slamming her hard hot bottom against the sink, standing on the heels of her shoes, until she seemed to rise over me, twisting straight up and screaming. And then flopped forward.

Exhausted.

Panting.

Limp. With her belly pressing against my head, her hands holding the back of my belt, her cheeks spread loosely against the sink. I blew gently against her hairless curves and clefts. And then she shuddered again and slid away and rolled onto her back on the polished floor. She lay there with her eyes closed. I entered her without undressing.

I never want this to end, she said, bathing my raw left hand in Epsom salts, as I lay on the bed where she had placed me, drained and empty. Never. Never, never.

Neither do I, I whispered.

And I know, she said, I shouldn't oughtta be saying that. We're here. We could be here lots of nights. I want it never to end. Even though, well, you know . . .

Don't say even though, I said.

She said nothing.

I want us to last forever, I said.

She rubbed my hand in the warm water, but she was looking at the wall.

We *won't* last forever, you know, she said gently. One fine day, you gonna meet a girl your own age. Probly younger. And she'll want to go to Paris with you and help make you a painter, and all that stuff, like you say you want. And she'll want to have *kids* and so will you. And she'll want to meet your *friends* and read the books you're reading and see you at *breakfast* every day of her life. You'll see her like she just came into this world, all beautiful and sweet and fresh and new. And you'll fall in love with her. And then you'll feel bad because you won't know how to tell *me.* You'll walk around in a fog, you'll pick fights with me, you'll see the lines in my face for the very first time and the way my titties are droppin and you'll see my kids go off and have kids of their own and you'll think that it's very strange, you being with a damn *grand*mother, and so you'll screw up your courage and come to me and tell me you love another woman. And maybe you *will* love her and maybe you *won't,* but in the end, you'll go away.

I won't, I said (the words still clear and fresh in my ears now). I swear it, Eden. I won't *ever* go away. I won't *ever* leave you.

Please don't say those words, she said. I hear them words in every rotten movie.

I said, my voice rising with the panic, I don't know any other words. But I *gotta* say them. Especially to you. I mean them.

You mean it now, she said calmly, but you won't even remember what you just said to me . . . When it's time to move on.

Then the words came pouring out of me, she lying beside me

now, her head on my chest, my hand playing with her hair, the smell of soap and cunt in the air, mixed with the thick scent of magnolias from the lake. I wanted her beside me for the rest of my life, I said, the two of us, Eden and Michael Devlin, and her kids too, and so what if she became a grandmother, what the hell difference would *that* make? I knew I couldn't be a father to her kids, they *had* a father, a real father, but I could be *good* to them, and maybe *teach* them a few things, and show them good *books* and take them to *museums* and if we all went to Paris, they could learn French while *we* were learning French and we'd all be happy. If I couldn't make money as a painter, and couldn't live on the GI Bill, I'd get a *job,* any kind of work to bring in the bucks, lots of them, and feed the kids and Eden and clothe them too and raise them up right and save what was left and . . . I could paint at *night* and on the *week* ends. And then, hey, sooner or later I'd have a breakthrough and I could give up the job and paint all the time. I knew I could do it, with Eden beside me, helping me make my way in the world while I was learning my craft. I *needed* her (I told her). I *wanted* her. Now. *And* later. When we both were old.

I couldn't stop myself. The words just kept coming, the foolish and pathetic words. The words of an eighteen-year-old boy who was far from home. She listened in silence, never moving; if anything, her body seemed slowly to stiffen. Then at last I ran down and finally I stopped talking. I turned to kiss her and saw that her face was wet with tears.

Nobody ever said things like that to me before, she whispered (she who had once forced me to tell her I loved her, in the woods beyond the railroad track). You damn crazy child.

I love you, I said, as if maybe she didn't yet understand me completely, and as if that ancient phrase explained everything. *I love you . . .*

She was silent. The insects droned. A loon made a crazy laughing sound.

I said, When your hair grows back—down *there*—it'll be mine. That hair, that new hair, that fresh-grown hair: nobody in the whole world will ever see it except me.

And she laughed.

Oh, Michael, child, of all the people in the whole wide world, only *you* would ever *think* such a thing.

I smiled, trying to be cool. But I was embarrassed, pleased only that it was too dark for her to see me blush. She had *laughed* at me!

But it's *true,* isn't it? I said. Nobody else will *ever* see it.

As soon as I'd said it, I was sorry. It was as if I were forcing her to say what I wanted so much to hear.

Who knows? she said casually.

I *want* it to be true, I said.

Then maybe it will be.

She was up on one elbow now, staring at me.

You ain't a man *yet,* she said. But you're gettin there, child.

I love you, I said one final time.

She sighed and touched my mouth with cool fingertips and said, I guess I love you too.

Chapter

54

From The Blue Notebook

SHE LETS ME *enter everything except her mind.*

Red Cannon was in a fight somewhere. When I saw him in the chow hall this morning, his hands were raw and skinned, but his face was untouched. Whoever the guy was, he never laid a hand on Red. Sal said the gouge on the base was that Red beat the shit out of some cracker down at Trader Vic's. After Red finished beating him senseless, the Shore Patrol came. They were all friends of Red's, so when the cracker came around, the SPs beat the shit out of him too. Will I have to fight Red some day? I have to admit, it scares me; Red is a man, tough and hard, and there's something dead in his eyes, like he's seen too many people die. I don't know if I can go up against that kind of man knowing I might have to kill him if it looks as if he's going to kill me. I guess if I ever fight him, I have to get off first; can't give him time to get set, to gather up all his craziness and anger and hatred. Take it out of him real fast. Still, it's scary.

E.: a stubble returns. She says it's itchy.

Stories about Dodgers going to Los Angeles in newspaper clippings sent by my father. Horace Stoneham is mumbling about taking the Giants. The majors won't let one team go because it wouldn't be worth all the cost of flying out there on the road to play one team. So the Giants gotta go with the Dodgers. Possible, they could both be gone: just like that. Next year, year after. O'Malley wants the big television bucks, the papers say. Can't believe it. In the papers here, the sports news is all stuff from Associated Press (that's where Caniff worked when he first came to NY, drawing cartoons). The Los Angeles *Dodgers? Sounds ridiculous.*

But . . .

Great pictures by a guy named Titian in a book MR owns. You can see the figures glow. All old cardinals and popes, with cruel faces; but the glow, like gold, comes off them. How does he make that happen with just paint and oil and turpentine? Gotta ask M.

I made 46 bucks this month drawing pictures. MR suggested I switch to chalk and charcoal, so the women's faces would be softer. He's right. I love smearing the chalk with my hands, grading it. It's almost as if you were rubbing your hand on a woman's face. With the money, I bought two more shirts, and a book called The Great Gatsby *for E. I read the book when Dunbar told me about it and it's a great book, even though I don't understand people like that, except Wolfsheim, the bootlegger. I was going to buy E. some earrings, but I couldn't do it at the end, because I didn't trust my own taste. Actually* ran *out of the store . . .*

The comics go on, but I don't care much about them anymore. I'd rather see red shoes.

Chapter

55

THE NAVY WENT on like a lumpy road beside a swift river. Routine and habit made it easy; my true life took place at night. I still visited with the blacks, doing their portraits for free and eating when I wanted. I even made a point of entering the chow hall with them, knowing it would drive Harrelson nuts. But I didn't go into town with them very much anymore. I made excuses about being too busy with my drawings or needing to see my girl or having the duty.

But the truth was I didn't want to see Winnie.

The truth was I didn't want to hear that she was pregnant, or in love with me, didn't want her to start hanging around the gate, the knocked-up black girl crazy for a white man. Most of all, I didn't want her confronting Eden. I didn't want her to throw a scene, didn't want to have to sit down with Eden later and explain what happened that one night when she was in New Orleans. I was also afraid of my own feelings.

The truth was that sometimes, making love to Eden, Winnie's syrupy body came into my head. I was on the floor again in her little house, betraying Eden while Winnie betrayed her husband. I could hear her furry innocent voice, the sense she gave me of being abandoned. At least once, making love to Eden, I came again in Winnie. And I was afraid that if I saw her I would want her again, in some powerful way that seemed to transcend my feelings for Eden. I loved Eden, I was sure, but Winnie's hot desperate body wouldn't leave my mind.

And there was one further truth: I was afraid that if Eden found out about Winnie, she would use the knowledge like a permit, and would go out and play around with other guys the way I had with Winnie. I had convinced myself that there was an unspoken agreement binding me and Eden Santana. I didn't want it to break. I told myself that I needed her the way I needed food and sleep and air to breathe.

Meanwhile, the war in Korea was grinding down and so was the activity at the base. The Navy had stopped all new enlistments, so there were no new arrivals among us, no sudden transfers to sea duty in the waters of Asia. We were trapped at Ellyson Field: officers and enlisted men, Yankees and Shitkickers. Each of had to deal with the increasing boredom. Max and Sal applied for sea duty and were told they'd have to wait. Dunbar filled out the forms for an early discharge. I started going to the gym each afternoon with Max.

My hair filled out. I did a lot of drawing and some awful painting (the colors muddied up and I could never get the light right). I read more books. I weighed myself one afternoon in Bobby Bolden's office in the infirmary and was certain the scale was wrong; I'd gained twelve pounds without getting fat. At night sometimes, Eden would dig a thumb into my biceps, and when it began to hurt, I'd grit my teeth and harden the muscle and pop her thumb out of my flesh. I even grew a half inch taller.

Late one afternoon, I was walking with Miles Rayfield along Copter Road on the base. He started talking about his wife. I remember feeling that I had a part in some play and Miles was really an actor reading some other guy's lines. He talked about her in a bitter way. She hadn't written to him in two weeks, he said, maybe three, he wasn't ever sure anymore; maybe he should just get a divorce. It was as if he were asking me to support him, to advise him. I was trying to sort this out, when we heard someone tap a car horn. It was Mercado, in the tan full-dress uniform of the Mexican Army. He was behind the wheel of his convertible, the top down, the back seat full of suitcases.

"Hey, I'll see you guys," he said, smiling widely, waving. "I'm off."

We went over and Mercado told us that he'd finished the helicopter training and he had his certificate, signed by Captain Pritchett and the Secretary of Defense. Now he was going back to Mexico.

"But stay in touch," he said, and handed us each a business card, with the name of a company printed on it in Spanish, an address, a phone number. "You can get me here most of the time, if you ever come to Mexico. Actually, it's my father's company. But they always know where I am. *Mi casa es su casa,* as we say. My house is your house . . ."

Miles said, "If everybody you've invited comes to Mexico at the same time, you'll have to rent a *stadium.*"

"My father *owns* a stadium," Mercado said, and smiled. "So what the hell . . ."

We shook hands and he waved and drove on to the gate. I felt sad. Mercado was decent. He wasn't one of those officers who acted like pricks. And then I felt a different emotion. *Relief.* Relief that began shifting into happiness.

Mercado was gone at last.

Now I'd never have to worry that Eden Santana was off somewhere with Mercado on the nights when I was a prisoner of the United States Navy.

He was *gone.*

And I was happy.

For about thirty seconds. Then a small commotion arose in me. Suppose Mercado was making one final stop in Pensacola before vanishing into Mexico and the future? Suppose the friendly good-bye was just an act, to make me relax before he went off for a few hot hours with Eden Santana on the silk sheets of the San Carlos Hotel? She might do it for one reason: *curiosity.* A tempting word from Roberta, who had slept with Mercado. A look at him in the passing convertible. He would be gone by nightfall anyway, and I would never know, so why not?

"Jesus Christ, what's with *you?*" Miles said. "Your face is jumping all over the place."

"Nothing. Nothing. I was thinking about something else."

"It must have been a bitch."

"Yeah."

That night, Miles had the duty in the Supply Shack. Eden was working late. I knew if I lay around the barracks my head might fill with still more unhappy visions, so I decided to work. I owed drawings to almost a dozen sailors and I needed the money. I took

a nap after dinner, to store up strength for a long night's work. I
awoke in the dark. And then, my face freshly washed, I took my
chalk, pad and photographs over to the Supply Shack. A soft rain
was falling but there were a few helicopters in the sky. The lights
burned warmly in the shack. Miles was probably busy; his bitching
would be good company. Between Miles Rayfield and the work, I
wouldn't think about Eden Santana.

But when I walked into the Shack, Miles wasn't there. Nobody
was. I went to his desk and saw cigarette butts in an ashtray and a
Navy white hat plunked on the chair, with Rayfield stenciled inside
the brim. But there was no Miles Rayfield. I went to my desk, stared
at the vapid face of a young blonde and started drawing. Then the
front door opened and a mechanic walked in waving a requisition
slip.

I took the slip, exchanged some small talk, and then walked to
the back to find a swash plate, wondering where the hell Miles was.
As soon as I stepped into the storeroom, I heard voices. Low,
murmuring. Coming from the secret studio beyond the wall of
packing crates. One of them belonged to Miles Rayfield. The other
was the voice of Freddie Harada.

I gave the mechanic the plate and had him sign the forms, but
when he was gone, I decided not to stick around. I left the signed
slip on top of Miles's hat and then packed my stuff and hurried
through the soft rain to the barracks. I worked there in the dim
light, sitting on my bunk, trying to draw what I could see and not
what I could imagine.

At lights out, I moved into the head and kept working, sitting
on a toilet seat with the drawing pad in my lap. Various sailors
came in and out, handling the usual ablutions before going off to
sleep. They were used to me by now; they didn't even bother to
kibitz. Then I was alone for a long time in the quiet. I was working on my third dark-eyed blonde; she was too pretty to be inter-
esting, and blonde hair was always harder to draw than black. But
the chalk worked for me; I kept repeating the tricks I'd learned
from Miles Rayfield and they were beginning to feel natural.

Then I heard a screen door open and close, followed by footsteps. I looked toward the sleeping bay and saw Captain Pritchett and Red Cannon staring at me. I started to get up. Cannon

took a step into the head and held up both hands, palms out.

"Stay there, sailor," he said, his voice soft but his eyes angry. It was as if he were making an arrest. "Captain wants to talk to you."

Pritchett stepped into the head.

"Thank you, Cannon," he said, his voice a dismissal.

"Good night, sir," Cannon said, snapping off a salute. He walked out quickly but was careful not to slam the door. *Ass kisser,* I thought. *Bullshit artist.* The captain waited until Cannon was gone and then he turned to me.

"So *you're* the guy doing those portraits I see everywhere," he said, looking at the unfinished drawing on my pad.

"I guess so, sir," I said.

"They're in lockers, the damned pictures. They're in the hangars. They're even turning up in *officer's* country."

I wanted to say: Yeah, *so* what? But I kept my mouth shut.

"And they're not half bad," Pritchett said.

He looked closer at the blonde on the pad.

"You got a *knack,* Devlin. Maybe even a gift."

"Thank you, sir," I said.

" 'Course, I been around so damned long now, I've seen all sorts of artists come and go and come again, in this man's Navy. Usually they pick up a discharge and go out into the civilian world thinking they're the next Picasso. They go to *art* school. They try to get *jobs* in their art racket. And then they find out they're not all that good, or they gotta make a living, or worst of all, they get *married.* And you never hear about them again. And then, a lot of times, they even re-up, come back to the Navy, where they can be big wheels again. You understand what I'm saying, sailor?"

"I think so, sir."

"No, you don't. You're too damned *young* to understand anything."

He sighed and then took his wallet from the back pocket of his suntans. He started flipping through a plastic insert. He took out a photograph.

"But you do have a knack," he said, handing me a photograph of his wife, the woman whose picture was in his office. "So try this. A nice big one, if you can do it."

"Yes, sir."

"What do you charge?"

"Uh, well, *any*thing, sir. I—"

"Stop the crap, sailor. I'll pay what the others pay. I don't want a deal, just cause I'm your commanding office."

"Five bucks."

"Do a nice job and I'll get you ten."

"Yes, sir."

"Good night, sailor," he said, and turned on his heel without saluting. He walked out to where his beds of flowers were drowsing in the soft Gulf rain.

I stared at the woman's face. A round head, crisp features, the cheeks a little dimpled, clear eyes. She was younger in this picture than in the one at his office. On the back, she had written: "For Ensign Jack Pritchett, Love Always, Catherine."

And I thought: *I've made hundreds of drawings of Eden Santana, but I don't have a single photograph,* nothing at all, *that says on it, "Love always."* All I had was her hurried note, scribbled before she left for New Orleans. That did say *love* but didn't add *always.* And I wondered how I would feel if Eden died on me, the way Pritchett's wife had died on him. What would I carry around for the rest of my days that would remind me of the way love for her once drowned my heart?

I slipped the picture of the captain's wife inside the pad and finished drawing the girlfriend of a man named Schlesinger, who was stationed at Mainside. Then Miles Rayfield came in.

"I thought you were going to come over," he said.

"I did," I said.

"Oh." He looked embarassed, and then walked quickly to the sleeping bay.

I gazed at myself for a moment in the mirror, remembering that first day so long ago when I showed up here, still loving a woman in Brooklyn whose face I no longer clearly remembered. Now I wanted Eden to appear behind me in the mirror, her eyes out of focus. I would turn and she would be wearing the red shoes.

The screen door slammed. Then slammed again. Nobody came in. I walked to the door and slipped the hook and closed the main door too. Outside, the streets glistened with rain. I remembered standing at the door to the roof in the house in Brooklyn, watching the rain on summer afternoons. That rooftop seemed a million miles away. I thought: *I'd better write to the boys, too. My little brothers. I'd better tell them what I'm learning about the confusions of the world. They should learn it too.*

And then thought: *No.*

They'll have to learn about it for themselves.

Chapter

56

THE NEXT NIGHT I tried to explain to Eden about Miles Rayfield. About his talent and kindness and generosity. About how much he'd taught me but how the other part of him made me uneasy. I told her about the wife Miles claimed to have. About Freddie Harada and the nude drawings I'd seen in the sktetchbook. I didn't think that such talk would take me where it did. That night changed everything.

We were in the trailer, facing each other across the small table. She was smoking a cigarette, her eyes as blurry as the smoke.

She said, Say, this Miles really is, you know . . . *funny*.

She took a drag.

But you don't really *know*, do you, child? I mean, you never seen him *do* somethin with a man.

No.

But say he *is*, say he's *that* way. Say he got somethin goin with that Filipino boy.

She paused.

Well, if that's the case, why, maybe you're *jealous*.

I felt jolted. I said, Hey, come on. . . . You know better than that—

She went on, a small smile on her mouth: Suppose he decided to run off with that Filipino boy? What would *you* do?

Nothing. I don't—

You *sure* of that? You sure you wouldn't miss him just a *little* bit? You sure you wouldn't wish he'd come back?

I didn't answer.

Why, you been jealous of *me* with no good reason, child. Why wouldn't you be jealous of this *Miles* fella?

Cause he's a *man.* And I'm not—

A faggot? she said.

Damn right!

She smiled and reached over and touched my hand.

She said, Child, you better learn quick that human beings are *complicated.* You hear me? Every woman got a little *man* in her. Every man got a little woman in *him.* Nobody's all *one* thing. Your friend Miles Rayfield is not one thing. Most people ain't.

I hated the way she was looking at me. Smiling. Self-satisfied, like a grade school teacher instructing an infant.

Okay, I said, with heat: Say that's true. Why should I be *jealous,* for Christ's sakes?

She tamped out the cigarette.

Cause the way you *talk* about him, if this Miles fella runs off, you'll be heartbroken.

You saying I'm *queer?*

No. Just saying maybe you want Miles in your life for a long time.

Oh bullshit, I said, in an annoyed way.

She made a small A with her hands and peered at me over the point.

Why you talking like that? she said.

Cause you're talking bullshit!

Her brow furrowed and her eyes narrowed.

Don't raise your voice to me, she said in a cold flat voice.

It was there again. The tone of authority. I slammed the table with the palm of my hand. The ashtray bounced and fell to the floor.

I'm not queer.

I never said that!

Well, what the *fuck* did you say?

She tried to reply, but I was standing now, the words rising.

I said, You should talk. *You!* The way *you* act with Roberta. Are you kid—

She looked at once furious and terrified, standing up too and backing away.

Shut up.

I knew I'd gone too far, and mumbled something, a lot of maybes and who knows, and reached for the ashtray and pawed at the

cigarette butts on the floor. The anger was gone; but I couldn't get
the words back.

She said, Maybe you better go off to the Navy, child. Maybe you
better sleep this anger of yours *off.* Maybe you better *go.* Right now.
What?

The words then came rolling out of her too. Her face was creased
and contorted. For the first time, she seemed ugly to me. And old.

She screamed: I said, go back to the *base.* Right *now.* Back to
Ellyson Field. With all the other sailor boys. I don't want *trouble.*
Not with you, not with no one. I had enough trouble to last me ten
lifetimes. And you look like you want to *hit* someone, Michael
Devlin. Fact, you look just like *another* man I knew once. Man
didn't want to hear *no hard things.* No *difficult* things. So I don't
want you here tonight. Go.

I threw the ashtray against the wall.

Jesus Christ! I said, panting. Jesus *fuckin* Christ.

I jerked the door open, slammed it behind me and went out.

I walked down the road toward the highway. And then felt
nauseated. We'd never argued before. Never even raised our
voices at each other. And here we were . . . Screaming. Smashing
things. Or at least I was. I'd said cruel words. I'd gone out of
control. Here we were . . . breaking up. Over words. Over the
word *queer.* The word *faggot.* Not over Mercado or a husband or
another lover. Over Miles Rayfield. A possible faggot. What the
hell did she *mean?* Trying to tell me I had some faggot in me? With
that smug schoolteacher look on her face. Why'd she *start* this crap?
I'm trying to explain about Miles and she turns it around, makes
it about me. And when I object, she gets harder. She pushed me
and like always, *I pushed back.* Yeah. That was it. She couldn't take
the way I pushed back. She thought I was this sweet boy. *Child,* she
always called me. Well, I wasn't a child. Maybe she knew that now.
Push me and I push back harder. Like a man does. She should've
know that and she made one big goddamn mistake. Does she think
she can find someone as good as me? Hey, *come on* . . . Or maybe
I made the mistake. If I did, then she'd never let me back. If I made
the mistake, it was *over,* just like that. Over? The way it ended for
all the men I knew. All the men who loved women and weren't
loved back. *No.* Jesus, no.

I stopped, started to go back.

Thinking: *I can still beg her forgiveness.*

And answered myself: *No.* I can say I'm sorry for losing my temper. For saying the rotten things about Roberta. For breaking the ashtray. But I won't beg. Maybe I can even say she was right about Miles Rayfield. I *would* miss him if he went away. But not because I'm interested in his prick. She doesn't know everything. But I just can't run off like this. I have to go back. Even if I have to plead with her. But suppose she says no? Suppose she won't even open the door? And what if she was just looking for some excuse to break up? Maybe that's why she started all this. And *she* started it. Not *me.* Eden. She started the whole goddamned thing. Fuck her. No, I *want* her. I want *her.* No. She started it. Let her come to me, call me at the base, beg me to come back. *Right now,* I thought, *I'm going to O Street. To the Dirt Bar. See Sal and Max and the others. Get a blow job from Dixie Shafer. How do you like* that, *baby? Get drunk. Who needs you, lady?*

I get along without you very well.

Of course, I do . . .

I stopped.

There was something in the bushes beside the road. Something moving. I reached down for a rock and eased into the shadows. Another movement. Then I heard a thick grunting sound, full of pain. Then shoes scraping on gravel, as if trying to get traction. I hefted the rock. Then moved closer to the sounds of pain.

And saw Bobby Bolden.

He was facedown in the gravel, his shirt torn off, deep bleeding wounds sliced into his back. His arms were stretched out in front of him, his hands flopping loosely at the wrists. He was digging his elbows into the gravel, trying to move forward. His face was so consumed with pain that he couldn't recognize me or anyone else on this earth.

I turned to the trailer.

Eden!

His body writhed as I reached under his arms and started to lift him. He was bigger and heavier than I imagined. The gouged skin was slippery with blood. Eden took his legs and we heaved and got him into the back seat of her car and laid him face down across the floor. His hands flopped loosely. His jaw moved and words came out but no sentences.

Mothafuck. The House. Get me. Hey you. Oh, *you.* Go ahead

you. Catty. Oh *you.* Scrapple from the apple and a bottle of ocean. *Oh.*

We started to pull out and then Eden saw a glow through the trees. *The house.* I turned the car around and pushed hard on the accelerator, moving down the road away from the highway. The house where Bobby and Catty lived together was burning beyond the screen of trees. I saw black men running through the trees, most without shirts, all carrying buckets of water. Kids darted across the road and I slowed down. Eden shrunk low in the seat beside me, biting her lower lip, her eyes wide and afraid.

Then up ahead I saw something else.

By the side of the lake, only thirty feet away, tied to the branch of a tree with her hands above her head and naked from the waist up was Catty.

Her head was thrown back. She wasn't moving. I could see her back had been split open.

Oh my God, Eden whispered.

Her hands became fists. She gnawed on a knuckle.

Oh Jesus *God.*

I pulled over and stopped the car and got out, but Eden stayed where she was. I saw an elderly black man coming through the trees carrying a shotgun. Six black teenagers were behind him. Their faces were blank.

"You kin keep on goin," the older man said.

I pointed at Catty and said I had to get her to a hospital.

"You just leave her be," he said. "She deserve whut she get. She come in here, dont care fo decency, cause nuthin but *trouble.* Things here is peaceful till this white trash show up. And look whut she *do.* She brung down the affliction on us. She brung down the damn Klan."

The Klan. Like Bobby Bolden said. Like all the blacks said. The damned Klan.

"You can't let her *hang* here," I said. Catty's bare feet were not touching the ground. She was hanging there, a dead weight. I wondered if arms really did get pulled out of sockets. The small black kids had moved around now to the far side of the tree for their first sight of a white woman's bare breasts.

"Hey you kids, git *away* fum there!" the old man said. The kids looked at him, then at Catty's breasts, then hurried away to see the fire. The orange glow had faded but the air was acrid with smoke.

I glanced back at the car. Eden and Bobby Bolden were both out of sight. I turned my back on the old man and walked over to the tree. Two black kids were still huddled in a bush.

"Who's got a knife?" I said.

One of the kids handed over a curved blade with a taped wooden handle.

"Leave her be, white man!" the old man shouted.

I stepped over to Catty and cut her down, trying to brake her fall with my shoulder. As she hit the ground, limp and hurt and bleeding, with her jaw slack and red welts noticeable now across her breasts, there was an immense ferocious roar.

I heard Eden scream my name.

I turned and saw the old man holding the shotgun. The stock was propped against his hip. But I felt nothing. He must have aimed at the sky. I stared at him. He stared at me.

"I'm gonna pick this woman up now," I said. "Right now. If you want to kill me, go ahead. But I don't think it'd be worth it."

I bent down and lifted Catty, waiting to be shot. I carried her to the car. Eden was hunkered down low in the front and I put Catty beside her. The light of the fire was gone. There was smoke everywhere. Animals and humans crashed around in the woods.

"Git out now, heah me?" the old man said. His voice seemed old and worn and sad. "Don't ever come back to these parts. Just go and leave us be. You come back, ah'll have to kill you."

I drove quickly to Mainside, but not too quickly, afraid of bouncing Bobby and Catty. Eden threw a coat over Catty and cradled her in her arms. We had no choice but Mainside. There was no night corpsman on duty at Ellyson and no hospital in all of Pensacola that would accept a damaged black man and a hurting white woman in the same emergency room. Bobby talked in a slurred voice, his mouth bubbling with bloody saliva:

All the way *hey.* Yeah. They comin down the ridge. In the snow. You watch the snow. Yeah. *Oh.* In formation, gonna march, mothafucka. He got. No, he *got.* Bottle of ocean and two dimes plus *her.* Yeah. *No.* The house. Oh Catty. *Yeah.* Oh Catty.

Eden was silent all the way. I kept wondering if Bobby Bolden had paid the price for rescuing me from Buster and his friends; then dismissed that; thought if *that* was so, it was only part of it, a small part. He was a black man fucking a white woman in the South. He couldn't expect to keep that a secret forever. The old black man was bitter, so even the blacks must have disapproved and the whites would have been crazy. I wondered too if there was some black woman out there by the lake who loved Bobby Bolden from a distance, and then in rage and jealousy made a call or sent a letter. I remembered that night months before when there was a sudden sharp knock on Bolden's door. . . . But maybe someone came here out of *Catty's* life. A husband. A lover. Followed her from Mainside. Watched where she went. *Then* called in the Klan. I remembered the photographs of the Klan in old newspapers and in Bill Mauldin's cartoons: assholes in white sheets watching fiery crosses burn in the night. Degenerate white assholes. They always seemed funny to me, looking at them back in Brooklyn. What did they tell their wives and kids when they went out for the night wearing sheets? That they were saving the good old Yew Ess of Ay from the niggers and the Jews and the Catholics? Ridiculous. But they weren't funny to me anymore. They had maimed and hurt two of my friends.

I glanced at Eden as we turned into the long avenue leading to the gates of Mainside. She was staring off in the distance. Her face was slack now, her hair disheveled. She looked older.

A Marine corporal blocked the gate when I pulled up. I pointed at Bobby and Catty and explained that they were sailors, one from Mainside, the other from Ellyson Field. The Marine's name was stamped on his chest. Gabree. Blond and sunburned. He didn't move or wave us on.

"This car doesn't have a sticker," he said. "*You're* out of uniform. So are *they*. And this other—*woman* isn't in the service." He blinked his blond eyelashes. "You can't come on board. Sorry."

"Are you fucking *crazy?*" I shouted.

Gabree narrowed his eyes and gave me the all-purpose Marine Corps hard-guy look, taught daily at Parris Island.

"You better lower your voice, sailor. Or you'll be in deep shit. *Real* fast."

"Where's your superior officer?" I said, getting out of the car. Gabree inhaled, trying to look more chesty. His hand went to his service revolver.

"He's asleep, sailor. And besides, I don't even have to *answer* you."

"Then you better wake him up, jackoff. If these people die, I'm gonna hold you responsible."

Gabree said, "You know something? I might just arrest you on general principles."

I pointed at Bobby Bolden's writhing body.

"This man was a Naval corpsman at the Chosen reservoir," I shouted. "He saved more Marines than you'll ever even *meet*. If you let him die, then you oughtta die too, fuckhead."

"That's a *threat,* sailor."

"You're fucking right it's a *threat*. Just stop the bullshit and get these people to a hospital."

He started to take the .45 from its holster. His face was cold. I heard Bolden groan. I couldn't see Eden, who was behind Catty.

"You better kill me with that, pal," I said. "If you don't, I'm taking it off you and you'll end up with an extra asshole."

Then another car pulled up behind Eden's and the horn beeped. There were two lieutenants in the car. I turned my back on Gabree and walked over to them and explained what was going on. They were both Marine pilots.

"Oh, these goddamned chickenshit assholes," said the officer behind the wheel. He got out of the car and shouted: "Corporal, get your ass over here!"

They had that squinty-eyed pilot look, the shambling bony bodies. But they took over. They made Corporal Gabree help them lift Catty and Bobby Bolden into their car, then raced past us through the gate into the great slumbering base. I pulled Eden's car around in a circle, stopping just short of the gate. Gabree was standing there.

"I'll see you around, Corporal."

He looked at me without blinking and then I pulled away. Eden huddled against the door, away from me. She didn't speak until we were on the road back to Ellyson Field.

What a night, I said, trying to get her to talk.

She looked at me, shook her head.

I'm sorry for all those rotten things I said. I'm sorry I blew my stack.

Forget it, she said in a soft voice. I shouldn't've egged you on.

It should have felt like a reconciliation; it didn't. We passed a lot of closed bars and churches. Just short of the base, she asked me to pull over.

I can't go back to the trailer tonight, she said.

I mumbled something about not letting the idiots scare her off and how she didn't really have anything to be afraid of, since this was really about Bobby Bolden and Catty.

She said, Are you kidding?

I said, No. In a way, maybe Bobby brought this on himself, with the Klan and all. You know, having a white woman and all that. Even the black people there—well, you saw that old man.

Then Eden Santana began to sob, shaking her head, her body racked.

Oh you poor damn silly *fool,* she said, through tears. You poor damn kid. You poor child.

I put my arms around her and held her close and the hopeless sobbing got heavier and then slowly eased.

What is it, baby? I whispered. What *is* it?

She pulled away and looked at me with her eyes all wet and the tracks of tears on her cheeks.

Don't you see *anything?* she said.

I looked and waited and then she said it.

I'm black, you damn fool. I'm *black.*

Chapter

57

What Eden Told Me (II)

I'M ONE OF *The People, child. And maybe you don't know about them, and for sure you don't know about me, so listen up, you hear? Don't sit there with that damfool white boy look on your face. You should've seen. You should've listened. You should've thought: Who was this James Robinson and why are there no pictures of her children on the walls and why is there a kink in her hair and why does she live by the lake with the niggers? You should've known. Yeah, I hid it. The truth be told, I didn't want you backing up, didn't want you going away. But I knew that if you knew, you'd go away. I learned long ago that I could pass in the white man's world. But I couldn't do it forever, child. Sooner or later, the white man smells niggers and forces them to pay for the white man's own degraded sins. That's what The People learned, too. Though it took em quite a while before they paid for the sin of pride and for all their sad treasons.*

I knew that from the beginning: when you touched my hand and when you entered my body: because it was all in The Story that was passed to me by my daddy and to him from his daddy, The Story passed down through all the generations, like a curse.

The People came from a place called Isle Brevelle, twenty-five miles from Natchitoches, way up in the northwest of Louisiana. This was long ago, you hear me? Before there was a United States, before your people came here, before everybody that was to come and fill the great empty land. Before all of them, The People was here. Americans from the start.

They were like two giant rivers joining to make a new one: the Africa river, the Europe river. The French were down here then, the whole damned

Gulf was theirs and the big river too, all the way to Canada, and later the Spanish were here, and always the Indians were here, and together they brought to America the men and women of Africa. All of them made us, and later they called us the gens de couleur libre, *the free people of color, the Creoles. We just called ourselves The People. We came from all those fucks of Africans and Europeans, fucks in the woods of the empty land, fucks in the August fields, fucks in slave quarters and masters' beds, fucks at gunpoint and fucks freely given.*

The white men looked at us, at the women most of all, and they wanted us. They had no women here, or their women were pale and scrawny things, their heads full of Christian damnation (though some of the women did wander to the woods with black men and add to The People and that's in The Story too). The white man tried to label us, ignoring the fact that before we ever saw a white skin or a blue eye we had the names of Africa, where we had lived since time began, and where later the Arabs chained us and put us in the holds of ships to be carried across oceans. The white men labeled us as if we were goods, and of course, to many of the whites, that's what we were. But late at night it didn't matter how white we were or how black. The white men wanted us.

Maybe that was the beginning of the pride: their wanting us. Maybe that was why we went with them, to break them down, to make them love us, knowing that if they loved us, we owned *them. Maybe that led to the pride. The true sin.*

So you look at me now, here in this place in the fifties, and I guess you think I'm one woman walking in the world. But the truth be told, looking at me you're also looking at people long dead and gone. Their blood's in me. The blood of The People. I can't even go all the way to the beginning of The Story. Can't go to Africa, child.

But I know that in 1742, on a plantation near Natchitoches, a woman named Coincoin was born. Her parents were from Africa, slaves of a French family, they gave her a Christian name, Marie Thereze, but always called her Coincoin in the old language. In The Story, that's the name that was always used.

That slave couple had other kids, but Coincoin was the smart one, the beautiful one, black and smooth and big-assed and ripe. She knew the language that came across the ocean in the slave ships, but she spoke French and Spanish too, and could read all the books in the master's house. She also knew all the healing that could be done with the simple things of God's earth, roots and herbs and plants and magic mud. And though she was Catholic and read the Bible and went to the church, she had the old religion too. She knew all about the gods of the rivers and forests and wind, the sun and the moon. By the time she was twelve, she was famous all over for healing. White folks came to her and black folks too.

But for all the respect they gave her, Coincoin knew one terrible thing. You hear me? She was the property of other men. She and her mother, her father and sisters and brothers did other men's work: cooked their food, plowed their fields, picked their crops, nursed their babies. And because they were property they never got paid, no more than a mule got paid. And though the Code Noir said they couldn't, the white men could grab the girl children and make them sleep with them. And then they could sell them off the way you might sell a saddle or a cart or a mule.

One night when she was sixteen, Coincoin found herself on her own. On that single night her mother died, her father died and the master died in an epidemic that ran through the whole area and killed hundreds. They tell how the master's wife got sick too and how Coincoin drew on the old medicine and saved that woman's life. They say her father on his deathbed asked her to look for the kee-ah root, and Coincoin went foraging in the deep woods, was gone for four days. But when she came back with the secret root, it was too late to help her own father and mother. The Story says Coincoin hated the master and let him die. But when she was certain the man was gone, she saved his wife.

When the plague was over, her slave family was split apart. Coincoin and a brother were given to the master's son. And The Story says that he was kind to her; after all, she had saved his mother. But for all the kindness, she was still property. And in those days, the females were like brood mares to the damned masters. The more children they had, the more human beings the master could sell at a profit, or keep around to work the plantations. So the new master made Coincoin live with a fresh new slave from the old country. She must've felt something for the man because she had four children with him, one after the other, and along the way, started knowing better about the true world.

And then, so The Story goes, when Coincoin was twenty-five, the Frenchman came to Natchitoches.

Her Frenchman.

He was tall and blue-eyed and kind, two years younger than Coincoin, free of family and responsibility, come to Louisiana to make his fortune. His name was Metoyer. He met Coincoin. They fell in love. And within a few months, Coincoin's black man was gone, sold off into the country, her children by him were sold, and Coincoin was living in the Frenchman's house.

This wasn't easy to do, child. She was someone else's *property, not the Frenchman's. She couldn't come and go when and where she pleased. But the Frenchman wanted her, and she wanted the Frenchman's wanting. So the Frenchman went to Coincoin's owner and made a deal. He* rented *her, like you might rent an ox to work your fields. And there, in the Frenchman's house, the Frenchman and Coincoin began to make The People.*

They stayed together for twenty-five years. She gave him seven children. The humiliation was always there, I guess, because though he leased her, all her children belonged to the original master. Still, they lived a moral life. She was his woman, simple as that, his black wife living in the house and taking him inside her and giving him children.

It wasn't always easy. A Spanish priest came to Natchitoches and tried to break them up. But Metoyer loved his Coincoin, and he fought the authorities and they stayed together until, when the owner was on his own deathbed, Metoyer bought Coincoin from him. Bought her outright. And then, because the Code Noir said that no owner was allowed to father a child by one of his own slaves, the Frenchman freed her. And she stayed there in the house with him and their children.

Finally, Coincoin started to get old. And the Frenchman came to her one night and said he wanted to break up with her. This was after twenty-five years and seven children. See, he was rich now and prosperous, this Metoyer, the owner of more slaves than anyone else in the region and thousands of acres of land. He said he wanted to marry a white woman that he'd met in New Orleans. That was the only way under the law that he could pass on his lands to someone, because he wasn't allowed to pass it on to black people. Well, we just don't know what Coincoin said to him when he brung her this news. I like to think she looked at him across a table and said, Go ahead, Frenchman, go to your white woman, but you ain't ever gonna find no woman like me again. Not in your bed. Not by your side. Not ever.

Whatever was said, they stayed friends for the rest of their lives. He arranged to buy her some land on the banks of the Cane River. He gave her money. He made sure all their children together were free and that they carried his name and that they knew how to read and write.

And in spite of her years, Coincoin used her freedom.

She and her children, with their brown hair and blue eyes, set about making something of the wild land along the Cane. They planted tobacco, and loaded it on the boats that would take it to New Orleans and then to Havana to be made into cigars. She raised chickens and turkeys, selling them in the market at Natchitoches, and then bought more land, and planted indigo, which made the dye used in the uniforms worn by the soldiers of Europe. In the early years, she and the children acted like they had no money, lived off the land, and with the money they made, bought more land. Coincoin found empty land along the river and asked for it from the King of Spain (who now owned it all) and got herself a deed written in the king's name. Because the king's deed said they had to, they cleared the land, hunted off the bears, built roads and bridges during those hot and endless days.

Coincoin built two small houses, and saved her money and then went chasing through all the plantations until she found her lost black children, and she took her saved money to their masters and bought them back too. If she was free, she said, then her flesh and blood had to be free. And maybe, someday, they would all be free.

And then came the part that was like a curse, certainly a sin, because more than anyone else in the region, Coincoin knew what she was doing.

She began to buy slaves of her own.

I think of her sometimes deciding to buy that first slave. She who had been the property of others. She who had seen her black children taken off like puppies from a litter. And I wonder what she was thinking and I can't ever get it right. She was a woman alone except for her children, and maybe she thought the only safety was in land: If you owned the land, they couldn't take it from you. But you had to work the land to make it valuable, to defend it, see? And she was getting older, and would never have another man, and maybe she thought, well, just for now I'll play the white man's game, cause eventually this crime will end. I live in the white man's world. I got no momma, no daddy, no husband, and I have to live and build and grow.

So she bought the slaves, and even had a jail built for slaves who didn't do her bidding, she the queen bee now, the mother of the land. She lived on until 1816. It's in the histories. You could look it up. But her slaves—well, when she died, they weren't freed. And her children, held together so long by Coincoin, didn't fall apart. They too wanted to grow and make themselves safe, and so they went down the river from Natchitoches and found the Isle Brevelle. It wasn't really an island, just a giant hunk of land formed by the old and new channels of the Red River. The old channel was called the Cane. The children had been there with Coincoin (chasing bears through the unfenced wilderness) and she had showed them how deep and rich the soil was and how easy it would be to defend.

So even before Coincoin died, The People had begun to buy the land on the Isle Brevelle. They built houses of mud held together with deer hair or Spanish moss. They turned their profits into more land and more slaves, always telling Coincoin what they were doing, and listening for her approval.

And by the time Coincoin died, The People owned twelve thousand acres and more than a hundred slaves.

They knew they couldn't exist on their Isle without fresh blood. But that too brought them up against the sin of pride. You see, they wouldn't mate with blacks: they didn't want to darken their skins again. Blackness, nothing more, had made them the property of strangers. So they wanted to be lighter and lighter. That made it all right to mate with white men. Or with men and women like themselves, part African, part European. But never with pure blacks, for that would be to go back. So they had to go looking. The young men traveled into New Orleans and saw there the beautiful women at the octoroon balls, parading their beauty for the rich young whites in hopes of finding lifelong protection. But not many octoroon beauties came to Isle Brevelle, because they too were part of The People, and would only mate with whites. The young men of New Orleans were something else, those poor lost men with mixed blood; nobody would set them up in houses, as white men did for their quadroon beauties. So some of the men came upriver to marry the women of Isle Brevelle. They had no money, no property other than their bodies and blood. But they were needed, and they came.

The Isle grew fat and rich. The land was turned to cotton and corn, the cotton sold in New Orleans, the corn for cash in Natchitoches. By 1840, The People owned the richest plantations in the parish, owned more slaves than the white men. King Cotton made The People rich. It allowed them to loan money to white planters, and invite them over to the mansions that had replaced the mud huts. It brought tutors from New Orleans to teach their children. It built a Catholic church where whites came to pray. It brought silk stockings and perfume and bands to play waltzes.

But cotton also came from oxen and mules and niggers.

I wonder now what happened sometimes in the evenings, when the masters walked out on their porches while the orchestras played. They could see in the distance the mud huts of the slave quarters. Did they hear forbidden drums playing? Did they hear Africa coming across the lawns?

You pay for your sins. You know that, child. You're a Catholic too. Like The People were. Like me. Pride goeth before a fall. Right? And that's what The People carry around with them to this day. The Story of the Fall.

It came in waves. The first was natural: there was only so much land, and when people died, they divided it among their children so that all the plots got smaller and harder to make money from. The Americans came. All of them Protestants, bony men with cold eyes. At first The People tried to ignore them, sticking to the old ways, speaking French and Spanish (the old

*language gone now), remaining Catholics as the Protestant tide flowed
around them. They couldn't believe that these pitiful river rats would forever
replace the men of Europe. Paris was a thousand years old and Madrid was
older. Washington was a village.*

*But the Americans kept filling the surrounding lands, then running the
banks and businesses and imposing a harder, more heartless attitude about
color. Some of The People tried to befriend the Americans. They invited them
to their homes, they loaned them money.*

*But the Americans saw The People in a different way. Instead of marvel-
ing at what we had made with sweat and sacrifice, they envied it. And after
a while they wanted to take it from The People without working for it as
Coincoin and her sons had, plows strapped to their shoulders, hunting bear
in the dark woods. So the Americans began to challenge the land grants
given by the kings of France and Spain, scheming and cheating and calling
upon God as their primary witness. They exhausted us in courtrooms. They
sat down to play cards with our men, not for a few reales as in the old days,
but for entire plantations. And sometimes they won: leaving families without land, and more women and children to be taken in by The People,
further dividing the limited acres.*

*So when the cotton market collapsed, and the Depression came, and the
banks failed and the whole country was full of starving people, the Americans were waiting like vultures. All the cotton planters, white and colored,
lived on credit, taking money from the banks at the beginning of the season
that was paid back at harvest time. But the Depression went on and on for
almost ten years. Everywhere, land, slaves, and tools were taken away to
pay the debts, everybody thinking: This is just for now, soon the Depression
will end and we can go back and do what we always did. Our young men
were still told to walk straight and proud. The People still worshiped each
Sunday in the church on Isle Brevelle where half the parishioners were
white. There were still parties and marriages and love affairs. But the
Americans were chopping away at us.*

So was God.

*For then one spring the Cane flooded and destroyed half the crops and
a horde of caterpillars came behind it and ate the rest. The budworms came
the following year, and then the price of cotton collapsed again all over the
world. The banks failed. Again the Americans grabbed what they could of
the good land cleared and made abundant by The People. It was as if the
great sin of pride had brought down the full punishing wrath of God.*

*And so when the last act of the tragedy began, they didn't see it for what
it was. The Civil War. The War Between the States. That was it, the final*

blow. And The People showed that they were no different in the end from other human beings. It was simple. They owned slaves. So they sided with the Confederacy.

And when the war bounced off the North and drove back deeper into the South and the Confederates retreated, The People helped. The Confederates destroyed much of what had been built by The People and their slaves. And then the Union army arrived, chasing the rebels, and destroying the rest. They raped our women. They tortured our men. For one long weekend there was no night in the land as everything from Natchitoches to Isle Brevelle was set to the Yankee torch. They called us niggers. And then they moved on. Talking about freedom.

Isle Brevelle never recovered. The slaves were gone, looking for the Promised Land, and The People had no money to hire new help. Crops rotted. Land went fallow. Families moved into the slave quarters, squatting on dirt floors, sleeping against mud and deer-hair walls. Reconstruction ended and the Americans made clear that all their talk of freedom was a lie. And The People learned permanently what they should have known from the beginning: to the white man, they would always be niggers.

Some stayed along the Cane. Most drifted moved on. My folks went to New Orleans. For a long time after the war, The People were still allowed to live there. I mean, really live. Not live the way the white man wanted you to live. But free. Marrying who you want. Eating where you want. That didn't last long. The rednecks took the South. They used their damn Bible to keep people down, to make them feel inferior, denying them even simple education and honest work, denying them freedom. They made sure you knew that no damn Yankee ever won a war.

So here I am, child. You sittin there with your eyes wide open and your chin droppin. Sittin here with me. How's it feel to know the damn Klan could do to me any minute what it did to Bobby Bolden? More: How's it feel to know you been in love for a long time now with a nigger?

Chapter

58

SHE DROVE AWAY in the chilly morning fog. I stumbled through the woods, heading for the hole in the fence, my head full of pictures that weren't there a few days before: Bobby Bolden's ruined hands with the music beaten out of them; Coincoin hunting bears in the dark woods and punishing her slaves; the Klan lashing at Catty's flesh, eyes red from white lightning and fear; the old black man with the shotgun warning me off the land. Rage was everywhere: my own and the rage of others.

But most of all I was full of Eden Santana and The Story. My own small tale seemed puny by comparison to her tapestry of history, myth, forgotten languages, old crimes. How could she care for my own small ambitions, my little fairy tales of Paris and art, when she was one of the secret bearers of The Story? A few hundred feet from the base, I sat down in the dark with my back to a tree and started to cry.

I felt like such a goddamned fool. Why *hadn't* I seen it? The clues were there from the moment I met her on that New Year's Eve bus: the frizzy hair and the dark skin and the way she slurred certain words. I had refused to notice the absent things: pictures of family and children and friends. Drawing from photographs late at night, I arrogantly thought I understood the lives of other men from the evidence of wrinkled snapshots slipped from wallets. But I never clearly saw the woman who was there before me in all her nakedness. She didn't have the black skin, broad nose or thick lips of a cartoon Negro. But Bobby Bolden must've seen what she was that time we picked him up in the rain. Maybe the blacks out by the lake always knew when one of their own kind was trying to pass in the white man's world, and maybe they liked what they saw, knew she was making me hers as so many black women had done with so many white men across the centuries. But I would never know the answers to such questions and that's what made me feel such a fool. I had made love to her and she to me; but James Robinson had gone there first. And I remembered Waleski's maxim: *I thought I fucked a colored girl until I saw a colored guy fuck a colored girl.*

My body trembled, I shuddered, felt very hot, then cold. I tried to get angry, to use fury to force out the shame. Why didn't she *tell* me? If she loved me, how could she keep such a secret from me? Was she waiting for some moment when she would sit me down and tell me and laugh at me, thus becoming my master, the owner of my broken pride? Did she make me love her as an act of revenge? But wait, I thought: *you wanted her to keep some secrets. You told her that her secrets would keep you loving her for the rest of your life. That's what you kept saying to her, right? So how can you get angry for going along with your desire? You want secrets, and then you learn a big secret and first get sick and then get angry. Come on.*

But then I knew that I wasn't crying simply because I felt shame or had been fooled. I was sobbing in the empty woods because everything I wanted to do with Eden Santana now seemed impossible. Say it straight, I said. And spoke out loud: *How can I ever marry a nigger?* Saying the word. The word that I knew had broken Bobby Bolden's hands and sent the Klan to hang women from trees. I'd thought of myself as the hip New Yorker, who knew all about Charlie Parker and Max Roach and Billie Holiday, and here I was, saying the word. *Nigger,* I said out loud. *You're a nigger, Eden.* And saw myself walking the streets with her nigger kids and our own kids with a touch of nigger in them. And people would stop us in restaurants and say, *Hey, no niggers here, pal.* And no niggers in this school. And *sorry, but ain't no room in this bus, you'll have to sit up front, sailor,* and put your nigger woman in the back.

Nigger, I said to the cold woods.

Nigger nigger nigger nigger nigger nigger nigger nigger nigger nigger nigger nigger nigger.

The word lost all meaning and I stood up, walking slowly now, drying my tears on my jumper. And new pictures formed in my head. I saw myself in New Orleans, sitting in the parlor with Eden's parents, the two of them looking at me the way that old man had looked at me when I went to cut down Cathy; his eyes cold and his shotgun cradled in his arms. There were photographs of The People on the mantel. The parents were looking at me very hard and saw that I was young. They stared at my Navy uniform and my poorly shined shoes and made their own labels, their own categories, and placed me in the bin for poor white trash. Her children were in the next room, closer to my age than Eden was to mine, the two of them coal black staring at the white boy and wondering how he could ever be their daddy. That vision made me laugh. But then I imagined Harrelson seeing us strolling together down Palafox Street on our way to Mass at the Catholic church. I saw him smirking. Heard him say something about pickaninnies. And then suddenly knew: *It was Harrelson tipped off the Klan.*

Of course.

It *had* to be him.

He'd seen us that day. Coming up out of the side road from the lake, going to the highway.

Harrelson.

You prick.

And then I began to hurry, brushing aside branches and pushing through wet shrubs. I found the hole in the back fence and slipped through. It was almost four in the morning. I moved through the emptiness of the landing strip, staying in the dark, then hugged the sides of hangars. I slipped into the barracks and went straight to Harrelson's bunk.

He wasn't there.

I felt cheated. I wanted to hurt him. I wasn't going to waste time in any court of law. I *knew* and I was going to punish the son of a bitch. But goddamnit, he wasn't there.

I got into bed and lay there trembling for a long time. In one night, my whole world had changed and I didn't know how I was going to live in it.

Chapter

59

I NEVER SAW Bobby Bolden again. The scuttlebutt came in from Mainside about how they treated him at the hospital, his hands broken, ribs smashed, jaw fractured. The first morning, we heard about his concussion and how the brass came to talk to him about what happened and how Bobby Bolden told them to go away. We heard about how they stationed a Marine guard at his door, who turned away all visitors. Later we saw two MPs come to the Kingdom of Darkness and pack Bobby's gear, taking everything with them, including the horn. Before the day was over, we heard they had flown him to Norfolk: out of Ellyson, out of Mainside, out of Pensacola, out of the South, and out of our lives.

We heard about Catty too. How they'd cleaned up her wounds and wired her broken shoulder and bandaged her ribs where someone had kicked her; how they'd listened to her as she made official statements; how the Navy brass had secured her hospital room too and then turned their backs as they transferred her to San Diego. They were shipping her as far from Bobby Bolden as they could send her. And as far as possible from anyone who might demand to know what had been done to her that night.

I was still so young that I was shocked when I discovered that there wasn't a word about it in the Pensacola newspaper. As far as the paper was concerned, it had never happened. I called Maher in the administration building, since yeomen knew what was going on better than the officers did, and asked him why there was nothing in the newspaper. He was busy, but he said he'd try to find out. Twenty minutes later he called me back to say that it was very simple: the beatings had never been reported to the Pensacola police. And if there was no police report, the newspapers would never know.

"Why don't *we* call the newspapers?" I said.

"You can," he said. "But the first thing they would do is call the Navy PIO guys. And they wouldn't confirm it. They'd just say that all Navy personnel records are confidential, or something like that.... And, of course, the Klan doesn't give out press releases."

I went over to see Sal and Max and they were in a fury. They wanted to hunt down Buster and give him the beating of his life, because they were sure that Bobby had been tracked by Buster's boys after rescuing me that day on the road.

"Set him on fire," Sal said. "Hang him on a meat hook."

Max said, "Break *his* hands and ankles."

But as we stood in the sunlight beside the hangar, we slowly realized that we weren't sure that it *was* Buster. We didn't know how many others had come in the night to beat Bobby Bolden and Catty Wolverton and burn their house to the ground. We didn't even know what had happened to Bobby Bolden's Mercury. The anger seeped out of us.

"There oughtta be *something* we can do," Sal said. "There oughtta be *some* ass we could kick."

Max shook his head: "It's going after ghosts."

After the MPs left with the artifacts of Bobby Bolden's life, I went up to the Kingdom of Darkness. The door was locked. I knocked and Rhode Island Freddie answered. He looked at me and started to close the door without saying a word.

"Hey, man, *wait*!" I said.

"Git outta here, mothafucka."

"Hey, *I* didn't do it!" I said. "*I* drove him to Mainside. *I* cut down Catty. It wasn't *me*. I just came up here to say I was *sorry* and—"

"You know somethin, boy?" he said. "You *dumb*. Dumber than shit. And Bobby, he was even *more* dumb. He take you as a friend. He take the white bitch as a friend. What it *get* him, huh? Answer me that? What it *get* him? You *seen* whut it get him. You *seen* it. Man never get to play that fuckin horn the rest of his fuckin life, that what it get him. *Why?* Answer me that. And you *know* why. *White folks!*"

"Yeah, but—"

"You *all* white. You and the bitch and the Klan and Abe Lincoln and the fuckin president and every fuckin officer in the Navy. *All* white. And all the fuckin same."

He slammed the door. On me, on all whites.

And it didn't end there.

At lunch time, the food was disgusting. Greasy, half cooked. The messcooks seemed to be wearing masks as they made their protest. I said hello. Nobody answered. They just looked past me. I gazed at the greasy vegetables and the pink half-boiled chicken on my tray. And then saw Harrelson at a table.

I went over to him.

"You prick," I said.

He smirked at me.

"Oh, *my*," he said. "We got us an angry nigger lover, don't we?"

I reached across the table and grabbed the front of his jumper and lifted him toward me.

"Say another word and I'll bite your nose right off your face, shithead."

"You touch *me*, Yankee," he hissed, "you might git what the nigger got."

I let go of him but I wasn't finished. The mess hall was quiet. I faced him, talking louder.

"It *was* you, wasn't it?" I said. "You fingered Bobby Bolden for the Klan."

"I don't know what you're talking about, sailor."

"You knew he was living down there by the lake."

"The whole damn world knew *that,* boy."

"Maybe so. But the rest of the world didn't *care* and you did."

Harrelson got up and lifted his tray, still covered with uneaten food. He looked at me.

"You sure lookin to git yore *ass* whupped, nigger lover."

I came around and grabbed his arm.

"Not by you, prick."

I was ready to hammer him, make him eat the tray itself, and then Red Cannon was beside us, and I could see Chief McDaid standing at the door.

"Ten-*shun!*" Red barked.

We both came to attention, Harrelson still holding his tray. The chow hall was absolutely silent now, except for the whistling of a coffee urn.

"What's this all about, Mister Harrelson?" Cannon said.

"The Yankee here's got a big mouth, *that's* whut it's about."

"Ask him about Bobby Bolden," I said. "Ask him when he called up the Klan."

"I wuddint addressin' you, sailor," Cannon said.

"You asked what it's *about.* Well, it's about Bobby Bolden. That's what it's *about.* This prick called down the *Klan* on him."

McDaid came over, smiling in an oily way.

"At ease, sailors," he said. He cleared his throat, knowing that others could hear him. "We all feel bad about what happened to Bobby Bolden. But you two aren't going to help matters by fighting each other. Let's both of you go back to work."

He nodded at Red and then they walked across the chow hall and left. McDaid was clearly washing his hands of the whole matter and letting Red Cannon know it wasn't his business either. Harrelson smiled thinly at me.

"Fuck you," he said.

"Not me," I said. "Your mother."

Harrelson turned his back and walked quickly to the garbage disposal as the room gradually filled with the murmur of conversation. None of the blacks behind the steam tables would look at me.

That afternoon, Harrelson was transferred to Mainside.

I had the duty in the Supply Shack that night and for once I was glad. I knew that Eden must have spent the night at Roberta's. She certainly didn't go back to the trailer. But even if I could find her, I didn't know what I would say to her. So when Donnie Ray gave me the duty, I was relieved. I took my pad and chalks with me to the shack and worked on the portrait of Captain Pritchett's dead wife for a few hours. There wasn't much business at the front counter; it was as if the base had emptied so that everyone could go somewhere and mourn Bobby Bolden's murdered hands.

I kept trying to get Pritchett's wife right, but her face wouldn't come off the page. I threw sheet after sheet into the trash basket. And I soon realized what was happening: the long-dead Catherine, the woman the Captain loved, the woman whose memory had been turned by him into banks of flowers, kept coming out looking like Eden Santana.

Around midnight, Miles came in. His skin looked yellow. His eyeglasses were dirty. He sat down at his desk and stared at his hands and talked about Bobby Bolden.

"I kept thinking about his hands," he said. "Kept thinking how he used to play in the afternoon for us. For himself, first, I guess. But for *us* too. And then I thought of those shitass rednecks and how much they must have enjoyed smashing up the hands of a colored man who had more talent and brains and heart than all of them combined. They must've loved it."

"You *know* they loved it."

"But I could've warned him."

"Everybody warned him, Miles."

"Then maybe he wanted it to happen."

"Don't be stupid, Miles."

"Maybe he *did.* Some people are so afraid of their own talent, they'd rather have someone else destroy it than have to do it themselves. They *provoke.* They make death happen."

"Bobby Bolden wouldn't have given these dirtbags that satisfaction."

A mechanic came in and I waited on him and when I was finished, Miles Rayfield was gone. He didn't know how crucial a part he'd played the night before; in a strange way, his existence might have saved Bobby Bolden's life; if I hadn't argued about him with Eden, I wouldn't have stormed into the night and found Bobby writhing in the bushes. I looked at my drawing. Miles had made a few marks on it, a tuck here, an emphasis there. I saw clearly what I'd done wrong. I started over one final time and finished quickly. And when I was done with Catherine Pritchett, I did a drawing of Eden Santana.

In chalk on paper. She was sitting on a chair in the trailer, with one leg up over the arm. The hair had grown back between her legs, frizzy and thick. The hair on her head was more clearly the hair of a black woman, and so were her features, the nose slightly wider, the lips fuller. She was looking at me in a cool direct way, wearing the high-heeled shoes. And she was more beautiful than ever.

I closed the Supply Shack at twenty minutes after midnight. I walked slowly to the barracks and sat on my bunk for a long while before I knew what I had to do.

I had to go to Eden Santana.

Right away.

If I didn't, I would lose her.

Chapter

60

THERE WAS NO moon. I avoided the road, because it went past Billy's where Red Cannon did his drinking, and past the boat shop where Buster's presence hung like an evil smell, and past too many gas stations where the lights of pickup trucks could snap on suddenly and find me in the darkness. I chose the woods instead, and I was almost immediately lost, slowly moving forward, going around thickets and tangles of wet brush. I had never gone this way before; until this night, all I needed to know was the trail to the highway. But now I was alone, going the other way, into the unknown.

After a while my body ached and my shoes were soaked. But I plunged on. I wanted Eden and I wanted her tonight. I was going to tell her I was with her forever. I didn't care if she was black, colored, Negro, nigger. I didn't fall in love with her because she was black and I wasn't going to stop loving her because she was black. I didn't care what anybody else thought. Not her mother or her father or my friends back home; not old blacks with shotguns or whites with whips. On the subject of Eden Santana, the opinions of others didn't interest me.

Speeches rolled around in my head, as I pushed through the brush and the thickets and bumped into trees, my arms and face scratched now, the words a kind of fuel, driving me on. *We can't quit, baby.* They'll win, the Klan will win. *The rednecks will win. Harrelson will win. We gotta be together against all of them. Me, you, your kids, our kids. Wherever we go. Paris. New York. We gotta do it. We got to fight this out together.*

Until at last I saw the lake. Black and sullen and silent.

I walked along the shore and found a flat-bottomed boat tied to a dock. The oars were leaning against a piling. I picked up the oars and untied the boat and began to row across the lake. I knew that I'd just committed the crime of stealing a boat. But I didn't care. On the far shore was Eden Santana.

There were no lights anywhere, and no stars. But I was still afraid of being watched as I came across the lake: watched by the Klan or the blacks. Waiting there for me in the dark. I rowed softly on, trying to stay low. If they were waiting for me, I didn't want to give them a good target. The oars seemed to make a sound that said Eden. Eden. Dip and pull and Eden.

And then I was at the far shore. The boat made a squashing sound as it drove into weeds and mud. I stepped into a foot of water and then pulled the boat up another foot into the mud until it was firmly wedged. I was about a half mile from the trailer, closer to where Bobby Bolden lived with Catty than to the place where Eden and I had played our games. I started walking through the woods in my soaked shoes. I saw the tree where Catty had been whipped into unconsciousness. I looked at the bushes where the old man had aimed his shotgun at me. It all seemed part of a dream I'd had a hundred years before. I paused, listened, heard nothing. And then moved ahead.

Soon I could see the trailer, small and silvery in the dim light. And my heart pounded. The car wasn't there. I began to run. A few feet from the trailer, I stopped, listening again, afraid. And then tried the door. It was open, but when I flicked on the switch, nothing happened; there was no electricity. But I didn't really need light.

From the moment I stepped inside, I knew that everything was gone and so was Eden Santana.

PART
FIVE

Chapter

61

From The Blue Notebook

NOTHING MATTERS.

Chapter
62

SO IT HAD happened to me, as it had happened to Turner and Sal and Maher, to all the other poor lost sailors I'd come to know: the thing I feared most: suddenly, after sickening violence, she was gone. The boy I was then went down to Sears and talked to some counter girls, and was told they hadn't seen her, no, they'd seen no sign of Eden Santana. The boy I was then went to see the store manager, a fat pig-eyed man named Rudolph. "Damn woman never even called," he said. "Just stuck me with her counter. Never called. And I got her pay check here for her too. Well, she comes to get paid, I'm gone to give her a nice fat piece of ma mind . . ."

On those nights in the fifties, when people all over America were sitting in their safe little houses talking about Gorgeous George and Howard Unruh, Miss Hush and pyramid clubs, I was searching the streets of a city that was not my own, trying to find a woman I was sure I loved more than anyone on earth. On the third night, I took a bus over to Roberta's and told her what had happened. We sat together in the living room in the fading light. She cried twice. I comforted her. Then she put my hand on her breast and started to move to the bedroom. I shook my head no.

"You helped *me* when I was hurting," she said. "Now I want to help *you.*"

"Only thing could help me, Roberta, was if she walked in that door."

She started sobbing again.

"Me too," she said. "Me too."

She looked suddenly old, and now the trouble, the loss, the departure was all about her and no longer about me.

"My friend is *gawn*," she said. "My sweet friend Eden is *gawn*."
She was still sobbing when I left.

I drifted through an agony of days, desperate for a letter, a note, some proof that Eden Santana had existed, was not conjured or invented by the boy I was then. I wanted something that said at the end "love always," like the picture of Captain Pritchett's wife. In bed, in the woods, in rivers and on beaches, she had made me almost a man. And then, through the simple act of departure, she'd broken me down again into a child. Not a word arrived from her. Some sick bastards had come out of the swamp and scared her and she had run. And I couldn't run after her. She had the car and the open roads of the great wide country. But I was trapped in the Navy, the prisoner of an easy oath.

And so, after those first few days, I went back to what I was before I met her. I didn't have to explain to Sal and Max and Maher and the others. I just showed up one evening at the gate and then all of us were racing to O Street. And once again, Webb Pierce was singing on the juke and Tons of Fun showed up with their van and then Hank Williams was singing about how he was so lonesome he could die.

While Dixie Shafer laughed and opened bottles.

The whole gang was there and nobody asked where I'd been and why I was back. But I was sure they knew. I drank beer and talked about Bobby Bolden and the Navy's great cover-up and drank more beer and said Harrelson had to be the finger man and then we all talked about what we should have done to save Bobby Bolden and then we chug-a-lugged more beers and then I was leaning against the concrete blocks outside, throwing up in the dirt while the night sky whirled around and the ground pitched and Dixie Shafer told us all it was time to go back to the base.

O Eden.

The next morning, my tongue was thick and slimy. My brains felt diced. I stood in the shower for a long time and when my brain started working again I still wanted Eden Santana. Instead of eating lunch, I went to the barracks and lay down on my bunk and tried to sleep and still I wanted Eden Santana. I went back to the Supply Shack and filled out forms and swabbed the deck and tried jokes with Becket and talked about college with Charlie Dunbar and still I wanted Eden Santana.

She had changed me. All those secret things we had done had changed me. A thousand images flooded through me and I was

filled with such longing, such desperation, such need for flesh and
hair and teeth, that I thought about going down to the black bars
to find Winnie, to fuck her real good while my brain flooded with
Eden's face and Eden's hair and Eden's hoarse morning voice.

But I never did go after Winnie. I just went back and back and
back to O Street and sometimes down to Trader Jon's and after
those first few nights we stopped talking about Bobby Bolden
because we knew it was just talk, knew we couldn't do anything,
knew we couldn't save him or Catty or anybody else, not even
ourselves.

So we talked about ball games and fighters and the peace talks
at Panmunjon and the shitheads from Washington whose pictures
were in the papers. I never mentioned Eden Santana. And one of
those nights, someone mentioned that Friday was Sal's birthday and
it was payday too and why didn't we have a party? I don't know who
suggested the Miss Texas Club. I'd never been in the place. All I
knew about it was that it was a strip joint out on the edge of
Pensacola on the highway heading east. We'd chip in some money.
We'd get through the door with the Navy ID, which meant we had
to wear uniforms.

Yeah.

And we'd get one of those strippers for Sal. Pay her some money
to pinch his nose with her twat.

O yeah.

And drink and shout and sing. On a summer night in the year
of Our Lord Nineteen Hundred and Fiftyfuckinthree.

Yeah, yeah.

And the next morning, Becket came into the Shack waving a
letter at me and said, "Got something for you." I trembled, thinking *Eden.* I stood there, thinking *At last.* And took it from him,
looking out the window, until he moved away, and then stared at
the writing.

It was from my father.

Christ.

A letter from the world I'd left behind when my heart was in a
world I could not even prove had existed. I opened it slowly.

> My son,
> It's hard for me to write a letter. You know I was never much for
> "words." They always say the Irish have the gift of the "gab" but

I just never had it. My father was that way too, may he "rest" in peace.

But your last letter made me proud of you. I know you are doing your part for your country. And even though the Korea war seems about to be over, we really need men like you. The "commies" are everywhere, son. Listen to this McCarthy. He's wise to them. You might not ever get to Korea but I bet the "Reds" are down there too in the south of "good old" USA.

Your brothers are fine. Danny has your gift with "words." He got two strate A's on his compositions at Holy Name. Isn't that hot "stuff"? I don't understand his stories. They are sort of "crazy." But he sits up all night and writes them like he was hipnotized. Something for a boy 11. He says he wants a typewriter for his birthday, in order to be a sportswriter, like "Dick" Young. He's a real dreamer like you.

Rory seems to have your gift for "art." He draws all the time. He loved the drawings you sent him from the Navy. He's not as good as you but I think he has the gift from his mother and "then" he's only nine.

Well I better finish this up. You sound happy son. How is the girl you "mentioned" in your last letter? You sound like your very serious about her. She sounds swell. I saw that girl you used to keep company with at church. Sad to say she looked fat. No "bargain" if you ask me.

Well try to write when you have time. Everything here is the same. We all hope you will come home soon.

He signed it "love always, Your Father."

I put it down, folding and unfolding it. I had my "love always."

And I suddenly wanted to be with him. I wanted to be in New York. I wanted away from the Navy and from people who broke the hands of a man who made music. I didn't want to see any of the places where I'd been with Eden Santana. Not alone. Never again. I wanted to be in the third floor right at 378 Seventh Avenue, Brooklyn 15, New York. In a place without orders or oaths or Red Cannon, without swash plates or palm trees or duty.

I wanted to be home.

The night before Sal's birthday, I woke from a dream to hear voices out in the street. The barracks were empty. The night was very hot. One of the voices belonged to Miles Rayfield.

"Please," he was saying. "Don't do it *this* way." I heard panic and fear in his voice. *"Please,* can't you—"

I hurried to the door in my shorts and paused behind the screen. Across the street, Miles Rayfield was pleading with Red Cannon while two young sailors carried Miles's things out of the Supply Shack and into a waiting panel truck. Paintings. Brushes. The palette and the tin water cans and the tubes of casein. The sketchbooks. Everything that had been a part of Miles's secret studio, everything that made his life a life. I went back to my bunk and pulled on dungarees and shoes and a T-shirt and then crossed the street.

"Red, *don't* let them slam the paintings around," Miles said. Then he saw me and his eyes were a plea. They said *Save me please save me now save me.* He was trying to sound reasonable. "Come on, Red."

"Shut up, sailor," Cannon said. "You are already on report. Don't make it worse."

I said, "Hey, Red, what did he *do* that's so wrong?"

"You shut up too. Or you'll join him in the court martial."

"Court martial?" I said. Miles looked ashen. "For *what?*"

"You seen them *sketchbooks,* sailor?" Cannon said. "If you have, then you could be a witness. All you *artistes,* you're the same way, ain't you? If you haven't seen em, then you'll never know what I mean."

Miles leaned a hand on the wood frame around the door. His jaw hung loose. I went over to him and put a hand on his shoulder. He pulled away. I turned to look at Red Cannon. He smiled tightly and got in the truck, and pulled away. Miles Rayfield's life and work bumped loosely in the back.

"I'm dead," Miles whispered.

He sat down hard on the ground and leaned back against the wall in a heavy ruined way. I squatted and faced him.

"What's he *got* on you?" I said.

Knowing the answer.

He didn't say a word. He just shook his head slowly, then hopelessly, and then began to sob. The pain and grief rushed out of some scary place.

I sat down beside him and put an arm around him and pulled him close and hugged him for a long time.

Chapter

63

THAT NIGHT, I went to the chow hall with Miles. He didn't eat. Later, we walked in the long summer evening, while I tried to get him to talk. But the brackets that framed his mouth had gone loose, making him look younger and more helpless, and words, which had been his defense against the world, had abandoned him. He stopped and wept three separate times. I waited until he was finished and then nudged him along and we walked some more. We even passed the hole in the fence, which I showed to Miles. He didn't react. Near the end, he said again, as he'd done a million times since I'd known him, *This goddamned Navy.* Nothing else. Then I walked him back to the barracks in the dark and waited while he undressed and stood there while he fell heavily and without words into his rack. He closed his eyes and slept.

I thought about him for a long time as I lay without sleep in my own rack. In the morning I'd have to find Freddie Harada and warn him. Make certain that he didn't say anything that would hurt Miles or himself. Tell him that Red Cannon and Chief McDaid were probably coming to interrogate him. Using guile or threats to get Freddie on the record, to nail Miles to the fucking cross. Sodomy, they would call it. Another word I'd looked up in the dictionary. I imagined them giving the news to the wife in Atlanta: *Your husband's a faggot, lady.* And then to the mother: *Your son's problem is dick, ma'am.* Whatever had gone on between them, Freddie had to deny everything. If he did, I couldn't believe that Captain Pritchett would call a court martial for the monstrous crime of having a painting studio on United States government property. Sure, it was against the rules. But it wasn't like Miles was selling secrets to the goddamned Chinese communists. This was strictly minor crap. Housekeeping. That's all. Except for those sketchbooks. And later I thought that even if they court-martialed Miles and booted him out of the Navy, there would be some good in it. Miles would be free. He'd be out of the goddamned Navy, out of Anus Mundi, free to roam the world. He could just *go.*

He would, in fact, be freer than I was, because I couldn't go anywhere. And then the notion blossomed in my mind: I wanted to *go.* Not simply home, to the safety of the third floor left. I wanted out of that place, out of the goddamned rules and regs, out of the boring prison of Ellyson Field. I wanted to find Eden. I didn't care who she had been and what color she was and where she came from. I didn't care where she was living or even what she was doing now or wanted to do for the rest of her life.

I wanted to be with my loving woman.

When I woke in the morning, Miles was already gone. His bunk was neatly made up, the sheets and blanket crisp in the lemon-colored morning light. I showered and dressed quickly and walked to the chow hall. Sal and Max were already there, full of plans for the party that night, already spending the payday money. But Miles wasn't around. I saw Freddie Harada behind the servers in the kitchen and waved him outside. He slipped out the side door.

"Hey, man, I'm busy," he said. "What you want?"

I told him about Miles Rayfield and warned him that Cannon and McDaid were sure to come looking for him. He looked scared. I asked him where Miles was.

"He was here when we opened," he said, his eyes darting everywhere. "About six. He just had coffee and a roll and sat 'way in the back for a long time, writing letters."

"He look okay?"

"Same as always."

We went back inside. Sal was talking about a girl Max had met in the Dirt Bar the night before. Six foot three and ninety pounds.

"You could open a letter with her and Max falls right in love," Sal said.

"It was lust, Sal, not love."

"It must have been like banging a pair of scissors."

"Worse," Max said.

I asked if they'd seen Miles Rayfield.

"Yeah, matter of fact," Sal said. "He was out on the steps of the barber shop. Oh, half an hour ago. Writing letters. Why? What's up?"

"Nothing," I said.

Boswell came over and sat down and told us that Harrelson had been transferred to the U.S.S. *Saratoga*. "Out of Pearl," he said, rolling his eyes. "Oh, my, how I'd like to get one of them Hawaiian leis."

"That's a truly terrible joke, Bos," Sal said.

"Yeah," Max said. "Leave the jokes to the Jews."

"Well," Boswell said, "he's gone."

I thought: Good riddance, you rat stool pigeon.

After breakfast Sal and Max said they'd see us tonight and headed for the hangars, while Boswell and I walked together to the Supply Shack. Donnie Ray called muster. Everybody was there except Miles Rayfield.

"He was just at breakfast," I said. "Let me go find him."

"Make it snappy," Donnie Ray said, sounding annoyed. "The man's technically over the hill."

I hurried out. But Miles wasn't at the barber shop or in the barracks, the chow hall, the infirmary or the post office. Yeah, he'd been *at* the post office, all right, the civilian said. Bought two dollars worth of stamps. Quite a while ago. Nobody'd seen him at the other places. I went back to the Supply Shack and told Donnie Ray.

"Goddamn, I'll have to mark him AWOL," he said with a sigh.

"Why don't you alert the infirmary first?" I said. "Maybe he got sick somewhere and they'll find him."

Donnie Ray sighed. "Yeah, and maybe he's halfway to Mobile right now." He glanced at his watch and chewed the inside of his mouth. "Well, you better start swabbin down, sailor. It's your turn."

He stared at the telephone. The aroma of fresh-cut grass drifted through the screened windows. Insects buzzed. Helicopters started chugging into the sky. I walked down to the closet where we stored the mops and buckets and soap, and opened the door.

Miles was hanging from a length of gray clothesline tied around a water pipe. His neck was bent at a right angle, the rope digging deep into his flesh. His face was blue.

Chapter

64

I GUESS BECKET CUT him down. Or maybe it was Donnie Ray. I don't know for sure. I do know that Boswell and Parsons and Donnie all were shouting for an ambulance, for medics, for someone who could do mouth-to-mouth: *Hurry now still a chance that's it easy boy okay hold him soft.* I remember hands reaching, then all lifting, then tearing open a shirt; rubber heels on the concrete floor; an empty wash bucket going over and men grunting. *Jesuschrist now what in the fuck would he wanna do that for?* And more shouts and doors slamming and the incessant ringing of a single telephone. All that happened: the logistics of death.

I remember staring at the gouged skin of Miles's neck. I remember him lying on the painted concrete deck that he would never walk again or curse again or swab down again on a Friday afternoon. I cursed the Navy. And I cursed God. And I cursed Red Cannon. I cried too, cradling my dead friend's head, feeling the heat drain away; just sobbed like a boy, until the medic came at last and tried to thump the dead heart back into life before saying that it was too late, the man was dead and hey, sailor, what was his service number?

Becket walked me outside.

Just like that (I said to Becket, in some fumbling way), Miles Rayfield was gone. And now that it had happened, I realized that he had been going away for days. First they took his work away. The paintings, drawings, paints and chalks: all had disappeared. Then they took his tongue, forcing him into tears and silence. And now he'd done what they couldn't do: removed himself from the Navy and the earth itself.

Miles you son of a bitch, I said out loud. *Why'd you do this, you dumb fuck? Why didn't you just run? Why'd you have to loop a rope around your goddamned neck?*

And then finally Becket said "Okay, dat's enough. Be a man, Michael. Right now."

So I wiped my eyes and took a deep breath and straightened up and exhaled hard and then walked back to the Supply Shack. Becket let me go alone, and I reached the building just as the corpsmen were carrying Miles's body on a stretcher to a waiting Navy ambulance. The body was covered with a blanket. The corpsmen looked vaguely puzzled as they heaved Miles up into the back, slammed the double doors, then drove away. I went inside and saw Donnie Ray looking at me strangely.

"Maybe you ought to take the rest of the day off," he said.

"No. It's all right."

He looked out at the field.

"It's a tough thing, seeing somethin like that," he said. "Combat's a lot easier."

"I said I was all right."

"You don't *look* all right."

"He was my *friend.* I *liked* him. That's all."

"Okay," he said. "But you can get lost if you want."

"There's some things to do. Like calling his wife."

"His wife?"

"Yeah, he talked about her all the time. . . . A wife. Back in Atlanta. And he's got a mother too. Same town."

"Christ."

"Someone's gotta call them."

"Yeah. Someone's gotta call them."

He picked up the phone on my desk and asked for Maher in the admin building. I heard him speaking about next of kin and turned around to examine Miles's desk. There was no sign that he was thinking of checking out, just an ashtray, a pile of requisition forms, some pencils. I put one of the pencils in my pocket. Then stood there and looked out through the screened windows at the hot June morning. Nothing had changed. Sailors ambled down the crosswalks. Helicopters thumped in the sky. I tried to imagine what Miles was thinking a few hours earlier, his heart beating as he came to his decision. Whatever he thought, whatever pain or grief or shame he felt, it had ended forever.

Donnie Ray hung up.

"The captain's calling his mother," he said.

"What about the wife?"

He looked at me with pitying eyes.

"There was no wife."

He turned to go to the counter.

"I think you better take the day off," he said gently. "He was your friend."

That was true. He was my friend. Not a friend of Sal or Max or Maher or any of the others. Except Freddie. Miles wasn't part of the O Street nights. He wasn't there on any wild evenings. He didn't care when Hank died and didn't know the words of any Webb Pierce songs. So I didn't go first to Sal and Max to tell them the news. They were probably talking about Sal's big birthday party at the Miss Texas Club.

I went to Freddie.

I found him sitting on the steps leading up to the shuttered doors of the Kingdom of Darkness. He looked at me when I reached the stairs but didn't say anything.

"Freddie?"

"Yeah?"

"Miles is dead, Freddie."

"What?"

"He killed himself this morning."

Freddie rose slowly, carefully, standing three steps above me, looking at me as if I might be playing some awful joke.

"I'm *not* kidding," I said.

"You better not be," he said.

"He hung himself. In the mop locker."

The phrase "mop locker" would have made Miles laugh. Maybe that's why he chose it.

"He—he *say* anything? Like leave a *note* or whatnot?"

"Not that I know of."

He seemed relieved and looked past me in the direction of the Supply Shack. Then he gripped the railing and sat down hard on the steps and began to cry.

By noon, his locker was empty, his sea bag packed, his transfer papers typed up by Maher and signed by Captain Pritchett, and he was on his way to Port Lyautey. He never said good-bye. And I remember thinking: *Maybe Freddie Harada would get to see the Red Shadow.* I knew that I never would. Nor, of course, would Miles Rayfield.

Chapter

65

W E WENT OUT TO the Miss Texas Club in a cab, all of us in
uniform: Sal and Max whooping and joking, Maher sipping from
Boswell's bottle of white lightning, and the cab driver acting as if
the ride was surely the most distasteful job of his life. On this day
Sal was twenty-one; it was payday too and we were all going out
to get drunk and get laid. There were no further ambitions. If the
world thought we were just a bunch of goddamned lonesome sailors, then by God, we were going to act that way. *If ya got the name
ya might as well have the game.*

Nobody mentioned Miles Rayfield. The silence wasn't because
they didn't care what had happened to him. There just wasn't
anything that could be done about it. Not tears, revenge, or prayer.
Squashed in the back seat of the cab, I remembered my mother's
wake, all the uncles and cousins drinking, singing, even laughing,
and how enraged I was at them; yet riding through the Pensacola
night, I forgave everybody. You might as well sing, and declare the
existence of the living. And (here, down in the Gulf, with rain
scattering on the motel windows) remembering my remembering,
other bodies force their way into me, dead on meaningless hills in
the Asian jungles, dead on blasted deserts in the Sinai, dead without
mourning. Their deaths never chilled me nor attacked my bowels.
For years it has been my pride that I can look at dead strangers and
photograph them with the remorseless eye of an assassin. But I
am like all other men on earth: wounded by the death of people I
love. And of those, Miles Rayfield was the first. That night long
ago, I churned with fear, anger, mystery and guilt. My friend was
dead and I should have known it was coming. And now there

was nothing to be *done* except get drunk, get laid, and remember.

There was a huge parking lot outside the place, which was a big red-painted barn with a red neon sign saying MISS TEXAS CLUB and a large suety bouncer posted at the door. We chipped in a dollar each for the cab, paid the man, and piled out. The bouncer was checking most IDs but we were all in dress whites, and he recognized that as sufficient credentials, took two dollars from each of us and waved us in.

"Enjoy yissef, boys," he said.

And Sal whooped and said, "Yeah, brother, oh yeah. En-*Joy*. We want some *joy!*"

About five hundred people were already inside and the place was only half full. There were tables on the near side and a wide wooden dance floor and a stage where a country band was playing hard. Off to the right, people sat on stools at a large circular bar. I saw a few sailors dancing with young girls and wondered where Eden was.

We went to one of the tables and ordered three pitchers of beer from a round-legged blonde waitress dressed in a short buckskin skirt and sneakers. After half a beer, Max angled over to dance with a thin redhaired woman who was alone at the bar. Then Becket came in with Dunbar, and a little later Larry Parsons arrived too, and then a couple of guys from the hangars. Then Dixie Shafer arrived from the Dirt Bar carrying a box with a chocolate birthday cake and candles.

She yelled out to Max on the dance floor: "Get back *over* here, boy. Her *tits* are too small!"

I sipped some beer and looked up and saw Tons of Fun waddling through the room, each of them carrying delicately wrapped presents for Sal (a Hawaiian shirt, a leather belt) and Betty yelled at a table full of Marines: "Who wants a blow job in the parking lot?"

And Dixie Shafer said to me, "They're so *crude.*"

And Sal said, "*Me!* I do!"

And Betty grabbed his cock as she sat down and Sal giggled and the band played the Webb Pierce song and we all began to sing:

> *There stands the glass*
> *Fill it up to the brim*
> *Till mah troubles grow dim*
> *It's mah first one todaaaaaaaay . . .*

And singing the anthem of O Street, I remembered the first time
I heard it, almost six months before. And I didn't feel like a kid
anymore. I remembered how lonesome I was that night and how
then Eden Santana was only a nameless face glimpsed in a dark bus.

I wonder where you are tonight
I wonder if you are all right
I wonder if you think of me
In mah mis-ereeeeee . . .

We shouted the chorus and the Marines looked at us and Dixie
Shafer slid over beside me, her hair redder than a sunset, and Sal
got up and went after a dark girl with a violet blouse and Maher
started drinking straight from the beer pitcher and then I glanced
at the door and saw Red Cannon coming in.
Ah Miles ah poor sad Miles Rayfield.
Red Cannon was wearing tan chinos and a bright Hawaiian shirt.
He squinted through the smoke as if looking for someone and then
he walked to the bar and leaned over and said something to the
barmaid. If he saw us through the nicotine haze, he didn't bother
to let us know.
You killed him Red you put the nails in his coffin You son of a bitch.
Then the music ended and the lights dimmed and Sal yelled at
us (the girl with the violet dress gone off): "They just executed the
chef." Dixie Shafer lit the candles and we sang "Happy Birthday"
to Sal and the Marines booed and Sal told them to go fuck themselves and reached down and grabbed a handful of the cake and
shoved it at Max's mouth. We all cheered and Sal opened his
presents and kissed Tons of Fun on the breasts and pretended to
whip out his dick and then we heard a tom-tom beating in a Gene
Krupa style and then a different band started playing "Caravan."
There was a sudden spotlight on the stage and a voice from a
hidden microphone saying, "Ladies and gennulmin, the Miss Texas
Club is proud to present one of the greatest dancers of her tahm,
straight from a trah-umphant tore of Havana . . . *Madame Nareeta!*"
A tall red-haired woman stepped into the spotlight, dressed from
chin to feet in a black satin gown. She wore white gloves up to her
elbows. There was no expression on her face. I drained my beer and
poured another as she began to move sensuously to the old Ellington tune. The light defined the hard mound of her belly and I forgot

Red Cannon for the moment and wondered about the color of the hair between her legs. She did a few gentle bumps and ground her hips, and then she began to peel off the gloves and the crowd roared. Sal said, "It's like she's taking a rubber off a dick." Madame Nareeta moved her naked fingers slowly to the tune, and did a few more bumps and then, still expressionless, put a hand behind her back and shook and shimmied until the gown fell away and she was standing there, still moving slowly to the music, dressed in black bra and black panties and black high-heeled shoes. A roar rose from the dark. My cock was hard. Madame Nareeta's skin was very white in the pale-blue spotlight and she moved her hands over her heavy thighs, her belly, along the sides of her breasts, her eyes half closed, her tongue moving over her lips. Dixie Shafer whispered to me: "You look too damned sad, boy."

"Yeah," I said. "Maybe I am."

Now Madame Nareeta moved her hand behind her back again and the crowd roared and then she unhooked the bra and I wished that Dixie would slide under the table and open my fly.

"You got woman trouble on your face, boy," she said. "And somethin' else . . ."

"A friend of mine died."

"I heard that."

"He was my best friend, I think."

"And what was the woman?"

The crowd roared as Madame Nareeta bent forward, shaking and shuddering, letting the unhooked bra hang loose, then wriggling out of it.

"I don't know *what* the woman was," I said.

"Then you'll never get over it," Dixie Shafer said.

Staring at Madame Nareeta I felt like crying. She had little red plastic stars pasted over her nipples, and was dancing with more movement, writhing and bending, while someone yelled from the dark: "What color is your *hair,* honey?"

And I turned to Dixie and kissed her on the mouth, running my hands through her piled hair, wanting to get lost in her abundance, my cock so hard I thought I would come. She whispered, "Happy Sal's birthday, sailor," and the crowd roared as Madame Nareeta stepped out of her panties, wearing only a G-string now, all glittery and promising more.

I glanced over at the bar and my hard-on vanished. Red Cannon was talking to a sailor in uniform. And I saw the man's face as he turned. Jack Turner. From that first long lonesome bus ride from New York. They watched Madame Nareeta in a clinical way. She was now down on the floor, her legs bent back under her, her crotch aimed at the audience. I finished my fourth beer. And as Madame Nareeta played with her G-string, teasing the roaring crowd about the color of her hair, I got up.

I eased between the packed tables. A lot of sailors and Marines were standing along the back wall. I headed for the bar. Maybe this was foolish. Maybe it made no sense. But it was time for me to do something about Miles.

Jack Turner saw me first.

"Well, hello there, sailor. Long time. How *are* ya?"

I shook his hand and said hello at the moment that Madame Nareeta flipped the G-string aside. The roar was gigantic. Sailors and Marines stomped on the floor, beat hands and glasses against tables. I leaned past Turner.

"Red," I said, "I want you outside."

He didn't even blink. "Get outta here, boy," he said, " 'fore I call yore momma."

Turner put a hand on my forearm.

"Hey, what's this all about?"

"It's none of your business, Jack. This is strictly between me and Red."

"What you mean?"

"Red killed a friend of mine."

Red said, "You mean that damned *queer*?"

He sipped a drink casually and watched coldly as Madame Nareeta did a farewell bump for the crowd, which was standing and pleading from the hot darkness "more, more, more." I wished I had words to use against Red Cannon, some amazing set of arguments and lines. I didn't. So I reached over and grabbed him by the front of his shirt. Turner muscled his way between us, his face next to mine, and said in a hard way: "You better *leave,* sailor."

Red smiled thinly and put a hand on Turner's shoulder.

"Leave 'im be, Jack," he said. "I think mebbe I'd better kick his gahdam ass."

Then we were bumping our way through the crowd and out past the bouncer to the parking lot. I was suddenly afraid and feeling weak. But it was too late. I led the way. When I turned around to face Red Cannon, he hit me and knocked me down. I felt no pain. Just a whiteness. I rolled, expecting a kick and a stomp and I wanted to protect my balls. The kick never came.

"Better git up, boy," Red said calmly, "an' take yo beating."

I got up and faced him and saw a short, hard-muscled man, his hands held at chest level, his face blank. He looked as if he knew what he was doing, and was going to enjoy it; if I let him, he was sure to give me that beating. I moved away from him, feeling lightheaded, and raised my hands and tried to remember everything I'd ever learned in Brooklyn. I was going to need it all.

He came in a rush and threw another right hand and I bent at the knees to go under it and the punch glanced off the side of my head. I hooked hard to his belly, threw a right that missed, then hooked again and heard him grunt. That one hurt. Now I heard shouts and saw Turner's anxious face and about six Marines coming from a car and then I got knocked down again. One of the Marines shouted, "Go *Navy*! On you *ass.*" And Red said, "Get the hell out of here, jarhead." And then I was up and feeling panicky, afraid not of pain but embarrassment, and the fear drove me at Red and I got punched hard in the belly and bent over and punched in the upper arms and heard a voice say: "*Kick* his ass, *kick* his fucking niggerloving ass." And was punched again and felt nauseated and hit again and then saw Gabree.

The Marine from the Mainside gate.

From the night I took Bobby Bolden to the hospital.

From the night Eden Santana got scared right out of my life.

He was leaning against the hood of a car, watching me take my beating.

I decided not to take the beating. I shoved Red off me and stood up behind a jab and speared him with it. Once. Twice. Again. Backing him up. Then as he came at me I slammed home a right hand, hitting him between the eyes. Blood spurted from his nose. He looked surprised. I stepped to the left and drove a hook to his body, stopped, twisted inside with an uppercut and hit him on the chin and knocked him down.

I wanted to finish him off right there, end my own fear by stomping him into the gravel. But he'd let *me* up; I had to let *him* up. There were more Marines watching us and they cheered as Red got up slowly, a small tentative smile on his bloodied face. He came at me and I hit him, knowing now that I had to time my punches to his rush, and then he paused, turned as if quitting, then suddenly rushed again. I stepped aside and he plowed past me into the group of Marines.

That's when the fight changed.

One of the Marines shoved him. Then another. They formed a circle around him, trapping him, punching him on the shoulders and back, shoving him. He seemed suddenly small and bedraggled and sad. I saw blood leaking from his brow and dripping from his nose.

I looked at Turner.

We didn't wait.

We rushed at the Marines, and I went crazy, a roar coming from inside me, fighting now without rules, a sailor leaping on jarhead backs to break the circle around another sailor named Red. I ripped an elbow across Gabree's face, bent him over with a knee in the balls, then kicked him hard on the side of the face. Someone knocked me down with a punch from my blind side. I grabbed a thick-soled boot and pulled and a Marine went down and I stood up and stomped him hard. Red Cannon was fighting two of them, his face a ghastly smear, his shirt torn off his back and I knocked one of them down and then saw Turner on his belly on the ground, not moving, and then there were more Marines coming at me and Red, and I was heaved through the air and bounced off the hood of a car.

I got up slowly.

Everything hurt.

I leaned on the car and saw three Marines trying to hammer Red Cannon into the gravel. I couldn't move. It was as if I were watching some movie. Red stood with his legs spread apart and his hands up, refusing to let them knock him down. Then they stopped for a moment. One of them stared at him, measuring. Another slipped off his garrison belt, wrapped it around his hand. They started taking shots at Red. First one. Then the other. Red sneered.

Finally I moved, climbing up on the car hood. I screamed and jumped toward the nearest Marine and brought him down. Suddenly Gabree was coming at me, swinging his belt too, the buckle huge, and then behind him I saw Sal.

And Max.

Maher and Dunbar and Parsons.

And Dixie Shafer too, reaching for something in her bag.

The cavalry.

Gabree turned. I got up. And saw more Marines and other sailors coming out of the Miss Texas Club and then we were fighting all over the parking lot.

I trapped Gabree between two parked cars and grabbed him by the hair and beat his head against a fender until he fell away. Thinking: *for Bobby Bolden.* Thinking: *for Miles Rayfield.* Thinking: *for Eden Santana.* Until I was spun around and whacked in the head by a tall freckled Marine and then saw him pulled back, turned, and hit by Sal. The freckled Marine went down. Sal stomped on his ankles and went back for another Marine, looking joyous, laughing like a maniac. I saw Max about forty feet away, holding a Marine by the wrists and whirling him around and around, faster and faster, as if playing a kids' game. Then he let him go. The man sailed about ten feet and made a sick thumping sound against the side of a pickup truck.

Sailors and Marines were fighting everywhere. Dixie was cracking fallen Marines on the head with a short blackjack. There were sailors down too. Jack Turner hadn't moved yet. I started for him and then a Marine sergeant pulled me around. I felt as if I couldn't lift my hands.

"*Freeze* there, sailor," he shouted. "Don't *move.*"

I threw a punch at his face, and he blinked, and then he threw a punch, and I went under it and took a deep breath and ripped a punch into his belly and he went down to a sitting position, his hands out on either side of him as if looking for something to grab on to, and I kicked him in the face.

Then I heard Sal yelling, his voice wild and urgent.

"Here they *come!*"

The Shore Patrol.

Three jeeploads of them were racing down the highway, heading for the parking lot of the Miss Texas Club.

The fight was over.

I looked at the woods beyond the parking lot and started to run. Then I heard a voice on a bullhorn.

"Everybody stop where they are. You are all under arrest. Don't move or you'll be shot!"

Nobody obeyed. Sailors and Marines started running in various directions. I stayed low, moving between the parked cars, heading for the woods. I heard a gunshot. Then another. I was very scared now but kept moving. There was a third gunshot, far behind me. Muffled shouts. A trace of music from the Miss Texas Club. And then I was in the woods.

I stopped behind a tree and looked back. Two Shore Patrolmen were leading Maher to a waiting jeep. Jack Turner was up, looking hurt, a Shore Patrolman talking to him. Dixie was shaking her fists. I had a stitch in my side from running and my hands hurt and there was a dull throb at the base of my skull. I heard sirens in the distance. An ambulance or more Shore Patrol. I moved deeper into the woods. The others would find their way back to Ellyson. I'd have to do it too.

Soon everything was dark. I could smell salt on the light breeze. The night was cooler. The ground rose and the woods thinned, the trees more frail and the earth sandier beneath my feet. Up ahead, through the thin stands of trees, I could see the sky brightening. I climbed up a sandy ridge and stopped.

Before me lay the sea.

The empty beach was silvery under the quarter moon. I stood there for a long moment, gulping the salt air, listening for pursuers. My nose was tender, clogged with blood. My side teeth were loose. My hands throbbed. I started walking toward the sea, pulling my jumper over my head, stripping away my T-shirt. I wanted everything off me, the clothes, the dirt, the blood. And by the time I reached the sea, I was naked.

I made a pile of the uniform, my shorts and T-shirt, socks and shoes. I had seventy-eight dollars in my wallet, the great payday haul. I pushed the wallet into the sand under the uniform. And then I turned, walking quickly, and plunged into the cold waters of the Gulf.

Weightless now, turning in the sea, feeling it against my balls and back, the pain seemed to leave me. I dove under the surface, where there were no Marines and no Red Cannon, no musicians with broken hands, no painters with broken necks, no sailors with broken hearts, except me. I wanted to stay there forever. And realized suddenly how easy it would be to die. To just stay there until everything turned black and I was gone too. I would be at peace. There would be no scandal, as there was with Miles Rayfield, and no shame either; they would all just believe that I drowned. Exhausted from the great fight at the Miss Texas Club. Sad. A tragedy.

Good-bye. It would all be over. And then, plunging deeper, my lungs hurting, I panicked.

I didn't want to die.

Not in the dark of the roadless sea.

I wanted to see Eden Santana at least one more time. Just once. To say what I'd never had a chance to say. A final plea. Or a proper good-bye.

I kicked and pushed against the sea, and felt a current dragging at me, and pushed harder, and felt my lungs bursting, and a whiteness blossoming in my brain; kicked harder, pushed, heading for the surface, panicked again when I thought I was going the wrong way, that I was plunging deeper, suddenly afraid that I'd never make it, that I would die without choosing, without saying good-bye, and then burst to the surface, gulping air, treading water, staring up at thick clusters of stars.

I lived.

And living, floating on the water, eyes closed, hearing the roar of the surf and a distant foghorn, I wanted to be finished with the Navy. I had two years to go. More. An endless time. And I didn't want to go back. I wanted to float here, weightless, naked, forever. Thinking of dying and how easy it was, I was no longer afraid of the Navy. If I went to find Eden, what could they do? *Kill* me?

Suddenly I was exhilarated and began to swim to shore. I came up on the beach and clasped my knees and sucked in air. I could feel the sea salt drying on my naked skin. I stood up straight and then immediately crouched low. There was someone about fifty yards down the beach standing where my clothes were piled.

For a moment I was full of fear. It could be the Shore Patrol, tracking me from the woods and the parking lot. Maybe some Marine was dead. Stomped to death between parked cars. I considered slipping back into the sea. I thought about running. But I was naked. I wouldn't last long on a highway trying to get back to Ellyson Field. And my money was there, tucked into the sand under the uniform. I had no real choice. If it was the Shore Patrol, my ass had had it. But it could be just a beachcomber, some rummy washed up on the Gulf. Either way, I had to get my clothes and money. Whatever the risk. I started walking through the sand toward the person who was standing beside my clothes.

When I came close I saw that it was Red Cannon.

I stopped.

Jesus Christ.

Now, sore and naked and exhausted, I'd have to finish what had begun in the parking lot of the Miss Texas Club.

Red was waiting for me, battered, unbeaten. Three great waves of exhaustion moved through me. I wanted to lie down naked in the sand and go to sleep. I didn't have any strength left to fight him nor will to beat him. I would have to contrive some rage and use it as fuel. So I thought about Miles Rayfield. His face blue and swollen. The cord digging into his flesh. But the anger wouldn't come. And I still needed those clothes.

I walked closer, on an angle, giving him a smaller target if he came at me in a rush, protecting my cock and balls. He was shirtless. His face was a mess of caked blood, dried by the Gulf breeze. He smiled, but I couldn't see his eyes. The surf broke on the shore. I stopped six feet away from him and waited.

"I need those clothes, Red," I said.

"Come and get em."

"I don't want to fight you for them, but I will if I have to."

"It's your gear. Whut the hell do I want with it?"

I took a step forward and so did he. Then we both stopped. I could see his eyes now. One was almost closed and was turning purple. The other just looked sad.

He held out his hand.

I shook it.

"You're okay, Devlin," he said.

"And you're still a prick," I said and released his hand and went for my clothes and started dressing. I looked at Red. He was gazing out at the sea. And then he toppled over and fell face down in the sand.

I went to help him.

Chapter
66

What Red Cannon Told Me

I SHOULDA SEEN THEY was shit the day they showed. *Green snotnose shit, enlisted men and officers both. We were in the buildingways up at Mare Island near San Francisco. They was fixin everything that was ripped up by the kamikazes at Okinawa, the hull and the water supply and the bridge, every damned thing on the ship. This was the summer of '45, just before the war ended, and I was a third-class gunner's mate on the* U.S.S. Indianapolis. *Bet you never heard of her, right, Devlin? Well you ain't alone. Most nobody ever heard of her, then or now. The Navy don't want it out, what happened to her. The goddamn politicians don't, either.*

But she was a death ship, Devlin: a great big heavy cruiser, that was what we call tender. That means she was about as heavy above the waterline as below, loaded down with all sorts of shit that wasn't there when they built her. Just walkin the deck, you knew it wouldn't take much ocean to tip her over. The Navy brass didn't give much of a fiddler's fuck. All those Annapolis boys loved cruisers cause the next stop was usually a battle wagon and that was the top in them days, before the carriers became the big deal. So they gave you a big So What? if you told them the ship didn't right itself too quick after a sharp turn. They didn't care she was tender. They even made her the flagship of the Fifth Fleet, and did all kinds of ceremonial shit whenever Admiral Spruance came aboard. And they gave her a captain, McVay was his name, a gray-haired guy with coal-black eyes, always smilin like a goddamned politician.

Yeah.

The Indianapolis.

A nice big cruiser.

They thought it looked good in pictures, I guess, though it wasn't worth a fuck at sea. So in July, we were gettin her ready, the war over in Europe, thinkin we was all gonna be part of the invasion of Japan. I wunt too big on that. I seen the way the Japs fought at Okinawa and figured theyd take a lot of us with them in Japan. Say what you will about the Jap, but he's a fightin man, sailor. Still although they was beat, and must've known it, the Japs wouldn't quit, so there was nothin to be done except invade. It was a war and we had to finish it and in the Navy, on the Indianapolis, *we'd play our part like everybody else, tender ship or no tender ship.*

The trouble was most of the old crew was dead now or scattered around, and one bright morning along comes this new crew. Talk about haulin green shit. Two hundred and fifty wiseass kids fresh out of boot camp and thirty officers out of the Academy and I knew right off we gonna have us some trouble. They made up almost a third of the crew and they showed up like they was goin to a Fourth of July picnic, instead of a war against a real tough son of a bitch. I knew we'd have to break their asses real good. But almost as soon's they were piped on board, we got orders to get ready to ship out. In twenty-four hours. The ship wunt ready. They wunt enough chow. The livin quarters wunt finished. Didn't matter. We had to go. And it was all because of the goddamn bucket and the goddamn box.

They swung them on board in the morning, usin a giant goddamn gantry. The bucket weighed maybe three hundred pounds, cast iron, sealed, and we welded it right to the deck, holdin it down with straps. It couldn't move or slide. If the ship went down, so did the bucket. The box was a crate really, eight feet high, and they took it below decks and wedged it in real tight. But then they called me and Big Nose Bernardi below decks and we met these two army guys, lookin like perfessers with guns, and they opened the box and took out a steel cylinder maybe three feet long and had us carry it into Captains Country, where Captain McVay gave us part of the mess, sealed off, and watched as we strapped this cylinder to the deck and welded the straps tight. The army guys never said a word. They stayed with the cylinder and never came above decks again.

Well, we pulled anchor at three ayem on July 16 and sailed out of San Francisco and started haulin ass. There was all sorts of scuttlebutt about the box and the bucket. Most of the crew thought they had to contain germs. That we was gonna use germs on the Japs. Or some kind of gas that would paralyze every last Jap in the country, something we captured from the Germans. It wunt till well after the war that I learnt that the bucket and the box was full of parts of the atom bomb.

Now out at sea, we were supposed to break in the new crew. Not for any atom bomb. For war. Suppose to do it right off. Dont give em tahm to think. That was the general plan. Real simple. Well, we didn't get to break em in. There wunt tahm and the ship was a complete fuckin mess. Somehow we picked up a bunch of hitchhikers, officers mostly, all tryin to git to Pearl, which was our first stop. Their luggage was all over the damned deck. Worse, some of em was Army and didn't know shit from shinola about livin on a ship. And the green kids was the real problem. Some of em was moonin over women. Some even cried for their mommas. They got lost and dint know port from starboard. Real green shit.

Things got so bad, there was a fire on deck cause these green shitbirds left suitcases next to one of the stacks. Suitcases! On a Navy ship. And they was no room in the chow hall, so people ate all over and left food and plates layin around and I seen roaches too. I swear. Cockroaches. On a flagship of the United States Navy.

Nobody paid much attention though. That was just housekeepin. And Captain McVay was haulin ass for Pearl. The Indianapolis *was thirteen years old and beat up. But he got her doin twenty-nine knots. We tested the systems. Radio. Radar. There wunt any sonar, though, and that hurt us later. There just wunt time to install it. We was haulin ass with the atom bomb. When we hit Pearl that Monday morning, we discovered that we broke the damned record. Two thousand and ninety one miles in seventy-four-and-a-half hours. I'm still amazed.*

But there wunt tahm for celebration in Pearl, for taking pictures, and bragging to reporters. We let the passengers off, and then we were told to get ready to git under way. And seen again that we could have bad trouble. I actually seen some of that green-shit crew start to cry. *They wanted to get off. They wanted to call their girlfriends or their mommas. They wanted liberty when they haddin even done nothin yet. They dint want to hear we had no tahm. They dint want to hear we were going to fuckin war.*

So we lifted anchor and started out for some little goddamn island called Tinian.

I yelled and hollared, I said we gotta do basic drills, we gotta do abandon ship and fire and rescue and anti-aircraft and man overboard. Nobody listened. I think maybe the captain thought he was gonna be part of history and all he had to worry about was posing for the pictures. And besides, we were in safe water. There wasn't a Jap for a thousand miles, everybody said. We'd do the trainin later. After Tinian. When we got to Leyte in the Philippines . . . Well, I did whut I could.

We made Tinian on Friday. It was one of those islands I used to see in the fillums at the Mosque Theater in Montgomery during the Depression. You know, fine ladies in grass skirts and some rummy doctor layin in a hammock with a bottle under the palm trees. There was a landing strip for airplanes but no dock for ships the size of the Indianapolis. *So we had to unload the box and the bucket onto an LCT out in the open sea. We cut the straps on the cylinder and put it in the box and started the job. But the wire was too short and I remember that goddam box swingin around in the breeze, six feet above the LCT. And then all them snotnose kids started jeerin. But we got it done. The mission was finished. At least that's what we thought. We delivered the goddam box and bucket, and now all we had to do was beat Japan.*

We sailed west, with a stop at Guam before going on to Leyte. And at last I started bustin balls on the housekeepin. Some shitbird of an officer had ordered 2500 life jackets for a crew of twelve hundred and they was layin all over the deck so I had them tied and stacked against the bulkheads. I had them clean up all the dirty food. I had them paintin and chippin. But most of the time it was like shovelin shit against the tide.

Wait till Leyte.

That's what they all said.

We'll get shipshape after Leyte.

Yeah.

After Guam we passed a spot called The Crossroads and went into the Forward Zone. That meant we were no longer under the command of Pearl Harbor. Now we reported to Leyte. And I dint like the conditions out there. I felt it from the minute we went through The Crossroads.

To begin with, we was alone.

Usually, a heavy cruiser sails with four or five other ships, and that was specially important with the Indianapolis *cause she was tender. But we was alone. In the Pacific. That's a big fuckin ocean, Devlin. Another thing I didn't like, there was a rule that when you wuh in the Forward Area, you could only do sixteen knots. To save fuel. The third thing was the basic thing.*

The crew.

That damned green crew.

Well, we left Guam at nine in the morning on Saturday and even at sixteen knots we should've reached Layte about eleven in the morning on Tuesday.

A weekend cruise.

Yeah.

Saturday was peaceful. I pulled a twelve to four and on Sunday morning

I slept in. I remember lunch wunt half bad. Hamburgers and mashed potatoes. I couldn't finish the potatoes, and in the next few days I thought about them uneaten potatoes a lot. A lot, sailor. In the afternoon I sat in the shade on deck while the green kids got cholera shots for the Philippines. In the afternoon, the weather changed. There was a haze on the sea now and a heavy chop. We were followin the normal zigzag pattern—normal that is in the Forward Zone, where you want to fuck up the other guy's listening devices, just in case he's around somewhere.

I wished we had sonar.

I wished we wunt alone.

That night I had an eight to twelve. It was fuckin hot. I remember walking through the quarters when I went on duty and noticin a lot of watertight doors open. I wondered who in the fuck was in charge of them and I went up on deck, pissed off, needin a smoke, followin the smell of the coffee pot. The deck was disgustin. Sailors had pulled mattresses and cots on deck and were lyin around bullshittin and sleepin. Hundreds of them. There was only one air conditioner on board, down in sick bay, and the Captain didn't give a rat's ass where they slept, I guess. I saw some guys shootin craps in a compartment and told them to make sure the light dint show and kept thinkin: There's too many doors open.

I went up on the bridge and looked out for a while, standin on the side. For some reason, we had stopped the zigzag. We were going due west. The sea was pretty calm. There was a quarter moon. I smoked half a pack of Camels, goin up and down and around the ship, fore and aft, port and starboard. The guys on deck stopped their bullshittin and grabassin and went to sleep.

And maybe cause it was quiet, maybe cause we wuz alone, I don't know why: for the first tahm in years, I started thinkin about home.

I had a wife back home once, married when we were both sixteen, and we used to talk all the tahm about gettin us a little house somewhere beside a lake so we'd always see a piece of water. I wondered what happened to that woman that was once mah wife, whether she married someone half decent, whether she had kids (we didn't), whether some new fella gave her what I never could give her.

You see, she was a good lovin woman. It wunt her fault we split. The truth was, I just couldn't take her lovin. Somethin in me. Dont' know what. Couldn't take her huggin and kissin and lovin. And besides, I couldn't stay put. I couldn't stand the idea of plowin them Alabama fields every spring and every fall for the rest of mah fuckin life. I always felt that way. Saw them fields kill my daddy and my uncles and make my momma old. When

I married that lovin woman, I thought I wouldn't feel that way no more. But I did. The feelin just never went away. I'd see the dirt fields and feel already dead. Even now, close as we are to Alabama from Pensacola, I never go home. Never. Never want to see it again.

So one night while my lovin woman slept, I packed a bag and took a bus to Mobile and joined the Navy and never seen that lovin woman again.

But sometimes she'd come to me in the night. And out there on the Indianapolis, *doing the eight to twelve, I wondered about her and whether she ever thought about me and I was tryin to remember all the details of her face and the way she smelled on them hot Alabama nights, rich as dirt, and what her hair felt like, and all the things about her body, I was thinkin all them things when the first Jap torpedo hit.*

The goddamn thing just tore the bow off the fuckin ship. Forty feet ripped right off, anchors, capstans and all. The niggers all lived up there, stewards and messmen, and not one of them lived. Thirty-two of em. And the fleet Marines. Thirty of them just died. The ship rose up in the air and fell hard with a bright red flash and a column of water as high as the bridge and I was holding on to a rail and then someone was screamin and then, maybe three seconds later, the second one hit.

Midships.

Right about where the bridge was on the starboard side, and that knocked me to the deck and then everyone started goin apeshit.

I pulled myself up and grabbed a phone off the bulkhead, but it wasn't working. Nothin electric was workin. No lights, no sound, and I thought: Please God make sure the radio aint hit, make sure Sparks is gettin out the location, make sure someone knows we been hit, cause we're out in a great big fuckin ocean. I saw a kid run by bawlin and then knew we were still plowing ahead, eatin the fuckin ocean through that hole where the bow used to be and I immediately saw all them open doors in my head and knew that belowdecks sailors were dyin.

There was gray smoke everywhere now, smellin like burnt paint. Then I saw Captain McVay comin at me through the smoke. He was ballsass naked, carryin parts of his uniform and tryin to get to the bridge. He didn't say a word to me, but he looked at the sea and the green kids runnin all over and up ahead where the bow was already underwater and fire was runnin across the deck and I knew what he was thinkin: We're gonna have to give her up.

I felt us list a few degrees and heard some godawful noises from belowdecks and then the Captain was gone into the smoke and I could hear him yellin, shut the engines down, shut down the goddamned engines.

While we kept plowin ahead.

I pulled on a kapok life jacket and tied it tight and started moving aft. There were scared kids everywhere, not knowin what to do, where their battle stations were, but knowin, like sailors do, even green-shit recruits, that they were goin into the sea.

I turned some of them around, told them to get to the fan tail, tie on life jackets, get ready to go. I tried to help some guys get the whaleboats out of the chocks, but then we listed another six or seven degrees, and one of the guys lost his grip and went into the sea and the boats were hanging beyond our reach. And I could see others jumpin in, some without life jackets, some just in skivvies, cause they'd been sleeping when the Japs whacked us. A guy sat on the deck, his whole body black and burnt. A corpsman was giving him morphine, but then we listed again, and the burned guy started slidin away.

There were maybe five hundred sailors on the fantail, now, all half dressed. None of them had flashlights or guns or knives. And the ship was still driving forward. There were a lot of officers runnin around now, all the green shitbirds from the Academy, and they were all yellin about stoppin the ship, like it was a truck on a road someplace. They were useless. Most of em didn't even know how to find the fuckin engine room never mind go down there and shut off the engines. A few kids started going off the fantail. I yelled to the others to get the floater nets ready, these great big nets with floats attached. Then there was a big jolt. The whole fuckin ship just twisted, and we went over another twenty-five degrees, the port side high up in the air, and kids were fallin all over the ocean. Along with equipment and bunks and all that loose gear that had littered the deck. The number 3 screw was still turnin and I saw two kids hold hands and jump off the fantail and get chopped to pieces by one of the propellers. The company bugler went into the sea, holding the goddamned bugle.

It was a mess.

A real fuckin mess.

Then I started climbin up the deck. It was like the whole world turned on its side. What I used to walk on was now a wall and I had to get up the wall. I pulled myself over the top and found I was standin on the side of the ship. There was maybe a hundred other sailors doing the same thing. Later I learned we got hit at 12:02 and the ship went down at 12:18.

Sixteen minutes.

It seemed a hell of a lot longer than that.

I stood on the port side, and then just walked straight ahead and stepped into the sea.

I started swimmin hard, trying to get away from her, afraid of suction. I'm a good goddamned swimmer, but I could barely move in the water. And then I knew why. It was full of thick black fuel oil. I tried goin under the oil and made some time and came up and looked back. The Indianapolis *was layin real low in the water. I could hear shouts. A few screams. And I thought I was still too close. That the suction would pull me down. I didn't know. I'd never had to abandon a ship before. But I looked back and all I could hear from her was the lappin of waves against the steel hull and then she just slipped away under the sea.*

No suction.

No whirlpool.

She was just gone.

Then . . . hell, I aint afraid to admit I was scared. I was alone in the sea, covered with oil. I was afraid the SOS never got off the ship. I was afraid the Japs would come to the surface and shoot the shit out of us. I was afraid of being alone in the biggest goddamned ocean in the fuckin universe. I didn't know if any rafts had been cut loose and I didn't know how many others were in the sea with me and whether I'd find them.

Then somethin hard bumped into me. I grabbed for it. A crate of potatoes. I held on to that and then a part of a desk floated by and I held that too, an arm on each one, just floatin, savin my strength. I could hear voices everywhere but I couldn't see anyone. I heard a kid screamin for his momma. Someone was prayin too, the good old Baptist shit. Then a kid come along, swimmin, no life jacket. I told him to grab the piece of desk.

It ain't enough, he said. I ain't strong enough.

Grab the motherfucker, I said.

And he did and drifted off. Later I found the desk but not the kid.

I held on to that potato crate as long as I could. But the potatoes must've started takin on water and it started ridin lower. I tore a slat off and started dumpin the spuds, shoving a few inside my shirt. I didn't think after that. I just floated for the rest of the night.

In the mornin, I could see other sailors. Maybe a hundred and fifty of us, scattered all over the ocean. And not a raft among us. I learned later that about eight hundred went in the water and some of them had rafts, including the captain. But we were scattered over miles of ocean because the ship kept goin after she was hit. We were so low in the water we couldn't see where the rafts were and nobody had flares. Nobody had food either. I saw an orange float by and grabbed it and shoved it in my shirt along with the two potatoes. I was looking for the rest of the potatoes when a guy bobbed right up to me. His face was black from the oil. And worse. He was fuckin charred, boy. His eyelids were burned off his eyes and he couldn't see anything. He said to me, What is this?

And slipped under the sea.

In the daylight, it looked like a sea full of niggers. Everybody was covered with oil. Some guys were in uniform but others didn't have shirts or even pants. We started movin toward each other. And I saw that some guys didn't have life jackets either. The sun started risin, the biggest hottest most orange sun I ever saw.

Then I heard a guy scream, looked over, saw him tear off his life jacket and go under. That was the beginning.

I started yellin at them all: Don't drink the sea water. Whatever you do, don't drink it. I knew that drinkin sea water was death. First you go crazy and then you get sick and then you die. I told the ones closest to me to pass it on: Don't drink the fuckin sea water. And then I started trying to calm the ones near me. Sure, I said, the wireless must've gone off. And if it didn't, as soon as we don't show on Leyte, they'll come lookin for us. Don't worry, I said. Stay calm, I said. Don't use up your energy. Most of all, don't drink from the sea.

I gave two of them a potato.

Then the strange shit started.

First of all, guys started goin blind. Later on I heard this was called photophobia. Comes from the sun, the oil, the reflection on the ocean, all combined. I saw three guys screamin they couldn't see anything. Then I thought about myself. With my skin, I wouldn't last the day. I was covered with oil. But if I didn't do something the sun would still get me. I saw a guy float by face down in the water. The back of his head was shredded. I unleashed his jacket and then tied it over my head like a bonnet. It didn't work perfect. You see my skin here? You see these scars? You see where the nerve ends was just burnt off? Well, I didn't get that jacket for a bonnet, it mighta been worse.

Late in the afternoon that first day, Monday, the sharks came.

We saw the fins, just like in a movie. Three of em. Circlin around us. The first thing they hit was one of the dead guys out on the edge of the group. Just smashed into him and pulled him under. But they wasn't finished. One of the kids suddenly screamed, the goddamnedest bloodcurdlin scream I ever heard, and then he was gone. Blood mixed with the oil. The others started thrashin around, splashin and kickin, but I remembered somethin from some magazine saying the best thing was to just lie on your back very still. The shark sees you kickin and he thinks you're already done for and you're

an easy kill. I told this to the ones near me and flopped over on my back.
I felt somethin bump me and then go away and then another godawful
scream and I just lay there for a long time.

I was layin there when I saw the plane. Not too high. Maybe three, four
thousand feet. Everybody else seen it too. And we start shoutin and yellin
and beating on the oily ocean. But the plane just kept on goin. It never came
back. And I thought: The SOS never left the ship. And I was scared. Never
said a word to the others, never said that if the message got off, there'd be
a dozen planes here, circlin in the sky. Never mentioned any of that. But
knew it.

The day was scaldin. I sealed my mouth, afraid of the sea water. Held
it so tight my muscles hurt. The sharks must of been full. They didn't come
back either. We all lolled there in the water, just taking it. That night, we
heard another plane. Then I saw star flares fired from somewhere on the
ocean. That was the first time I knew for sure that there were others out
there. And if they had flares they had Very pistols and if they had Very
pistols then somebody had found a raft. The pistols were part of the gear
on every raft. And I thought, the planes had *to see that. Durin the day,*
maybe the ocean was like some big mirror if you looked at it from the sky.
But at night, the flares meant that people *were down here. They couldn't*
miss us. Now they'd come for us. I bobbed in the sea and heard someone
start to sing.

Pardon me boy
Is this the Chattanooga choo-choo . . .

And someone else said, Track Twenty nine, and another, Well, can you
give me a shine. They were happy. They'd seen the flare and heard the plane
and they were sure now we'd be found. In the morning. As soon as it got
light.

But the plane didn't come back in the mornin, or the mornin after that.
And then people started going crazy. They must have been drinkin the sea
water. Or if they wunt, the sea water was gettin into their mouths anyway
and down their throats.

The craziness came in waves. Some ensign said that there was an island
only a mile away, with palm trees and freshwater streams and beautiful
girls like Dorothy Lamour. He got a dozen guys to follow him and they all
started swimmin away and we never saw them again. Another guy said that
he could see the Indianapolis *right below us, about thirty feet down, and*
there was fresh water down there, hundreds of gallons of it, and Betty
Grable was on the deck and everything was beautiful. I told him that the
bottom was 10,000 feet down. He said You're crazy, man, said, Look, said,

There it is, the ship! He stripped off the life jacket and started swimmin down and three other guys did the same and that was the end of them too.

A lot of guys started fightin each other, they'd be punchin and thrashin around and beatin at the ocean and each other and then this brown shit would start burblin up from their mouths, and they'd be dead. Some guys had knives. They used them to keep the food for themselves. They used them to get fresh life jackets. They threatened officers with them. There was no discipline, no rules, no Navy regs, no feeling of being in this thing together. It was every man for himself, for four fucking days and nights. You think human beings are decent? You think human beings love their neighbors? Go out in the ocean with them sometime. Eight hundred guys went in the water when the Indianapolis went down. At the end, only three hundred were left.

It went on and on. I ate the orange but was afraid of the salt water on the potato and threw it away. By the second night, the kapok lifejackets were gettin waterlogged. We were ridin lower and lower in the sea. I started playin mind games, trying not to go crazy, tryin to stay alive. What time was it? Yesterday today was tomorrow. Right this minute was yesterday's future. Night will become dawn. But when does dawn become morning and what makes afternoon different from morning and when does it happen and why are we all here in this fuckin ocean which has no beginning and no end except when the fuckin sharks come to get us? I thought like that.

Finally I thought if I didn't want anything then it wouldn't matter if I died. So I said to myself over and over, I don't want anything, I don't care for anything, I don't love anything or anyone or anyplace. I'm nothin. I'm just here on the ocean. A speck. Bein alive, that was nothin. Dead, I'm nothin.

And that way I was able to live.

We saw more planes high in the sky and they never came back and that was nothin. We saw a squall in the distance comin across the ocean and we thought we'd have fresh water in our mouths and then the squall turned and the rain went away to the west without coming near us and that was nothin. I saw guys keel over and die and that was nothin. I saw a guy with a knife cut another guy's throat for his life jacket and that was nothin. Prayin was nothin and day was nothin and singin was nothin and night was nothin.

And then on Thursday, a PV-1 flew over and circled and circled and finally landed on the water, bouncin, skiddin, hittin the tops of waves and settlin.

We were saved.

And even that was nothin.

I couldn't cheer. Only my nose was above water. I couldn't get excited.
I was saved.
I was alive.
Nothin.

Only later, after we were picked up and taken to a can named the Doyle, only then did I want to live. They took us to Peleliu and the hospital. I drank too much water and puked and ate too much food and puked. I slept for eighteen hours. And when I woke up I knew that if I stayed in this man's Navy, I wouldn't ever again be in a place where green snotnosed kids panicked and died and got other people dead.

You think I'm a shit, don't you, Devlin?
Maybe I am.
Maybe I'll always be a shit.

But I wunt born a shit. Maybe I left somethin out there in that fuckin ocean. Maybe I'll never find it again. I know I sure ain't gonna find it on land. Hey, git your ass up off the sand, sailor. We gotta git back to the base.

Chapter

67

IT WAS GRAY and chilly when we got back to the base. Sunday morning on the Gulf. The sky empty. Red Cannon left me without a word, as if he had no words left, or was vaguely ashamed that he had used words at all. My uniform was filthy. My body hurt. I showered for a long time. My mind was as blank as the sky.

Then, clean again and most of the aching gone, I climbed into the sack. Longing for sleep. I shoved my hand under the pillow and found the letter.

Dear Michael,

By the time you read this, I'll be dead. They've taken everything away from me at last. My work—my pride—my need for love. There'll be a court martial and they'll say all sorts of filthy things about me and make filthy jokes in the corridors and write filthy things into my record. And all of that will follow me everywhere. Well, I don't want any of that. I don't want the shame or the tears or the cheap laughs. I want out of Anus Mundi. Forever.

All my life I had to hide what I was. When I was young, it didn't matter. Nobody cared. But when I was twelve or thirteen, I started to think I was a woman in a man's body. It wasn't a sudden thing. I just looked at boys instead of girls. I wanted to dress in women's clothes. I had urges—desires—they weren't what boys were supposed to feel—weren't what I saw in the movies—weren't what I heard on the radio. I can't explain it all. I die, not understanding it all.

But once when I was in art school I loved a boy and he loved me and I understood for the first time how hard my life was going to

be. You see, we couldn't ever do what other people did. Not in
Atlanta. Not in the South. Maybe not anywhere. We couldn't walk
down the corridors at school, holding hands. We couldn't kiss each
other in the balcony at the movies. I couldn't sit in the living room
with him at his parents' house, necking, while they slept upstairs. We
had to hide and sneak around. Until there was a big school party out
at a lake and we all got a little drunk and one of the advertising
people—a designer—a real shithead—found us in the woods. Maybe
that's why I joined the Navy. To get away from that boy—to get
away from the shame and the talk—to get away from Atlanta. But
I loved that boy. He was my wife. That bitch. And it's been a long
long time since he loved me. Or since anybody loved me.

But it turns out that running away and joining the Navy was a
terrible mistake. The Navy was just too tough for me. I'd see bodies
in the showers—muscles and asses and cocks—have you stopped
reading this? have you thrown it down in disgust?—and I'd want to
touch them—kiss them—hug them—and have them hug me back
and make love to me as if I were one of those women whose bodies
were taped inside their lockers. To tell the truth, I'd see you like that
sometimes. Do you understand why I could never go with you to
O Street? I didn't want to see you dancing with your sluts. And I was
afraid that I'd have too much to drink and then I would do something or say something that I'd be sorry for later. I loved you. But
you were my friend too. Maybe the only one I had in this goddamned Navy. I didn't want to love you so much that I lost the
friendship. Do you understand?

So I was a coward and that's why I went with You Know Who.
He was small and beautiful and didn't care about anything except
money. He couldn't find a girl in the great American South. Too
dark. Too small. So he found me. Or I found him. I'm not sure now
who started it, but it doesn't really matter anymore. He let me draw
him at first (and how jealous I was of your woman when I saw your
drawings of her). He posed for me for money, of course. And then
he let me take photographs of him, for money (Cannon must have
those now). And then later he let me do what I wanted to do with
him, and that was for money too. I had a crush on him in some ways,
because he was so perfect—so small—like a doll. . . . But he didn't
love me and I didn't love him. I couldn't—because I loved you.
Does that embarrass you? Will you burn this letter? I guess you'd
better. . . . But you knew it, didn't you? You're a damned innocent
in a lot of ways, for all your Brooklyn crap, but you aren't a fool.
You must have seen . . .

But I knew that it was never to be. Nothing ever was to be. I had poor little amoral You Know Who. And what broke me—after Cannon took away everything—was that I would be disgraced over a tart. Someone I didn't even love.

Well, I just don't want to live anymore in a world without love. I don't want to live alone.

I used to tell myself that maybe art was enough. That I'd put everything into my painting and that would give me a life. But the truth is—my work just isn't good enough. I have craft, but no art—an eye, but no vision. There's always been something missing right from the start—some center—something that would focus the vision—bind all the elements . . . and I guess that the name of that thing is love.

So I'm going out of this. I want you to have all my stuff—my paints—pads—books—if the Navy will give them to you. If you ever get to Atlanta, go to see my mother. But don't tell her everything you know and don't show her all of my work. You know what I mean. . . . I've written to her to explain everything in a way that she will accept.

But I can't give you anything else. You know what you have to do. You have to go and get love. Any goddamned way you have to do it. You have to get it and hold on to it because that's what makes art art and a life a life. I go. But I hope that some day, years from now, when you're a famous painter or a father of six, when you have met ten thousand new people and seen the great cities of the earth, you will pause on a summer morning when there's a wet wind like the wind off the Gulf and you'll remember me.

Love,
Miles

Aw, Christ.
Aw, Miles.
I slipped the letter back into the envelope, folded it, thought about tearing it into a thousand pieces but didn't. I opened my locker and slipped it into Miles's copy of *The Art Spirit*. Then I lay down. Wanting to answer him. Wanting to go to his bunk and wake him up and tell him to take some more time, to outlast the Navy and then go to New York or Paris or some other gigantic place where nobody cared what he was and he could find someone to love.

I wanted to say some magic words to him that would save his life.
But it was too fucking late.
I fell into a deep, exhausted, trembling sleep.

I slept through breakfast. I slept through lunch. I woke at last around three, my hands and head hurting. I was in the shower before I remembered the letter. And thought: *What if someone finds it?* Suppose they came to search all the lockers, looking for evidence of something or other? A board of inquiry. An investigation. And I felt instantly ashamed, as if I were betraying Miles even after his death. Then, still showering, scrubbing my teeth under the nozzle, letting the water drill into my mouth, the fragments of the night moved through me. Red Cannon in the endless Pacific at the end of the war, with dead men everywhere. Dixie Shafer's abundance. Madame Nareeta. The fight in the parking lot of the Miss Texas Club. *You have to go and get love.* There were too many men without women in this world, fighting and hurting one another. And I'm one of them again.

I dried myself and dressed in clean whites and hurried out. I was very hungry. I went to the EM Club. Becket was sitting at a corner table. He looked up in a grim way aand told me that Sal, Max, Dunbar and six Marines were all in the brig. There were seven Marines in the Mainside hospital and the scuttlebutt said that one might die. A guy named Gabree. If he did, everyone would be charged with manslaughter.

"Manslaughter?"

The word sounded huge, scary.

"I'm going to Mass," Becket said. "Wanta come?"

"No."

"You're a Catlick, right?"

"Retired," I said.

Becket smiled and tapped me on the shoulder and went out through the door into the hot afternoon. I ate a burger and drank a Coke and added a cup of coffee. I wondered if the Marine guards were banging around Sal and Max and Maher. The way I'd booted and stomped Gabree, who had called me a niggerloving swabbie. I thought about Bobby Bolden in the ice hills of Korea and the way the Marines marched back, hurt and wounded and crippled with frostbite, and how much Bobby loved them for that and how stupid the endless rivalry was between sailors and Marines. It was a fight between uniforms. If we'd gone to the Miss Texas Club in civvies, the brawl might never have happéned. It would have been a simple fair one: me and Red Cannon.

I looked out through the screened windows and saw Captain Pritchett staring at his flowers. I didn't want him to see me. I didn't want to talk to him about what happened the night before or what was going to happen. I got up and slipped out the door and walked across the base, my T-shirt clinging to my back in the heat.

Back in the barracks, I read the letter from Miles again. *You have to go and get love,* he whispered from the grave. *Any goddamned way you have to do it. You have to get it and hold on to it because that's what makes art art and a life a life.* I went outside and glanced into the brightly lit chow hall. Red Cannon was sitting alone, staring at his soup, his face lumpy, the skin shiny from the Pacific sun.

It was time to go.

I packed a small flight bag with the Thomas Craven book, *The Art Spirit,* The Blue Notebook, socks and underwear and shaving stuff. Nothing except my shoes would say Navy. I left the packed bag in the locker and waited until everyone was asleep. Then I slipped out the side door. The base was very quiet. I crossed to the Shack and went along the side of the building and stopped just before the window that opened into the secret studio where Miles Rayfield had tried to live his life. For a moment, I hoped that none of this had happened and if the shade was up I'd see the stacked paintings and the brushes and tubes and tins of turpentine laid upon a sheet of glass. I'd see Miles Rayfield's furrowed face. I'd see an orange filling a room.

The shade was up. But all I could see were crates.

I moved carefully along the perimeter of the field. I saw no guards. Not even at the dumpster. I went out through the hole in the fence into the woods, circled to the highway and slipped into the locker club. I hung my uniform on a wire hanger. Then, dressed in sport shirt and chinos, carrying the small bag, I went behind the locker club and stayed in the shadows, moving west. There was a river to cross, a chance of capture, and I was afraid. I was doing something now that would change everything. Doing this, I could land in the brig or become a fugitive for all the years of my life.

But there was no real choice.

I was going to New Orleans.

To find my loving woman.

Chapter

68

I STOPPED AT THE gravel road that led to the trailer and for a moment considered staying there for the night: to sleep one final time in the tight small bed where Eden changed me and maybe I changed her. But then I saw lights burning dimly beyond the trailer, and I moved on, safe in the darkness. By dawn, I wanted to be far from Ellyson Field.

I walked for a long time. I trudged past the railroad trestle where Eden once stood in her red shoes and tempted or terrified some railroad men. For the moment, hitchhiking was out; I couldn't risk being picked up by Buster and his cruising friends, didn't want to be spotted by anyone who might recognize me from the base. If that Marine died from his beating, they'd want me for more than being AWOL. The word *manslaughter* chilled me again. And I wished I could just disappear. If I was never seen or heard from again, what difference would it make to the world? I was nobody. Nameless. Faceless. Walking to New Orleans, with seventy-eight dollars in my pocket. What was important to me didn't matter to anyone else in the world except Eden. Possibly not even to her. But I would get there. I would find her. Even if I had to walk all the way.

The hours went by. The lights of a thousand cars flashed past while I moved behind a screen of bushes and billboards. Then up ahead I saw a road sign saying Foley and I knew I'd walked into Alabama. My legs felt heavier. My feet hurt. *Enough.* Now I'd have to take the chance of hitchhiking. I stepped out on the road, trying to look like a sweet all-American boy and not some trunk murderer. After a while a dark-blue pickup stopped, the engine racing. An old man was behind the wheel, thin and toothless and smiling.

"Hurry up, sailor," he said. "I ain't got all goddamn night."

I got in and he put the truck in gear and started tearing down the road, wavering from time to time, heaving up gravel from the shoulder. The radio was tuned to a black station. Hank Ballard. *Work with Me, Annie.* They used to sing it in the Kingdom of Darkness, everybody stopping to shout the chorus.

"How'd you know I was a sailor?" I said.

"Hitchhikin in these parts, you ain't no Royal Canadian Mountie. Course, I ain't no Sherlock Holmes either. Just, I drive these damn roads all the time and that's who I see. Sailors. Most you people look the same. Where you fum?"

"Miami," I lied.

"Lots of Jews down there, ain't they?"

"Some."

"Hell, they's Jews all over nowadays. I seen them even in *Memphis.* Can you *beat* that?"

"Amazing. Memphis . . ."

"Where you bound fer?"

"Mobile. The bus station."

"I'll drop you off."

We were on a four-lane road now and all around us I could see marsh grass writhing under the graying sky. The air was thickening with heat. A mosquito landed on my arm and I slapped it and the old man laughed. "Skeeters down here big enough ta play basketball with," he said. I laughed too. Then we were on a causeway, shooting out over the swamps. "Six miles long hit is," the old man said. "One of the longest damn bridges in the world." He told me his name was Woods. I said my name was Lee. I was surprised how easy it was to make up names and places and histories.

The black radio station faded and Woods fiddled with the dial and found another one. Lloyd Price. "Love that damned *nigger* music," he said, as Lloyd Price shouted his delight with Miz Clawdy. "Ho, *boy!*" He slammed the dashboard with the palm of his hand and moved against the rhythm as he drove. Up ahead was the Bankhead Tunnel. He slowed down and fumbled for change to pay the toll. I handed him a dime.

"Thanks, sailor," he said, palming the coin.

I could see cops around the change booth. And I thought: *They could be looking for me.* For killing that Marine guard, that Gabree. I thought about feigning sleep but decided it was easier simply to look casual. The cops were bored and tired, with big sweat stains under their arms. Woods handed over his dime and we eased into the traffic as Billy Ward began to sing *Sixty-Minute Man.* I wondered where Bobby Bolden was and whether he did much thinking about the rest of his life.

The tunnel was two lanes wide, with a few cars coming at us in the other lane. Woods moved the truck smoothly, both hands gripping the wheel. He didn't drift. Not down there. Then he started to pick up speed. The tiled walls were dripping with summer perspiration. I had a feeling that we would come up on the other end in Manhattan. I'd see the Hudson behind me and the docks of the ocean liners and the Empire State Building off to the left. The faces would be familiar. There would be plenty of Jews. And black people too. And Puerto Ricans. I'd thank Woods and get out of the truck and go to the newsstand on the corner and buy the *News* and *Mirror* and the *Journal-American.* Maybe I'd take the train to Ebbets Field. The Dodgers would be playing the Cardinals. And when the game was over, I'd go down to Coney Island and buy some hotdogs at Nathan's and walk out to the beach and look at the girls in their bathing suits, their skin still white with winter, and I'd call my father and tell him I was home, and I'd be there soon and none of this would have happened.

But when we came up out of the tunnel we were still in Alabama. Going farther and farther away from New York. And then I felt light, boneless, runny with fear; in a few hours, what I had done would be irreversible. Donnie Ray would call the roll and I would not be there. He would run through the motions, as he had the morning that Boswell didn't show; but when he was certain I was gone, he would mark me AWOL. And I knew that I might never be able to go back to New York. I would never see my father and brothers, except from the shadows. I felt like crying.

Over on the left, jammed around the flat mouth of the Mobile River, I could see cargo ships tied to docks, being loaded with bauxite. The air smelled of salt. It was very hot and there was not yet a sign of the sun.

"Ugly goddamn place ain't it?" Woods said.

"Depends," I said.

"On what?"

"On whether you're *from* here. Maybe if you're *from* here, it's beautiful."

"*I'm* from here, sailor. And I say it's *ugly.*"

Then we were passing summer houses with bicycles lying on the lawns. The trees were plump and green. I saw at least one swimming pool. Woods made a series of turns and we were suddenly on Government Street, a main drag full of grand houses. We drove a few blocks under a high canopy of live oaks. We turned again, into a seedy treeless district, with For Rent signs in some of the stores. An abandoned car rusted in a side street, its tires gone, the windows punched out. And up ahead I could see the sign for the Greyhound station.

"There you are, sailor."

"Well, I certainly appreciate the ride."

"Ah preciate the comp'ny. Hey, you ain't in no *trouble* now, are ya?"

"No. Why do you ask?"

"You don't look too damned *good.*"

"Just tired. I'll be all right when I get to where I'm going."

"Won't we *all.*"

He pulled over to the curb across the street from the bus station. I opened the door and got out.

"See you, bub," he said, and then drove away, a crazy white man who listened to nigger music and thought Jews were weird. I took a breath and started across the empty street.

My heart stopped.

Two Shore Patrolmen in dress whites were standing in front of the newsstand. Their backs were to me. They were looking at the newspapers and I suddenly imagined myself on page one, along with Sal and Max and Maher and Dunbar, all of us charged with manslaughter. Bigger than our pictures was the photograph of the dead Marine.

I turned around and walked slowly away from there. Down the side streets. Left. Right. Left again. Expecting to see the Shore Patrol hurrying after me. Expecting a jeep to come screaming around a corner. Sweat poured down my face. My hands were wet. Up ahead, I saw a heavy black woman in a violet housedress come out on the porch of one of the houses. She had a yellow rag over her head and a cigarette clamped in her mouth. She was barefoot. I slowed down to a stroll, trying to look cool, as she bent over for a milk bottle. There was a cardboard sign in the window behind her. Rooms.

"Excuse me," I said. "Which way's the main drag?"

"You mean Gubmint Street?"

"The one with the big live oaks."

"Ova yonduh. Bout three blocks."

"Thanks."

"Hey."

"Yeah?"

"What the hell you doin roun heah?"

"Tryin to get to New Orleans.

"You look tebble."

"Just tired."

"You tahd, you betta sleep, white boy."

"Gotta go."

"Ah gotta room, you needs it. One dolla."

She flipped the cigarette into the street.

"No, I better get to New Orleans."

"Mah bruvva-in-low, he be goin that way this aftanoon . . ."

"Can I get a bath?

"That be a quota extra."

I woke up soaked in sweat. I could see wallpaper peeling above me in the small cramped room. Beside the bed, a green painted bureau was greasy with heat. Old cooking smells hung in the air. I pushed my hand under the pillow. *The wallet!* I'd placed it there before falling off to sleep. Now it was gone. I sat up straight, my heart pounding. My clothes were draped over a chair. Then I looked at the door, thinking that I might be trapped here, locked in, my money stolen, like a traveler in one of those old fairy tales who went to spend a night at a country inn and ended up as meat pie.

I went to the door.

And sighed in relief.

It was open. I could see a landing and stairs going down to the first floor. I closed the door and got down on my knees to look under the bed. There was the wallet. The money was still inside. For a moment, the wallet and money had been the most important things in my life; now they seemed without any value. Now I would have to gather myself and start moving again. AWOL. Over the hill. Into the scary world.

Then there was a knock at the door and I jumped.

The door cracked open. I tensed.

And saw the black woman.

She had a large yellow towel for me and a pitcher of ice cubes and lemonade.

"Yo baff is ready," she said. "Next door."

"Thanks."

"You look ready too," she said and smiled.

"Your brother-in-law here yet?"

"Oh hell, boy, I dint mean you looks ready for *him.* I mean you looks ready fo, oh . . . somefin else."

"I better just take a bath and go."

"You sho?"

The brother-in-law's name was Roderick. He was thin and knuckly and forty-two-years old and he had a load of pipe to deliver to Pascagoula. I didn't know where Pascagoula was, but he sure did. And he wasn't happy about going there.

"Anything I can do," he said, "I stays outta Mississippi. They *crazy* ovuh there."

"What about New Orleans?"

"Oh, that's a different matter, all-to-gether. *They* crazy too. But crazy *diffrunt.*"

There was no radio in the one-ton truck, which Roderick said he'd bought as war surplus in '46. We drove in silence through dark pine forest which gave way to groves of what Roderick said were pecan trees, drooping in the heat. We cut down a two-lane blacktop toward the Gulf. A breeze began to rustle the trees and I could hear a clacking sound. Roderick said it was the pecans. Smacking each other in the wind like a million castanets.

The sound of the pecans followed us most of the way to Biloxi. When we came into the town, Roderick said nothing. This was Mississippi and he damn well didn't like it. Directly in front of us, planted in the middle of the highway, with the eastbound and westbound lanes swerving around it, was a giant whitewashed light-house.

"You think they *planned* this lighthouse this way?" I said.

Roderick laughed.

"Hell, no. This used to be the *water.* All this be *landfill* we drivin on."

To the left now was the Gulf. Charter boats, docks, bait shops, food stores, souvenir places, a long crowded white beach that seemed to go for miles, and beyond the beach, out in the water, about five hundred shrimp and oyster boats riding at anchor. It looked like a postcard and I wished I could get out of the truck and enter the postcard and have a vacation the way ordinary people did. The streets were packed. Girls in bathing suits. Rednecks. Cops. Air force guys from Keesler. What looked like college boys. Their bodies were tanned and oiled and some of them were gliding in and out of the motels and all of them were white.

I looked at Roderick.

His eyes were fixed directly ahead of him on the slow-moving traffic.

Then the honky-tonks were gone and giant white mansions rose on a bluff: rich, smug, defiantly facing the sea. They all had tall white pillars holding up the roofs, like great houses in Civil War movies, and vast rolling lawns, and on the distant porches I could see tiny people in rockers watching the road and the ocean and the horizon. Biloxi vanished and Gulfport appeared, quieter, with a divided highway and palm trees and more grand houses, but no bait shops or charter boats or oiled blondes drifting to motels. I saw some odd-shaped trees. For the tung nuts, Roderick said.

"Years ago, buncha crazy peoples all tho't they get themselfs rich wid de *tung nut.* Befo that, they tho't the same wif the *awnges.* When I'se a boy, they's *awnge* trees all up and down the damn coast. But the awnge trees died and so did the tung nuts. So now peoples still gotta make money the way they always done. Fum the damn Gulf. Fum the big blue water."

Roderick drove quickly through Gulfport. The light was almost behind us and the Gulf looked large and scary. We could hear the ding-dinging of buoys and see the fishing boats cleaving through the water as if going to battle. Then up ahead we could see giant shipyard cranes rising off the flats, looking odd and disjointed against the lavender sky. Signs appeared, directing trucks with deliveries for the Ingalls Shipbuilding Corporation to make the next left. Roderick pulled over on a wide shoulder. Marsh grass swayed on both sides of the road. A sour smell rose from the baking earth.

"Ah don't go no futhuh," Roderick said. "You gotta git you the rest of the way to New Awlins on you own."

"Thanks for the ride," I said. I felt clumsy. He held the wheel with both hands. "It sure is beautiful country along here."

"Yeah," he said. "Yeah, it sho is."

I walked about a mile and saw a gas station with a small seafood
store attached to the office. I bought a pound of shrimp for a dollar
and crossed the highway and sat down on a damp log. I peeled the
shrimp and ate quickly and wanted more. Thinking: *They know I'm
gone now for sure.* I imagined Donnie Ray calling Red Cannon and
asking if I was locked up somewhere and Red saying, *Locked up?*
Hell, *no.* He came home with *me* on Sunday morning.

I was AWOL.

They'd come after me for that.

And maybe worse.

Maybe murder.

I finished the shrimp and looked back at the gas station across the
road. The sun was now gone. A blue '49 Chevy was parked at the
pump with an Air Force sticker in the rear window. Two guys were
at the Coke machine. Another came around the side of the building
where he'd obviously just taken a leak. A tiny man in coveralls was
gassing up the car. One of the three young men went into the
shrimp place. I walked over.

"Hey, can I hitch a ride with you guys?" I said.

The tallest one squinted at me. He was wearing a starched sleeveless white shirt and chinos. He went around to the driver's side, and
started to get in, without giving me an answer. The other one paid
for the gas. The third came out with a large bag of shrimp.

"Where you goin?" the tall one said.

"New Awlins," I said, trying to pronounce the words the way
Roderick did. Not New Or-leeens.

"You got a couple of bucks for gas?" he said.

"Yeah."

"Get in."

They were all enlisted men, stationed at Keesler, and were starting a ten-day leave. All were from Texas and they were going
home. Dave, the tall one, was from Austin, and he drove as if trying
to establish a speed record. Harry, who bought the shrimp, was
from Fort Worth. Jake was from Dallas. He was the crew's paymas-
ter and after I got in beside him in the back seat, I gave him three
bucks. As Dave drove with ferocious concentration, passing trucks,
dodging oncoming cars, the others pulled the shells off the shrimp
and threw them out the open windows into the steaming air and
then passed around a bottle of Jack Daniels.

"Have a belt."

"I better not."

"It's Mister Daniels."

"I got some business in New Awlins. I don't want to get there plastered."

"Suit yisself."

It was hard to see them in the dark. I huddled in the back seat in a corner behind the driver, feigning sleep or staring into the darkness. I was Miller from Miami but I didn't want them to know me, to catch me in some dumb little lie. The bottle moved around. I thought: *Be sharp, be cool. Get drunk and you'll lose control. You'll get caught. You'll see a brig before you see New Orleans. Before you find what you're looking for. And you can't tell these guys. They're not your friends. They're just Air Force guys going home.*

We stopped five times. Someone had to piss. Someone wanted sandwiches. Someone had to puke. Once I came suddenly awake as the car swerved, spun around on the empty road, came to a coughing stop. Dave had almost rammed a wandering cow.

"Open range!" Jake shouted. "Bounty hunter!"

We got out and they all laughed and passed around the bottle and this time I took a slug. The bourbon was hot, burning, good. We all pissed into the dark.

Then a vast swarm of mosquitoes found us, thick, dense, silvery in the moonlight, filling our noses and mouths, and we were slapping our faces and arms and running to the car. Dave pulled away, cursing and slapping, the windows wide open to blow the rest of the mosquitoes out. My arms and neck were bumpy from bites. Harry said we should rub whiskey on the bites and Dave said that was a hell of waste of good bourbon and Jake said, Well, let's try it a little. I didn't do it. Where I was going, I didn't want to smell of bourbon. I didn't drink anymore after that.

The night air smelled different now: hot, salty. I saw patches of black water, then great open swatches like lakes, with shanties up on stilts over the water. We crossed a steel drawbridge and then we saw a sign. Chef Menteur. Two gas pumps, some fishing shanties and a bar.

"Goddamn, a real metropolis."

"Named after a chef!"

"You know you in Louisiana now."

"Wuddint that the Pearl River?"

We all went into the bar. I was hot and thirsty, because of the bourbon. Inside, there were two guys playing a shuffleboard machine and a red-haired woman behind a small bar. She looked up when we came in. She was wearing a lot of makeup and her tits were too pointy to be real.

"You boys old enough to drink?" she said.

"We're old enough to die in Korea," Dave said, laying two singles on the bar.

"Then you're old enough to drink," she said and smiled and gave her tits a little shake.

There was a crude map on the wall between the two windows, with a sign above it saying: DON'T ASK WHERE YOU ARE. YOU'RE HERE. The arrow pointed at Chef Menteur. We were on a kind of island, and at the western end there were a lot of little streams called the Rigolets and a half dozen places marked SWAMP. Using the map as a guide, I looked out in that direction. In the distance, the sky was glowing. I turned to the barmaid.

"How far are we from New Awlins?" I said.

"You're in it, boy."

Chapter

69

WHOOPING, HOLLERING, CALLING to women and drinking from a fresh bottle, they dropped me off on the corner of Canal and Rampart and then sped away. In all the years since, I've spent too much time showing up in strange cities at night. None of them have ever looked to me the way New Orleans did that first time. I stared around me and for a long strange moment felt as if I were home. There were office buildings, all brightly lit, souvenir stores and camera shops and jewelry joints, restaurants and huge hotels and big-assed women with yellow dresses and pairs of cops smoking cigarettes in doorways. Just like New York. And there were trolley cars. That's what did it to me, reached out, hugged me, promised me the salvation of the familiar. The trolley cars: their steel wheels clacking on steel rails, squealing as they turned from a side street into Canal, the conductors ding-donging their warning bells. They were the older cars, made in part of wood, with square Toonerville Trolley faces, the kind that ran along Fifth Avenue in Brooklyn, not the streamlined gray trolleys that now raced along the Seventh Avenue line. And I thought: *I'm a long way from home.*

And thought again: *I'll be all right.*

So I started to walk. *New Awlins.* Almost midnight. The heat still rising off the sidewalks. The gutters soft from the blaze of day. I needed a place to stay but I knew the big hotels were beyond me; I just couldn't spend that kind of money or risk a demand for identification. And I sensed that if Canal Street was like Times Square, then the Shore Patrol would be around here somewhere, picking up strays. I had to get off into the side streets to where

ordinary people lived and there'd be a boarding house with no
questions asked, a hideout where the Shore Patrol was never seen.

Suddenly I was at the river. There were people on line, waiting
for a ferry marked Algiers. A line of cars too. *Algiers?* Jesus. Wasn't
that in *North Africa*? I walked past the waiting lines, out to the edge
of the ferry slip and looked down.

The Mississippi.

Black and glossy and moving slowly.

I heard a deep voice behind me.

"Help you, son?"

I turned and saw a cop staring at me. Old guy. Maybe fifty. Fat.
Pouchy eyes. His face shiny with the heat.

"Uh, no, no, I'm fine. Why?"

"Oh, just we get a lotta jumpers along here. Dey stand here and
den dey go in da water and dat's all she wrote." He was closer now,
looking into my eyes. "You aint thinkin of doin nuttin *foolish,* are
ya?"

He sounded like Becket. Or Brooklyn. I smiled, trying to look
like the All-American boy I wasn't.

"Hell, no, officer. I'm just lookin for a boardin house. I'm headin
for California. Start a new job out there next month."

"Where in California?"

"Uh, San Diego. Ever been there?"

"Durn da war. I gotta sister in Santa Barbara. She loves it out
dere. Me, I like *here.* Da food out dere—hey, eat before ya go."

"What about that boardin house?"

He scratched the side of his cheek and then pointed me toward
Decatur Street, where, he said, there were plenty of rooming
houses. The fastest way was through the railroad yards, but I'd
better be careful of the trains and the hoboes.

"The other way to get to da same place is go back down Canal,
right here, to, say, Charters Street. Den cut right into the French
Quarters, into the Voo Kuhray. On da right. You keep goin to
Jackson Square and make another right over to the waterfront
and—"

There was a sudden squeal of brakes, and the sound of rammed
metal. Two cars angling for position on the Algiers ferry had
smacked into each other.

The cop hurried over. I drifted back down Canal Street. At
Chartres, I turned right. The street was narrow and badly lit, with

high rough walls rising on either side and cobblestoned streets and a sickly rotting odor seeping from somewhere, as if the heat were boiling sewage beneath the streets. There were several winos sitting on the sidewalk, their backs to the walls. All white. One of them came over to me. His eyes looked scraped. His skin was loose. He put a hand on my flight bag and grinned. In the dim light, he had almost no teeth.

"Whatchoo *got* there, boy?"

"Hands off," I said.

He jerked on the bag and I pulled it away and shoved him. He whirled and faced me, both hands poised, a blade in his hand.

Shit.

The other winos didn't move. They didn't even seem very interested.

This is stupid. This ain't why I came here.

I backed up.

I don't want to die this way. I don't want to die at all. I have to find my loving woman.

The wino said, "You got somefin you wanna *do,* boy?"

I turned and ran.

Along Chartres Street, then right, then left again. I ran for a long time, until I got brave enough to look behind me and saw steam rising on the empty streets but no wino with scraped eyes. I slowed to a walk. There were more little bars, with yellow light spilling onto the sidewalks. Scraps of music filled the air. Distant Dixieland. Bebop. Black music. The notes came from here and the bass lines from there. I imagined people dancing in hidden rooms. I was very hot.

Then I saw the OTEL.

The H was out in the red neon sign and the place had no other name. It was on a corner. The front door was open, so I went in. There was a small lobby, with fluorescent lights on the high ceilings and a fan beating slowly and doing nothing to the thick hot air. A fat whore sat on a couch watching TV. There was no reception counter, only a booth, like the kind you see outside movie houses. A thin man with yellow skin looked up at me. He had a cigarillo stuck in his mouth.

"Yeah?"

"I need a room," I said. "What are the rates?"

"Three bills a night. In *advance.* A buck extra if you bring in a broad."

"Three nights," I said, and gave him a ten-dollar bill. He handed me back a dollar and the key to room 127.

"One flight up," he said, without removing the cigarillo. A staircase behind the Coke machine led upstairs.

The room was narrow, with a bare yellow light on the high ceiling. The furnishings revealed themselves in bits and pieces: a bed, a bureau, a night table; a 1952 calendar with a picture of Miami Beach; a small sink; a pale-blue spread over the bed, with little white wool balls all over it.

No telephone.

No bath.

I sat down heavily on the edge of the bed.

I noticed a wire mesh over the windows. A stain on the wall looked like Italy. I was very hot. I leaned back and was soon asleep.

In New Orleans.

Where Eden Santana lived her life.

Chapter

———

70

FOR TWO DAYS, I searched for her through the streets of the city. I started with the telephone book (none in the room, none in the lobby, found them hanging in a post office), looking up all the Santanas in New Orleans, calling each of them, receiving baffled replies as I begged for information. After each call, I left my name and the number of the hotel. I remembered old movies and detective stories and the way private eyes relentlessly tracked the missing. I went to the gas company, asking for records on Eden Santana or James Robinson. The woman behind the counter looked at me as if I were crazed and then called over a superior.

"That's confidential info'mation, son," a hairless blue-eyed man said. "Why you want that?"

I couldn't tell him, so I fled. Then I thought of going to the newspapers, the *Times-Picayune* or the *States-Item,* and asking to look at their clippings for James Robinson. If he was so bad, there must have been stories about him in the papers. But when I called up and asked if I could look at their clippings they wanted to know why I needed to see them and I said I was a student writing a term paper and a woman said, "Well, honey, whyn't you git yaw *pifessor* to write you a *letter,* and we see what we can do . . ."

And, of course, I couldn't go to the police.

By noon of the first day, I was exhausted and hot, sitting on a bench in Jackson Square. I was very thirsty. I saw a guy selling shaved ice dyed with juice and asked for cherry. It was sweet and cold and when I finished, I ordered another. They were three cents each. I gazed around the square and saw painters with easels setting up under the arcade and I wondered what would happen if I did find Eden and then thought, *Well, maybe we could just live here.*

For I had come to think of New Orleans as the most beautiful city I'd ever seen. Hour after hour, I walked through the cobblestoned streets of the French Quarter, peering into dark entryways to the gardens within, with their fountains and plants and birds. I was filled with a sweet sense that they were from another century, the time of the French and the Spaniards, sealed off and protected from the present by their heavy iron gates. Leaning on the rough plaster walls, my body burning from the summer heat, I gazed into the cool interiors and thought of Eden's people long ago, coming down the river to find husbands here for their women, while white dandies went to the quadroon balls and picked out their own women and installed them in these houses. Upstairs, behind the balconies with their scrolled ironwork, I could see bedrooms with high ceilings and they must have lain there in the hot summer afternoons, naked to the breeze or the stirred air made by ceiling fans. The rooms made me think of a painting in the Craven book, a naked woman lying on a couch, in the company of a black cat and a black woman. Except that here in New Orleans, in *my* version of the painting, the naked woman was black and the cat was white and an even blacker woman was looking on.

On that first night I wandered everywhere, drawn not only by Eden now, but by the city itself. Before going out, I made a drawing of her face and carried it with me as I started visiting the bars. I went down to Bourbon Street, where Dixieland music blared from the honky-tonks, and I talked to bartenders and doormen and whores, showing the picture, asking if they knew her.

As the hours passed, the air grew thicker, more feminine. Around midnight, I stood for a long while at the corner of St. Peter's and Bourbon, listening to a white Dixieland band, looking at faces. There were hundreds of tourists and locals moving down the packed street, speaking a dozen dialects of English, talking in French and Spanish and German. There were a stream of faces: flabby, compressed, blank, sharp, beautiful. None was hers. I could smell coffee somewhere, and came again to Jackson Square, and saw lights along the Mississippi. I was very hungry. Across the street, beside the river, was a place with outdoor tables and black waiters. The Café du Monde. I didn't know French but thought about my high school Latin and figured it out.

The Café of the World.

I crossed the street and sat down at an empty table. It was cooler there, with a breeze lifting off the black river. There were only two items on the menu: coffee and beignets. I didn't know what beignets were but when the waiter came over I ordered them anyway.

"Chicory in da coffee?"

I didn't know what chicory was either, but I said *sure, why not?* He came back with a plate of doughnuts without holes, covered with confectioners' sugar. Beignets. I sipped the coffee, which was more powdery than ordinary coffee, the taste somehow grainy, and it was delicious. I gulped down the beignets, waved for more, and ate them in a kind of frenzy. Then I sat back, belching, swollen, as if exhausted by the sudden gorging. A riverboat went by with its lights all dazzling and bright and a band playing and people on deck and I wished that Eden was with me, drinking that special coffee, watching that river, sitting in the Café of the World.

I woke late and everything was wet: my body, the sheets, the walls. I reached for the towel beside the sink. It was damp. I got out of there in a hurry.

This time I followed the black people's faces through the city until I came to a district where the architecture was different, the houses low and tin-roofed. If the doors were open, I could see all the way through them into the backyards. Black people sat on the front porches fanning themselves, drinking cold tea or lemonade, laughing in growly voices. I started showing them the drawing of Eden, but most were suspicious. Who was this white man and what he *want?* And then retreated into icy lemonade and muffled laughter.

Toward late morning I felt heavier, damper, hotter, oddly drowsy, thinking: *Maybe she just told me a mess of lies. Maybe she wasn't from New Orleans at all. Maybe she was from Memphis or Texas or some other goddamned place in America. Maybe she wasn't even from the South. And if that was true* (I thought, moving into laundries and barber shops and bars), *then I'd ruined my life for a lie. And for sure, I would never find her.*

And then a woman with sad yellow eyes and heavy breasts and a long pink housecoat looked at the picture and said, "Why, dat's Eden."

I felt weak.

"Do you know where she lives?" I said.

"Oh, she moved away long tahm ago."

"How long?"

"Two, t'ree years?"

"Do you know where she went? I said.

"Feared ah don't. Her man Mist' Rob'son in trouble again?"

"James Robinson?"

"Yeah . . . Big ole handsome fella. But *bad news.*"

"It's Eden I'm looking for. Not him."

"You trah da choich?"

"What church?"

"Da *Catlick* choich. Up by da square. Da St. Louis Cathedral. Where else a Catlick goil might be found?"

I told the woman that if she saw Eden Santana, to tell her I was in New Orleans. I tore a corner off the drawing and wrote down the address of the hotel on Chartres Street. I handed it to her and thanked her. And then started for the Cathedral.

The sky grew dark and tumultuous. Trees filled and bent in the wind. People started hurrying along the streets. A few shopkeepers began to lower their shutters. A storm was coming, but I didn't care. This trip, this journey, was *not* the result of a series of lies. Eden Santana really *was* from here. She really had been married to a man named James Robinson. And I was sure she was still there in New Orleans. Somewhere. Maybe round this next corner.

Jackson Square was deserted when I reached the cathedral. The main door was closed, but I found an open side door and went inside. I could smell the familiar traces of incense and burning wax; the odor made me feel like a Catholic. There was no Mass being celebrated, but there were a lot of women in black scattered around the pews, and a few black men, all of them praying in solitude. Off to the right, men and women waited on line outside a confessional booth.

I walked slowly down a side aisle to the altar, glancing at faces, hoping to see Eden. She wasn't there. I bought a candle for a nickel and lit it and knelt at the altar rail, wishing I still believed enough to pray. I didn't but my face felt as hot as the flame of the candle. I tried to understand the layout of the cathedral, so that I could get back into the sacristy and find a priest. There was a door over to the right, as there was back home at Holy Name. I crossed the front of the cathedral, genuflecting in the center out of old habit, and went into the sacristy.

There were rotting flowers on a table, an open closet holding cassocks and surplices for altar boys, boxes of candles from Benziger Brothers, New York. I walked over to the dark passageway that led behind the altar and saw a figure coming toward me. I felt weak. Small. As if I was an altar boy again, serving in contempt and fear. I needed something cold to drink.

The figure came closer, his face obscure in the unlighted passage. And then emerged into the dim light of the sacristy.

An old priest, dressed in black.

"Can I help you?" he said in a soft voice.

"Yes, yes, Father. I'm looking for someone . . . A friend. She's Catholic. And I thought maybe you might have some address for her, a telephone number."

"Well—"

I took out the drawing, which was smudged now, and told him Eden's name and a little about her husband. The priest's voice was whispery and dry, like dead leaves.

"Both names are common in New Orleans," he said, "although Santana is a lot more . . . *Catholic* than Robinson." He scratched his scalp, then gazed at his nails. They were dirty. "I would have to look though church records. Is there any, er, *trouble* in this?"

"No. No trouble. I'm a *friend.* She knows me."

"Because I couldn't, well—"

"If you could find her, don't even tell *me* where she lives, if that's what you're worried about. Just tell *her* that I'm here and where I am. She can come to me."

He took a pack of Camels from under his habit and lighted one. It was the first time I'd seen a priest smoke.

"You know, *last* year, someone came looking for one of my parishioners. . . . And I was taken in. I gave my visitor the address and my poor parishioner is now serving twenty years at Angola. That's the prison farm. . . . You're not from New Orleans, are you?"

"No."

He waited for me to tell him where I was from. But I said nothing. Something in me made it hard to lie to a priest, even if I didn't believe what he believed anymore.

"You don't have to tell me where you're from," he said. He took a deep drag and then made a smoke ring and gazed proudly at its perfection. "But maybe you should tell me what kind of trouble you're in."

"I can't."

"Nobody will know."

"I don't believe in confession anymore, Father."

"But you did once."

"Yes."

"I might be able to help."

"Thank you, Father. But I don't think you can . . ."

"Is the woman part of the trouble?"

"No."

"That bad, huh?"

"I'm in love with her. . . . That's all."

"That's everything."

"Father?"

"Yes."

"Can I have a glass of water?"

The summer storm hammered at the city, all water and wind, with garbage cans going over and awnings flapping and broken umbrellas careening away. Dozens of people huddled in the entrance of the Cathedral, making nervous jokes about hurricanes and disasters. There was a tremendous *ka-pow* and the square was instantly bright with lightning and everybody backed up, laughing and afraid. We were all huddled together, blacks and whites joined in a common need for safety.

But I had to get out of there. The rain was blowing hard and cold. A shower of hailstones clattered across the square. And yet I felt as if I were being boiled. I shivered. I thought I was going to throw up. Another bolt of lightning split the sky over the river. My eyes burned.

I had to go.

To run.

To get into the room and the bed.

I broke out of the dense packed crowd and ran into the pelting rain, the water above my ankles.

And then the water rose and the sidewalk came with it and hit me in the face and I was gone.

Chapter

71

THE FOG WAS the color of piss and it came through the window and under the door of the high white room. Miles Rayfield stood in the cloud, wearing his white hat and his horn-rimmed glasses, his lips a bright red smear. And behind him came all the others: Sal and Max and Winnie, Buster and the Red Shadow, Captain Pritchett and Steve Canyon. As someone shouted: *Everyone meet at the Café of the World!*

O Bobby Bolden!

O Buz Sawyer!

I remember them all, from that visit to the fever zone: Dwight Eisenhower was there, and Mercado from Mexico. Hank Williams entered with John Foster Dulles, and there was Tons of Fun . . . and Dixie Shafer too. They came in a smiling progression, looking down at me sadly and without pity. Roberta arrived holding blue-veined white flowers. Turner showed up in a Hawaiian shirt. And that was Chief McDaid and this was Tintoretto . . . Freddie Harada held hands with Harrelson . . . and there, advancing and receding, smiling and frowning, touching my face and then wide-eyed in fear: Eden Santana.

Did she whisper to me about Joe Stalin? Did she urge me to read Ernest Hemingway? In the piss-colored fog, there was no precision. Boswell wept for Hank Williams while Eden touched my hand and then released it. I tried to rise . . . to join her . . . to dance . . . but my legs wouldn't move. My hands were thick tubes. My father wept for my mother. Miles Rayfield waved in the fog. Then Eden came close and spoke to me softly in some language I didn't know. The language of The People. The language of the Cane River. The language of Africa. I turned away, trying to conjure a cool green world, plunging deeper and deeper, going for the fresh water, past the gnawed bodies and the sharks, down into the whiteness . . .

And then opened my eyes.

Eden Santana was standing at the foot of the bed, staring at me. Her hair was brushed back. She was wearing a black blouse and a white skirt. Her eyes were glittery, intense.

"Hello, Michael," she whispered.

"Eden . . ."

She came around to the side of the bed and took one of my hands in both of hers. Her hands were very cool.

"You've got malaria," she said.

"Malaria?"

I looked at the room, its whiteness and emptiness. Saw a chair, a bureau, a night table.

"Where is this?"

"Charity Hospital. They brought you here two days ago. You collapsed on Chartres Street in the middle of a thunderstorm."

"Two *days* ago?"

"That's what the nurses tell me."

Two days ago?

"How'd you know I was here?"

"Father Bienville came to my sister's house. That's where I'm stayin. He told me you were in New Orleans. You gave him the name of your hotel, remember? I went there and they said you hadn't been in. And you owed a day's rent. I paid it and got your stuff."

She nodded at my flight bag, on the floor against the wall.

"Then I started calling around."

"You call the police?"

She blinked. "No. And I didn't call the Navy either—if that's what you're worried about."

I squeezed her hand. And whispered: "I've got to get out of here, Eden. I'm in big trouble."

"I know," she said.

The doctor was from Honduras and he wasn't happy about letting me leave the hospital. But I told him I was in the Air Force and would go right to my base doctor and tell him what was wrong.

He gave me some tablets to take every four hours and then I got dressed and Eden led me down the white corridor past the white nurses and the white rooms filled with white people. I felt very light. As if I could fly. And then stopped when we reached the elevator bank. Eden squeezed my hand, as if trying to keep me from running.

Red Cannon was sitting in a chair beside the elevators, smoking a cigarette. He was wearing his dress whites with an SP armband. There was a .45 caliber pistol in a holster hanging off his cartridge belt. He put out the cigarette in a metal ashtray and stood up. He looked from me to Eden. Then back to me.

"You okay, sailor?" he said, his voice quiet, even soft.

"I guess. . . . It's malaria."

"Well, they got a lot of experience with that over at Mainside."

I looked at Eden but she kept her eyes on the floor.

"I don't want to go back, Red."

"Neither do I. But we're both goin."

"What if I refuse?" I said. "What if I just run?"

"Then I have to shoot you."

"You aren't kidding, are you?"

"Hit's my job. I'd ruther bring you back walkin than bring you back in a box. But I promised Captain Pritchett I'd find you and bring you back. I did, and I will. So we can go now, sailor, nice and quiet."

Eden stepped between us and for a moment, Red bristled, as if afraid she was trying to help me escape. There were a lot of people looking at us now. Patients and doctors and nurses.

"Can we talk about this downstairs, Mister Cannon?" she said quietly.

"Suits me."

We went down in the elevator and out through the main lobby to the parking lot. A gray U.S. Navy car was parked near the entrance. It was empty, so I was certain that Red had come alone. I looked out at the streets beyond the lot.

"Don't even think about runnin, sailor," Red said.

I shrugged, and stared at the ground, feeling small and trapped and vaguely ashamed. I'd made a mess of things. Eden put her arm around my back. When I looked up, Red was lighting a cigarette and staring at some giant magnolias beyond the lot.

"Tell you what," he said, still not looking at me. "I'll give you till tomorrow morning. Sunday. Ten o'clock. You meet me in Jackson Square, right at the foot of that statue of Jackson, you hear me? We'll go back together . . ."

Then he looked at me, took a drag, let the smoke leak from his mouth, and said: "If you don't show, I'll hunt you down and kill you."

Chapter 72

EDEN HAD SEVENTY dollars and I had thirty-five, an immense fortune; we pooled the money and checked into the Royal Orleans Hotel. She handled everything. She registered us and paid cash in advance and led us across the hushed lobby under the crystal chandeliers to the elevators. All the while, she acted as if she were escorting a prince instead of a malarial AWOL sailor in filthy clothes. At the door of room 401, she slid the key into the lock and looked at me in an odd way and then opened the door and waved me in first.

The room was large and dim with a huge double bed and French doors leading to a small balcony. She turned on one muted light and then pulled down a corner of the bed coverings. On the walls, there were dark-brown landscapes in gilt frames and whorling velvet wallpaper out of another century. Then she took my face in her cool hands and kissed me gently. I held her tightly for a long time, trying not to cry, and then we fell together to the bed: everything in me entering her, midnight bus rides, beaches, nights at the shrimp place, the trailer, the woods; again we were on the flat rock in the middle of a nameless stream, the water Alabama red and flowing around us; again we were in the time before she taught me the names of birds and trees, animals and clouds; we were among thorns, smoke, vines, sand, petals, stones, clay, in blood too and kisses and magnolia and fear.

Eden, I said, mouth to her ear, sweat of my belly mixed with sweat of hers. *I want you forever, Eden.*

And she said, *No,* digging nails into my flesh, *No, there'll be nothing after this,* biting my lower lip, saying *This is all this is everything there is only this and this and this.*

Until we rose and fell and twisted, hissing each other's names, and dug heels and nails into silk sheets; and fell back.

Empty.

Cool.

Drained.

We ate shrimp and steak from room service and drank a bottle of champagne (my first) and she laughed at the way I held the dainty glass and then she belched loudly for a joke and I laughed too and we didn't talk, didn't say what we had to say, didn't accuse, account, define; and then were in bed again, more desperately than ever, full of loss and departure. I wanted to drink the darkness, the champagne darkness of Eden Santana.

You must go, she said. *You must find out. With me you would live only a retreat. My retreat.*

Then I was lost again, in some gray and chilly corridor, with the piss-colored fog seeping into my skull, hearing music, Charlie Parker and Gregorian chant, Webb Pierce and Little Richard, bagpipes from the Antrim fields and drums from the Cane River, and I knew what was beyond the fog: the endless cemetery where love was buried.

You must go.

Fear shaped itself in the fog, fear with the same dense volume as desire, fear that could grip me and smother me, and I was afraid then of dying the way love dies, to be placed in some stainless-steel drawer where there was no loving woman. The fog advanced.

You must find out.

And almost dying, I rose in final anger, and grabbed life.

It's all right, child. Don't you worry none.

Eden Santana: with a cool cloth to my brow, kissing me, handing over tablet and water, the glass cold in my hand. Gray light leaked through the shutters. I heard the thin distant sound of a saxophone, announcing closing time in a honky-tonk. She eased back into bed beside me and held my hand. Her dark skin felt very cool.

Don't die, she said. *Don't die on your own. Don't die of fear or doubt or darkness, child. You got too much living to do yet. You gotta go from here, from me, and remember that the going is the easy part. It's the living that's hard. I'll be with you wherever you go now. You know that, don't you? But you must go. Not go back. Go on. Put your hair beside the hair of a thousand women. Kiss a thousand mouths. Give them all what we gave each other. Love them all and let them love you back. Then you'll know I'll always be there. They won't know, but you will. Because when it's over and you have made love and she has got what she wanted and you have got what you wanted, you will still be alone, Michael. Still loving me. As I love you. Wherever we are.*

Her voice was a whisper in the dark high-ceilinged room. She was certain: with me she'd finished things. I was no longer what I was the night I first saw her on the bus, and wanted her, and felt her hands in the dark. I wasn't that boy anymore. But I was still only a perhaps.

So you'll go from here like a man, she whispered. *And you won't be afraid. Not of the world, not of the Navy. They can't do anything permanent to you, Michael, no matter how hard they try, just as long as you're alive. So kiss me one last time now. You gotta go all too soon. Gotta go like a man. Got to go on and live.*

Chapter

73

I AM DRIVING THROUGH the Gulf night, the radio playing in its permanent present tense. It is four in the morning. Pensacola is behind me. The news announcer says that the Attorney General of the United States has appeared before still another grand jury. The Challenger space shuttle has been delayed again because of shoddy work. A new strain of AIDS has arrived from Africa. The weather will be hot with scattered showers. Suddenly, the news is over and Frank Sinatra is singing. In the South once ruled by Hank Williams and Webb Pierce.

Each time I see a crowd of people
Just like a fool, I stop and stare
I know it's not the proper thing to do
But maybe you'll be there . . .

The song is old. Out of the fifties. When Sinatra was aching for Ava Gardner and proving that even artists can be fools. I begin to sing along, as if old dead skin is being peeled away, and for the first time in years, I can feel the emotions behind the banal words. The window is open to the warm night. I see houses, shopping centers and factories where there was once only emptiness. And I fill with the woman I loved across all the years, the woman who went with me to all those other beds, and into three marriages, the first and best loving woman among all the women I've loved.

I say her name out loud.

And again.

And once more.

Eden.

On this road, years before, Red Cannon took me back to the Navy. I went without struggle. For the first hour out of New Orleans, he drove in silence, the .45 slung to his hip. In Gulfport, I looked out at the pine woods and the little streams and the great stretches of swamp. I felt forlorn. As we turned down to the beach, we could see thunderheads over the ocean. Then Red said, "Need to take a leak?"

"Yeah," I said. "I do."

"Figured. Those goddamned malaria pills do it to you."

He pulled across the highway into a gas station and sat there while I went around the side to the men's room. For a moment, I thought about running. But I'd given Red my word. And I knew that if I ran, I'd be running for the rest of my life.

When I came out, Red was leaning on the fender of the car, drinking a Coke. His back was to me. He must have known I wouldn't run. I came around to his side. He was staring out past the beach at the sea. The SP band was off his arm and the cartridge belt and holster were gone from his hip. They were lying on the front seat, the .45 still in the holster. We had become two sailors heading back to base. He drained the Coke bottle and dropped it in a trashcan, still gazing at the Gulf.

"Wish I was out there now," he said.

I smiled. "Me too."

Red looked at me for the first time, and shook his head.

"You'll get there," he said. "Soon enough."

"I doubt it," I said. "Not from where I'm going."

He curled his lip.

"Where in the hell you think you're *goin,* sailor?"

"Portsmouth prison?"

"Shit," he said, and sneered. "You ain't *important* enough for Portsmouth prison."

He got in behind the wheel and I slid in on the passenger side. He lifted the gun and cartridge belt into the back seat, then started the car and pulled out onto the road. He glanced at me in a disappointed way, as if I were just another one of the people who had failed him.

"You're lucky, sailor. That jarhead's okay. Just a busted head, which won't ever do a Marine no damage. You're lucky for another thing too: the captain likes you, for some goddamned reason that's beyond mah ken."

Someday when all my prayers are answered
I'll hear a footstep on the stair . . .

I shut off the radio.

Remembering that Red was right. Pritchett called me before a captain's mast, which was less than a court martial, allowed me to blame the malaria, restricted me to the base for a week. I shipped out a few weeks later and truly began my long hard run through the world. I don't know what happened to Red Cannon. I never heard another word about Bobby Bolden. I don't know what became of Becket or Harrelson or Boswell, Captain Pritchett or Chief McDaid. Max and I wrote to each other for a while, and I saw Sal once when I was on leave in New York. But then the addresses changed, as they do when you're young, and we moved around some more, and we lost all contact. I started three different letters to Miles Rayfield's mother, but never could get the words right and gave it up. Out at sea, waiting to go ashore in Cannes, I got one letter from Dixie Shafer saying she was selling the Dirt Bar because it just wasn't as much fun anymore. I sent a card back, but she too vanished into the darkness. I suppose some of them are dead, casualties of the cigarettes or the whiskey or the Nam. The others live on, full of golden stories.

But as the years slipped by, I would sometimes hear a fragment of a forgotten song, or feel a breeze on a deserted beach; I'd see a river on a summer morning or a house trailer at the side of a road or a woman in red shoes—and I'd want to know what happened to Eden Santana. And across all those years I was afraid to find out. I never went back to New Orleans. I didn't want to learn that she had grown old. I didn't want to hear that she had made her peace with James Robinson. I didn't want to believe that she was dead. But in a thousand places and a thousand dreams she lived on in me as she had said she would one fevered morning long ago, under the chandeliers of the Royal Orleans.

O Eden!

Suddenly, illuminated briefly in the high beams, I see a sailor in dress whites. I haven't picked up a hitchhiker in twenty years, but

I slow down, the car's momentum taking me past him. I stop and wait and see him in the rearview mirror, running toward me, an overnight bag in his hand. I unlock the door on the passenger side.

"Hey, thanks, man," he says. He has the two pathetic stripes of a seaman deuce, a sunburned face, crooked teeth. A kid.

"Where you going?" I ask, pulling onto the highway.

"New Orleans," he says.

"It's a good town."

"The best," he says. "My girl's there."

"So's mine," I say, driving fast across the dark tidal fields of the Gulf. My heart is racing. My palms are damp. I am no longer old.

About the Author

PETE HAMILL was born in Brooklyn in 1935. He has been a professional writer since 1960, when he gave up a career as a graphic artist to become a general assignment reporter for the *New York Post*. He has since published six novels, one collection of short stories, one collection of journalism, and has written many movie and TV scripts.

He is the father of two daughters, Adriene and Deirdre, and is married to writer Fukiko Aoki. They live in New York City.